BREAKOUT
FROM
SUGAR ISLAND

BREAKOUT FROM SUGAR ISLAND

Seamus Beirne

FIRESHIP PRESS

Breakout from Sugar Island by Seamus Beirne

This is a work of historical fiction. While based upon historical events, any similarity to any person, circumstance or event is purely coincidental and related to the efforts of the author to portray the characters in historically accurate representations.

ISBN: 978-1-61179-335-2 (Paperback)
ISBN: 978-1-61179-336-9 (e-book)

10 9 8 7 6 5 4 3 2

BISAC Subject Headings:
FIC002000 FICTION / Action & Adventure
FIC014000 FICTION / Historical
FIC047000 FICTION / Sea Stories

Address all correspondence to:
Fireship Press, LLC
P.O. Box 68412
Tucson, AZ 85737
info@fireshippress.com

Or visit our website at:
www.fireshippress.com

ACKNOWLEDGMENTS

Someone once said that editing a novel is like sanding a piece of wood. The more you sand, the more you discover still more to be sanded. That being the case, my wife Ann must have splinters in her fingertips from her numerous trips across the rough terrain of *Breakout from Sugar Island.* My thanks to her for sticking with it. Thanks also to our adult children, Katie, Brendan, and Courtney for their insights and advice. Thanks to Lynda Gibbs, Steve Veenstra, Gene O'Toole, Donal McCarthy, Bill Holder and Ken Crilly for volunteering to read the rough drafts and provide valuable feedback.

A special thanks to my professional editor Matt Pallamary, award winning author of *Land Without Evil, The Infinity Zone* and many others. Also, an all around great guy. These acknowledgments would not be complete without mentioning my debt to Peter Duffy, author of *The Killing of Major Denis Mahon, The Bielski Brothers,* and his most recent, *Double Agent.* His thorough research on 19th century Ireland, specifically on Strokestown, the place of my birth, provided me with the germ from which the novel grew.

SOURCES

The following books were an invaluable
help in the creation of the story.

On Ireland:

The Killing of Major Denis Mahon
by Peter Duffy

The Big House in Ireland
by Valerie Pakenham

A History of Ireland
by Jonathan Bardon

Modern Ireland 1600-1972
by R.F.Foster

On Barbados:

To Hell or Barbados
by Sean O'Callaghan

AUTHOR'S NOTE

First it must be said that *Breakout From Sugar Island* is a work of historical fiction not an actual historical account of the events portrayed in the novel. While this story covers the experience of Irish slaves in the sugar colony of Barbados, it is not about the actual mass deportation of Irish slaves by Cromwell in the 17th century. For the purpose of the story, I've taken some liberties with the chronology and set the events in 18th century Ireland and Barbados rather than the previous century. Primarily, it traces the fortunes of one white slave, Michael Redferne.

Another discrepancy in the service of the tale: the mention of the Grand Canal as the waterway by which the smugglers reached Dublin. The Grand Canal link to Dublin wasn't finished until 1779 which is beyond the time frame of the story. I hope these historical adjustments don't impact your enjoyment of the novel.

GLOSSARY OF IRISH WORDS AND REFERENCES

A Sassenach: *an Englishman.*

Amadan: *A fool.*

Awalye: *home.*

Boreen: *A small unpaved road.*

Céili: *An Irish community dance or get-together.*

Clachan: *A village.*

Conacre: *A system of letting land for tillage, usually on an eleven-month basis.*

Demesne: *The parklands surrounding the Big House.*

Dudeen: *A tobacco pipe usually made of chalk.*

Fawg on beallach: *Get out of the way, or the road.*

Gale days: *Rent collection days, usually during May and November.*

Gasun: *A young boy.*

Loblolly: *A concoction of gruel fed to slaves in Barbados.*

Naggin: *A small quantity of alcohol, usually one gil.*

Naw bach lesh: *Don't bother about it.*

Poteen: *Home distilled whiskey. The Irish equivalent of moonshine.*

Rapparee: *An armed Irish rebel of the 17th century.*

Rundale: *A system of land distribution.*

Scalpeens: *Make-shift shelters with straw roofs.*

Scathlain: *A sod hut.*

Sugan chair: *A chair with a straw seat.*

Townland: *A geographical subdivision unique to Ireland.*

Uisge beatha: *Irish word for whiskey. Literally, water of life.*

Ullaloo: *Lamentation.*

MAP OF IRELAND

CHAPTER 1

The West of Ireland, 1773

Padraig pointed to a red stain under the lake ice about twenty feet from shore. "Out there at the edge of the bulrushes, Father."

Redferne knuckled his eyes. "God bless your sight, Son. I don't see a damn thing."

The lad brushed the drip from the tip of his nose and redirected his finger at the spot near the rushes. "You must be blind then."

"Not yet, son, but I'm getting there. Need me a pair of them spectacles like His Lordship has." He shaded his eyes to see what his son was pointing at.

The lad took a few steps onto the ice.

"Come back. You'll get yourself drowned, so you will." Water in all its forms frightened him.

"But there's something strange out there, Father." The boy blew into his cupped hands.

"It's probably a sheep or a calf. It's none of our business. We're here to cut ice. His Lordship won't be none too pleased if we return to the Big House with a cart load of slush. The sun's coming up."

"I never seen a sheep with red hair." Padraig edged forward.

"Didn't I tell you not to do that?" Redferne followed his son onto the ice threading gently, with arms outspread as if on a tightrope, until they were over the stain, their breath escaping in steamy plumes.

His belly tightened. "Oh, merciful Jesus." He made the sign of the cross and dropped to his knees, brushing leaves and powdered ice from the red blotch.

1

Though distorted by the ice, there was no mistaking the ghostlike face, or the red hair that trailed behind it like the tail of a fiery comet. Maureen Kelly, recently departed for America, fixed them with an icy stare. Their last night together swam before his eyes. Dancing around the bonfire at the crossroads. The feel of her breasts. The curve of her thigh. His heart thumping. The wail of the uilleann pipes. The fight with his wife.

Padraig grabbed his elbow. "Father, Father. Are you all right?"

Redferne shook his head to break free from the web of memories. "Quick, Son, go back to the cart and get the saw and the rope."

"Shouldn't I bring the sledge?"

"Yes, and the ice pick too." His pulse raced and his hands shook so badly he thought he might pass out. *I should've followed my initial instinct and gone on about my business.* Beads of sweat ran down his back as he looked at the beautiful face entombed at his feet, the light now gone from the large blue eyes. He wanted to cry, but Padraig wouldn't understand, or perhaps he would, so he turned his face away.

It was assumed that Maureen Kelly had reached her destination across the Atlantic safely. What right had he now to shatter that illusion? She had asked him to go with her that night, her eyes pleading with him, but he refused, although God knows he was sorely tempted.

"Father, is that...?" Padraig asked, coming up behind him with the ice tools.

"One of Pat Kelly's girls? Yes. Don't tell a sinner till I figure out what to do. You hear me?" Redferne raised his arm and wiped the cold sweat from his forehead with the sleeve of his coat.

"Not even Mother?"

"Especially not your mother."

"What about the Kellys?"

"Until I can muster more nerve than I have right now, we have to keep this quiet."

"Why?"

He dropped his head. "I can't face them with this horrible news." He paused and looked down at the wan figure. "If we remove her, it might endanger all of us. If we don't, we could end up in a worse fix. That's all I can tell you right now, so do as you're told. "

Redferne sawed around the outline of the body and chipped away at the ice covering the feet until he exposed the dead woman's ankles, to which he attached the end of the rope. He instructed Padraig to smash a channel to the shore with the sledgehammer. The shallow water allowed them to pull the ice coffin to the lake's edge. Getting it into the cart was another matter.

"Padraig, we need to take this poor creature away from here and hide her, but we have to find a way to lift her into the cart first."

"Father, even if I was as strong as you we couldn't do that on our own."

Redferne raised his hand. "Hold on. That cattle shed on the boreen awhile back…" He set off at a run across a thistle field, wet grass spattering the toes of his boots with spray.

Seamus Beirne

CHAPTER 2

A hawk floated on the morning updrafts, wheeling in lazy circles over the lakeshore. Periodically, Howard Bannister, the wily land agent for the Preston estate, glanced up, wondering if the bird was stalking him. He wasn't superstitious or anything, but as he trudged along the edge of the lake examining the ice and checking the bulrushes poking from the frozen lake like green spikes, his eyes twitched. The hawk moved up the shoreline with him in ever-tightening circles. He picked up a smooth brown stone and hurled it.

"Off with you; get the hell out of here."

The hawk's desolate screech echoed off the frozen landscape as it gracefully avoided the missile. Although it was after eight o'clock, the sun barely penetrated the grey haze that obscured the lake, making his search all the more difficult.

He looked behind him before moving toward a low ditch topped by a wooden fence that straggled about fifteen feet out into the ice. Should he cross it on dry land or circumvent it where it ended on the ice? He chose the ice. As he approached a clump of rushes, the hawk landed on the last fence post, raising and lowering its wings like a man wrapped in a cloak elevating and lowering his arms.

That damn bird, I'll settle this once and for all. Scrambling to the shore, he grabbed a piece of driftwood and charged back onto the ice. The hawk took flight gracefully. Bannister lost his footing and slammed against the now-deserted post, skidding off into the bulrushes.

He lay there for a minute winded. The ice shattered. He sank to his hips. "Ah, fuck. Jesus Christ!" The cold wrapped itself around him like a predator clasping him fast to its frozen mass. He kicked and flailed, gasping for breath. Voices. No telling where they were coming from. Rather than risk being seen, he remained where he was. His teeth rattled. He had to clench his jaws to avoid biting his tongue.

He parted the bulrushes. Some distance down the shoreline two figures milled around a horse and cart. They appeared to be quarreling. The man, bundled in a frieze coat and a woolen scarf, stood about six feet. The boy, similarly clad, had close-cropped black hair. He recognized the adult as Michael Redferne, the ice harvester from the Big House on the Preston estate. The other, a lad of about sixteen, was his son. They gathered ice to cool the drinks of the gentry during the hot summer months.

Bannister hauled himself up on the ice shelf, but it broke under his weight and he sank face first into the water. With his remaining strength, he broke the ice in front of him with his fists and elbows and staggered through the bullrushes towards the shore, keeping low so the ice gatherers wouldn't see him.

He hunkered down in the cover of the reeds near the water's edge, gasping for breath. He glanced down the beach. The ice gatherers were no longer visible, but their voices were clearly audible in the stillness of the morning. This was his chance while they were out of sight. The exertion of smashing the ice had sent blood pumping through his veins, giving him enough energy to limp up the bluff to the cover of the scrubby pines.

The hawk continued to circle, now above the ice gatherers. As Bannister lifted his head to observe it, something scratched the back of his neck. He tried to swat away the annoyance and discovered it was his long braid, frozen solid. He had to get to a fire and dry his clothes or he would freeze to death.

Something about the bird's screeching frightened him, but he remained riveted where he lay underneath the pine tree, watching. Redferne was nowhere to be seen. The boy was on his own, pulling a rope attached to large slab of ice. *Idiot! Why doesn't he break it up? Make the job easier?* This was odd. He needed to get closer for a better look. He forced his frozen limbs into a sprint along the bluff behind the scrubby pines until the trees ran out. But he was still too far away to see what the lad was doing. Where had the father gone? When the hawk stopped its raucous circling and headed toward him, Bannister abandoned his hiding place, sticking close to the hedges so as not to be seen from the road. What if he ran into Redferne? *I will kill him. That's what.*

Leaving the cover of the hedgerows, he traversed fields laced with stone walls until he reached a river swollen by winter rains. He avoided a bridge downstream near the town for fear of running into someone. Turning up stream, he crossed a narrow plank that put him out onto a rocky plateau of large cracked limestone slabs. The place was in all respects a desert save for the hardy plants that flourished in the cracks, even in winter. As he hop-scotched from slab to slab, he had to be careful in his debilitated condition not to get his frozen feet caught in fissures, in some places a foot wide. Halfway across the cracked limestone, the wind kicked up and it started to snow, adding to his misery.

Shivering, he thought of stopping to rest, but decided against it for fear of losing consciousness in such a barren place. Finally, the outlines of a hazel wood emerged and he plunged among the trees, happy to be off the exposed plateau.

Another ten minutes of hard slogging brought him to a little clearing with an abandoned scathlain—a sod hut with a thatched roof where fugitive priests once said Mass for their beleaguered flock during periods of repression.

Once inside, he peeled off his sodden clothes and wrapped himself in a coarse wool blanket that he had secreted under a pile of straw that served as a bed. Gradually heat came back into his body, but he would not survive the day without a fire.

Temperatures had dropped to abnormal levels for the past few winters, shortening the growing season by as much as six weeks, causing the potato crop to fail. Thousands died of hunger. During the worst of it, emaciated bodies littered the fields and byways, their mouths green from eating grass. Even in his misery, he smiled. *Their loss; my gain.* He dug further into the straw and pulled out a rucksack holding a woolen shirt and a pair of pants. He donned them with shaking hands.

Cold air fell through the smoke hole in the roof like a steel spike. The best way to block it was with the heat of a good fire. He stacked a few handfuls of straw against a collection of flat stones set loosely on the ground to form a hearth. Over the straw he placed fragments of dry, half-decayed branches. The tricky part was getting flame to the straw.

He reached into his canvas bag and pulled out a flintlock pistol with a skull emblem embedded in the wooden stock. Sticking the barrel into the straw, he put a powder charge in the pan, drew the hammer back, and pulled the trigger. As flint struck steel it threw a spark, igniting the powder and setting the straw ablaze. He piled on more branches and a few sods of turf. Soon he had a roaring fire. Reflecting on the vagaries of chance, he wrapped himself in the blanket and stretched out on the straw beside the fire. His close call today rattled him. His task was fairly simple, but danger jumped out of the lake like a wild boar and nearly did him in. If Redferne and the kid found the body, there could be trouble, but better Redferne than another.

He needed to find out what young Redferne was pulling from the lake. He went outside and cut a sturdy hazel rod that he wedged between the two sod walls of the hut in front of the fire, draping his wet clothes over the makeshift rack.

Almost dead from exhaustion, he barricaded the door and stretched out in front of the fire, the loaded pistol by his side. As he dropped off, the fire cast shadows on the walls and danced along the chains and manacles embedded in the wooden post sunk in a corner of the hut.

CHAPTER 3

Within minutes Redferne was back, dragging a shed door. Reversing the cart to the water's edge, he propped the door against the back of it. After a half hour of exhausting pulling and shoving, they succeeded in sliding the ice coffin up the ramp, onto the cart where they covered it with a layer of straw.

All the tugging and pushing jarred one of the corpse's arms loose from the frozen mass. Inside the forearm, half way between the wrist and the bend of the elbow, he spotted a faded brand about three inches long with the letters *WS* still visible. The imprint of a fern-like plant separated the letters vertically. It had not been there before Maureen went to America.

"What's that, Father?" Padraig asked, pointing.

"Some marking that's meaningless to me." He brushed back a shaggy strand of brown hair that drooped over his eye and tucked it under his battered felt hat. The sun cast a yellow sheen on the frozen lake as it burned off the fog. If they didn't get a move on, they might end up with a thawed-out corpse. "Let's pile a few slabs of ice on top in case we get stopped."

"Why would we get stopped?"

"Because when you're doing something you shouldn't be doing, you think the whole world is on to you." Redferne walked around the cart to make sure the side crates were anchored. Satisfied, he set off with Padraig sitting on the shaft driving the horse, while he walked alongside.

9

"Son, careful you don't fall off that shaft or you'll have the wheel across your neck."

"Father, I've done this hundreds of times. If I fall, I'll roll outta' the way quick enough."

By the time they turned in the direction of the Big House, water dripped from frozen branches. At this hour on a winter's morning, few people were out. With any luck, they'd make it all the way to the ice house without encountering anyone.

As they rumbled along the frozen lane, their iron-shod wheels smashed the delicate membranes of ice that camouflaged the ruts, sounding like the crushing of a thousand eggshells. Several goldfinches picked at a clump of blackheads sticking from a hay reek adjacent to a farmhouse. A vigilant sheepdog charged after them, retreating when Redferne turned on him with his blackthorn stick. "Get outta' here, you mangy cur, before you wake half the country."

The horse flared its nostrils and gave a gentle whinny. "Someone's coming, Padraig." He grabbed the horse by the bridle. When they rounded the next bend, a small cavalry detachment trotted toward them, pennants flying from their lances. Each rider wore a black-plumed silver helmet, bright red jacket, white pants, and black riding boots. In addition to the lance, each carried a pistol and a polished sword of Sheffield steel that hung in its scabbard from the rider's waist. Behind them, a ragtag crowbar brigade marched sullenly, bathed in sweat from the effort of keeping up with the horses. Redferne pulled the cart over to one side to make room. The captain of the detachment pulled abreast of them and raised his hand for the column to halt. Redferne's heart raced.

"You're out early my good fellow," he said, scanning the cart. "What is it you have there?"

"Ice, Captain, for The Lord of the Big House. Me and my boy here does gather it in the winter so the quality will have it during the summer." My God, man, Redferne thought, what the hell is all this? He's acting as if he doesn't know me, and him The Lord's son. The men on foot didn't conceal their contempt as they leaned on their crowbars, happy for a respite from the march.

"I see." The captain nudged his horse close to the cart and took a piece of ice in his gloved hand. "You work for Lord Preston?"

Redferne bit his tongue. *Bastard can't even acknowledge my existence.* "Off and on, Captain, as you well know, I do piecework for your father when he has something for me to do."

The captain dug deeper into the ice. Redferne's breath caught. Captain Reginald Preston, the only son of Lord Charles Preston, the local landlord, eyed Redferne, appearing irritated that the ice gatherer recognized him. The captain had a reputation as a hot head, a bully, and a notorious womanizer who was fond of his liquor and prone to act impulsively on little or no provocation. Bad blood existed between him and Redferne over Maureen Kelly. Were it not for the captain's father, Redferne would have been thrown in jail, or worse.

Rumor had it that Maureen was pregnant with the captain's child. Under threat of physical harm he persuaded her to emigrate, not wanting an heir with a commoner. Another rumor pegged Redferne as the culprit.

The captain pitched the chunk of ice back into the cart and brushed the shards from his gloved hands. "You were down at the lake this morning," he went on, still not acknowledging Redferne.

No, I excavated this from a potato pit, you moron. "Yes, Captain."

"Notice anything out of the ordinary?"

Redferne averted his gaze. "No, Captain."

"What about you, young man?" He kneed his mount over to where Padraig sat. The horse's breath shooting in spurts from its flared nostrils warmed the boy's face, but he did not flinch.

"No, Captain. We had the place all to ourselves."

"You lying Catholic whelp. A touch of the whip might loosen your tongue." He swung his mount's head around, striking Padraig, knocking him to the ground. The carthorse reared. Michael struggled to prevent the animal from trampling Padraig who lay stunned on the road close to the horse's hind legs. He backed the cart up and tied the horse's reins to a branch, then ran back to his son.

Redferne, face crimson, raised his fist and roared at the captain.

11

"That was uncalled for. You could've killed my boy; your father will hear about this." The captain looked shocked at being challenged before his men. He drew his pistol and leveled it at Redferne's head.

"You insolent pig. I should spatter your brains all over the road. Should have done it a long time ago." The crowbar men straightened themselves up, uneasy at the dangerous turn of events. The soldiers shifted in their saddles as their horses stomped and moved erratically.

"Put that gun away!" a voice ordered from the rear of the column. "You were sent to deal with the Whiteboy ruffians, not to harass our workmen." Lord Preston, the captain's father, stepped from his phaeton and tightened the fur collar of his great coat around his neck. He wore a grey tri-corn hat pulled down over his ears. His thin face looked weary as if worn out from dealing with his hotheaded offspring. All heads turned toward the captain, who slid his pistol back in its holster.

"But Father, this wretch threatened me."

"How can a man armed to the teeth, with a half dozen soldiers, likewise armed to the teeth, plus five men with crowbars, be threatened by one unarmed man and a mere boy?" Lord Preston never looked in the captain's direction. "Leave now and carry out my orders." The column moved off. Redferne had further antagonized one of the most hated and feared men in the county.

The Lord turned to Redferne. "And you. Better be on your way before my ice turns to mush." He stepped back into his phaeton. The driver flicked his whip at the horse's haunches and headed back to the Big House. Redferne put his arm around Padraig. They stood in the middle of the road for a long time staring after the phaeton. The day had hardly begun and it was already shaping up to be one of the worst in his life.

"Get back on the shaft, Gasun, and let's be on our way," he said quietly.

If there was any doubt in his mind before that he needed to hide Maureen Kelly's earthly remains, it was gone. Raising the sally rod, he snapped it lightly on the horse's rear. *The quicker we get off the road the better.* They entered the private parkland of the

Preston family, known as the demesne, through a large ornamental iron gate guarding one of the side entrances. Following a cart track, they crossed a small river with an enclosure for dipping sheep. Beyond that, a grove of beech trees spread its branches over a large circular earthen mound, not unlike a prehistoric burial site. This was the ice house.

Its interior consisted of a brick-lined well twenty feet deep by fifteen feet wide. It had a domed roof to control circulation. Redferne backed the cart up to an arched doorway that led into an antechamber overlooking the well. A flight of wooden stairs contoured to the circular wall led to the bottom where the ice was stacked between layers of straw. The stack already stood five feet high. From the lower level, a subterranean passage ran all the way to the kitchen in the Big House, providing easy access to the ice in inclement weather. Michael removed the back crate from the cart and instructed Padraig to light the lanterns hung on the wall in the antechamber. "Take two of them down to the lower level, and for God's sake be careful navigating those stairs."

Padraig rolled his eyes. "Father, I'm not a two-year old."

"Looking out for you, that's all."

"Stop looking out for me. I'm not an imbecile." When Padraig had the lanterns in place, he climbed back up and helped his father load the ice coffin onto a large wooden crate suspended by pulleys and chains from an iron frame over the well. They lowered the crate to the top of the ice stack and unloaded the body. Then they dug a cavity in the ice. An hour later, they placed the last blocks of fresh ice over Maureen's corpse and said a prayer over her frozen grave.

"This will have to do," Redferne said, crossing himself, "until we can give her a decent burial." His breath caught as he looked at the grave. Had he done the right thing?

Unhooking the lantern from the wall he did a quick survey of the chamber before hustling up the stairs behind Padraig. At the top, they doused their lanterns and exited through the arched door into the anemic sunlight of the winter morning.

Seamus Beirne

CHAPTER 4

Rory Blake, the hedge schoolmaster, handed Michael Redferne a mug of ale. "You look like you could use this."

Redferne accepted the drink, walked across the sawdust-covered floor of Gavin's pub, and settled in a corner near a blazing turf fire, away from the knot of locals that crowded the counter. Blake returned to the bar. A half dozen lanterns hung from the ceiling, creating islands of light on the floor that merged and separated as the lanterns swayed back and forth before drafts seeping through the doors and windows. An oak bar top extended along one wall behind which stood three large vats. Three barmen worked the vats, sliding mugs of local beer along the moist countertop to outstretched hands. Two windows, one on each corner, lit the room, allowing Redferne to observe both streets. The noise from the market entered in short bursts as the door opened and closed. After the day he'd had, Redferne wasn't in the mood for conversation and wanted time to himself to ponder his predicament. He had a feeling this was not to be. So far, Padraig had not told his mother about finding Maureen's body. That was good, but how long would that last?

Blake sauntered over with a mug of ale in one hand and a dudeen in the other. He was in his early forties, but didn't look it. His black curly hair topped a rugged face sporting several days' growth of beard. He filled his dudeen with tobacco and lit it with a coal from the fire which he arranged in the bowl with his calloused fingers. "Old Preston saved your arse today, I'm told." Rory blew a shaft of smoke from the side of his mouth as he sat across from Redferne.

Redferne bristled. "Is accepting your jibes the price of the ale?" He shoved the mug toward Blake, slopping its contents on the table.

Blake pushed it back. "No offense intended."

"Rory, what do you want?"

"Your help, Michael."

"For what?"

"You know right well, for what."

Redferne raised the mug to his lips. Taking another swallow, he gazed into the fire. "Indeed I do."

"Well, then, can I have your answer?"

"I don't believe in the Whiteboy creed of terror. You should stick to school mastering, Rory."

Blake clinched his fists. "We're protecting our people from Prescott and his crowbar goons."

"That's what you call it, eh? Maiming cattle and throwing neighbors naked into thorn pits?"

"None got thorned that didn't deserve it and hadn't been warned."

Redferne expelled a blast of air through his nostrils. "A rock through a window in the middle of the night is more apt to harden a man than get his cooperation."

"Good neighbors don't covet the houses of them cast out on the roads. Can't you see that?"

"Maybe so, but acting like the Prestons won't get you sympathy."

"Like the Prestons?" Blake stabbed his index finger several times in front of Redferne's face. "You'll come running when *you* want help, but know this, by God, we don't take kindly to malingerers." Then jumping up, he whipped the dudeen from his mouth, flung it into the fire and stormed toward the door. Redferne struggled to control himself. At six feet two, he had the look of a fella who saw the inside of too many taverns. Few dared to pick a fight with him, unless they were drunk. Rory Blake came close to doing that. He wasn't drunk either.

The lads at the bar grew quiet, looking from Blake to Redferne. They gazed Blake out the door and then leaned in to whisper. A few threw sidelong glances at Redferne, who stared into the fire.

A patron with a threadbare canvas cap tipped his head toward Redferne. "The priest says they might cast him out."

"If Father Duffy was going to do it, he'd have done it by now. Hasn't it been two years gone?"

"Ah shure, Redferne couldn't give a tinker's damn anyway. He's a rough ticket."

"That scar on his lip tells you he's no altar boy."

"That's hardly news."

"There's them that done a hell of a sight worse, strutting round like peacocks."

"Aye, the ones with money and acreage."

"It's said he talked to Parson Stack. Might be considering becoming a..." "Protestant?" another said. May he roast in hell 'til the trumpet blows!"

"Hold on now. Could be tolerable if that red-haired Kelly lassie ended up there with him."

"How could that happen with her in America and him in Ireland?"

"You amadán. Hell is universal." A trickle of laughter rippled through the group.

If Redferne overheard, he didn't let on. He emptied his mug and strode to the door beneath the swaying lanterns.

As he got closer to home, he slowed down. Despite the passage of time, things were tense with his wife Grace. She was on him for everything. Going to the tavern, coming home late, being unemployed—most of the time. It seemed as if she was looking for excuses to lay into him. He wasn't ready right now for a fight, so he turned around and walked back down the street. The confrontation with Blake, the leader of the secret Whiteboy agrarian society, also weighed on his mind. He would have to address it sooner or later. A light shone in his aunt's place, which didn't surprise him, as she slept little. He tapped lightly on the door.

"It's at home with your family you should be, not knocking on strange doors in the middle of the night," the small grey-haired woman said as Redferne stepped into her little kitchen. Aunt Kate lived on her own in the townland of Kildallogue, a community of twenty dwellings, since her husband died in the famine of 1745.

"For Christ's sake, I'm your nephew, Aunt Kate, what are you blathering about, 'strange doors.'" Redferne kissed her on the forehead.

She moved to her chair beside the struggling fire. "Things in a cock-up at home again?" A black shawl draped her shoulders and a white wool cap covered her head. Her face was the color of parchment.

"And anyway, what's an old woman like you doing up at one in the morning? In bed you should be saying your Rosary."

"If you're staying, you might as well bring us a few sods of turf from the creel in the corner and put the kettle on."

In minutes he had a blaze going that cast shadows on the whitewashed walls. The kettle began to sing. He sat on the other side of the hob, warming his hands on the flames. This had been his place of refuge since he was a kid, especially after his young brother drowned.

"Bit chilly out there tonight," he said, rubbing his hands together.

"What do you expect? There's snow on the ground."

He smiled. "Yes, Aunt Kate."

"Suppose you were at the tavern earlier." She pulled the shawl tightly around her thin shoulders.

He pointed to the moon, shining through the frayed weave of thatch. "When are you going to let me fix that hole?"

She eyed him critically. "You're getting a bit of a belly."

He raised his shoulders. "'Tis nothing. I'll work it off as soon as I get a real job."

She blew her nose on the hem of her apron. "Get up and make the tea, will ye? Don't forget the bottleen in the bottom shelf of the cupboard." He made them each a mug of tea and splashed a generous dollop from the little bottle into both.

"Me knees are killing me. Without the bottleen I'd be up all night. God in his mercy bless Sore Nose Paddy and his still, the scoundrel."

"But you *are* up all night."

"Maybe, but I'm a much happier night owl for it." They sat sipping tea and staring into the fire.

"Isn't it strange the way things work out in life?" Redferne said. "Something happens early on and it cripples you forever."

"How long are you going to let that strangle you? You were a wee lad of nine. You're not to blame."

"That's not the way Mother sees it. That's not the way Daddy saw it either, God rest his soul." Redferne raised the mug to his lips. A thin breeze came through the hole in the thatch and bent the fire sideways, scattering white ash across the toecaps of his boots. Redferne's mother, Tess, was Kate's sister, high-strung and not prone to forgiveness.

"You've honored your brother's memory. You named your son after him," Kate said. "He will walk this earth as long as Padraig does." She shifted her shoulders within the shawl, looking for a warmer spot.

"He was so young and I was reckless and stupid."

"You were both young; that's the point." Kate took another mouthful of fortified tea. "The drowning was an accident." A long silence ensued.

"Grace still hasn't forgiven me for my indiscretion with Maureen."

Kate cleared her throat. "Can you blame her? After all, that Kelly girl was ten years your junior. Not a smart move on your part."

"Much of what I do isn't smart, Aunt Kate. Sometimes I can't help myself when I think of the accident. And I think of it a lot."

"Don't lay your excuses on your dead brother. You know it's dishonest."

Redferne couldn't shake the memory of that day long ago on the lake. He had tried to save his brother, but he had failed. So he saved himself. That was his burden. No escaping it, although much of his life since was an attempt to outrun it.

As a consequence he wasn't given to introspection, not because it wasn't called for, but because introspection was a Pandora's box.

Once opened, it couldn't be slammed shut again. That's why he didn't dwell on his dalliance with Maureen Kelly. Self-reflection dragged him back to the accident.

He finished his tea and threw the leavings into the fire, and then stood to go. "I'll be back at the end of the week to patch that roof, Aunt Kate, as soon as Lord Preston pays me the few shillings he owes me."

"The blessings of God on you, Michael. Now go home to your wife and son."

Redferne kissed her on the forehead again and stooped through the small door into the moonlight. He pulled a crumpled frieze cap from his pocket and set it on his head.

He walked down the quiet street until he reached his own house where he checked his pocket watch. *Two a.m. Hate to wake them up.* He slipped the watch back into his waistcoat pocket. In reality, he didn't have the courage to go in and face the music. Better wait till morning, he thought, and headed for his neighbor's shed, where he bedded down for the night.

CHAPTER 5

Bannister pricked the horse's flanks with his spurs as he rode through the early morning fog along a country lane to a rundale collective in the townland of Kildallogue. The rundale, an archaic Irish system of land distribution, allowed a group of tenants to lease several plots in common from a landlord, a system which often led to disputes among the participants and headaches for the owner. On Gale days in May and November, an elder in the townland collected the rent and delivered it in a lump sum to the landlord.

This particular rundale was the biggest disaster on the Preston estate. Over half the tenants were in arrears and the other half so inconsistent in their payments that evicting the beggars and leveling their hovels seemed the only solution. But it was difficult to sort out those who paid from those who didn't, since the elders weren't forthcoming about the identities of the slackers. As Lord Preston's agent, Bannister was supposed to make eviction recommendations to his boss, who sometimes forgot that the vast estate of 15,000 acres, with its hierarchy of middlemen, small farmers, cottiers, subtenants, and landless peasants needed a steady hand at the helm.

This meant running the estate as a business, not as a philanthropic organization. Bannister saw it as his mission in life to put some backbone into Lord Preston, even if he had to bend the rules, and if his instincts were correct, he would soon be bending the rules.

This morning he was out early to check on the results of yesterday's clearances by Captain Preston, Lord Preston's son. The bailiff had assured Bannister that the crowbar brigade tumbled everything, and with the help of the soldiers, turned the occupants out onto the road. Problem was, many of the evicted often returned, setting up scalpeens—makeshift shelters—near the original dwellings.

Bannister reached the crest of a hill and turned into a field with several spent potato plots. Running alongside them, an aboveground pit covered with straw and earth protected the potatoes from the winter frost. The fact that the evicted had forfeited their potatoes, their only food source, which they planted and harvested, did not bother Bannister. He regarded them as part payment toward uncollected rent, allowing him to squeeze extra cash from the next tenant.

He eventually planned to get rid of all these small plots and turn them into larger fields for dairy farming, a venture far more profitable than renting land as tillage to paupers. So far, Lord Preston had resisted his advice, but Bannister had no doubt that he could overcome his boss's scruples by demonstrating how profitable such a scheme could be. If the Lord proved obdurate, he would turn to his son who was more flexible and ruthless.

At the end of the field, he dismounted and led his horse to a grove of trees where two men with pistols in their belts sat smoking pipes. Seeing Bannister, they stood up and tried to look awake. The elder of the two, a barrel-chested man in his forties named Skelton, came toward him, arms akimbo, his fists dug into his hips as if expecting an argument. Ringlets of unkempt hair escaped from under a woolen cap, meshing with a black beard that dropped from his chin in four disheveled tufts.

"Are they all tumbled, Skelton?" Bannister asked.

"'Fraid not, Boss. That is, they were tumbled yesterday right enough, but the crowbar men didn't burn the thatched roofs, so the paupers came back and built scalpeens."

Bannister smiled thinly. "My orders were to burn the roofs."

"I know, Boss, but the bailiff got word from the Lord to leave them be. Not much me and Devine could do." He nodded in his mate's direction, a tall thin man with a ferret face and sloe-colored eyes.

"Wasn't his son there?" Bannister said.

Devine pulled the pipe from his mouth and lofted a fulsome tobacco spit into the hawthorn bushes. "Aye, he fussed and he fumed but the old man's orders carried the day."

The captain can't afford to lose his allowance, Bannister thought, *so he does his ranting behind daddy's back. Fortunately, I'm not bound by the Lord's scruples or his son's cravenness, even if I'm running a risk countermanding the old man's wishes. Oh, well, I'll cross that bridge when I come to it. I'll have to persuade His Lordship to allow me to supervise future evictions.*

"Right, let's get to it then." He mounted his horse and withdrew a carbine from its sheath. Skelton and Devine cocked their pistols. Leaving the cover of the trees, they followed Bannister down the slope at a trot toward a row of scalpeens that followed the contours of a boreen. Steam rose from the thatch roofs as the sun burned off the early morning mist. Birds chirped and flitted through the nearby pine trees but the occupants of the scalpeens slumbered. At Bannister's signal, Skelton used a tinder box to set a torch ablaze. Bannister touched it to the straw roof of the first scalpeen, and then yelling at the top of his lungs, rode up and down the lane, brandishing the torch in front of him. He didn't stop until the whole lane blazed in a fiery inferno.

Mothers with babies, men and women, both young and old, piled into the lane coughing and choking. A tall dark-haired lad named Clancy charged Bannister with a spade. Bannister dropped him in his tracks with a blow from the barrel of his carbine.

"Hold him," he shouted to Devine. "Skelton, you follow me." He spurred his horse through the throng of women and children. Seeing two young men running up the spent potato field, he reined his horse off the lane and followed. They headed for a gap in the hedge, but Bannister got there ahead of them. With Skelton's help, he herded the fugitives with his whip back down the furrows into the arms of his other henchman.

The faster of the two broke free and cut across the potato plot toward the gap. Bannister wheeled his mount and undid his bullwhip, flailing it in circles around his head as he pursued the fugitive, ensnaring him around the ankles and bringing him to the ground with a sickening thud.

Dismounting, he inspected the cowering runaway. He wore a frieze jacket over breeches that went to mid-calf and were tied at the waist with a length of rope. He had no shoes. Grabbing him by the scruff of the neck, he led him back to where two other young men lay face down in the dirt under the watchful eyes of Skelton and Devine.

"Not a bad morning's catch, if I say so." He eyed the captives from head to toe as if evaluating prize animals. The men, in their mid-twenties, appeared in good physical condition.

Devine pointed to one of them. "Boss, do you think this bloke you clipped with your carbine is in shape to travel?"

"I didn't clip him that hard. After a good meal of potatoes and a night's rest, he'll be as right as rain. After all, it wouldn't do to send them off hungry."

Surprise registered on the captives' faces. One of them muttered something in Irish. Bannister didn't understand him. At the age of five his mother had taken him with her to France in search of his father who had enlisted in the armies of Louis XIV. She never found him.

Bannister lost his native tongue as he had little use for it wandering the world as a soldier of fortune, so when the captive spoke in Irish, Bannister became agitated.

"*Dites moi.* Tell me. What kind of gibberish was he mumbling?"

"I think he said, *'Thaw rud me cearth,'* or something like that," Devine replied.

"What the hell does that mean?"

"*There's something wrong,*" Skelton answered.

Bannister threw back his head and laughed. "Something wrong? That's it? *Merde,* he doesn't know the half of it." His mates joined in the laughter and the captives showed fear.

"That's a bloody good one. Enough of this nonsense. You know the drill. Take them to the hut. Stay off the main roads. In the meantime, keep a sharp lookout, and no boozing. I'll join you later."

"Where's Luke?"

"He's at the hut getting things ready for our guests."

Bannister mounted his horse. His men led the captives away bound to each other at the wrists. A purifying wind scoured the lane of the acrid smoke of burning straw and the stinking smell of squalid mattresses. As he spurred his horse toward the Big House, he released the long braid from under his tricorne hat and let it tumble down his back.

Seamus Beirne

CHAPTER 6

After midnight, Bannister mounted his horse and galloped through the demesne to the main gate. The town slumbered under a mantle of snow, not a sinner to be seen, not even a stray dog. Across his saddle hung a sack with a slab of bacon, legs of mutton, potatoes, and a few pounds of butter.

By one o'clock, he reached the cracked limestone plateau, detouring around it to avoid the fissures between the slabs, a treacherous route for a horse, especially since it was masked by snow.

A hundred yards from the scathlain, a gruff voice challenged him. "Halt! The password, friend, or you die."

"Captain Tolliver," Bannister shouted.

"Hello, Boss." Skelton emerged from the shadows and unloaded the food sack from Bannister's horse.

"Everything under control?"

"Everything's shipshape, Boss," Skelton replied.

Bannister dismounted and followed Skelton into the scathlain.

A turf fire heated the interior. The three captives bound at the hands and chained to a post, appeared desolate and afraid.

Bannister pointed to one with congealed blood on the side of his head. "What happened to him? Did he fall?"

Luke, a handsome young lad in his twenties with wavy brown hair and a stubbly beard, stood in the middle of the cabin, glowering at the captives. "Against my fist," he snickered. "He wouldn't stop yelling."

"Luke, dammit, next time use your pistol."

27

"Shoot them?" he asked, his mouth agape.

"No, fool. Use it to threaten them. The better condition they're in, the better the price they'll fetch, and the better your cut." Skelton and Devine boiled the bacon, the potatoes and the legs of mutton in the same iron pot. When the meal was ready they freed the captives' hands so they could eat. They went at the bacon and mutton like famished wolves attacking a deer carcass. They peeled the potatoes with their fingernails and slathering them in butter, stuffed them in their mouths and washed everything down with ale.

Bannister viewed them with amusement. "Probably the best meal those paupers had in a year."

His henchmen guffawed. "Probably ever," Skelton said.

When the prisoners ate their fill, their captors reshackled them and settled down to eat themselves. Bannister limited their beer consumption to one mug. They needed to be alert on the long night journey to Sligo harbor.

After two hours sleep, they unchained the captives and herded them toward a coach. Before boarding, Bannister drew his pistol with the Medusa head and leveled it at one of them. "Don't anybody get the bright idea of calling for help unless you want a pistol ball in the skull."

One of Bannister's hirelings translated his warning into Irish. Satiated by the good food and drink, the prisoners offered no resistance, stepping into the coach one after the other like sheep into a shearing pen, except for the tall dark-haired lad named Clancy who had attacked Bannister with a spade.

"*Caw will amuid eg dhul?*" he asked in a thick Connaught accent. Bannister looked to Luke, frowning.

"He'd like to know where they're going, Boss."

Bannister laughed.

Luke grinned and said, "Should I tell him?"

"Why not, but make it sound good, all right?"

Luke lifted the canvas flap of the coach window and stuck his head in.

"You lads want to know where you're going, eh? You're off to seek employment in a much warmer climate than this Godforsaken place. The pay is good and the women are amazing, especially the mulattos; and I hear tell the supply is unlimited. You get free food and lodging and if..." Two manacled fists flew out of the coach window, smashing his handsome face. He fell backwards onto the side of the road. Blood spurting from his nose melted red holes as big as copper pennies deep in the snow. Skelton and Devine rushed forward with drawn pistols, but Bannister intervened.

"Leave it be. No time for payback."

"Are you going to let them away with this?" Skelton said glowering.

"Luke's a fool. You don't mock a man and hold your face inches from his fists, especially if you're as handsome as Luke thinks he is. Besides they are more valuable to me than him." A cheer went up from the captives. Skelton and Devine rushed the coach. A pistol shot brought the assault to an abrupt halt, jolting the night awake. Little creatures scurried through the withered grass under the crusted snow.

Bannister pointed a double-barreled horse pistol at his men bunched around the carriage door. One barrel disgorged black smoke. "Are you imbeciles deaf as well as stupid? Now mount up."

"What about Luke, Mr. Bannister? He's out cold," Skelton ventured.

"What about him?" Bannister swung his horse around. "Either he wakes up or he freezes to death. Simple as that. Stupidity has its price."

After the driver finished lighting the lanterns at the front of the coach, they trundled off, leaving Luke crumpled by the roadside, his blood expanding the red stain in the snow.

Bannister and his crew arrived at a warehouse along the Garavogue River around six in the evening. They offloaded their passengers and stowed them in the rear of the building behind chests of tea and bales of linen. Leaving his men to guard the captives, he went in search of Captain Tolliver, master of the ship *Kate O'Dwyer*.

The O'Dwyer, a brig with two square-rigged masts, fore and main, was bound that evening for the West Indies and the American colonies with a cargo of salt beef, pork, butter, and linen. Bannister recognized her from the green and gold figurehead of a mermaid mounted on her prow.

The tide surged through the Garavogue as Bannister hurried down the wharf. It was already halfway up the stone stairways, constructed along the waterfront for loading and unloading of ships. There wasn't much time to spare. By the looks of it, the tide would be at its highest within the hour. The brig strained her hawser, her masts silhouetted against the winter sky like barbed spears. Sailors swarmed up the rigging to unfurl the sails in preparation for departure.

"Bannister, began to think you'd come to grief," Captain Tolliver called from the deck.

"Caution begged delay." Bannister scrambled up the gang plank and joined Tolliver in his cabin. Tolliver didn't look like a captain. He wore a round grey hat with a broad brim and a full-length blue frock coat trimmed with a lace binding. Woven red brocade adorned the cuffs, collar, and pockets. His face looked rough from a week-old beard and he had an upper tooth missing.

"Where's the merchandise?" he asked, pouring two glasses of claret from a half-empty decanter. He studied Bannister under hooded eyelids.

"Right close. As soon as I see the color of your money, I will hand them over. Fifty pounds per head, as I recall," Bannister said.

"Not so fast my friend. The fifty pounds agreement was not sight unseen. I don't buy pigs in a poke. Might be getting a bunch of half-starved peasants who could end up food for sharks."

"I have three strapping farm boys in their mid-twenties, who will command the highest prices in the slave auctions of Barbados."

"Providing they survive the voyage and the tropical heat," Tolliver drained the last of his claret glass.

"That's no concern of yours or mine," Bannister said.

"They are your countrymen, are they not?"

"Come Robert, that high moral tone ill suits you, given that you run a slaver back of your legitimate business," Bannister said, pursing his lips.

"I didn't mean to give offense or sound disapproving. Merely intellectual curiosity as to whether nationality has any bearing in these matters," Tolliver continued matter-of-factly, tapping his fingers on the arm of his chair.

"I found out long ago that money is a great salve for a delicate conscience, but to answer your question: I don't know and I don't care. I never dwell on such things. The world is an ugly place. One must fight to survive," Bannister said crossing and uncrossing his legs.

"Let's get on with it then, shall we. The hour is late and we are up against the tide."

Bannister couldn't risk walking the chained captives down the pier with its grog houses and taverns, so he advised the captain to send a skiff to collect them.

Once on board, the captives were chained together in a hold jammed with linen bales and barrels of salted meat. They resisted by shouting and kicking, but they were no match for truncheons and hobnail boots. The captain examined them by lantern light. Prime specimens. He took a leather pouch from his pocket and counted out the agreed-upon sum to Bannister in front of the condemned men.

They toasted their good fortune with a shot of rum provided by the bursar who stood by with a silver tray holding a bottle of Jamaica's best. When they finished, Bannister followed the captain through the hatch, out onto the deck. He turned and looked as the captives were being led into the bowels of the ship. Their ankle chains beat a rhythmic jangle on the floorboards as they shuffled away.

Seamus Beirne

CHAPTER 7

One year later

Crickets chirped when Michael Redferne lifted the canvas flap covering the shed door. It took a while for his eyes to adjust to the darkness inside. He thought schoolmaster Rory Blake had moved the hedge school to a new venue because its location had been compromised. The Penal Laws of 1702 made Irish schools illegal, so they frequently relocated to out-of-the-way places like bogs or foothills. He was about to leave when a light flickered in the darkness, revealing a man sitting on his hunkers behind a makeshift table, holding a lantern. He wore a grey frieze jacket over what was once a white shirt. Six or seven young students arrayed in front of him sat in a similar fashion.

"We heard someone approaching but there wasn't time enough to disperse so I covered the lantern and hoped for the best," the man said, "but I'm right glad to see you, Michael Redferne."

"Rory Blake, is that you? Sorry for barging in like this, but I've come on an errand of some importance."

"It's not to refresh your Latin that you come then." Blake rose from the floor and approached Redferne.

"Faith, it's not Rory, though my Latin could do with a little shoring up. It's been quite some time since we were together in old Master Casserly's classroom." He reached for Blake's outstretched hand.

"Thought so, but you're welcome nonetheless," Blake said. "I'm afraid I'm not as vigilant as old Casserly. He would have spotted you a mile off."

"Jaysus, the times must be rough. At least you and I had a door to our school," Redferne said. The voices of the students filled the shed talking and laughing, glad to get a break from their lessons.

"We have a door sure enough, but these days you have to be resourceful, so we put it to a more creative use." Blake pointed to the table which was the shed door sitting on two large turf baskets.

"Well I'll be damned," Redferne said laughing. "Irish ingenuity."

"Despite that ingenuity the Sassenach has held his heel on our throats for six centuries." Resentment dripped from Blake's voice like sap from a wounded tree.

"The English may have held us down, but they haven't quenched our spirit, by God," Redferne said. The crescendo of young voices made it difficult for them to communicate, so Blake clapped his hands.

"Children, I've some bad news. School is out for the day." The kids cheered and scrambled for the door. "Wait, wait! Be careful on the way home and as usual leave your books and school material with me. We don't want you stopped by an unfriendly and have to explain why you're carrying pencil and paper. Remember it's a crime against the State." The canvas flapped back and forth like a punching bag as the kids rushed outside.

"Isn't it a hell of a situation that our children must live like this?" Redferne followed Blake to the table and sat down opposite him on a bag of straw. "It makes my blood boil."

"And it will continue so unless we stop talking and do something about it." Blake reached into his pants pocket and took out a chalk pipe, filling it with pre-cut slivers of tobacco from a leather pouch. "I hope what you've come to talk about is a step in that direction." He lit a twisted piece of paper from the lantern and put the flame to his pipe, puffing vigorously.

"If you can't answer me that, then take your problems elsewhere. I'm no priest who can fix your moral dilemmas." He passed the pipe to Redferne, who wasn't a stranger to priests. Over the years he had consulted them to cope with his brother's death. Telling him it was God's will didn't help, so he wasn't about to seek their advice now. They trotted out God's will to keep the poor in their place. He was as angry at the purveyors of this callous creed as he was at the ruling class.

He took a few puffs of the sweet-smelling tobacco smoke and returned the pipe, then proceeded to tell Blake about finding Maureen's body. When he was finished, Blake got up and poked his head through the canvas flap, looking to the left and right, before returning.

He leaned into Redferne's face, squinting as if trying to decipher the scrawl of an errant schoolboy. "Are you a raging lunatic? Tell me again why you thought taking the body and hiding it wouldn't land you in a deeper manure pit than you were already in." He locked his fingers behind his head and waited.

"Rory, I panicked, that's all. When I saw it was Maureen, I couldn't think straight. I thought for sure that when Captain Preston got wind of this, he would implicate me, not because he cared a damn for her, but because he blamed me for having bested him with Maureen. He's a prick, that's all. A pompous ass. He doesn't like to lose. It would be a way to get back at me." He studied Blake as if pleading for understanding.

Blake removed his hands from his head. "Did Preston get into Maureen Kelly's knickers?"

"Absolutely not."

"How do you know?"

"Because she told me, and I believe her. That's why Preston has it in for me."

"Did you?" Blake knocked the bowl of the pipe against the heel of his boot.

Redferne looked away.

Seamus Beirne

CHAPTER 8

Captain Preston and his detachment of cavalry were out early that morning on an eviction run. After leveling houses and turning the rabble out on the road, they burned the thatched roofs. It was against his father's wishes, but Bannister was along, having persuaded His Lordship to put him in charge of the eviction detail. If there was any fallout, Bannister would get the blame.

To the younger Preston, Bannister had far too much authority, but regarding evictions, he was Bannister's ally. Go easy on this rabble and they'd sprout up somewhere else like mushrooms. If he had his way, he would clear the estate of every last one of the beggars. Only when the land was rid of these indolent Papist pigs could the estate grow into its potential. Then he could lead a life befitting his station, no longer humiliated before his peers by his thin purse. He needed several additional horses and at least a dozen more hounds for his foxhunting enterprise, but was stymied by a lack of cash.

He left the cleanup to Bannister and headed back to the Big House with his troopers. He couldn't stand the screams and wails of the evicted, and the stench from their mud wall dwellings, shared with cows and pigs, was atrocious. It was a beautiful crisp winter day with a light dusting of snow on the hard ground. As the detachment cantered along, the horses kicked up a swirl of fine powder and knocked sparks from the rocky terrain with their iron hooves. He took a short cut through a copse of white ash and came out on the crest of a hill.

A road gang toiled at its base. The road snaked through a desolate landscape punctuated by solitary clumps of bare trees. He turned to his sergeant. "Nice to see these lazy bastards working for a change. Let's pay them a visit."

A group of poorly clad men wielding sledge hammers broke large rocks into fragments. Women and children stooped over, loading the fragments into wicker baskets. Many had no shoes. Blood speckled the stones where sharp edges tore at bare fingers and toes.

Preston signaled the detachment to halt alongside the workers. Walking up and down the edge of the road, a short, middle-aged man in a battered cap surveyed the rock breakers with the caution of one looking for a lost sixpenny bit in a thistle field. His cheeks had the overripe, purple color of a rotten peach that hinted at a fondness for an illegal brew called poteen. His hands were sunk into the pockets of an old British Army red coat. Tucked under his arm was a small ledger with a tattered grey cover. The strained look on his face suggested a mixture of curiosity and fear. He was not wielding a sledgehammer, so Preston suspected that he was in charge.

"Are you the ganger?"

He tipped his cap. "Yes, Yer Honor."

Preston, gestured toward the group. "How much is this lot being paid per day?"

"A penny, Yer Honor."

"Even the kids?"

"They get a farthing."

"More than they're worth."

None of the laborers lifted their heads or made eye contact with the captain. Such a move could be interpreted as disrespect which might result in a flogging with the lead-tipped thong hanging from the captain's saddle. The horses stamped their feet and shook their heads. The jingling of their bridles sounded like dinner bells. Breath flared from their nostrils like steam.

Preston snapped his fingers at the ganger.

"Give me that." The ganger passed him the ledger containing the names of the laborers and their attendance records. He scanned it briefly before returning it, then he pointed to a middle-aged woman wrapped in a black shawl. "I say, woman. Don't I know you?"

The woman didn't reply or look up. Preston went for his whip.

"Cait, Cait, his honor is talking to you," the ganger shouted.

The woman lifted her head. Her eyes darted back and forth like a trapped fox.

Preston took his hand off the whip. "What's your name, woman?"

"Cait McLoughlin, Yer Honor."

"Don't you have an older boy?"

"Yes, Yer Honor."

"How come the younger one is here and not him?"

The woman looked down. "He's home sick, Yer Honor."

Something was odd here. Most of the children were young. Where were the older ones? Were they all sick? He wanted to investigate further but then he remembered an assignation with a young wife whose husband was in Dublin on business. He spurred his horse and gave the order to move out. They had cantered along the road about a quarter of a mile when a tall gangly lad in his mid-twenties came running across the fields waving his arms and shouting.

One of the rock breakers. Hard to forget him dressed as he was. He wore a frieze greatcoat, tightened around the waist with a frayed cloth belt. A battered felt hat adorned his head. The hat band had pulled loose on one side and hung down by his right ear. In the past he had supplied Preston with valuable information. Preston raised his hand and halted the column as the young informant, out of breath, scrambled across the stone wall onto the road.

"What is it, O'Rourke?"

"Yer Honor, sir," the lad said bending over, grasping for breath. "I know why the older lads are off the work gang."

Preston straightened in his saddle. "Go ahead."

"They're at the hedge school, sir."

A nervous spasm shot through Preston's stomach. His instincts had been right. "Where?"

"I don't know, Yer Honor, but 'tis around here somewheres. This morning, the older McLoughlin fella and two others were on the job for about an hour before they slipped off."

"Good work." Preston reached into his purse and gave the informant two pennies. He had to make a decision. Keep his appointment with young Lady Osborne, or look for the school. He hated to forego the charms of another man's wife, but if he put the Papist den of ignorance out of commission, it would be a feather in his cap. He ordered his horsemen to fan out in a skirmish line and scour the area. "If those kids walked from the work site, it can't be too far hence. We're looking for a shed or an abandoned dwelling."

After searching for a half hour, a shout came down the line. One of his dragoons rode up. "You better come down here, Captain; I think we found what we're after." Preston followed the horseman over a small hill where four of his riders had pulled their mounts in a circle. A young freckle-faced, red-haired boy with blood running from a gash in his forehead stood in the middle.

"We ordered him to stop, Captain, but he put up a fight," one of his men said, still grasping the struggling boy by the back of his collar. Another rider handed the captain a canvas bag with a jotter, a pencil, and a small volume of Irish poems.

"Is this yours, boy?" the captain said, inspecting the canvas bag. The boy bit his lower lip trying not to cry. "Listen, you young whelp." The captain uncurled his whip and pitched the bag across the heads of the horsemen, scattering its contents all over the field. "Either tell me where that Papist school is, or I'll flay you within an inch of your life."

CHAPTER 9

"She was carrying my child," Redferne replied, covering his face with his hands.

"So the rumors were true. You knocked Maureen Kelly up and then disowned her," Blake said.

"It wasn't as crude as you're putting it," Redferne said.

"Oh, I'll wager it's every bit as crude as I'm putting it, even a damn sight cruder," Blake's face gathered into an angry frown.

"You can't afford to get up on your high horse given your own spotty reputation," Redferne shouted.

"I don't have a wife and kid and I'm not running to Mass every Sunday, you hypocrite."

"Why don't you come out and say what's getting under your skin. You're sore at me for not throwing my lot in with the Whiteboys."

"You were unwavering in your refusal to fight for your neighbors, but a damn sight more flexible when it came to abandoning a young woman who was carrying your child."

"This is not a bed of roses for me either, I'll have you know." The veins stood out on Redferne's forehead.

"Maybe not, but it seems to me you got the sweet-smelling blooms and she got the thorns," Blake said.

The stinging truth of Blake's words roiled Redferne's gut. He hadn't expected to be rebuked by him, and if *he* felt this way, what would the more rigid members of the community think?

The eerie sound of the wind whistling through the spaces in the stone walls deepened his sense of foreboding. A thin shaft of light filtered through a hole in the roof turned blue with tobacco smoke.

Blake gathered his books and put them into a leather bag. "Are you sure she was pregnant, or could she have conned you?"

"Before she went away, she visited Grainne Dysart. She confirmed it."

"That old hag, with her keening, fairy tales, and her so-called medical cures. I wouldn't trust a word she uttered."

"If we could have gotten the opinion of a right doctor, we would've, but those people wouldn't give poor folk the time of day." Redferne lowered his eyes and scraped the heel of his boot back and forth across the dirt floor.

"A bunch of quacks, if you ask me," Blake answered with a turn-your-stomach expression on his face. "The bigger questions are, how long was Maureen back from America, who killed her, and why?"

"That's guesswork at this point. Maybe it was an accident and she fell into the lake."

"Pity you weren't that cool and analytical when you cut her from the ice," Blake scoffed, adjusting the strap of his leather bag and looping it over his head. "I bet old Benjamin Strange would have a fair idea of what led to her demise."

"He lodges in the Big House so I'm not going into the lion's den to test that theory right now," Redferne said, "but something else doesn't sit right. Where did Maureen come by the passage money home in so short a time? Most people can never afford to return."

"Your hunch that Preston killed her to protect his reputation is ludicrous," Blake said. "He already has illegitimate progeny running all over the townland. Not only does he not try to disown them, he's proud of it. Sees himself as a Lothario."

"Never made that claim."

"No, but you were thinking it," Blake said.

"Now you're a mind reader? But be that as it may, thanks for removing him from the suspect list and putting me back on it."

"Unless Preston killed her for another reason," Blake said more to himself. Redferne studied the palms of his hands as if the answers to his problems were written there.

"I know our last conversation about me signing on to your cause wasn't a friendly one. But things have changed since then."

"The only thing that's changed is that Maureen Kelly appears to have been murdered, which has raised your awareness about the state of things in our fair island. Otherwise it's pretty much the status quo," Blake said, the old sarcasm returning.

"Hasn't the status quo grown worse?" Redferne said straightening himself and rubbing his knuckles against the small of his back.

"When Maureen left two years ago, there were evictions and clearances. These outrages are still taking place today, so no, the status quo hasn't..." Blake jumped up, pulled the canvas flap aside, and peered out.

Redferne half rose. "Anything wrong?"

"Probably the wind. Running a hedge school makes you paranoid. You're always on edge."

He dropped the flap and returned to his seat.

Redferne sat back down. "There's one major event that's put the people up in arms that wasn't on the horizon two years ago."

Blake rolled his eyeballs. "Enlighten me."

"Begod, Rory, I'm not sure any mere mortal is capable of doing that. But I'll try. The cursed landlords are fencing in the commons. Poor folk can no longer use it for tillage or grazing."

Blake scoffed. "There are so many outrages being perpetrated against our people that I'm losing track. It's all the same viper's nest of injustice as far as I'm concerned."

"The country is on the verge of a bloody revolution," Redferne said, standing up. "I need to take a leak." He didn't, but it was an excuse to get out of the claustrophobic shed. He paced a little, then stopped and cupped his ear. Was that the clink of bells or the chafing of ice-covered branches against each other in the wind? Probably his imagination playing tricks on him. The hostile reception from Blake unsettled him. He thought about leaving but went back inside and resumed his position on the bag of hay. Blake relit his pipe and passed it to him.

"I shudder to think of the bloodshed that will result from an uprising," Redferne continued. "Our side doesn't have the firepower to stand up to the British Army. Never did, never will." He returned the pipe to Blake, shaking his head.

"I wouldn't be that pessimistic if I were you. There are them out there that are willing and able to give us firepower."

"For money I'll bet, which our poor country doesn't have."

"For political and military advantage."

"And who might this generous benefactor be? What's the trade-off?"

"France. The trade-off is to stick it to the British."

"I don't see Louis XV as a hell of an improvement over George III. It's trading one tyrant for another," Redferne said.

"I'm willing to bet that in this case, the 'devil you don't know' is an improvement over one that's tormented us for centuries, but we're getting ahead of ourselves. Let's cut to the chase. Are you in or out?"

"As I told you in Gavin's pub that night," Redferne finally said, "I don't hold with maiming defenseless cattle and sheep to prove a point."

"Neither do I, Michael, but if there's a choice between maiming the animals of the parasites and gougers, or maiming decent people, I'll go with the former." Blake stood up to go.

Redferne followed suit, brushing straw from the seat of his pants. "If you care so much about our people, how did John Ryan find himself naked in a thorn pit last month? If it weren't for the grace of God that Eileen Dysart happened by, he would have bled to death."

"Ryan was willing to suck the life blood from a poor widow and her young son thrown out on the road in the dead of winter for failure to pay rent. He and his clan were right in there to take her little house and claim her forfeited potato pit."

"Outrageous, I'll give you that," Redferne said.

"If some kind neighbors hadn't taken them in, the woman and her boy would have perished."

"You make a compelling argument, Rory. I can see why you went into the school mastering business. God help me, I hope I'm doing the right thing but, yes, I'm in." He crossed himself, his tone revealing relief at having made a decision.

"Let's shake on it." The two men clasped hands. "We are sorely in need of men like you," Blake said, lifting the lantern.

A horse whinnied. Before Blake had time to douse the light, the canvas flap burst open. Captain Preston, followed by a half dozen dragoons, rushed in, their spurs jangling, with swords and pistols at the ready.

Preston's dragoons came out of the makeshift school carrying armfuls of books and writing slates. They lofted them atop the thatched roof before setting it ablaze. Blake roared and strained to break free of the bonds that tied him to Redferne. His little store of precious materials that took years to gather went up in smoke before his eyes. Not only was his meager livelihood gone, but the means to educate poor Irish children went up in smoke as well. Redferne felt Blake's white-hot rage through the ropes that bound them back to back. They both cursed Preston.

One of the dragoons fixed his bayonet and advanced on them. Preston called him off. "Let them continue. I'm enjoying this almost as much as the whipping I gave that young McLoughlin brat back on the road."

"That's all you're good at, beating and breaking innocent women and children, you ignorant, cowardly bastard," Redferne roared. "If it wasn't for Daddy you'd be in debtor's prison where you belong." Preston's eyes narrowed and his lips grew thin as rubber bands. He turned on his heel and retrieved the whip from his saddle.

"Sergeant, would you please cut Mr. Redferne loose from the schoolmaster and secure him to that tree yonder." It took four men to carry out Preston's orders. The blazing roof collapsed into the shed in a cloud of smoke and sparks. Crinkled shards of burnt paper floated on the updraft through the bare trees, like large black snowflakes. They pulled Redferne's arms around a tree trunk and tied his wrists together. With his chest jammed against the tree, he found breathing painful. Blood pounded in his ears. Next, they ripped the shirt from his back and retreated to give the captain leeway. Two magpies lifted off a tree branch as the punishment began. Redferne clinched his teeth and closed his eyes in an effort not to cry out. The lash made its own song as it hissed and crackled through the cold air, landing on his back with a "thwack." Preston relented after thirty lashes.

He sank to his knees when they cut him free. Preston fetched a cart from the Big House and loaded Redferne on it. One of the dragoons attached a rope around Blake's neck and dragged him along behind his horse.

It was dark by the time the strange procession made its way past the market house, down the broad tree-lined thoroughfare of Cloonfin toward the large Gothic entrance of the demesne. People came to the doors and watched in hushed silence, but mostly they peeped through the curtains. Word spread like wildfire that Redferne had been flogged and that Master Blake was a prisoner. Their little school was no more.

CHAPTER 10

Benjamin Strange, Lord Preston's veteran footman, woke with a start. Two a.m. Something crunched the gravel path below his second-story window in the servants' quarters. The pain from his stooped back restricted his movements, however, his undying curiosity overcame his disability. That along with being a light sleeper may have saved Michael Redferne's life.

Benjamin pulled the curtain back. A horse and cart moved off the gravel path onto the lawn toward the stables. Whoever drove the cart apparently didn't want to be heard. He threw his clothes on over his long johns and headed in the same direction through the interior of the mansion along a damp, poorly lit passageway.

When he reached the stable area, he heard several voices, one of which was Captain Preston's. Strange did his utmost to avoid any contact with the younger Preston in daylight and had no desire to meet him in the dead of night. He lingered in the passageway until the captain departed. Hearing the squeal of a rusty gate and the snap of a lock, he figured that whatever was going on had something to do with the rarely used hundred-year-old jail cell off the horse stables. Dubbed the "equine cathedral" by the family because of their Gothic arches and soaring vaulted ceilings, these stables were often cited by the poor as gross examples of Preston excess.

He lit a small candle from a brazier in the passageway and tiptoed toward the old cell. It was a grungy enclosure that a man could cross in ten steps either direction. Clumps of grass and moss grew from crevices between the stones in the walls, where time and neglect had stripped the plaster clean. Near the ceiling, a small barred opening provided the only exterior lighting. A layer of fetid straw covered the cobbled floor giving off a pungent smell. A stout wooden door with bars guarded the entrance. Benjamin's nose twitched as he looked inside. Rory Blake was on his knees bending over the prone figure of Michael Redferne. Both were old friends, but he had a special relationship with Rory Blake, chief of the Whiteboys, an agrarian secret society. Strange was Blake's eyes and ears in the Big House.

"Jaysus, Rory, is it you that's in it? How did this happen at all?"

"God, am I glad to see you, Ben," Rory whispered. "You need to tend to Michael. He's in a bad way."

Strange handed the candle to Blake through the bars and asked him to shine it on Redferne who sprawled on his belly. "Suffering Jaysus," he swore when the light revealed the bloody welts on Redferne's back.

Blake returned the candle. "He's lost a lot of blood, Ben."

"I'll be back," Strange whispered and hurried off. A while later he returned with a basin of warm water and a satchel with bandages, plasters, and several ointments of his own concoction.

Instructing Blake to hold the candle, Benjamin took a selection of files and picks from a leather pouch hanging around his neck. He selected a pick and within seconds the door creaked open.

After washing Redferne's back with warm water and cleaning the lacerations, he disinfected them with a chlorine-based solution before applying a sticky plaster to both sides of the deeper wounds. Then he put strips of cloth with ointment over the cuts and pulled the plasters together to close the wounds. To keep the bandages in place, he wrapped clean linen strips around Redferne's chest and back and then placed a small brick of opium under his tongue as a sedative.

Benjamin turned to Blake. "You both best stay here tonight, Rory. Michael cannot be moved in his condition."

"Are you out of your mind? We need to get to hell out of here before the captain returns."

"Trust me, it's best you stay. If you run, you'll become fugitives. That will allow some hot-head like Preston to make a name for himself by shooting you on sight."

"What's to stop the captain from coming back here tonight and blowing our brains out?" Blake asked holding his hands to his head.

"Two things: fear of his old man, and brandy," Benjamin said, "Otherwise he'd have done it already. I will alert Lord Preston about what happened here at first light. He will not condone this. It'll stir up a hornet's nest of trouble that he can ill afford."

"And the brandy. How does that play into it?" Blake asked, his face pinched as if contemplating a chess move.

"The captain is fond of it as you know. After a night carousing he will be incapacitated. According to Betty, one of our scullery maids whom Preston bedded last evening, he has plans to spend the night with Lady Osborne." As insurance, Benjamin reset the cell-door lock so that Captain Preston's key wouldn't work.

Blake shook Benjamin's hand, as if they had sealed a contract. "Our lives are in your care, physician."

After a final check on Redferne, Benjamin locked the door on his two friends and returned to his room hoping his appraisal of Preston's state of mind proved accurate. If he was wrong, not only would Redferne and Blake suffer the consequences, but so would he for helping them. He needed a plausible story to account for unlocking the cell door. The Lord would be more than concerned if he discovered that his stooped footman had the skill to pick the lock of any room in the mansion.

Against the odds, Captain Preston and his men showed up at the cell early next morning, his appetites unsatisfied, apparently, by drink or Mrs. Osborne. Overcoming the debilitating effect of brandy, and emboldened by the false courage it often induced, he decided to handle the prisoner issue himself. To hell with his father.

He turned the key in the cell door. Nothing. He unleashed a stream of abuse, kicking and pulling the iron bars.

"You there," he shouted, cuffing one of his men over the head, "find the fucking locksmith."

"It's six in the morning, Captain. Old Davie won't be in till eight."

Prescott got within inches of the man's face. "Go rouse Old Davie's arse." The underling fled through the door. Preston drew his pistol and began pacing.

He glowered at the prisoners, now fully awake. Closing the outer door he stepped toward the cell and cocked his pistol. "You two think you're getting away with this," He aimed his pistol at the lock. Blake pulled Redferne into a corner. Footsteps sounded in the passage and the outer door flung open as Lord Preston, wearing a white nightcap and a grey flannel nightgown, preceded Ben Strange into the stable. He snatched the riding gloves from his son's belt and slapped him across the face.

"You imbecile, you haven't the sense God gave a rabbit. That pistol ball could have ricocheted and killed you or one of the prisoners. Get out and take your hooligans with you or I swear I will lock you up for being a public nuisance."

The captain, his face twitching with rage and embarrassment, swung the pistol on his father. Lord Preston brusquely shoved the mouth of the pistol to one side. "Put that away before you shame yourself further." It might have been the unaccustomed fire in his father's eyes that caused the captain to back down--Redferne couldn't tell. But he breathed easier when the captain holstered his pistol and left, his companions trailing behind.

Lord Preston looked into the cell. "My apologies for what happened. I do not approve of my son's methods; nevertheless, I cannot release you since you broke the law."

"What's to become of us?" Redferne asked, his face taut with pain.

"You will be tried at the court in Roscommon town the next time the circuit judge presides here. I give you my word I will speak on your behalf. In the meantime, Benjamin will continue to minister to your wounds. There's not a better doctor around." He started to walk away, then stopped short. "Mr. Strange, one thing puzzles me. Since my son had the key, how did you gain entry to the cell?"

"Your Honor, as you know, that lock is a century old, at least. It took but the tap of a hammer in the right place to disengage it."

"Then we'll need to get the locksmith to remedy that, won't we?" Lord Preston took a final look around the room and left.

"Cheer up lads, there's not a locksmith in all of Ireland who can make a lock I can't crack," Benjamin said after The Lord left. "If things turn ugly before the court session, I can always spring yez." He gave a reassuring nod. "The Lord is posturing now to buy some time. In the end, wiser heads will prevail. Ah sure, ye'll be out of here in no time."

Redferne gazed up at the barred vent near the ceiling. "What about the circuit judge?"

"Circuit judge, my arse," Benjamin sniffed, stepping into the cell and sitting with Redferne and Blake on the straw. "His Lordship can't afford to let this get that far, mark my words."

Redferne's eyes became slits. "I'm not sure I follow."

"Nor do I," Blake added. "Your first assumption about the captain's reaction was wrong."

Benjamin sighed. "Yes, but as is evident, I reconsidered it."

"What kind of a physic did you give me last night? I feel like I've been asleep for ten years," Redferne blurted, stifling a yawn.

Benjamin laughed. "A little something to get you through the worst of it. The Lord has enough problems on his hands as it is with the ongoing evictions and all. The last thing he wants is more anger and resentment in the townlands. The other landlords, them that have any brains, don't want the peasants riled up more than they are over a so-called illegal school."

Blake shook his head. "It makes not a whit of difference if the schoolmaster stays in jail or not. My school, illegal or otherwise, is gone."

"What are you talking about?" Redferne said in a scratchy voice. "All the kids are still here and the old shed they destroyed is hardly a prime piece of property, now is it?"

"That whipping must have addled your brain. Are you forgetting that the captain and his men not only burned the shed, they burned all the books that took me a lifetime to gather? The captain understood what he was doing."

A gust of wind blew through the vent, rustling the straw and kicking up eddies of dust from the floor. Benjamin took a handkerchief from his pocket to stifle a sneeze.

"If that damn McLoughlin kid left his books in the shed as he was told, we wouldn't be in this fix right now," Redferne wheezed, scrutinizing the moss and grass growing from the dilapidated cell walls.

Blake shook his head. "He's a kid. The irony is, it was your arrival that distracted my class."

"God's blood! I hadn't thought of that. He got whipped because of me. Now I have to carry that burden along with everything else."

"Look on the bright side. Guilt you can work off," Blake said, "by becoming an active member of the Whiteboys. I bet the sting of Preston's whip has shored up your resolve."

"That bastard has been in my face half my life. First it was over Maureen, then the incident with Padraig on the ice cart. Now this."

"Why don't you challenge him to a duel?" Blake said.

Benjamin laughed. "You can forget that idea, boys. The gentry don't duel with peasants. It's beneath them."

"We'll have to find some way for the captain to overcome that reluctance." Blake eyeballed Redferne. "That could be your first assignment."

Redferne got up and ran his hand across the ruined walls. "Say, Rory, doesn't this place remind you of your school?"

"Never thought of my school as a prison." Blake and Benjamin exchanged looks.

"Wonder how many men died here, rotting away from abuse and boredom?"

"Again, not a flattering comparison," Blake said.

Benjamin stretched out his hand. "Help me up, Rory. There's a good chap. How does a bowl of stirabout, a few cuts of soda bread lathered with butter, and a couple of boiled eggs sound?"

Redferne hadn't thought of food in the turmoil of the morning. Now that the topic came up his stomach growled. "Any chance you could add a few mugs of buttermilk?" His eyes lit up in anticipation.

Blake let out a hearty, "That would be great."

"I already checked with cook and she is in a generous mood this morning. It's not often we have guests of your station among us." Taking the key from his pocket, Benjamin left and locked the door behind him. Then turning, he bowed to the men behind the bars. "Now that you've had time to reflect aren't you chaps better off here for the time being instead of having your arses chased over hill and dale by that vicious twit and his motley crew?"

Blake massaged his chin. "Time will tell, Benjamin. Time will tell."

"Another thing," Benjamin continued. "Once you get out of here, Rory, I've no doubt you'll be back in the school business in no time."

Blake's mouth fell open. "Apparently Ben, you didn't hear me the first time. All my books went up in smoke at the hands of that bully and his thugs."

"Oh I heard you all right, and I repeat: You'll be back in business in no time." Blake and Redferne exchanged puzzled looks.

"You have me at a disadvantage," Blake said.

"Leave it to me. While I get your grub, you might mentally prepare a list of the books you lost in the fire." Then turning to Redferne he said, "A few mugs of buttermilk, right?"

"Oh, God, yes, before I collapse."

With that the stooped footman shuffled down the hallway.

"What if he's wrong about all of this?" Redferne said, turning to Blake.

"Then both of us are royally screwed."

Seamus Beirne

CHAPTER 11

It was market day in Cloonfin. Lord Preston was uneasy. Horse and donkey carts filled with farm produce crowded both sides of the wide street beyond the great gothic arch. Poultry and pigs corralled in pens scurried about as people went from one to the other, bargaining and haggling with the farmers. Large hanks of brown linen lay stacked in stalls as drapers circulated among the tables examining merchandise. Buyers came from as far away as Northern Ireland, drawn to the Cloonfin market because of its reputation for high-quality linen.

Mingling with the well-to-do was a large number of subsistence farmers and conacre renters who could not afford most of the goods on display.

The phaeton taking Lord Preston to the Protestant church creaked as it struggled to get through the milling crowd.

Then. "The curse of God on the Prestons," echoed off the buildings. Followed by "Release Redferne and Blake, release Redferne and Blake." The horse shied and bucked.

"Should I turn down Bridge Street, M'Lord?" the driver, Vinny Deaver, asked.

"Absolutely not! Go straight up Church Street. We mustn't show fear." A young man who looked like he hadn't bathed in two months grabbed the horse's bridle. "Halt!" Preston ordered Deaver. He stood to address the crowd that was fast becoming a mob. Whether startled by Lord Preston's action or scared by their own audacity, the people quieted down.

"Let justice take its course," the Lord began. "Redferne and Blake will be treated fairly."

"The word of a Preston ain't worth shite," someone yelled out. "There's no justice for the poor. Bring your own son to justice, why don't you?"

The crowd roared. After a few more futile attempts to reason with them, Lord Preston sat back down. "Proceed to the church, Deaver." Miraculously the crowd parted and let them through, appearing too intimidated to take on the powerful man who controlled their lives and upon whose good will their meager fortunes depended.

Preston's hands shook like a man recovering from a heavy night of drinking by the time they turned into the Church of Ireland compound enclosed by a six feet-high spiked iron fence. To the left of the existing church, the walls of a much larger structure rose starkly into the winter sky without roof or belfry. To the right sat the cemetery with tombstones dating from the previous century along with the mausoleum housing the bones of the patriarch William Preston, who would have turned in his grave had he witnessed the scene in the marketplace, or more likely turned out a company of dragoons on the protesters. William never bargained with peasants, especially Papists, whom he regarded as little better than animals needing to be controlled by fear.

The decision to hold the meeting in the parsonage was part strategic and part political. It shifted the focus from the Prestons and implicated the Church in whatever verdict was reached regarding Redferne and Blake. It also flattered Parson Stack, on whose moral support Preston depended, to release the prisoners with all possible speed, which was underscored by the ugly scene in the marketplace.

The phaeton crunched up the gravel driveway and stopped before the parsonage, a large two-story house draped in ivy. The parson, a man in his sixties with a great shock of white hair and a prominent belly, waited to greet them. He walked with a limp, which Preston thought had worsened since their last meeting.

Lord Preston stepped from the phaeton and extended a still-trembling hand which the parson pumped vigorously. "How are you keeping, Parson?"

"Gamely enough sir, gamely enough, except for this confounded leg." He bent to stroke his right knee. "They tell me it's the gout, but beyond identifying the malady, they're at their wits' end to come up with a remedy."

"Are you under professional care?"

"One chap I'm seeing swears by a regimen of Rhenish and Moselle wines. I must say I find it a most agreeable approach to the problem." His belly rippled with laughter.

"Perhaps you should let my man Benjamin take a look at it," The Lord said. "He's good, you know."

"Bishop Berkeley himself is suffering from the same ailment and he with the finest physicians in the country." Groaning, the parson led the Lord into a comfortable drawing room. A large mahogany table surrounded by several stiff-back chairs sat in the center of the room. A silver tray with a dozen glasses and a decanter of Rémy Martin cognac rested on it. Two sofas with an abundance of cushions occupied a space on either side of a blazing log fire. John French, a neighboring landlord with a holding of twenty thousand acres, slouched on one, a glass of cognac in his fist. A tight-fitting beige wig framed his oval face which sagged to a point at his chin. He wore a yellow waistcoat with pewter buttons down the center and stains to match the color of his brown frock coat. Whatever decision was reached would affect him as well. Howard Bannister arrived next and, to everyone's surprise, Reggie Preston came in behind him.

"You are all most welcome to my humble abode," the parson began when everyone sat happily with a glass of cognac. "I've arranged for us to gather in the most comfortable room of the house in hopes of facilitating a speedy solution to a most vexing problem. Now I will turn the discussion over to the Honorable Lord Preston."

The elder Preston rose and surveyed the group, making mental notes on the likely positions of the participants. Then he coughed and began. "Let me start by saying I struggled with the idea of having my son, the architect of our present difficulty, attend this meeting."

He nodded toward Reggie. "Since his point of view is contrary to mine, I thought it fitting that he be here to present it, but that is not the only reason I think he should be present. I hope he might learn that following the letter of the law is not always the wisest course."

"I must say," French interrupted, straightening his slouch and spilling cognac on his waistcoat, "I find myself coming down on your son's side in this affair. If we allow our subjects to challenge and insult us, it may be a short step from that to insurrection, as the history of this country so often demonstrates."

"I agree," the Lord said, "Redferne's behavior was unacceptable, but did the punishment fit the crime? Because we have the power to do something doesn't mean we should always do it. Power should be exercised prudently, lest we dig ourselves into a hole and get mired there."

"I'm inclined to agree with the honorable gentleman," the parson said, his words punctuated by deep wheezing. "Power is a two-edged sword that if exercised unwisely can cut off the hand that wields it. Especially at a time when there is so much agitation in the land."

Bannister drummed his fingers on the arm of the sofa.

"I may have overreacted in my treatment of Redferne," Reggie Preston said, his tone suggesting that his sentiment came more from a desire to ingratiate himself back into his father's favor than from any deep-seated conviction. "However, he attacked my honor as a gentleman in the vilest fashion and demonstrated further contempt by being present in a Papist school. Our standing is on borrowed time as long as we tolerate such insolence and allow the Papists to grow and prosper."

Bannister burst out laughing and stood to pour himself another glass of cognac. Reggie Preston's face turned the color of beetroot. He shifted in his chair.

"Look around you." Bannister stood waving the cognac bottle as he spoke. "How many Papists do you know who continue to prosper? The danger is not from the one chance in a million that they will prosper, but from the scientific certainty that they will not.

That's why we need a coherent approach to move them off the land before the genie gets out of the bottle."

Lord Preston raised his eyebrows. "I'm all ears, Mr. Bannister. Tell us how."

Bannister shifted his eyes left and right. "It's a matter of timing and tactics, M'Lord. More cognac anyone?" French and Reggie held out their glasses.

"Remind me to pursue that matter with you later," Preston said, dabbing his forehead with his handkerchief.

The parson wheezed loudly. "Regarding the Papist school. The Penal Code is a powerful tool, but not through strict enforcement. It's the threat of enforcement that keeps the Papists in line. As long as they are not out pillaging and burning, let them have their schools. The end result is the same."

"Fact is, it has never been uniformly enforced. It was and still is a form of blackmail," Lord Preston added.

"I don't follow," Reggie said.

The parson opened his hands wide as if he was about to pray. "What your father means, young man, is that the state achieves compliance by holding the sword of Damocles over the Papists' heads—not by dropping it."

Bannister threw back his head and laughed. "What the *parson* really means, Captain, is that the Catholics, if provoked, might cease paying tithes to his church to which they don't belong, bringing the construction of his new building to a grinding halt. Isn't that right, Parson?"

The parson's face turned crimson. He cleared his throat and took a sip of cognac.

"So, it's in his best interest to release the prisoners forthwith," Bannister added.

"That's outrageous, Parson," French huffed. Reggie bared his lips in a thin smile.

Lord Preston shuffled his feet and stared at Bannister. *He is sabotaging the meeting. He is trying to bully me. Well, it won't work.*

Lord Preston pursed his lips. "Despite Mr. Bannister's narrow interpretation, it's in everyone's best interest to talk and act cautiously. The parson makes a good point. Catholic unrest is not something to be scoffed at." He recounted the ugly scene in the market place earlier that morning. But French and Reggie Preston remained unconvinced. French wanted to put the militia on alert. Reggie, buoyed by French's support, suggested transporting the prisoners to the jurisdiction of Dennis Brown, known as the hanging sheriff of County Mayo.

The meeting devolved into bickering. Everyone left with the same convictions they had coming in. The fates of Redferne and Blake lay in the hands of Lord Preston. With only the parson in his corner, he was now virtually on his own. He feared Whiteboy retaliation if he retained Blake, and Protestant anger if he released Redferne, so he split the difference.

He released Blake that afternoon. Under the guise of humanitarianism, Redferne would remain incarcerated until he recuperated. This decision gave him political running room. Redferne's eventual release would be gauged on community reaction. Insurrection hung in the air and he didn't want his son's desire for revenge to be the spark that ignited it.

Benjamin Strange stood before the bars of the prison cell trying to convince Redferne to enjoy Lord Preston's hospitality. "It's not as if you have any choice in the matter, so you might as well make the most of it until your strength returns." Redferne's back was healing nicely due to Benjamin's expert care. An hour before, Blake had left with a parcel of books under his arm filched by Benjamin from Lord Preston's library.

Redferne had mixed feelings. "I don't trust Reggie Preston."

"I don't either, but I do trust His Lordship. *He* made the decision to retain you."

"All good and well, but there's nothing to prevent Reggie from sending one of his thugs back here in the dead of night to put a pistol ball through my head."

"I thought of that and The Lord said that you can move into my quarters."

Redferne snapped his head around. "He said what?"

"You can move in with me."

His eyes danced. "Isn't he afraid I'm going take off at the first opportunity?"

"He believes that if you treat a man honorably, he will do the honorable thing."

"I'm not sure I have that much honor in me, Ben."

"Don't sell yourself short, my friend."

Here we go again, Redferne thought. Others' expectations that he rarely lived up to. The sad fact was, his life up to now was not all that honorable. Much of it was wasted on self-pity and regret. The honorable thing for him to do was go home. On the other hand, if he took off, he would be a wanted man.

Where was the honor on the Prestons' side? They imprisoned him unjustly. Ben's place might be the cheese in the mouse trap. Maybe they wanted him to break out. *That's it*, he thought, *they'll be lying in wait for me if I run.*

Seamus Beirne

CHAPTER 12

Captain Preston and a few hand-picked men huddled in the ruins of an eighth-century abbey nestled in a grove of trees on the perimeter of the demense. Across the open expanse, lights flickered in the Big House, visible through a grove of beech trees. Donning white sheets and hoods, they mounted their horses. Captain Preston turned to the informer, O'Rourke. "Let's hear what you're going to shout when the action begins. The rest of you pay close attention. If we are to be convincing stand-ins for the Whiteboy rabble, someone needs to be speaking Irish."

O'Rourke pulled his felt hat down over the white hood and shouted: *"Fawgh on beallach, fawgh on beallach."*

"What the hell does that mean?" one of the men asked.

"Get the hell out of the way," the captain replied.

"Why don't we all yell that? It doesn't sound that difficult to imitate," the sergeant said. "It'll scare the bejaysus out of them."

"Sound phony as hell pronounced with an English accent. Stick to the plan and rely on the native. You're sure you're up to this, O'Rourke?"

The gangly youth sat hunched on his horse, looking like a gargoyle in the white sheet and crazy hat. "Shure, why wouldn't I be, Yer Honor?" O'Rourke cleared his throat and struggled to stay astride his mount as it pranced around on the flagstones of the ruined church.

The captain knew that the informer was unfamiliar with horses. His kind was not allowed to own one, and couldn't afford one, even

63

if they were. All he had to do was stay mounted until they reached the Big House. The captain pulled the sergeant aside. "Your part is crucial if this is to work as it should."

"Never fear, Boss. Once we're through, they'll blame the Whiteboys all right. Your old man won't be a bit the wiser."

"Let's hope so, for all our sakes." The captain mounted his horse and waited behind the sheltering walls of the church. When the moon passed behind a cumulous cloud, the six hooded figures dashed from their hiding place. They raced across the open fields, kicking up divots of snow. The muffled beat of hooves and the rhythmic breathing of horses were the only sounds of their coming. They entered the demesne yard and dismounted behind the wing that housed the equine stables. The captain checked his pocket-watch. Half past ten. Most of the house was dark except for the library and an upstairs apartment. Leaving one man in charge of the horses, the captain led the way to the servants' quarters.

At the foot of a stone stairs, he dispatched two men to the library. The remaining three followed him up the stone steps to Benjamin's bedchamber. He peeped through the key hole. The stooped servant sat at a table running his finger down pages of a book. Redferne leaned over his shoulder. The captain stood to one side while the sergeant kicked the door in.

"*Fawgh on beallach,*" O'Rourke yelled. The captain pushed Benjamin against the wall.

"Hey, you clowns, no need to rough Benjamin up," Redferne said, probably thinking the intruders had come to rescue him. "He's not my jailer. Don't you lads know that?" Two of the assailants grabbed him by the elbows and hustled him toward the door. Shaking himself free of his attackers, Redferne grabbed one of them by the forearms and threw him against the wall.

"*Fawgh on beallach,*" O'Rourke yelled again, doing an awkward two-step as if some agitated footwork was called for.

"Watch out behind, Michael," Benjamin shouted, picking himself up from the floor. The captain lunged and Redferne ducked. Straightening up, he rammed his head into the captain's belly. The captain doubled over. His face collided with Redferne's fist on the upswing, sending him sprawling across the table, shattering it. A red stain spread across the captain's hood. Redferne kicked a chair out of the way and attempted to rip the hood from his attacker. A pistol blow to the back of the head knocked him to the floor.

"Fawgh on beallach." This time with less enthusiasm.

"Enough of that gibberish for Christ's sake. Get over here and help us," the sergeant roared. He and O'Rourke pulled the captain to his feet. Benjamin cowered in a corner alongside O'Rourke's hat that rested on its crown atop the splintered table. As his ruffians manhandled Redferne out the door, the captain picked up the hat and placed it on his head.

Then grabbing a fragment of the broken table, he lashed out at Benjamin. Before the blow landed, Benjamin coiled himself into a ball and covered his head with his hands.

"Fix that, physician." The captain cast the splintered board on top of the prone figure and staggered out the door, blood dripping from beneath his hood.

Loud voices echoed through the hallways. Lord Preston looked up from the book he was reading by the library fire. He checked the grandfather clock. Half eleven. Who could be making such a commotion at this late hour? He thought of retrieving his pistol from the top drawer of the sideboard seconds before the door burst open. Two white-robed figures stomped into the room. He put aside his book and stood with his back to the fire. "Gentlemen, what can I do for you?"

The gunmen looked at each other. "Shut yer yap, that's what you can do," one of them said, leveling his pistol at Lord Preston's chest. They stood like that in a silent face-off until, *"Fawgh on beallach"* sounded in the hallway and the captain, followed by O'Rourke, rushed through the open door. "I repeat. What do you gentlemen want?" the elder Preston asked in a steady voice. He bent down and added another log to the fire. "Perhaps a brandy for a cold night?" he gestured to a glass cabinet where he kept his private stock. He nodded toward the captain. "Looks like one of you needs some medical attention. I can have my man Benjamin take a look."

The captain let out a mocking laugh.

The others joined in.

"Fawgh on beallach!" O'Rourke's silly war whoop broke the spell. The captain aimed his pistol at his father, who straightened the lace kerchief around his neck and stood at attention.

He wanted to see his old man cower, but the cold eye of his great grandfather staring down at him from above the fireplace rattled him. He swung his pistol and fired, blowing a large hole in his ancestor's beribboned chest. Within the confines of the room the pistol shot sounded like a cannon. A wreath of black smoke curled toward the ceiling. The blast broke the stalemate, and the intruders hurried out the door.

Lord Preston slumped into a chair.

When they reached the stable, the others waited with the unconscious Redferne, anxious to put as much distance between them and the house as possible. The captain transferred the battered hat with the loose ribbon to O'Rourke's head.

"Can't send you home without your favorite hat," he said, in a voice muffled by the bloody hood.

"Thanks Guvn'r," O'Rourke replied. "Did I do good?"

"Better than you'll ever know." Everyone mounted except the sergeant, who stood in the shadows. As the group rode off with O'Rourke shouting, *"Fawgh on beallach,"* he raised his pistol and fired, hitting the informer in the base of the skull. He tumbled off his horse and rolled to the side of the lane, coming to rest in dirty brown snow.

CHAPTER 13

When Redferne came to, his face lay buried in the horse's mane, causing him to sneeze. Both wrists were tied together under the animal's neck. His captors laughed, but made no attempt to help him. He recognized them even before they discarded their white sheets and hoods. This operation had Reggie Preston written all over it.

If Lord Preston believed that his home had been terrorized by the Whiteboys, severe reprisals were bound to follow. He would go after Rory Blake, the presumed Whiteboy leader. This is turn would push the peasants into revolt, which was the real objective of the attack on the Big House, Redferne figured. Getting rid of him was merely the settling of a personal vendetta. If it helped to add fuel to the fires of insurrection, so much the better.

They moved at a slower pace as the horses floundered in deep snow. The icy wind pierced his light shirt. If his sense of direction was correct, they were getting close to a country inn named the Cock and Bull. Its proprietor, a disreputable character named Andrew Hicks, a retired sailor from His Majesty's Service, had a reputation as a skinflint whose allegiance went to the highest bidder. When the exhausted column dismounted at Hicks's place, Redferne bet that tonight that allegiance would go to Reggie Preston.

A sharp cough followed by a spit directed their attention to a corner of the inn where a figure emerged carrying a lantern, head high. Its light illuminated a stocky man with a whiskey nose set in a round face. He wore a shabby brown overcoat and had tufts of grey curls peeking from under a grimy wool cap. One could roll a barrel between his legs. After a short conversation with the captain, he said, "Follow me, Guvn'r." Affecting a half-bow, he led them to the coach house and stables. Before putting the horses inside, a soldier pulled Redferne off the saddle, letting him tumble to the ground. He landed face down in a snowdrift against the stable wall. Laughter erupted. Redferne twisted and turned to get his head out of the suffocating snow.

"Maybe we should leave the bugger here for the night, eh, Captain," one of them said, pulling Redferne to a standing position.

"And deprive the hanging sheriff of his prey? Not bloody likely. We must get this man inside and fatten him up for the noose."

"Why wait for the sheriff," Redferne shouted. "Let's you and me settle this right now fair and square. No need to travel a mile farther."

"You'd love that, wouldn't you?" The captain ripped the front of Redferne's shirt. "Look at that for a physique, boys." He traced the contours of Redferne's chest muscles with the braided handle of his whip. "Got those muscles from turf-cutting, I bet."

"That's what happens when you work, something you and the fops you hang around with know little of."

The captain got within inches of Redferne's face. "You're so right. What a distasteful activity." He rubbed his bloody nose, "Did Maureen like those muscles?"

"She sure as hell preferred them to yours, didn't she?"

The captain stepped back and uncoiled his whip, then stopped. "Sadly for her, yes, but it wasn't a well thought-out decision, and since you're a dead man, perhaps I'll tell you about it before your rendezvous with the sheriff." He strode away, shouting, "Get the prisoner out of the weather."

Inside the tavern the innkeeper threw a blanket over Redferne's shoulders. A roaring fire set in a large fireplace of contoured sandstone from a nearby stream dominated the sparse room. The furniture consisted of wooden tables surrounded by rough-hewn wooden benches. The grease and grime of years had accumulated on the table tops as a glossy sheen, underscoring the reputation of the Cock 'n Bull as a rough and ready establishment.

When the captain and his men had their fill of stew and local beer, he spoke to the innkeeper. "Untie the prisoner's hands so he can eat. We don't want to send a starving man to the gallows."

Hicks led Redferne across the room and sat him down on a bench by the fire. Then he untied his hands and placed a bowl of stew and a mug of beer before him. As he gorged on the piping hot stew, heat coursed through his body. He contemplated bolting but reconsidered after weighing the odds of surviving on a bitter cold night. Added to that were the pistols on the table at his captors' elbows.

As the night wore on, the captain and his henchmen grew more boisterous as the innkeeper kept the beer flowing. Throwing their arms around each other's shoulders, they sang a bawdy song about a "young girl from Madrid." One of the group sat alone in a corner, his face tight with anger, but cold sober. A cocked pistol rested on a bench beside him.

After an hour of drinking, the captain got to his feet and, wobbling toward Redferne, drew his rapier. "You'd like to fight me, wouldn't you, bog boy?" Redferne stiffened. If the captain had mustered the courage to break into the family residence and terrorize the household, even in disguise, no telling what he would do with an infusion of courage from cheap beer. His men gathered around him, egging him on.

"No, sir," Redferne said. "Given your reputation as a swordsman, putting an amateur like me away wouldn't enhance that reputation, would it?"

"C-c-lever bastard." The captain raised the tip of his rapier to Redferne's throat and ran the stinging point down his bare chest. A stream of hot blood seared his skin like a rivulet of fire. Preston's eyes looked glazed. Beads of sweat ran down the bridge of Redferne's nose. His heart rate increased, sounding like the pounding of a bass drum in his ears.

"Give Redferne a rapier," someone cried. While the captain pondered this, the inn door flew open and the sergeant of the dragoons strode in covered in snow.

He pulled the captain away from Redferne. The captain resisted and then fell backward into the sergeant's arms letting the rapier fall to the floor at Redferne's feet, its hilt rolling into the fire. The sergeant kicked it away from the coals. "You two," he said pointing. "Bring the captain to his room. The rest of you turn in for the night."

The sergeant turned to Redferne. "Count yourself lucky that I got here when I did. If you killed him, and in his condition even the fat innkeeper could have taken him, they'd have sliced your throat."

Redferne's breathing came in great gasps as he regarded the smirk on the sergeant's face. *Gotta' get out of here tonight despite the risk.* They were taking him to Castlebar, to Sheriff Brown. Once there, he was done for. Brown never gave a reprieve.

Hitting a nobleman was a crime which frequently brought the death penalty and the captain had a black eye and a broken nose. No matter that Redferne had acted in self-defense.

"Your prisoner can sleep in the kitchen," Hicks said, collecting mugs. The sergeant raised his eyebrows.

"The kitchen?"

"'Pon my word, sir, it's the most secure room in my establishment."

"Oh, it is, is it? Is that where you keep your cash, old man?"

"I keeps that under me pillow along with a horse pistol. Since I'd feel downright uncomfortable putting Mr. Redferne there, that location is out."

A smile crossed Redferne's face.

The sergeant didn't see the humor in it. "Show me the kitchen."

"It's the honest to God's truth, sir." Hicks slapped the whitewashed kitchen wall. "These walls are two feet thick and as you can see the window's got bars on it."

The sergeant removed his cap and scratched his head. "Who in hell turns a kitchen into a prison cell for bread and cheese? It's not as if your place has a high reputation for quality food. Most of the time, it tastes like shite."

Hicks didn't appear bothered by the slight. "If I didn't keep it this way, my thieving help would rob me blind." He stroked his beard with his thumb and forefinger watching the sergeant's every move. Redferne heard the sergeant rattle the window bars and examine the door lock.

Satisfied, he ordered Hicks to bring the prisoner in and tie him up. Hicks directed Redferne to sit on the floor with his back against the press and feet outstretched.

"Let's get more light in here," the sergeant yelled. "No wonder the grub stinks. You've been cooking in the dark. Probably putting dead mice into the pot, you tight bastard." Hicks ignored the insults and tied Redferne's hands and feet. But he did a sloppy job. The sergeant inspected the operation from a distance and failed to spot the innkeeper's careless handiwork, or Redferne flexing his muscles.

Hicks got off his knees and gave the sergeant a knowing wink, saying in the midst of a coughing bout, "He won't stir from there 'til hell freezes over."

"By that time, he'll be a resident of the place. All the captain cares about is getting him before Sheriff Brown." He laughed and left the kitchen, Hicks following. A short time later, Hicks reappeared with a greatcoat and a woolen cap which he hung on a wooden peg beside a grimy white apron. Taking a ring of keys from his pocket, he extracted a small double-barreled pistol from a drawer. He cocked the hammers, checking to see they worked, and then returned it to the drawer leaving it unlocked. Footsteps echoed from the outer room and the dragoon who sat watch with the pistol beside him, stepped into the kitchen.

"Out, innkeeper, I'll take over from here."

"Then you'll be needing this." Hicks handed him the key to the kitchen door.

"Right, on your way then." He grabbed the lantern and locked the door from the outside. The muscle-flexing combined with Hicks's lackluster performance allowed him to undo his bonds in no time. He rose and tiptoed to the window. It appeared to have stopped snowing. The guard outside the door cleared his throat.

Aided by the light of the winter moon through the little window, he surveyed his surroundings for an escape route, finding the walls to be as solid as Hicks claimed. He pulled on the window bars. They rattled, but stood firm. It reminded him of the night he tunneled his way out of a farmer's shed in Scotland with a spade, but those circumstances weren't as dire.

Hicks's kitchen had a flagged floor. There was no digging that, even if he had a spade. The guard's snores echoed from the dining room. He thought of calling out that he wanted to piss, then jump the guard when he came in to let him out. But the response was likely to be, "Piss on the floor." After his eyes became accustomed to the dark, he noticed an iron poker hanging from a hook on the wall by the stove. A good tool to dig with, but what to dig?

A gust of wind sounding like the skittering of dry leaves across a road on a stormy day reverberated through the thatch shaking loose a shower of fine dust. He had found a use for the poker.

As insurance against the guard waking up, he placed the back of a chair against the latch of the door and moved to the end of the kitchen, where an open door led to a small storage room, illuminated by a barred window. Sacks of potatoes, crates of vegetables, and bags of flour lined its walls. This was what Hicks was protecting from his "thieving employees."

After donning the innkeeper's coat and woolen cap, he took the pistol from the drawer along with a bag of black powder and half a dozen steel balls. He grabbed the poker and went back to the storage area. Unless the guard had the ears of a dog, he wouldn't hear anything from the outer room. He stacked bags of potatoes and sacks of flour on top of each other, putting him within easy reach of the ceiling.

He thrust the poker upward several times into the thatch between the rafters and pulled back. A gush of crusted snow dropped through the opening. By the time he had enlarged the hole enough to crawl through, a mound of snow lay on top of a flour sack beneath him. Hicks would be furious over the ruined flour, and probably curse whatever impulse had prompted him to help him.

Once on the roof, he lowered himself down the outside wall and dropped to a snowdrift beside the coach house. Snow came through the holes in his boots. He might find a suitable pair in the coach house. Guests often left their boots there for more comfortable footwear before entering the inn. The horses stamped in the stable as they muzzled their forage. Anger rose in him like bile. The horses of the gentry were better fed and sheltered than the average poor peasant.

Inside a coach he found a pair of brown leather riding boots stuffed with a pair of woolen socks, a pleasant turn of fortune in contrast to the disasters that had befallen him this past fortnight.

Moving cautiously into the stalls so as not to frighten the horses, he saddled the one closest to the door. He had one foot in the stirrup when something colder than snow touched the back of his head.

"Turn around, gently now, or I will blow yer head off, horse thief." Redferne's blood turned to ice at the utterance. Horse thievery was a hanging offense.

"You've made a bugger of me old roof, so you have, but never mind that." Andrew Hicks lowered the shotgun.

Redferne gasped for breath. "For a second there, my whole life passed before my eyes."

"My apologies for that. Wanted to be rock-solid sure that it was yourself that was in it, Mr. Redferne, before going off half-cocked."

Redferne wiped sweat from his forehead with the back of his hand. "You put the wind up in me, half-cocked or full."

"I was pondering how long it would take you to put the pieces together. Pretty damn fast by my calculation. You're a smart one all right, which will stand you in good stead against that shower o' bastards." He inclined his head toward the inn.

"The blessings of God on you, Mr. Hicks," Redferne wheezed, when he found his full voice.

"Don't believe in God, but on the outside chance he's up there, let me tell you that bucko doesn't want much truck with the likes of you and me. I learned that the hard way from crawling up and down the rigging of His Majesty's ship *Vengeance*, my nails shredded from wrestling canvas."

Redferne's eyes opened wide. "A sailor! But the careless way you tied me?"

Hicks smiled. "Laddie, you'd have stayed tied till the rope rotted had I a mind to."

"Well, I thank you kindly, sir. If it's okay with you there is something I wanted to do before saying farewell to your fine establishment."

"Go on," Hicks said, enlarging one eye like an owl.

"I wanted to turn the rest of the horses loose so those blackguards can't follow me right away." He studied Hicks's face for a reaction.

"I've a better idea. Can't turn those animals out on a freezing night like this. Once you're on your way I'll cut the saddle straps. That'll slow them down, and it won't harm the animals. Now get your arse outa here." He placed a flask of brandy in Redferne's pocket. "God speed and good luck with the captain's gelding."

Redferne smiled as he cantered silently down the snow-carpeted lane. Despite what his benefactor said, he was sure that the presence of divine goodness in the world was manifested tonight in the person of Andrew Hicks, the disreputable proprietor of the Cock and Bull.

CHAPTER 14

The morning after the attack on the Big House, Alex Reid, the master of the hounds, found the hooded corpse of Sean O'Rourke stiff as a frozen shirt on a line, a few hundred yards from the stables. Snagged on an elm branch above him, the battered hat with the loose ribbon fluttered in the breeze. The discovery of O'Rourke swaddled in white was all the proof that some needed to pin the outrage on the Whiteboys. Lord Preston identified O'Rourke from his hat as the one who threatened him in the library and fired a pistol ball at the portrait of the patriarch.

The Protestants in the town stormed the demesne, forming an angry mob in the front portico of the Big House.

"How could such a thing happen?" someone yelled. "If the Big House was not secure what little chance have we against the Whiteboy menace?" another said. "Where were Captain Preston and his cavalry detachment?"

That was the big question Lord Preston sought to answer before coming out on the balcony to address the agitated crowd.

He summoned Howard Bannister to the drawing room over the portico to assist him in crafting a plausible response.

"The cavalry detachment was away on maneuvers in the town of Athlone thirty miles distant," Bannister said. "Didn't you know that?"

"I did not. Was my son with his unit?"

"You know your son."

Indeed he did. It was why he hesitated to state with any degree of certainty where his son was last night.

"I can send a rider to Athlone to find out," Lord Preston said.

"You can, but it is thirty miles away. Listen to them out there. They won't wait that long for an explanation." Lord Preston rose and pulled back the curtain to scrutinize the faces of those gathered below the balcony.

Bannister joined him at the lace curtains. "Perhaps you should reinstate the militia."

Preston mopped his brow with a silk handkerchief. "I thought of that, but it carries risks."

"It does, but so does doing nothing."

Preston was on the horns of a dilemma. He had as much to fear from an out-of-control, well–armed Protestant minority as from the angry unarmed Catholic majority. He stepped onto the balcony to address the throng of merchants, small farmers, and middlemen milling around below him.

"Let me begin by saying I appreciate your solidarity with my family in this trying situation. I will move with all possible dispatch to bring the perpetrators of this affront to justice..."

"Where was the cavalry last night?" a man yelled.

"Did they turn tail and run?" another shouted.

"Unfortunately, Captain Preston and his detachment are on maneuvers in Athlone. I've sent a rider to have them return with all possible haste."

A chorus of derisive shouts rose from the crowd. Someone jeered, "Might be better if he maneuvered closer to home."

"Sending a rider won't help. We need action now!"

"Bloody right," another agreed. The mob yelled its support.

"You should've hanged Redferne and Blake while you had them."

"I am reestablishing the local militia."

"Now you're talking." They cheered and applauded, some smacking swords against the columns of the portico. "We'll show those cowards behind the sheets what it is to fight real men."

"The town bailiff will assist me in this effort, beginning tonight in the market house at seven o'clock. See you then. Now return to your work and your families." When The Lord came back inside, the back of his silk waistcoat had turned damp with sweat. The crowd dispersed and drifted away. Could the remedy be worse than the disease?

Bannister handed Prescott a glass of claret.

A large log fire burned in the iron fireplace decorated with an imposing image of Cerberus, the three-headed dog of Greek mythology, guarding the gates of Hell. Lord Preston sank into the red velvet armchair, drink in hand, realizing how desperately he needed his own Cerberus to keep the wolves at bay.

He had misgivings about Redferne's escape. Certain features of the attack didn't make sense. Benjamin Strange doubted Whiteboy involvement, given the violent manner of Redferne's abduction. Preston expressed his suspicions to Bannister.

"Something else that doesn't make sense, is O'Rourke's killing," Bannister said. "It's unlikely the Whiteboys did that."

Preston furrowed his brows. "Of course, the Whiteboys didn't kill one of their own."

"Exactly, which means one of our people had to do it. Except no shots were fired to repel the attackers."

Worry lines etched into Preston's face. Although only in his mid-fifties, he arose from his chair with difficulty. His joints ached from arthritis. He walked stiffly to a corner of the room and opened a closet containing an array of bell pulleys. He tugged one and returned to his seat by the fire. Within minutes, Benjamin limped into the room, his head swaddled in bandages.

"Benjamin, come sit by the fire." Preston drew up another chair for the stooped servant. "Could you detail again for Mr. Bannister what took place when you were assaulted?"

"Certainly, sir." Benjamin related the events of the night before.

"Is it possible that Redferne was faking it to pretend that he had no prior knowledge of the assault?" Bannister said.

"Allowing one's head to be pistol-whipped would be faking it in the extreme, don't you think."

"But someone spoke Irish," Bannister pressed.

"To be sure, but that in itself means nothing. It could have been a ruse to throw people off track. In my humble opinion, this was a setup. Redferne was kidnapped, not liberated."

"To what purpose?"

Benjamin shifted in his chair. "That's beyond my powers to divine, sir."

"I'm sure you could hazard a guess, my good man." Bannister's eyes brightened in anticipation.

"I could, sir, but I fear it would be a most imprudent road to go down, since as you said it would be guesswork." He glanced at Lord Preston.

"I fear we may be taxing Benjamin's strength," Preston said.

Bannister drained his glass of claret and stood up. "Of course. I will take my leave as I still have work to do on the accounts before our meeting this afternoon."

The Lord felt as if another weight had been placed on his shoulders. Bannister suspected what he himself now thought was a possibility and which Benjamin deftly avoided when pushed. He studied his servant who looked more uneasy by the minute.

Benjamin rose from his chair. "May I leave now, sir?"

"Not yet. It's a hard thing for a father to admit, but I feel my son is somehow involved in this. I value your opinion and I need you to be straight with me. Do you think that is so?"

Benjamin looked away. "There may be something to it all right, sir," he said, in a tone that betrayed the danger of speaking truth to power.

"You have nothing to fear from me, but I am binding you to silence until I've gotten to the bottom of this." He placed his hand on Benjamin's shoulder. "I know you have sources. Try to find out what has become of Redferne." Then he ushered the stooped servant to the door.

Benjamin Strange had a complicated relationship with his employer ever since that day forty years before when William Preston, Lord Preston's father, threw him off the hay loft where he had gone to steal a nap. Benjamin had turned fourteen and in an instant, his life changed forever. As the High Sheriff of County Roscommon and the area's biggest landowner, William Preston had little to fear from the law.

He was the law.

It was of little concern to him that young Benjamin nearly died that day when he collided with the upturned shaft of a horse cart before hitting the ground. Such was his brutal introduction to the family in whose employ he would spend most of his life.

Whether out of indifference or inattention, William Preston allowed Benjamin to stay on. He spent months recuperating from his injury and the doctor, such as he was, did a less than adequate job in attending him, leaving Benjamin with a stoop at fifteen. He never complained for fear of being lashed with the master's lead-tipped thong. William Preston went about his business with no more regard for what he had done than if he had pitched a rat from the hay loft. Gradually Benjamin worked his way up the ranks, from stable boy to cook's helper to footman, until he became the current Lord Preston's personal assistant.

Every night he laid out his master's clothes, and first thing every morning he brought him a cup of tea and a copy of the *Freeman's Journal* when it was available. Though docile, Benjamin swore revenge, if not on the perpetrator of the deed, then on one of his offspring, but over the years, the current Lord Preston's kindness mellowed his rage. Of late, The Lord had drawn him into his confidence, making him conflicted in his loyalties. Regardless, getting information to his master about Redferne was a good thing. It might not only save Redferne's life, but prevent further bloodshed, and it didn't compromise his support for Blake and the Whiteboys.

He thought about the upcoming meeting between The Lord and Bannister in the library. He didn't want to miss that since it sounded like it had something to do with the estate finances. The library was one of Benjamin's favorite haunts. Over the years, he had taught himself to read and write by spiriting books from it when he went in to tidy up. By hopping and trotting, he had amassed a store of knowledge that few of his class could even dream of, let alone attain.

He liked the library for another reason. The Preston manor, like other big houses throughout the country, was honeycombed with a secret labyrinth of back stairs and passageways, designed to segregate servants from their masters. Should a servant see one of the quality coming down a corridor, he was obliged to disappear into a concealed passageway so as not to offend the upstairs person by his presence. Failure to do so was seen as a breach of respect. Swift punishment was sure to follow. As a teenager, Benjamin was fascinated by this hidden world and soon knew every nook and cranny of it.

One day he discovered a stairway behind the library wall where the portrait of the patriarch hung above the fireplace. Nobody else appeared to know about it, or if they did, never used it. That stairway became one of his favorite haunts when he discovered that he could hear and see the goings on in the library through a crack in the crown molding near the ceiling.

Down the years he heard and saw embarrassing conversations and scenes. He recalled with clarity the time William Preston, father of the current lord, and the wife of a fellow landlord staying overnight for a foxhunt next day, took a tumble together on the large rug before the fire. Or the night Captain Preston lost one hundred pounds gambling to a local squire whom he later killed in a duel. The meeting between His Lordship and the estate agent would be far more significant, he felt, than those events.

CHAPTER 15

Redferne reined in his horse among the scrubby pines overlooking Lough Gorm, close to the spot where he and his son found the body of Maureen Kelly. He looked up at the starry sky. Should he take the more direct but risky road to Cloonfin or detour around the lake? The militia might have been mobilized, thinking he had been sprung from jail by the Whiteboys. Going around the lake would take hours, which would leave him traveling in daylight before he reached the Whiteboy safe house. A black shape appeared on the lake moving toward shore. He rubbed his eyes to see if the apparition disappeared, but the dark blob only grew larger.

Could it be the wandering monk that legend claimed haunted the Preston demesne? Although it was an idiotic impulse, he pulled the innkeeper's pistol and cocked the hammers. To human eyes he would be safely hidden among the pines, but to the eyes of a thousand year-old monk? Maybe not. He blessed himself in just in case. His horse raised its head from nuzzling the snow in search of moss and whinnied.

The dark shape stopped and whinnied back. Redferne started breathing again as the blob grew four legs and trotted off the ice down the shore. Something on the animal's back gave it an odd silhouette. Could it be a person? He holstered his pistol and gave chase.

Within minutes, he was abreast of a riderless runaway. Grabbing its bridle, he brought it to a halt. The odd shape turned out to be a canvas rucksack tied to the horse's back. He cut the ropes and it slid to the ground, landing on a crusted patch of snow with a crunch. The horse took off at a gallop and disappeared into the darkness. He cut the draw strings holding the mouth of the pack together and found bottles of Jamaican rum; small sacks of tea, sugar, indigo; blocks of cheese; and boxes of Virginia tobacco. Smugglers, he thought. Hicks's flask was almost empty.

The horse must have broken free of the train and wandered off unnoticed. Either that or its rider came to an untimely end. He chuckled when thinking, *don't look a gift horse in the mouth.* Although all alone on the frozen lake shore, he looked around, like a man about to rob a poor box, before liberating a bottle of rum, a box of tobacco, a sack of tea, and another of sugar.

He took a few swigs of rum and sat down on a rock protruding from the snow. Warmed by the alcohol, his mind wandered from his current predicament to the worsening problem at home.

After storming from the house that night to attend the farewell for Maureen Kelly, things had gone downhill faster than before. And there was always the chronic sense of guilt over his brother's death, a deep-rooted ache that was not just emotional, but physical as well. The only way to deaden that was to keep moving.

His life seemed to lack a sense of permanence or commitment. Aunt Kate was still waiting for him to patch the hole in her roof. The need to travel in search of work took him away from home for weeks at a time, widening the gulf between him and Grace. A six-week stint digging potatoes in Scotland signaled the end of his home life. When he finally pushed open his cabin door with only calloused hands and bloodshot eyes to show for his absence, it was difficult to make the case that he was out struggling to support his wife and son.

Battle lines were drawn and he lost. Padraig sided with his mother, so he stayed only sporadically at the house after that. When he announced that he was throwing in his lot with the Whiteboys, she demanded that he leave. He would stop by tonight if he survived, and make her a peace offering of the tea and sugar. He wouldn't mention the rum.

After burying the smugglers' sack under a snowdrift, he placed the items he'd taken in a saddlebag and returned to the spot where the animal had exited the lake. A brown track in the snow led out onto the ice, disappearing in a patch of frozen rushes. The snow had been fairly well compacted by animal hooves. Either animals were using it on their own or they were being driven across it by their owners--most likely smugglers.

Since the ice sustained the weight of what appeared to be multiple animal crossings, it could sustain him if he dismounted and led the horse. It would shorten his trip by hours and throw any pursuers off course. He broke into a sweat and began to shake. His heart raced. He took a deep breath. It wasn't the fear of walking across the frozen ice that scared him. It was the lake itself. His brother and Maureen Kelly had both perished here.

He kept breathing deeply until his panic subsided and then, blessing himself, he led the horse onto the ice. Skittish at first, with a little coaxing the horse took a few tentative steps.

Initially he walked as if stepping on eggs, fearing that he might plunge into the frozen depths. By the time he reached the rushes, he moved with more assurance until he found himself up to his knees in snow, the reins to the horse pulled taut. The horse stopped when Redferne strayed from the path. Although the sky was ablaze with stars, the light was not sufficient for this kind of travel, but the horse operated by a sense other than sight. He edged the horse back to the ice path and let it take the lead.

In a short time, they came to a small island where the path disappeared among driftwood washed up on shore. The horse continued until it found the ice path again on the other side of the island. From here he could make out the dark outline of the opposite shore.

A cold wind kicked up, pelting him in the face with chips of ice and powdered snow. He tightened his collar and took a sip of brandy from Hicks's replenished flask. Voices. Spectral shapes came toward him speaking Irish. Grabbing the horse by the bridle, he scrambled up a small rise and took cover behind some boulders.

Since the voices were Irish, they were probably friendly, but many of Reggie Preston's henchmen were Irish whose services went to the highest bidder. Tying his horse to a hazel bush, he pulled the pistol from the saddle holster and took up a position with a view of the ice path. Some of the men led horses with large packs on their backs. Others led donkeys similarly burdened. All wore white clothing and hoods. Whiteboys, or smugglers posing as Whiteboys?

Probably the latter.

He guessed that this operation originated in the port of Sligo and ended in Dublin. Cloonfin was only a transit point and hardly in the market for fine Jamaican rum. Neither was it the most direct route to Dublin. Curious.

After they passed, he set off again, following the horse toward the opposite shore. Periodically, the ice made snapping sounds like pistol shots. The man who had warned his son against venturing out too far on the ice when they found Maureen Kelly now walked across a frozen lake at the rear end of a horse. In the middle of the night, no less.

It was still dark when they stepped on dry land into a copse of ash trees. A thin wind hissed through the frozen branches, scattering shards of ice. He shivered and burrowed in the pack until he found the rum and took a few hurried swigs. It felt like fire coursing down his throat, all the way to his feet. But the pleasure turned sour when he thought of what drink had done to his life and marriage. He licked his lips and stifled the urge to fling the bottle out onto the ice. Instead he took another swallow and returned it to the pack.

The sun would be up in about two hours. He weighed the wisdom of stopping at his own place. It would delay him getting to the safe house under cover of darkness, but he wanted Grace to have the tea and sugar. It was worth the risk. He hadn't seen Padraig in over six weeks, so he spurred his horse and set off at a gallop.

As shards of light pierced the horizon, he reached the crossroads where they had lit the bonfire for Maureen Kelly on the eve of her departure to America. The tramp of dancing feet, the lilt of Maureen's voice, and the mournful sound of uilleann pipes echoed in his head as he momentarily relived the American wake organized to bid her farewell. He imagined he heard her voice, but it was only the wind. He spurred his horse and turned up the lane to his cabin. His erstwhile good mood at the prospect of seeing Grace and presenting her with enough tea and sugar for a year now darkened. Maybe she would invite him in for a cup which would be the Christian thing to do on a cold morning. He turned off the lane and dismounted on a hill overlooking his house in the shelter of some trees. Since he saved hours crossing the lake, it wasn't likely that the captain and his crew had gotten ahead of him, but to be safe, he hunkered down to listen.

Satisfied that the house was not under surveillance, he crept toward it and tapped on the bedroom window. The only reason the house had a window, unlike the majority of the dwellings in the townland, was that the previous tenant had been a game warden for the Preston family. The typical window was a hole with a piece of sack cloth or wicker covering. When no stir came from inside, he tapped the window again. "Grace, it's Michael. Let me in."

A sleepy voice asked, "Who's out there?"

"It's me—Michael. Got some presents for you."

"Go away," the scratchy voice said. "We're through."

"I've got tea from India and the finest sugar from Barbados. Enough to last a year," he answered hoping that might weaken her resolve.

"Don't believe you. How'd you pay for Indian tea when you can't even buy a loaf of bread when you're done in the tavern?" That last remark stabbed like a thorn, not only because she uttered the words, but more because they were true.

"I'm not lying," less certain now that his bribe would work.

The squeak of a latch being lifted raised his hopes, but she only cracked the door and asked him to pass the items through.

He stamped his feet and blew into his cupped hands. "I'm as cold as a stray dog on All Souls Night. You wouldn't believe what I've been through to get here. I could sure use a cuppa' hot tea and a stint at the fire."

"The militia already paid me a visit. If they find you, they'll hang you from the nearest tree. They blame the raid on the Big House on you and the Whiteboys."

"Grace. I was the victim not the perpetrator. Ask Ben Strange."

"Nobody believes that. You best be away from here." She edged the door back.

"A hot cuppa' tea would revive me powerful and help me on my way." He handed her the bags. Her eyes widened. He could tell that she had not expected him to come through. He spent his whole life making promises to her, but seldom delivered.

She opened the door wider and turned back into the tiny kitchen without a word. She grabbed the tongs by the hob and extracted coals from the ashes to revive the fire. "One cup and then you must be on your way." She added fresh turf to the embers, and soon she had a blazing fire. When the kettle sang she wet the tea, setting the pot to draw on a few crushed coals placed on the stone hearth. Crouching by the fire, he placed his hands close to the leaping flames. Snow cascaded off his cap and greatcoat. "Where did you get the tea and sugar?" she asked from behind him.

He turned to look at her. "If I tell you, you won't believe it."

She glanced at him while setting the table "This I do believe. If the revenuers find us with these items, we could hang."

He hadn't thought of that. The whole story gushed out of him: everything about the raid, the captain, Hicks, and the smugglers. He didn't mention the rum.

"This is not another one of your tall tales, is it?" She eyed him like a cat ready to pounce on a small bird.

"'Tis the God's truth, Grace. I couldn't make up that story if I wanted to."

Her face softened. "Come to the table." She poured him a mug of tea and placed two cuts of buttered soda bread and a boiled potato left over from dinner on a wooden plate.

"I could warm the potato if you'd like."

"You'll do no such thing. Give me some salt and I'll be as right as rain." The tea tasted wonderful, especially with the sugar from Barbados. He had never tasted sugar before, and judged it a fine addition to a mug of India's finest. She did not have any. She sat looking pale and careworn in her grey flannel nightshift. She wet the tip of her finger with her tongue, and dipped it into the sugar bag, then touched her tongue again.

"Never heard of Barbados," she said.

"Some fancy place across the water, I'm told, with beautiful palm trees and the sun cracking the stones. Not like this God-forsaken country with its infernal wind and rain."

She had a faraway look in her eyes. "Sounds like a nice place."

"Someplace you and I will never see, unfortunately, so don't worry your pretty head about it."

"It doesn't cost anything to dream." She dipped her finger into the sugar bag again.

"I'd like to see Padraig before I leave."

"So would I."

Redferne stopped eating and looked up at her. "What do you mean, 'So would I'?"

"Padraig's been gone for a month."

"You've lost me. The kid's sixteen. Where is he gone to? This is no time to play word games." His face flushed.

"I couldn't take care of him on my own," Grace shouted.

Redferne jumped up from his chair. "In other words..."

Tears filled her eyes. "He's gone, because his father was gone, most of his life."

"For Christ's sake, tell me where he is, or do I have to beat it out of you." He advanced on her with a raised hand. She retreated into a corner, alarm on her tear-stained face. Her startled look jolted him back to reality. He dropped his hand and sat back at the table. He had blown it. He best be on his way. In his most persuasive voice, he pleaded. "Please, Grace, tell me where he is. I can't leave without knowing. I can't live with that burden on top of everything else."

Grace had withdrawn behind a heavy chair by the fire for protection. "Parson Stack found him a job with a linen merchant in Sligo town."

His throat caught. "Parson Stack, that fat bastard that's sucking the life's blood from poor Catholics to build his fucking church. Are you out of your mind?"

She threw her hands in the air. "He was willing to take care of my child. That's all I care about. That's more than you were willing to do."

"Do you know the name of this merchant?"

"No," she replied, looking into the fire.

Redferne stood up, drained the last of the warm tea from his mug and jammed the remainder of the cold potato into his mouth. Without looking at Grace, he pulled the wool cap over his ears, tightened his belt, and walked out the door.

The cold penetrated Hicks's coat like a lance, but it was nothing compared to the chill that settled in the pit of his stomach at the news that his sixteen-year old had been spirited off to an unknown address in a seaport town fifty miles away.

CHAPTER 16

Lord Preston's stomach growled. He stared out the ten-foot-high windows of the library at the sweeping vista that went all the way to the abbey near the perimeter wall surrounding the demesne. The warping effect of the century-old glass made the ivy on the walls of the abbey coil like snakes every time he shifted his gaze. It was rumored to be haunted by a long-dead monk, killed by the Norsemen on a plundering raid.

According to popular belief, he walked the grounds at night, disappearing at the first rays of sunlight. Preston had little tolerance for superstitious twaddle, but it helped keep the gullible rabble off his grounds after the evictions.

Beyond the wall, the Preston estate extended for miles in all directions, encompassing grass, bog, and woodland. A hierarchy of squires, middle men, cottiers, and tenant farmers worked it, all roiling and squabbling among themselves for advantage. This didn't unduly trouble him as long as they paid their leases and rents on time. That was the problem. Many paid late, and some not at all. An unpleasant business, pounding on his door for a solution.

He removed a small silver box from his waistcoat pocket and, tapping a thin line of snuff along the side of his index finger, he slid it beneath his nose to inhale. This brought on a sneezing fit that sprayed tobacco juice all over his white waistcoat. He seemed oblivious and looked up at the bewigged portrait of the family patriarch now with a gaping hole in his chest. Dead almost half a century, William Preston still exerted a strong influence on all major family decisions from his place above the fireplace. After the break-in, Lord Preston could hardly look his ancestor in the eye without sensing shock and contempt. Underlying this lurked a greater disaster. Despite his best efforts, his estate of sixteen thousand acres was slipping into insolvency. He spent many sleepless nights fretting about the Encumbered Estates Court and the possibility of debtors' prison.

Most thought that such a vast holding guaranteed a luxurious life style, but the demands of a spendthrift wife and a wastrel son pushed his resources to the limit. He was embarrassed by his inability to maintain the estate in its traditional grandeur.

At times he felt unworthy to be in the library. It was once the patriarch's private study and one of the finest rooms in the mansion. Its handsome oak bookcases stretched from floor to ceiling, with paneled window seats and a crystal chandelier hanging from an exquisite *fleur de lis* ceiling medallion. A large log fire supported on two brass fire dogs emblazoned with ornamental lions' heads roared in the spacious cut-stone fireplace.

Preston considered himself a man of letters. The library handed down to him by his forebears carried volumes on local drainage schemes, horticulture, and sports, but he had upgraded its quality considerably. It now included the complete works of Shakespeare, Bunyan's *Pilgrim's Progress*, Chaucer's *Canterbury Tales*, plus copies of books representing the new-fangled literary form called the novel. To this he added volumes from the Greek and Roman worlds, including books by Aristotle and Plato, Ovid, Horace, Caesar, and Lucretius. Not many members of his household visited the library, and on most days he had it all to himself.

A sharp knock on the door broke his reverie. Benjamin Strange hobbled in.

"Will you be requiring some refreshment, sir?"

"Yes, Benjamin. A bottle of claret and two glasses if you please."

"Right away, sir." Benjamin bowed and left the room.

The long-case clock struck half-eleven. A little early for claret, but he needed to bolster his courage in light of last night's outrage. Another tap on the door and Benjamin returned with a bottle and two glasses on a silver tray. He placed them on the table and left.

Preston turned in his seat and looked at the portrait. "I know, I know. It's a little early, but…"

Another knock, followed by Benjamin. "Mr. Bannister is here, sir."

"Very well, Benjamin. Show him in." Prescott took his place at the library table.

Howard Bannister swept into the room with a large ledger under his arm, pushing past the stooped servant. Bannister dropped the ledger with a thud on the oak table. Preston was never any good with figures, so he hired Bannister to manage the daily affairs of the estate and bring it back to solvency. For Preston, commanding a British regiment in the French and Indian War was child's play in comparison to eking a profit from the land. Bannister sat at the table opposite Preston. Benjamin poured the first drink, bowed, and left the room.

"Tell us what you have found, Mr. Bannister." Preston's voice sounded strained.

"Your Honor, if the estate continues its current outlay, you could be facing the Encumbered Estates Court within a year."

Preston did not show any visible signs of panic, but beads of sweat rose on the nape of his neck and trickled down the small of his back.

Taking another gulp of wine, he said with an air of forced detachment, "That is your diagnosis. What is your prescription?"

"You have four thousand tenants on your estate. Evict half of them."

"I find our current incremental evictions odious enough, but this wholesale upheaval you suggest is madness. What would become of these wretched creatures?" he stammered, jumping to his feet. He moved to the fireplace where he stood with his back to the flames, hoping to absorb the energy of the burning logs.

"Wretched. You've hit the nail on the head. The wretched can't pay," Bannister scoffed, tapping the ledger. "The wretched are dragging this fine house and your entire enterprise into a quagmire.

They breed prodigiously and will eventually storm the walls of your isolated demesne and turn you and yours out on the road."

Preston forced himself to walk slowly toward Bannister and plant his hands on the table, leaning into his face. "I put the question to you once more, sir. What is to become of those people?"

Bannister reached for a glass of claret and took a sip. "What do you care?"

"There must be some options."

"There are, but they are all equally painful." Bannister opened the large ledger and thumbed through it. "How about this item, for instance?" He ran his finger down the lined page, stopped at an entry, then reached over and grasped the bottle of claret from the silver tray.

He held the bottle aloft. "Last year you spent three hundred pounds alone on claret, not to mention two hundred on brandy and white wine."

Preston waved his hands several times as if swatting flies. "Hold on, hold on, that's impossible."

"Do you order the claret?"

"My butler does and I will have a word with him right after our meeting." He made a notation in a small notebook.

"Save yourself the trouble, I already did. These are his figures. Now to the larger item of entertainment." Bannister flipped a few pages. "Last year you spent two thousand pounds on banquets, balls, and fox-hunting. You rarely have a meal without forty people beyond your own family in attendance. You routinely serve upwards of twelve courses. The amount of money you spend on beef is staggering. The expenditure would feed the townland of Kildallogue for a year."

Preston threw his arms open. "But I am following the hospitality code of my peers."

"And you will follow it right into bankruptcy unless you change your ways."

Preston shoulders drooped. "Is that all?"

"There is still the matter of your wife and son." Bannister closed the ledger and waved it in front of Preston's face. "It's not my duty to take on a challenge over which I have little influence or control. I will leave that to you." He slid the ledger over the polished table to Preston. "I should mention this: you can ill afford to import drapes from London at ten shillings a yard or buy hunting dogs at two pounds each."

Preston propped his arms under his chin and leaned on his knuckles, staring into space. He stayed silent for some moments before reaching for the ledger and tapping his index finger on its cover. "Are there other shocks in here I should be aware of?"

"There are many, but two stand out. One may seem trivial, even comical. For example the excessive amounts you spend on wax candles."

"What?" Preston slammed his right hand on the table. "We should live in the dark, is that it?"

"You don't need to have a hundred candles burning throughout the house every night."

"But what are the alternatives?"

"The first alternative is obvious. Burn fewer."

"And the other?"

"Make your own."

"Are you joking?"

"Have the cook render the mutton fat into tallow and dip your own candles. Many Big Houses have gone from beeswax to mutton tallow candles. They're a little smelly, but they do the job."

Preston studied his bookshelves. How long could he afford his prized library? He might have to take a second look at some of Bannister's remedies if the Prestons were to continue leading a lifestyle that befit gentlemen.

Preston gestured toward the ledger. "And the next?"

"Fox-hunting. Terminate it. You have fifty horses and thirty hounds dedicated to it. Sell them. It's costing you almost three hundred pounds a year to house and feed them, plus the expense of entertaining a large contingent of guests and hangers-on who eat and dine at every 'tally ho' you subsidize."

The blood drained from Preston's face. "But I would never be able to hold my head up again among my peers if I do that. I'd be the disgrace of the county."

"Not as much as when the Encumbered Estates Court forecloses your property." Preston's head pounded. He poured another glass of claret with trembling hands. "Couldn't we secure a loan?"

"You already have one. The estate is encumbered to the maximum and the bank in Dublin is not likely to extend more credit unless your balance is brought current."

Outside the pale winter sun disappeared and a strong wind kicked up, rattling the tall shutters of the window casings. The wind crept in through dozens of cracks and crannies like a hostile interloper, as if Preston needed another reminder that he was under siege.

"Putting this off is not going to make it any easier," Bannister said. "It will only hasten your ruin."

If Preston made the austere cuts Bannister suggested, his family would slip into the lower class gentry. "Half-mounted gentlemen," they were called, unwelcome and shunned by their peers. He was a member of the Irish Parliament and the high sheriff of County Roscommon. That should count for something.

If the only way to avoid such a disgrace was to evict two thousand tenants, that road might bring armed insurrection. The Whiteboys were pushing back against the small scale clearances that Bannister recommended. They burned the houses of those who claimed the land of evicted tenants, maiming cattle, and in some cases, resorted to murder.

He shuddered to think of what might happen in a large-scale eviction. "Lord John Russell," he blurted, "the speaker of the Irish Parliament, is a good friend. Surely he has influence with the Dublin bank."

Bannister pushed back from the table and crossed his legs. "All well and good if he has that kind of clout. Bankers are notorious for being impervious to rank and pressure, even from King George himself, when it comes to throwing good money after bad."

"I will travel to Dublin within the week to confer with Lord John."

"If Lord John is not the savior you anticipate, consider this as a back-up plan. You asked what would become of the rabble turned out on the road. I offer a solution. Pay their passage to America. It would be cheaper in the long run."

Preston's face lit up. "Has this ever been done? If it worked, it would eliminate a breeding ground of insurrection, and clear the land for more productive use."

"Precisely as to whether it's ever been done before, I'm not sure, but we could be trailblazers in a new venture." Bannister emptied his glass of claret and returned it to the table.

"What if they refuse to leave?"

"They'll jump at the chance when faced with the alternative of surviving on the roads in the dead of winter. We could add a little encouragement."

"Like what?"

"Hang a few Whiteboy leaders like Blake in the town square on a market day. That would get their attention."

"Because he's a hedge schoolmaster doesn't mean he's a Whiteboy."

"That's beside the point. All we need is an example, to scare the hell out of those criminals and those that harbor them."

Preston had a stricken look on his face. "I cannot abide that." He grabbed the bottle of claret and filled his glass with a shaky hand.

"But you are still interested in the overall concept?"

"Yes."

"The first step would be to secure ships and captains willing to get involved in such an enterprise. In that regard your wife could be most helpful."

Lord Preston's face went blank. "I beg your pardon."

"Come, Your Lordship, you know as well as I that your wife's family still has valuable contacts with ships' captains and the shipping industry." A sly smile crept across Bannister's face.

Preston shifted uneasily in his seat. After the collapse of the woolen industry in Ireland, his wife's people turned to the lucrative slave trade from Africa to America and the West Indies. That's what Bannister was hinting at.

Preston cleared his throat and, without committing himself, gave

Bannister the go-ahead to research the scheme. He walked Bannister to the door. "Be discrete and prudent in your inquiries. We don't want this to get out under any circumstances until we make a decision. If this information fell into the wrong hands, it could be a disaster for all of us," he said holding Bannister by the elbow.

"Don't worry, sir, I will be the soul of discretion."

"One final item," Preston said, opening the library door to let Bannister out. "I've been told that several young men from the townlands have gone missing in the past two months. You wouldn't know anything about that, would you?"

"The press gang has been active in our county of late. His Majesty's ships are in constant need of men."

"Isn't it unusual for the press gang to come this far inland?"

"Not if they're in dire need of recruits. The last time I talked with Captain Tolliver, he informed me they were, after the heavy losses at Minorca and Pondicherry."

CHAPTER 17

Redferne rode into the valley of the Black Pig, high in the Arigna Mountains, as the first streaks of light brushed the sky, with his mind in turmoil. The sun had risen but barely took the chill off the morning. His breath swirled around him like steam. Snow lay in swatches along the road, giving way at times to patches of ice in shallow pools. When he couldn't feel his fingers on the frozen reins, he dismounted and led the horse up the final stretch of the mountain trail. The horse's breath warmed his neck.

Topping a rise, he came upon a derelict house. It nestled in a hollow against the base of a limestone cliff, curtained in ivy all the way to the top. As he got closer he noticed plaster peeling off the walls and a door that hadn't seen paint in years. Holes peppered the thatch. A horse whinnied in a second building with a double door that sat at right angles to the first.

No sign of human activity. Reaching inside his jacket, he cocked the hammers of his pistol. The dilapidated door flew open and Rory Blake rushed out, rifle in hand. Several others followed, all armed.

"Redferne, as I live and breathe. I'm right glad to see you, friend. Wasn't sure I'd have that pleasure again, after what happened."

"Likewise." They pumped each other's hands.

"You'll understand why we were cautious. You snook up on us."

"No sentries out. Not a great recommendation for a safe house."

Blake looked a little sheepish. "We've grown lax due to our remote location."

"Grace told me that I'm a wanted man."

Blake propped his rifle against the side of the house. "That's putting it mildly. The whole county is after the man who broke out of the Big House and took a shot at the landlord."

"I've done neither, yet I've gotten under their skin," Redferne said, secretly enjoying his ill-deserved reputation.

"That's not the half of it. There's a price on your head, put up by the local landlords and the town merchants."

"How much?"

"One hundred pounds."

"Not bad for a spailpín. All that for getting bushwhacked by Reggie Preston."

"So Benjamin guessed right. It was Captain Preston."

"Indeed. Andrew Hicks of the Cock and Bull can give me an alibi."

"That alibi isn't worth spit," Blake said. "Who would believe you or take the word of a disreputable character like Hicks over the word of the landlord's son?"

"Why should I be singled out? They dressed as Whiteboys. You should be their number one suspect."

"So far I've escaped their attention. All I can think is that Reggie Preston wants you more than he does me."

How convenient.

Redferne stamped his feet against the cold.

"Better get you and this animal inside before you freeze to death."

Blake led Redferne's horse toward the stable. Redferne followed. The stable felt warm from the body heat of several horses munching hay along the back wall. Saddles and bridles hung from racks and wooden pegs on the wall opposite. Redferne removed his bulging saddlebag and laid it on the floor, and Blake's eyes drifted toward it.

"Why are they so all fired up about me? Are they afraid I'll start an insurrection or something?"

"I'm not sure your reputation has grown that much, but Parson Stack's condemnation of you from his pulpit last Sunday has riled the auld ascendancy class like never before."

"The fat prick, that's another score I've to settle with him." Redferne uncinched his saddle and hoisted it onto a wooden rack with a grunt.

"The militia has a free hand in harassing and terrorizing Catholics. They're searching homes and imposing curfews." Uninvited, Blake rummaged through the saddlebag and fished out the bottle of rum. "Ho, ho, ho, what do we have here?"

"Nobody's ever put a price on my head before. Wonder what the rest of me is worth?"

"It's no laughing matter," Blake responded, turning over the bottle of rum in his hands. "That kind of money could attract gunmen from Inniskillin."

A worried look crossed Redferne's face. "Bounty hunters from the North?"

"Exactly, but where in God's name did you come up with this?" He pointed to the Jamaican label on the bottle.

Redferne gave Blake the details of his kidnapping, his escape from the Cock and Bull, and his encounter with the smugglers.

"Whoever is running that smuggling operation has inside connections to get by customs with such luxury items as indigo dye, Jamaican rum, and Indian tea. These boys are not a bunch of moonshiners from the bog," Blake said, carrying the saddlebag as he and Redferne walked back to the house.

"They've also figured out a way to hoodwink the Inland Revenue Service by posing as Whiteboys," Redferne said.

Blake's face tightened. "Any connection, I wonder, between Reggie Preston and the smugglers? They both use the Whites as cover."

"Wouldn't put anything past Preston."

"True, but he's a hothead. Can't see him running the smuggling operation. That takes someone with a cooler head and brains."

"That rules Reggie out on both counts."

Blake opened the front door and placed the saddlebag on a rugged table set in the middle of a flagstone floor. A roaring fire supplied the only light. All the window flaps were down to keep the winter cold at bay. The whitewashed walls had turned yellow from turf smoke and time. Two young men slouching on benches played cards at a crude wooden table.

"Let me introduce you to the lads. This is Brendan." Blake pointed to a young man in his early twenties with blond hair and the beginnings of a beard. He put his hand on the shoulder of the other. "And this fella is Roger Courtney. He can knock a skylark from the heavens with a musket ball, when he's not distracted by a young lassie at the butt of the mountain." Roger's freckled face colored to the roots of his black hair and he fiddled with the buttons of his frieze jacket.

"Pleased to meet you both," Redferne said extending his hand. "Now, if you'll excuse me, I've got to get to the fire. My hands are about to drop off."

Blake retrieved four glasses from the dresser and liberated a bottle of Jamaican from the saddlebag. He inclined his head toward Redferne. "With your permission we'll break it in." He poured four drinks.

Settling by the fire beside Redferne, he raised his glass. "In honor of your safe return." The others joined in.

Redferne held up his glass and looked at it. "Begod, Rory, If not for this, I mightn't have." He downed the brandy in one gulp.

"Got to thinking," Blake said, "Reggie Preston may not be smart enough to run the smuggling operation, but he's brutal and vicious enough to be an enforcer, which a savvy person might need to protect his operation."

The heat of the fire and the rum soon had Redferne nodding off.

"Don't know, Rory. I'm dead to the world, your excellent company, and this fine rum notwithstanding."

Blake pointed to an unmade bed in a corner under a faded painting of the Last Supper. "You can bunk down over there." A woolen blanket lay crumpled in a ball at its foot. He looked at the picture as he drifted off to sleep. Had he let Grace down as Judas did Jesus?

CHAPTER 18

When he awoke hours later, he was on his own. He lay there in a dreamlike state. The Last Supper moved about the wall. Grace's words rang in his ears. "He's gone because his father was gone, most of his life." His wife's cutting words mingled with other voices, all conspiring, it seemed to him, in a choir of condemnation. "He's gone to serve his time with a linen merchant in Sligo," they chanted, like the chorus in a Greek play. He sat bolt upright, his head and neck wet from sweat. He swung his feet onto the floor and staggered outside to find the voices.

Blake and Brendan were helping Benjamin to dismount. Roger and several newcomers tended to the other horses. Redferne was surprised at how frail-looking Benjamin appeared in daylight. Benjamin grabbed his hand and gave a weak smile. "Delighted to see you well my friend, delighted."

"Likewise, Ben." Redferne's throat constricted. "Don't worry— we'll even the score with Preston." When Blake and Roger led Benjamin into the house, Redferne stayed behind to chat with Brendan who was on sentry duty. A refugee from one of Preston's evictions, Brendan depended on the Whiteboys for food and shelter. There were dozens like him in all the townlands. A ready-made army of recruits, Redferne thought, waiting for a signal to go on a rampage. "Brendan, is the path the only way up the mountain?"

He shifted his blunderbuss to the other hand "Unless you're a goat it is."

Redferne nodded at the gun. "Know how to use that thing?"

"Damn right I do. There's not a lot to know. Pull the trigger and it'll blow a hole the size of bucket in a barn door." Brendan looked as if he couldn't wait to try it out. Redferne shuddered at the slaughter a dozen or two angry young men could generate with weapons like that.

"What was that about the goat?" Redferne walked to the edge of the clearing by the barn and looked across the snow covered valley below. Brendan followed.

"What?" Brendan asked.

"You mentioned something about a goat."

"Oh, that. It's almost impossible to climb the mountain from the other side, unless you're a goat."

"Thanks, lad." Redferne gazed a little longer at the peak of the mountain and hurried inside. He needed to know the lay of the land, especially with a price on his head. If someone came after him, it wasn't likely they'd come up the path and knock on the front door.

When he entered the kitchen, the aroma of tobacco smoke filled his nostrils. Blake and Benjamin sat at the table, Benjamin cradling a mug of tea and Blake puffing on his pipe. Roger occupied a chair at the fire, cleaning the barrel of his musket. The newcomers lolled around the periphery, their chair backs propped against the wall, some smoking, others chatting. Redferne checked the Last Supper. It had returned to its place above the bed.

"We've been waiting for you." Blake pushed a chair toward him. "It's time we inducted you into the group. The Whiteboys are a secret society, requiring an oath of loyalty that the Catholic Church condemns. In some parts of the country, the bishops are threatening to excommunicate anyone who takes it. Is that a problem?"

"If that's the only problem, I can endure it. Let's get on with it."

Blake handed a sheet of paper to Benjamin, who placed a pair of spectacles on the bridge of his nose and said, "Repeat after me:

"I, Michael Redferne, swear to be true to our friends...to attend all meetings when warned...no cause to excuse absence but sickness...of which sufficient proof must be given...to keep all secrets...to suffer till death rather than betray each other or our cause...So help me God..."

Redferne gripped the seat of his chair. "So help me God."
Everyone smiled except Benjamin. "Isn't it strange," Redferne said,
"to invoke the name of God for an activity that God apparently isn't
too crazy about, if one is to believe the bishops?"

Benjamin looked over his spectacles. "The bishops don't speak
for God, least of all those who condemn the Whiteboy organization."
Blake presented Redferne with a large white shirt and hood. The
Whiteboys donned this attire on punishing raids both against the
landlord class and their own people—those who stepped out of line.

Redferne struggled to suppress a belly laugh. "Jaysus, I'll look
like a clown in this outfit."

Blake threw him a dark look. "As long as you don't act like one
when wearing it." Inflicting pain on his own kind was no laughing
matter to Redferne, but he was willing to tolerate it if it gave him an
opportunity to get back at the captain, and avenge Maureen Kelly.

Benjamin took the floor and reported on the library meeting
between Preston and Bannister. Blake looked gob-smacked. "You
mean the fuckers don't have enough money for candles? Well I'll be
dipped." Roger nearly burst a gut laughing at that.

The blood drained from Redferne's face at the mention of
evictions. "Forcibly transporting two thousand souls across the
Atlantic?" He shook his head. "That's monstrous!"

"Problem is, we don't have the power to stop them," Blake said,
his face etched with worry.

Redferne threw up his hands. "But people won't stand for it."
Blake avoided his gaze. Benjamin ran his fingers through his thin
hair, examining the table top.

Then Benjamin spoke.

"To Rory's point. We don't have enough manpower. We don't
have enough guns. We don't have enough horses. A few midnight
raids against Preston livestock or the shops of rapacious merchants
will not remedy that situation."

Redferne stood, his face flushed. "So that ridiculous oath I took.
The ballyhoo with the bloody clown suit. Nothing more than a
costume party, is that it?"

Blake jumped up and pushed his chair back. "The Johnny-come-lately has spoken. Sitting idle on your arse for the last two years doesn't give you the right to be critical."

Benjamin pounded the table. "Enough of this. Sit down, both of you."

Feeling embarrassed, Redferne dropped back into his chair. "You're right. I have no right to be a scold." A murmur went up from the group. Then it hit him. "But there is a way we could raise funds to buy more horses and guns, if we have the courage to do it."

Every head turned in his direction.

Blake and Benjamin exchanged glances. Those on the periphery eased their chairs forward onto all four legs.

"This we got to hear, brother, fire away," Blake leaned back on his chair.

"I propose we ambush the smugglers as they cross the ice path. Those are high quality goods they're carrying. They'd fetch a pretty penny on the black market."

Benjamin held up a shaky finger. "If they get hit once, they're not likely to fall into a trap a second time. Keeping that in mind how can we generate an ongoing stream of revenue?" A murmur of agreement followed.

"Aye," Rory said, "unless they're stupid, which fella's like that rarely are, they'll change their routes and avoid the lake altogether."

"I've thought of that. The purpose of the ambush should not be to put them out of business, but to share in the spoils. We don't want to kill the goose that lays the golden egg."

Everyone talked at once. "We could exact protection money from them?" Blake said.

"Not necessarily cash. Might be a share of the smuggled goods." Redferne looked around the room for reaction. Some moved their feet, others shifted in their seats, while others stared back at him with blank looks.

"That's all well and good," Blake said, "but how much can we make off a smuggling route that may only be used once a month?"

"I'm betting that it happens a lot more than that up and down the West Coast, especially from the port of Galway," Redferne countered, leaning into the table.

Blake stood and started to pace. "It would take a bloody army to monitor the comings and goings of smugglers over so large an area. We don't have such an army."

"It doesn't have to happen overnight," Redferne said. "As for manpower, there's an army of young evicted men wandering the roads in search of work."

Except for Benjamin, the enthusiasm of the group appeared to wane.

Benjamin took out his pipe and Roger jumped up to light it. Puffing vigorously, he pulled the shank from his mouth and expelled a cloud of smoke. "I think Red's idea has merit. Let's take it a step at a time and see what happens."

"Assuming we run with this," Blake said, "in the long run how is that going to persuade Preston and Bannister to halt evictions?"

A strong gust of wind echoed in the chimney like the guttural roar of a wild animal, swallowing Blake's question. It spewed a cloud of soot and ashes across the kitchen. Everyone broke into fits of coughing.

Blake got up and lifted the flap on the window. "Wind coming straight down. A bad sign. Roger, go check on Brendan. Sounds like a storm brewing."

"Right, Boss." Roger grabbed his musket and left.

Benjamin dabbed his watering eyes with a handkerchief. "Am I to cheat death at Reggie Preston's hands only to die of asphyxiation among my friends?"

"The chimney needs cleaning," Blake said.

Benjamin turned to Redferne. "So, can you answer Blake's question?"

"This morning Blake wondered if Reggie Preston had any connections to the smugglers. I'd lay odds he does. If the Prestons have to curtail their use of candles, they're in dire financial straits. Losing the smuggling money could be the last straw. So we present them with an ultimatum: Scrap the eviction plan, or get driven out of the smuggling business. This is a huge leap of faith, I know, but my gut tells me I'm right," Redferne said.

"It's not a leap, it's a bloody pole vault," Blake said to general laughter. "All we have is a hunch that the Prestons are involved. Still and all, it's worth pursuing. So, let's find out."

"How?" Roger asked.

"We set a watch on Lough Gorm. That will be the first task for our newest member."

"Then we'll have to keep that lake under constant nighttime surveillance," Benjamin said taking the pipe from his mouth.

"Not necessarily, Ben," Redferne said. "I believe there's a more efficient way to find out when and how often they make their runs."

"And pray what would that be?" Benjamin asked, his keen eyes focused on Redferne's face.

"Check the shipping arrivals into the port of Sligo from the American colonies and the West Indies. I bet the smuggling runs are clustered in and around those dates."

Blake smiled for the first time that night. "Now we're getting somewhere. I'll send someone down there right away to scout the port and taverns. Sailors are a garrulous lot."

Redferne looked at Blake. "Put my name in the hat for that job. I have another reason to go. My wife and that damn parson apprenticed my son to a linen merchant there. I want to get him back."

Benjamin put his hands together and puffed on his pipe. "Rather than attract unwanted attention in the taverns, we might check the local newspapers. They carry the departure and arrival times of sailing vessels on a monthly basis."

An ear-shattering boom echoed off the limestone cliff. A cry of pain.

Everyone save Benjamin grabbed weapons and ran for the door. Brendan, the smoking blunderbuss still in hand, stood over a young man convulsing on the ground, half his chest blown away.

"He climbed down the ivy," Brendan said.

Redferne looked up at the cliff. "He won't be the last. Inniskillin isn't that far away." Then he looked at Blake and knew Blake was thinking what he was. Redferne's presence here put them all in jeopardy.

CHAPTER 19

Life among the Whiteboys was anything but predictable. Tonight Redferne sat astride Preston's gelding among a group of men in white shirts and hoods. They crouched in the tree cover behind the equine cathedral, waiting for the lights in the Big House to go out. Between them they had but three horses which limited their ability to strike back with force and speed, but tonight Blake was determined to remedy that. If he couldn't buy horses, he would steal them, which was faster than waiting on the smuggling scheme that might never pay off.

An owl hoot from Blake brought Alex Reid, master of the hounds, around the corner of the building.

"Pull yer horses farther back into the woods," Alex whispered. "They're agitating those in the stable."

"Righto, Alex." Blake motioned for his men to move back.

He passed a key to Blake. "If they find out I'm involved in this, I'll be hung, drawn, and quartered. So for Christ's sake, don't get caught."

"You heard what the man said. Don't fuck up," Blake said. Reid melted back into the shadows.

"Redferne, lead the way, since you're familiar with this place."

"Okay, everyone take off your hobnail boots. They make a fearful clatter on cobblestones."

"But there's snow on the ground," someone protested.

"Better snow on yer feet than snow on your grave."

Blake positioned five men with muskets to stand guard outside the stables while the rest led the horses outside. Twenty minutes later they were on their way, all mounted. Captain Preston was minus seven of his finest hunters.

"That was simple enough," Redferne said to Blake, who rode up front.

"That was a one-off. They're not likely to get caught napping a second time."

They cantered for a while down a boreen that meandered through a terrain bounded by stone walls and bare-leafed trees, standing ghost-like in the moonlight. The horses, as if sensing the nervousness of the riders, strained at the bit, and soon the canter turned into a gallop.

Roger groaned from behind. "Jesus, I'm frozen. Need to get my feet in front of a fire."

"No time for that now. We've got something else on our docket before the night is out," Blake said.

"Nice if you'd tell us about this ahead of time," Redferne said.

"The fewer who know about our plans beforehand, the better."

A few miles from the Big House, they dismounted on a bluff overlooking a small valley. A prosperous-looking farmhouse with several chimneys and an array of windows that reflected the light of the winter moon nestled in its center.

"We don't have time to light a fire," Blake said, "so stamp your feet, dance around a bit to get the blood moving, only don't scare the horses."

Two large ricks of hay and an assortment of stables extended from the back of the dwelling in an L-shaped configuration. Numerous old-growth beech trees surrounded the house. In summer they must have provided luxuriant shade, but in winter they looked like naked sentinels, ice glistening on their bare branches.

"This is the farmstead of a Mr. John Tallford," Blake said to Redferne when he joined him on the perimeter of the bluff.

Redferne blew into his cupped hands. "And the reason you're giving us this tour at two in the morning is to further our knowledge of local geography. Is that it?"

"Mr. Tallford leases a thousand acres from Lord Preston which he subleases in small parcels to over a hundred tenants."

"Will there be a test on this tomorrow, teacher, sir?"

Blake shook his head. "As you know, middlemen like Tallford are often more ruthless and hardhearted than the landlords themselves."

"I take it our friend Tallford fits that description?" Redferne said.

"Despite several warnings to be patient, he evicted Mike Brennan and his family on a night with frost. They spent several hours in the open and almost froze to death. Brennan was suffering from tuberculosis, which Tallford knew about."

"Was?"

"He died last night in the house of a charitable neighbor, leaving a wife and four young kids."

The chill in Redferne's feet rose up through his legs and into his belly. He gazed at the sleeping house in the valley among the naked trees. The smell of burning pitch filled his nostrils.

Blake handed Redferne a torch. "Let's mount." Redferne dropped back to the rear of the column. They galloped down the slope, torches blazing. Without stopping to open the front gate, they raced up to the wall surrounding the farm. Preston's hunting horses showed their stuff. Not one faltered, but they carried their riders effortlessly across the barrier. They followed the boundary wall to the orchard, two fields back from the hay ricks. Dousing their torches, they set to work. The thud of axes and the hiss of saws echoed through the orchard. When they finished, over thirty trees lay spread across the frozen ground, like the skeletons of gutted fish. Redferne grew nauseous. What had taken thirty years to mature lay devastated in less than half an hour.

On Blake's order several men started digging a pit amidst the fallen trees. He assigned Redferne and two others to stand guard.

The ring of picks and spades against the rocks in the frozen ground. When the pit was finished, they relit the torches and mounted their horses. Spreading out in a skirmish line they advanced on the farm house at a canter, covering the front and back entrances to prevent escape. Redferne's heart pounded. A primitive impulse engulfed him when Blake and the others pulled out hunting horns and blew several short bursts followed by a long drawn-out whine. It sounded like the banshees of Irish mythology.

Picking up the energy, the horses galloped. Wailing horns, yelling riders, the pounding of iron hooves on frozen earth made a fearsome din. Lights appeared in the farmhouse. The skirmish line hit the house with musket fire and rocks, smashing the windows and peppering the doors.

The raw violence of it all went to Redferne's head. He threw himself off his horse and charged the door, but it held fast. Two other riders came up behind him with a battering ram and knocked the door back onto the kitchen flagstones with a bang. A woman with a defiant look on her face stood before a fireplace, her arms wrapped around two small children.

"Where is he?" Blake yelled. Her face looked like it was chiseled from bleached stone. The children screamed, breaking her stupor. She looked up toward the ceiling. Whether deliberate or involuntary was hard to tell, but the sound of breaking glass in the second story sent Redferne racing up the stairs. Blake dashed outside. Redferne cocked his pistol, tracking a draft of icy air to a room with a broken window. A man ran toward the orchard pursued by two mounted Whiteboys. Several farmhands scurried into the stables.

They caught Tallford near the ruined orchard and dragged him back to one of the barns where they set him on a milking stool.

Blake spoke: "You're charged with the murder of Michael Brennan late of Cloontuskart townland. Do you have anything to say in your defense?"

Redferne stood on the periphery watching the poor bugger slumped on the stool. Whatever mad fever overtook him before abated, and he pondered the terror that one man menaced by ten must be experiencing.

Tallford, a redhead in his mid-forties with muscular arms and a barrel chest, looked every inch a farmer. One could tell by his ruddy face that he spent most of his time in the fields. He straightened on the stool and opened his mouth, but no words came forth. Fear curled in his eyes like a worm on a fishing hook.

"Can't run a farm and support parasites," he blurted. "Like slugs in apples, they putrefy the system from within until the whole edifice crumbles. Can't have that."

"Neither can we have a bloodsucker like you who values money more than human life," Blake said. A chorus of ayes came from his comrades.

"At least I can face my accusers, unlike you cowards who hide behind masks." His voice rose as if his words gave him courage.

"You can explain your philosophy to your maker and see who he agrees with, you or Mike Brennan." They dragged him down to the orchard and buried him in the pit up to his chin. "Hold the wife and kids in the house until it's over," Blake ordered.

Redferne looked stricken. "How does leaving a widow and two small children right the evil done to Brennan? Isn't it a question of two wrongs don't make a..."

"No it's a question of an eye for an eye," Blake shot back. They gagged Tallford and took him to the orchard. Redferne reckoned he couldn't last more than two hours in the frozen ground.

When they galloped toward the boundary wall, torches blazing and horns blaring, Redferne pulled his horse up alongside Blake and said, "Why not torch the hay ricks. That will send a signal for miles that the Whiteboys struck again."

"No, I don't believe in pushing my luck. If you want to do it, go ahead, but you'd better get out of there fast because it will attract the attention of the militia."

Redferne peeled away from the group and headed for the ricks. He torched one, but with snow on its peak it produced more smoke than fire, a handy excuse, he thought, if he was late to catch up with Blake. He rode around the other side of the hay rick and collided with a young man trying to avoid him. Redferne dismounted and helped the man to his feet. Apart from being winded he appeared none the worse for wear. Seeing the Whiteboy attire, he cowered against the hay rick. "Please sir, I'm just a laborer."

"Where are the rest of your mates?"

"They took off as soon as the bedlam erupted."

"I want you to do something."

"Yes, sir."

"Grab a shovel and go to the orchard. You'll find your master up to his chin in a pit. Dig him out."

The young man's face went blank.

"Trust me."

"Y-y-yes sir."

"And don't tell anyone about our meeting. Understood? If you do, it will land you in trouble."

"Don't worry. I'm not that thick."

Grabbing a shovel from the barn, he ran to the orchard. Redferne finished torching the other hay rick. By the time he cleared the boundary wall and galloped up the incline, the hay was fully engulfed, lighting up the countryside like a harvest moon.

CHAPTER 20

Twenty families lived in the clachan of Kilmore in mud cabins circling a central compound. Redferne approached it near dusk, a pistol dangling from his right hand partially concealed by the horse's mane. Up ahead, sounds of children squabbling, parents laughing, dogs barking, and sporadic angry shouting filled the air. His saddle bags carried a bottle of rum in case he needed to loosen some tongues about the ice track.

The decision not to go to Sligo was painful. It meant putting off looking for his son, but he was battling a cold. He assuaged his guilt with the promise that when the weather warmed, he would search for him in earnest. Surveying the inhabitants near the ice path might be a quicker, more efficient route to the smuggling intelligence he sought, but there was another reason why he left the safe house without telling Blake. The man from Inniskillin was after *him* and he didn't feel secure there any longer. How safe was the safe house if they found him so quickly? Even more troubling, was there an informer there?

All that aside, the raid on the Tallford farm unnerved him the most. He wasn't cut out for that. And if Blake discovered what he had done, no telling what might happen, so he had to get out and do a little freelancing. When he had something solid on the smugglers, he would contact Blake and see which way the wind was blowing.

He planned his arrival at the clachan around evening mealtime. Most people would be indoors as the cold wind coming off the lake drove even the hardiest souls for shelter. By the looks of it, he had calculated right. The compound appeared deserted. So far nothing out of the ordinary. His nose picked up the smell of frying bacon. He hadn't tasted any in over a year because he couldn't afford it.

He dismounted near the perimeter, slipped the pistol into his waistband, and looped the horse's reins around a tree branch. He wanted to talk to Fergal O'Driscoll, the clachan chief, whom he knew only by name, figuring he ought to go straight to the horse's mouth while honoring the code of respect.

He strode up the middle of the compound as if he belonged there. Halfway through the village he spotted a horse cart tipped back. Its shafts pointed skyward like two cannon guns. Once past it, he sensed someone following him, like a cat creeping up a tree to spring on a wounded bird.

Something cold and hard touched the base of Redferne's skull. "That's far enough, Stranger."

Redferne raised his hands so as not to startle his challenger and risk getting his head blown off.

"Take it easy, take it easy. I come in friendship to talk to your chief."

"And friendship persuaded you to bring this." The voice reached around him and pulled the pistol from his waistband.

"A measure of precaution, that's all. We live in troubled times."

"It's a wise man that takes precaution. There's no harm in that, surely. The question is, are you a wise man or a fool?"

"Neither," Redferne said, "but the man who runs this clachan is wise, I'm told. It would be foolish not to take me to him as I've come to seek his advice." He wasn't quite sure how snooping for information on a smuggling operation would be regarded as looking for advice, in fact, it would come across as downright unfriendly, if it turned out that he was prying into their business. And this hostile reception got him to thinking that the inhabitants might be connected to the smugglers. He hadn't thought of that. He had better come up with a plausible excuse for his presence.

The man with the gun marched him toward one of the cabins. Maybe coming here on his own wasn't all that smart, but he had been in tighter situations before and always managed to pull through.

His confidence plummeted when the gunman pushed him through a flimsy burlap door. He found himself before a group of men sitting on a floor carpeted with rushes, all of them armed.

A large turf fire kept the cabin warm. Judging from the sacks of flour and grain stacked on top of each other, this cabin was not used as a dwelling. It was larger than the rest. Several white shirts and hoods hung from pegs along the back wall. *Oh fuck*, he thought, *I stepped in it now.* These people have bread and bacon aplenty unlike their neighbors in other clachans.

He had stumbled into the smugglers' lair.

A thin gangly man sat in the middle of the group. A full black beard sprouted from his sunken jaws like a tuft of grass in the hollow of a stone wall. His long hair dropped below his shoulders. He took the white clay pipe from his mouth and spat into the fire, motioning Redferne to the floor with its shank. "Not from 'round here, are you?" He put the pipe back in his mouth and puffed, sending clouds of smoke swirling into the matted straw ceiling.

"I'm a stranger sure enough, but I'm throwing myself on your hospitality."

"A stranger of some means I gather, judging from the pedigree of the horse I'm told you're riding."

"In my line of work, a fast reliable horse is a must. Without that I'd be out of business in no time."

The bearded man withdrew the pipe from his mouth. "And that line of work would be?"

"I'm almost embarrassed to admit it, talking to hard-working people like yourselves…"

"Admit what?"

Redferne struggled to devise a convincing lie. "I've gone into business for myself and now I live by my wits and my horse's heels."

A thin smile parted the bearded man's lips revealing a row of yellow teeth, stained by neglect and tobacco. "We too live by our wits, which makes me doubly suspicious of another plowing the same furrow."

"I'm what they call a knight of the road," Redferne said.

115

The speaker and his men looked at each other for a second before bursting into guffaws. "A fucking highwayman." They roared in unison, slapped their knees, and pointed him out to each other as if they could hardly believe their ears. Redferne smiled and acted sheepish.

When the situation quieted down, the bearded one became serious again and said with a straight face, "So did you come to pick our pockets, highwayman?"

Again the place erupted in laughter. This turn of events slowed Redferne's pounding heart, but he'd have to come up with a credible explanation as to why he had come to their clachan with a gun in his belt.

"No, sir, I didn't, but things have been kinda' slack lately. As I'm sure you know, the gentry are not out and about as much in the cold weather, so the pickings are slim."

"That didn't quite answer my question, Mr. Knight."

Redferne suspected this man to be the clachan chief Fergal O'Driscoll, but thought it best not to let on that he knew his name.

"I've never heard of a highwayman holding up a whole village, yet here you are armed and with a horse." The smile on his narrow face turned to menace.

Redferne coughed as if trying to find his voice and looked down at the palms of his hands spread out on his knees. "I suppose there is nothing for it but to get it out: I am so greatly reduced in means that I haven't eaten in two days. With armies of the evicted walking the roads begging for food, I hadn't a hope in hell of getting a meal." He raised his head to give the impression of pleading, scanning their faces to see how his story was going over.

"How did you stumble on us?" the chief asked. His demeanor softened.

"I could smell that blessed bacon frying a mile off." Redferne looked into his hands again. The room grew silent. Everyone in that room had been hungry at one time or another. Even if their circumstances had improved, they had long memories.

Several of the men looked at Redferne, slack-jawed. "What

are you staring at?" Fergal elbowed one of them in the ribs. "Fetch this man a meal and be sure it has lots of bacon." He extended his hand and said. "Welcome to Kilmore, friend, my name is Fergal O'Driscoll, what's yours?"

"Freyney, John Freyney," Redferne said, giving the name of a famous Irish highwayman from the midlands; one he hoped his hosts this far west did not know by sight.

Fergal gasped. "Freyney! Captain Freyney from Queen's County?" He looked startled.

"Some call me captain," Redferne said, maintaining his self-effacing attitude.

"Give this man back his pistol," Fergal said. "While you're at it, see to it his horse is stabled. This calls for a celebration."

"By the way, who are you stopping with in this neck of the woods?" Fergal asked.

Redferne struggled to come up with an answer. "When you're down on your luck, few want you, especially when you're a stranger, so I'm living rough in a wee stable down the road near the river bridge."

"A bloody outrage for a gentleman of your reputation. That settles it! You've found your new home with us." Within seconds, Redferne had a glass of Jamaican rum in his hand. When Fergal offered a toast, he enthusiastically raised his glass.

"This is not your moonshine from the bogs," Fergal boasted. He threw his shot back in one gulp. Redferne sipped it cautiously as a mouse might nibble the cheese in a trap. His eyes opened wide as the liquor crossed his lips, then froze. Christ! The rum in his saddle bags. If they found it, the jig was up.

Over the next hour, Redferne put away a hearty meal. His plate was constantly replenished with bacon, colcannon, shallots, a leg of mutton, and hunks of homemade bread slathered in butter. All the while the rum flowed freely, supplemented by mugs of local ale and wine from the Bordeaux region of France served in pewter mugs.

"You're no doubt wondering where all of this came from. Let me tell you, little of it hailed from this Godforsaken place," O'Driscoll gestured toward the door.

"I'm not one to look a gift horse in the mouth." Redferne tore at a hunk of mutton washing it down with mouthfuls of ale.

"Captain, this is your lucky day. We can use a man of your talents: a cunning rogue and a good horseman skilled with a pistol. Rather than rely on the pittance you collect from the idle rich, I can put you in the way of real money." His eyes danced with excitement and a touch of bravado.

When the meal ended, Fergal dismissed his men, but commanded Redferne to stay. Whether it was the rum or his infatuation with the highwayman Freyney, Fergal divulged more than he should have. He gave Redferne a rundown on the entire smuggling operation: the routes, the modes of transportation, the ships involved, and the ports of entry, but when it came to identifying the kingpin behind the operation, the chief was less forthcoming.

Redferne took Fergal's claim about the money that could be made from the illegal trade with a grain of salt. Someone made money all right, but judging by their living conditions, it wasn't Fergal O'Driscoll and his clachan. Yes, they had plenty of food and drink, but that was probably their compensation for supplying muscle to the smuggling operation.

"You can bed down here for the night." Fergal pointed to a bag of straw on the floor, then staggered to his feet and headed for the burlap-covered opening where a wooden door should have been— another sign that few gold coins or pound notes greased their palms. Although his mind was dulled by hours of drinking with his new friends, the hair stood on the nape of Redferne's neck when the rum in his saddle bags drifted back into memory. He sweated, waiting for the other shoe to drop. On the pretext of stretching his legs, he followed Fergal outside.

A crescent moon hung in the winter sky, giving off a pale sheen that painted the settlement in a ghostly light. He waited until O'Driscoll disappeared into a nearby cabin, and then went looking for his horse in case he needed to make a fast exit. He felt the pistol in his waistband. They wouldn't have returned it if they mistrusted him, and they sure as hell wouldn't have trusted him if they found the rum in his saddle bags. He breathed easier.

Since they used horses on their smuggling runs, there had to be a shelter or a shed for them somewhere. He went to the rear of the cabins and worked his way around until he found a mud-walled structure with a thatched roof situated near the cabin O'Driscoll entered. It was closed to the elements on three sides. The horses stood in a row munching hay from a stall on the back wall. Sensing his presence, they began to prance and nicker.

The dim light forced him to rely on touch to identify his black gelding, indistinguishable from the rest in the murky interior. He stroked each horse gently on the back before ducking under its neck and going on to the next. Better risk being bitten than getting kicked in the balls at the south end. Halfway down the line he stopped. He heard the crunch of footsteps on the frozen snow. A light appeared. Redferne crouched in front of one horse's forelegs and prayed that it didn't rear up and stomp him to death.

The man with the lantern talked in a soothing voice as he moved behind the horses, alternately raising the light over their backs or swinging it between them, agitating the animals even more. Redferne didn't dare look up to see if it was O'Driscoll. In the end, whether out of frustration or assurance that nothing was amiss, the man withdrew. Redferne continued his search. A horse at the opposite end of the shelter raised its head to nuzzle him when he drew close and didn't shiver when he stroked it. It was the gelding.

Missing were the saddle and saddlebags. Whoever stabled his horse could not have missed the rum. He searched until he found a saddle and a bridle in a tack enclosure adjacent to the shelter. Was the man with the lantern still out there, camouflaged between the half-light of the moon and the pallid snow?

He led the gelding from the shelter and retraced his steps around the rear of the dwellings. At the edge of the compound he jumped into the saddle and galloped down the lane that twisted around the lake, keeping his pistol ready. He had gathered some information on the smuggling operation, but would the smugglers change their plans when O'Driscoll discovered he had been hoodwinked?

The clachan chief might be loath to reveal to his overlords that he had spilled his guts to a stranger. He might even believe that Captain Freyney had paid them a visit and that an opportunistic lone wolf living by his wits wouldn't dare show his face in this part of the country again.

He followed the contours of the lane until he heard the burbling of a stream on its passage to Lough Gorm. The little humpbacked bridge, overhung by the branches of an alder tree, loomed ahead. As he crossed the bridge, a dark shape dropped from the alder tree landing on the horse's back behind Redferne. The animal, startled by the extra weight, lunged sideways and pitched the two riders across the parapet into the freezing waters below.

Redferne broke the surface gasping and spat out a mouthful of icy water. He couldn't feel his tongue. His limbs locked in place, yet his body spasmed. A head with long grey hair and tuft-like beard erupted from the water with a roar. Something flashed in the moonlight. Redferne grabbed the assailant's wrist and deflected a dagger away from his throat. As he scrabbled with the attacker he came within inches of the narrow face with the sunken eyes.

"Did you think you could outwit me, highwayman," O'Driscoll yelled as the two wrestled each other beneath the water. The strength of the man, who looked as thin as a broomstick, shocked Redferne. When they broke the surface again O'Driscoll wrapped his long legs around Redferne's hips, scissors-like, attempting to upend him. Redferne broke free and pushed the clachan chief away, but he quickly regained his footing and engaged Redferne once again.

"You eat my food, drink my rum, and then spit in my face, you damned spy," he grunted, bending the knife close to Redferne's jugular. Redferne's strength ebbed. O'Driscoll began to overpower him. He took a gamble and relaxed his grip on O'Driscoll's wrist and whipped his head sideways. The dagger sliced into the water inches from his neck.

Knocked off balance at missing the mark, O'Driscoll plunged into the stream face-first, connecting with the full force of Redferne's knee surging upward. The impact wrenched the knife from his grip, but not before it sliced into Redferne's thigh. The power of the collision propelled O'Driscoll back onto the snow-covered boulders on the bank. Redferne limped from the water gasping for breath. But O'Driscoll wasn't finished. He reached into his boot and whipped out a smaller dagger. Lurching at Redferne, blood streaming from his mouth and nose, he hissed, "May you burn in hell."

Twisting to one side, Redferne pulled the pistol from his belt and slammed the butt twice into the base of O'Driscoll's skull as he lunged past. The clachan chief's long body bent at the knees like a hinge and slipped beneath the rushing current. Redferne made an effort to grab him but didn't have the strength.

O'Driscoll drifted away, his long black hair trailing behind like sea weed amidst a swarm of bursting air bubbles. Redferne took a few halting steps upstream toward the bridge and collapsed on the snow-covered rocks.

Seamus Beirne

CHAPTER 21

"You took your precious time getting here," the lady in the blue evening gown said as she opened the door to Bannister, who held a gaily-decorated box festooned with a pink bow.

He set it down and put his arms around her slim waist. "Punctuality, my dear, is for those like yourself who have little to do. I, on the other hand, have many irons in the fire that need tending."

Lady Preston moved into his embrace. "Apparently I am not among those irons that need tending, for I have grown quite cool by your inattention."

"Perhaps, after the ball, I can meet you here and together we can work on raising your temperature."

She tapped him on the cheek with her silk-gloved hand. "Insolent man. I've a good mind to let you spend the night in your own apartments." She led him over to a brocaded French chaise with a Medusa head engraved on its mahogany back. "Now tell me," she asked as she sat and patted the seat beside her for him to join her. "Which of our enterprises has kept you so busy and distant?"

He took her hand, his face creased with concern. "First, let me express my relief that your person escaped the attention of those hooligans who violated the sanctuary of this house last week."

"A nasty episode that underscores our diminished standing, if riff-raff like that can breach our security without reprisal."

"I beg to differ; The Lord is not taking this lying down. He's mobilized the militia."

"Indeed, at your behest apparently, but enough of this. Let us move on to more pleasant topics."

Almost ten years his senior, Lady Preston found in Bannister the promise of what her much older husband could no longer guarantee: the continuation of a genteel lifestyle that befit her station as the wife of one of the biggest landowners in the county.

She was well aware what Bannister found in her: access to power and the potential for great wealth and title.

He put the decorated box on the chaise beside her.

"Pray what have we here?" she asked, feigning amazement.

"Go on—open it," he urged. She removed the lid and put her fingers to her lips on seeing an expensive bottle of French perfume, the fine bottle of Bordeaux, and two packets of indigo dye.

"I'm flabbergasted," She reached out and kissed him. "I've been told such items are not available in our country for love or money." She smiled coyly.

Bannister put his hand on her knee. "You heard right, but one of our enterprises is already paying handsome dividends as you can see."

"Well. then, let's toast our dividends." She held out a bottle of Bordeaux for him to uncork. "You will find a corkscrew and glasses on the nightstand."

He filled their glasses and together they toasted their good fortune. After the first sip, she said, "Now let's discuss this enterprise of ours that's producing such results." She put her wine glass on the table at the back of the chaise. "I trust there are more tangible benefits than these gifts, magnificent though they are, flowing from our little venture." A sly smile played across her lips.

"Indeed there are, Madam. 'Flowing' is an apt usage, as indeed much of our profit is flowing to us from overseas." He took a leather purse from his inside pocket and handed it to her.

She caressed it as she might a kitten. "How much joy is in here?"

"A fifty pound note short of five hundred, my dear." She locked the purse in the nightstand.

"You can tell me all about it after the banquet," she said, embracing him. "Now I must be off to the grand hall. Can't keep my guests on the long finger. I'm sure my husband is as nervous as a wet hen waiting for me to make an appearance." She rushed out the door, leaving Bannister standing in the middle of the room nursing a full glass of Bordeaux.

Lord Preston waited for his wife at the foot of the staircase as she swept down the wide steps into the great hall. Her black hair was arranged in soft curls close to her head. A gold pendant hung from her neck. She wore a long red gown bordered with black velvet piping that trailed behind her.

"You look beautiful, my dear." Lord Preston drew her fingers to his lips. Her smile looked forced. "Now let's join our company."

The great hall was the crown jewel of the big house and Preston delighted in showing it off. Coats of medieval armor interspersed with several antlered heads of Irish deer adorned its walls. Three Gothic arches running parallel to each other supported the ceiling, giving the room an ecclesiastical look without robbing it of its familial charm. The guests mingled and socialized in this large space without being diminished by its size.

Facing the staircase on the opposite wall, large beech logs blazed on medieval fire dogs in a spacious stone fireplace. In the center of the hall, a small contingent of servants and liveried footmen sporting the Preston colors of black and amber stood at attention on either side of a long banquet table. It was set with glistening silverware, decanters of wine, sparkling glasses, and settings for sixty people in preparation for the evening's festivities.

The Prestons walked over to greet their guests, who milled about awaiting their arrival. When the introductions were done, The Lord escorted the most senior lady to her place at the banquet table. As the host, he took his place at the head of the table and waited for his wife to approach with the other guests and take her place at the foot. Apart from the host and hostess, there was no prearranged seating. People were free to choose their places, allowing the young men and women to meet and court potential mates. Lord Preston had one unmarried daughter by his first wife, now deceased. Finding her a partner was always on his mind when hosting these gala affairs.

Lord Preston was about to welcome his guests when a door

slammed behind him and Captain Preston, his cravat askew and his shirt unbuttoned, tramped up the marble floor and took a seat beside Lady Osborne and her husband. "My apologies for my tardy a-arrival, but I was un-avoidably detained."

Lady Preston gave him a look that could have scaled a fish. His appearance set off a round of whispered speculation as to how he came by the black eye and swollen nose, giving rise to one theory that an irate husband or brother had finally caught up with him. Although separated by the length of the table, Lord Preston could feel his wife's contempt for his son.

She looked radiant, he thought, in her new gown. It set him back quite a penny to have it shipped from London, but tonight was a time of celebration. As he looked around the table, his chest swelled with pride at the magnificent feast he had laid on for them: saddles of mutton and lamb, platters of fish, venison, and quail, tureens of soup, bowls of white wine, and bottles of claret. He had spared no expense to impress his friends, and from the rollicking conversation and peals of laughter, he appeared to have succeeded. He noticed the wine bumpers of Lord Castlereagh and his wife running low so he called a footman to remedy the situation. He ate little but compensated for it by keeping a full bumper of claret within reach.

By the end of the first course when the tablecloth had been changed and the table reset, The Lord was slurring his speech and his normal reticence gave way to ebullience. He walked up and down, wine bumper in hand, gesturing flamboyantly and clapping guests on their backs, inquiring about their families, the state of their health, the disposition of their estates, all the while urging them to indulge themselves more in his lavish repast.

With the slightest nod of her head, Lady Preston beckoned her thirty-year-old stepdaughter, Pamela, who was seated near her father. "Sit him down, before he makes a show of us all."

Pamela bit her lip and conducted her father back to his seat. Once settled, he raised his empty glass to a servant.

Pamela put her hand on his arm. "No, Daddy," she whispered and waved the servant off.

Lord Preston looked at his daughter, her flowing black hair resting easily on the shoulder straps of her elegant blue gown. She had her mother's no-nonsense attitude and stern looks. He worried about her marriage prospects. "Whatever you say, my dear," he slurred.

When the second course ended, the tablecloth was replaced again and servants hovered around the diners like drones around a queen bee, restocking the table with bowls of raspberries and cream, platters of sweetmeats, Dutch cheese, and dishes laden with cheesecake and blancmange, as well as walnuts and dried fruit. Decanters of Rum Shrub, a cheap Irish whiskey flavored with raspberries, were placed strategically on each table to help settle the stomachs of those who overindulged on claret. Hundreds of candles set in wall sconces and candelabra burned brightly, their writhing flames casting shadows on the granite walls.

The Lord grew quiet, his joviality giving way to brooding until he glowered at his guests. The grinding and slurping sounds of eating and drinking clawed into his brain. Bannister's warnings hit him with blinding clarity. These parasites were eating him out of house and home. Worst of all, they were doing it at his invitation. The black candle smoke whispering up the granite arches was a visual reminder of the possibility of his ancestral estate going up in financial smoke before his eyes.

The clash of silverware, the clink of glasses, and the boisterous sounds of the diners congealed into a massive headache. His head began to swim until he slumped face down into a platter of cheesecake and passed out.

Lady Preston pulled the gold pendant from her neck and flung it into the jewelry box on the nightstand in her boudoir. Her husband had embarrassed her in front of the area's elite. His inability to hold his liquor was an apt reflection, she felt, of his inability to manage his estate.

Her reduced circumstances came from her husband's dithering and lack of spine to do what had to be done to make the estate solvent.

After her parents' wool business collapsed, she used her beauty and cunning to lure the much older Lord Preston into marriage.

When her revenues nose-dived for the second time in her life, she attached herself to Howard Bannister, a dashing soldier of fortune with the guile and guts to control his destiny. She looked around her boudoir with the flocked wallpaper, its floral blue pattern fading to a shabby grey. Catching her face in the oval mirror above the chest of drawers, she ran her fingers over an incipient wrinkle.

A light knock on the door interrupted her brooding. She opened it to Bannister. "I heard about Lord Preston, so I figured a more potent pick-me-up might be in order." He smiled and held up a bottle of Jamaican rum.

"You and half the county have heard it by now," she scowled, ushering him into the room.

"I'm sure it's not as bad as all that. He's hardly the first Irish landlord who overindulged in liquor."

"That's not the point." She picked at her high lace collar. "They're all a bunch of drunkards and braggarts, but few embarrass themselves so publicly."

"In a week it will blow over and the gossip will move to another topic." Bannister fetched a corkscrew from the nightstand and uncorked the rum.

"And I know where it will have blown to." She held out her hand for the glass of rum. "All the way to Dublin to lie in wait like a bird of prey and fly in my face at the first ball of the season." She took a generous gulp of rum, wincing as the blood rushed to her pretty face.

"Careful, my dear, careful," he said grabbing her around the waist, "or the next piece of gossip to hit the circuit might be 'Lady Preston succumbs to rum after husband overdoses on cheesecake.'"

She whipped around, angry, and then burst out laughing after considering the picture he had painted. Soon they were on the bed together.

She awoke in the middle of the night to the sound of a high wind ripping under the loose slates of the roof. It rumbled through the cavernous attic like the boom of a cannon. Although she felt and heard the comforting presence of her lover, she slipped out of bed and padded over to the dying fire. Shuffling the embers with the tongs, she soon had a small flame from which she lit a candelabrum, set it on the nightstand, and returned to bed. She lay there thinking while Bannister snored. He was ruthless, which was exactly what she needed, but she wasn't naïve enough to think that he wouldn't double-cross her. Men like Bannister did not get where they were by acting like choir boys.

He would be straight with her as long as it benefited him. She was well aware of that. Right now, he depended heavily on her contacts in the shipping business to ferry captives to Barbados and the American colonies. In that regard, her uncle's brig, the *Kate O'Dwyer*, played a double role.

She was a slaver on the outward journey and a smuggler on the return. Bannister wouldn't jeopardize that arrangement. If those ventures continued to generate revenues at the current pace, she would be independent of estate income in a year or so. Her husband was totally in the dark about all of it. Then there was the problem with her lout of a stepson Reggie. The mere thought of him prompted her to shake Bannister's shoulder.

"We have to get rid of him," she said, as Bannister sat up in bed and rubbed the sleep from his eyes.

"What in the hell has gotten into you? It's after two in the morning," he slurred, his voice thick with sleep. He pulled her to him under the bed clothes and kissed her. "Get rid of who?"

"Reggie," she said without a trace of feeling or fear in her voice.

At that, Bannister sat up and leaned back against the headboard. "Are you out of your mind? That would cause such an uproar as to endanger all our endeavors."

"All of our endeavors are in jeopardy as it is with him on the loose. He knows too much."

"He's a loose cannon, but his knowledge is limited to the Maureen Kelly affair."

Lady Preston ran her fingers through Bannister's hair while

staring distractedly into the candle light. "That piece of knowledge could hang us, if he talks."

"He can hardly talk given that it was he who did her in," Bannister added.

"At our urging, with the aid of a hefty bribe, or don't you remember?"

"Of course I do. You simply made the balls behind the scenes, while I threw them," Bannister said. He shot a quick glance at her before reaching across her nude body to take a swig from the bottle of rum on the night stand.

"I was a little bit more involved than that," she replied, looking pensively into the candle light.

"What do you mean?"

"You don't believe he choked the life out of that Kelly slut merely for money?" She arched her eyebrows.

"I'm afraid you have me at a disadvantage."

"Please! Do I have to spell it out? I had to come up with a down payment that was quite personal; that's why he did our bidding." She looked away.

Surprise rippled across his face. "I'll be damned. You slept with the cad?"

"For God's sake get down from your high horse. Moral outrage ill becomes you."

Bannister laughed and took her in his arms. "It's not fear. You want revenge. I love it!" He tightened his embrace.

She pushed him away. "You need to take this seriously. We've left ourselves open to blackmail or worse."

"*We* can blackmail him in turn. After all, he did the dirty deed." Bannister's tone sounded less confident.

"*He* is a member of the gentry, a gentleman, granted a misnomer. You and I are not. His father is High Sheriff of the county. If push comes to shove, they'll believe him, not us," Lady Preston said.

"Your standing as the High Sheriff's wife would have no bearing on the outcome?"

"Reggie is not above claiming that I slept with him. He knows that the consequences would be far more devastating for me than for him."

"You're a complicated woman, Lady Preston, but you have a point. If this little nugget of information hit the Dublin social scene, more than one bird of prey would fly in your face." Bannister tipped his head back to take another swallow of rum. He passed the bottle. The wind rumbled in the attic. She shivered and moved closer to him before taking a sip.

"However, Redferne and his spawn may pose a more immediate threat than Reggie," Bannister said. "And I don't believe he can be bought off for love or money."

She stayed silent as if mulling something over. Finally, she whispered. "I'm not sure about the love part. I think he's persuadable."

"Oh, for Christ's sake!" He lifted her toward the light to get a good look at her face. "Don't tell me…"

"You lout. I'm only playing with you."

"Let's get back to your concern about Redferne and the kid. We've never had any proof that Redferne and the boy found the body. It's all speculation at this point."

"We know the body was spotted by Reggie's informer, O'Rourke, in the ice the evening before. He gave a fair description of where it was."

"Yet when Reggie got there the next day, it was gone."

"I got there long before Reggie, and I know for certain Redferne and his son found something. Unfortunately, I couldn't stick around to find out what it was. Nearly froze to death." He pulled the blankets up around both of them.

"Why would they take the body?" Lady Preston asked.

"A body encased in ice doesn't up and walk away," Bannister said.

"Could wild animals have gotten to it?"

"No, unless you mean fish." She shuddered at the image. "They say he was involved with the Kelly girl before she went to America. Maybe he thought he'd be blamed," Bannister said.

Lady Preston grimaced and laid her head on his chest. "Still doesn't make much sense."

"Nevertheless, it's a loose end that needs tying up. If Reggie ever talked, Redferne might come forward and produce the body."

Lady Preston sat up. "Produce the body! Now it's you with the rum head. After all this time there would be nothing left but bones."

"Maybe not." He rose from the bed and paced the room. "He may have stowed it away in a place that would preserve it."

"Why would he produce the body? Wouldn't that amount to signing his death warrant?"

"Not if he found evidence on it pointing to someone else."

Lady Preston whipped her head around. "What kind of evidence?"

"I…I don't know, maybe Reggie was careless," Bannister said.

"You're panicking. Pull yourself together."

A powerful gust of wind rattled the window panes and shutters, bending the candle flames as if paying homage to an unseen presence.

CHAPTER 22

Blake and his men searched the area around Lough Gorm for days but found no trace of Redferne. As time wore on, they started thinking the worst.

"Maybe he lit out for Sligo town to find his boy," Brendan said. They were stopped at the mouth of the lane leading to the clachan of Kilmore.

"I'd like to believe that." Blake straightened in his saddle and scanned the path that meandered between bare hedgerows. "But I got the feeling that was all talk."

"Hard to credit that. Wouldn't any decent father want to find his son?" Roger dismounted and examined the compacted snow.

"Not if it meant crossing a wicked wife," Blake said.

"One reason why I'm not throwing my cap into any woman's kitchen," Brendan said, referring to the Irish courting custom.

Blake scoffed. "You needn't fret about that, Brendan. You'd get it back quick enough wrapped around a sod of turf." Everyone laughed.

Roger pointed at the snow. "A lot of animal tracks."

"About twenty families live in Kilmore. The more well-to-do have sheep and goats," Blake said.

Roger lifted his cap and scratched his head. "Aye, but they have more horses than they should have."

Bleating sounds. A barefoot boy came into view leading two kid goats. Fear gripped his freckled face and he dropped the tether and ran. Blake spurred his horse and nabbed him by the collar of his frayed jacket.

Blake dismounted. "Don't be afraid, young fella'. Not out to hurt you." The boy squirmed, eyes wide with fright. Blake moved his hand to the boy's shoulder. "We're looking for someone who was in this neighborhood a few days ago. Maybe you've seen him. A tall man with long brown hair. About your dad's age I'm guessing."

The boys eyes darted back and forth, suggesting he would bolt at the first opportunity. He looked down at his feet. "I'm not supposed to truck with strangers."

Blake raised the boy's chin and looked into his eyes. "The man we're looking for has a son a little older than you, who misses his daddy."

"Have a horse?" the boy asked.

"That he did."

"A strange man came here a few days ago. Said he was a pirate or something. My daddy said he wasn't and that he left in the middle of the night."

"Know why he left?" Blake asked.

"My daddy said he was a spy." The barefoot boy rubbed the sleeve of his jacket across his runny nose.

"A spy?"

"Yeah. He drowned Mr. O'Driscoll near the bridge," the boy continued, warming to his story. Blake's men looked at him and each other.

"Is Mr. O'Driscoll the chief of your clachan?"

"Aye," the boy replied.

Figuring they gleaned all the information they could, Blake gave him a farthing and sent him on his way.

"That's got to be the bridge we passed about ten minutes ago. Let's go. If Redferne killed O'Driscoll, then he encountered something dangerous in Kilmore."

"Smugglers," Brendan said.

"Aye, and had to get out of there fast."

They wheeled their horses and retraced their steps down the serpentine road guarded by alder trees until they came to the bridge where they dismounted.

"If it happened as the boy said, then either O'Driscoll followed Redferne here, or he was waiting in ambush here. Either way, there was a confrontation at this spot. Let's fan out and look for clues."

They left the path and walked both banks of the fast-flowing stream. A half hour of trudging through the snow brought them up empty-handed until Brendan spotted a pistol in the shallow water near the bridge.

Blake examined the firing piece and discovered a lead ball in both barrels. "It's Redferne's, but he didn't use it."

"So he didn't kill O'Driscoll with it then," Roger said.

Blake scanned the landscape in all directions. "Unless he reloaded. But why abandon a perfectly good weapon?"

"Come look at this. Maybe he was wounded and wasn't thinking clearly." Brendan pointed to blood stains on the rocks. "Assuming that's his blood and he went looking for help, where might he go?"

Blake cleared his throat and spat, leaving a dimple in the snow. "Not to Kilmore clachan. That's for sure. If he heads east, he has to cross the mountains. In this deep snow he'd be exhausted before going a mile."

Brendan blew into his cupped hands. "That leaves the way north and there's not a habitable dwelling for five miles along that cursed road, thanks to Preston's crowbar gang."

"Aren't we forgetting something?" Blake asked. "He could've gone west."

Roger looked across the fields of snow. "Toward Lough Gorm? What the hell good would that do? He'd end up at a frozen ice barrier almost a mile wide and six miles long."

"It's not an ice barrier this time of year," Blake said, "if you know the way across."

"The ice path," his men shouted in unison.

"The ice path," Blake agreed. "That's what started all of this and why, I'm guessing, he came to the Kilmore clachan in the first place."

"He knew where the path was and we don't," Roger said.

Blake stamped his feet. "I've a fair idea."

They mounted up and followed Blake down the left bank of the stream, a cloud of powdered snow swirling around them, kicked up by the hooves of their galloping horses. It was slow going, but at last they emerged on the other side of a birch wood onto the shores of Lough Gorm.

CHAPTER 23

Redferne watched the debris storm forming over the lake from his makeshift shelter under scrubby pines. A strong gale scooped up clusters of ice pellets, bundles of leaves, and stacks of withered branches, and piled them into ridges that snaked along the windward shore.

High above a hawk screamed, circling closer like a leaf caught in a whirlwind. The dark shadow broke from its orbit in the debris cloud and dove toward a group of horsemen moving up the shore in a skirmish line. Some of the horses reared, pitching their riders. The hawk swept in front of them trailing a high-pitched scream that echoed off the lake boulders.

Were the riders struggling to control their animals a search party or a hunting party?

If they were hunters, they would discover his crude shelter in the abandoned hut among the pine trees. If so, he needed to flee. If they were a search party, he ought to show himself.

The hawk kept up its attack until one of the frustrated riders fired his musket. The ball missed, but it forced the hawk to retreat. Its high-pitched cry faded away as it took refuge in the swirling cloud above the lake. Scrambling from his hiding place, Redferne hobbled back up the shore. using the pine trees as cover. Something about those riders made him suspicious.

If it was Blake and his men, they would not have fired a musket, fearing it would attract unwanted attention. And they would not deploy in a skirmish line that looked more like a military operation than a group of mates on a rescue mission. The wound in his leg throbbed as he tried to put as much distance as possible between himself and the riders. Another worry: he was leaving footprints in the snow like a string of breadcrumbs. His only option was the lake itself. If he could get to the ice path he had a chance, but to do that he had to cross open ground between the pine trees and the shore.

He looked down the shoreline to where the horsemen had bunched more closely together. In this formation they might miss his shelter, but Redferne didn't feel he could risk returning to it. His energy was ebbing, so he couldn't afford to wait. He made a dash for it. Not wanting to give away the location of the ice path, he headed for a large patch of bulrushes that extended along the shore and out onto the lake. Once under cover in this maze, he could make his way to the ice path and head for the little island.

Halfway through his sprint, a chorus of shouts came forth. Shots rang out. Musket balls ricocheted off the rocks with a whine. Then his wounded leg gave out, and he fell at the edge of the bulrushes. The riders surrounded him, their horses kicking up sand and divots of snow as they careened to a halt. He lifted up on one elbow, and found himself looking into the malevolent face of Reggie Preston, still astride his horse. Preston nodded to the group. One of them, with a well-manicured beard wearing a cavalier's tricorne hat and buckskin breeches, pulled a pistol from his holster and dismounted. When he got within a few feet of Redferne, he stopped. With his left hand, he reached beneath his jacket and withdrew a broadsheet which he shook loose.

"Let's see now." He looked at Redferne and back at the broadsheet, which featured a man's head and shoulders. "What say you lads? Is this the notorious outlaw Michael Redferne?" He held up the broadsheet and moved it in a semi-circle before them.

"Aye," they shouted.

The captain turned in his saddle and looked around.

Redferne grasped a fistful of snow and threw it at Preston, causing his horse to skitter. "What is it, Reggie? Don't have the balls to do the dirty deed yourself? You need a hired gun from Inniskillin?"

Preston's face turned white as the snowcap on the frozen ice. "Proceed, Mr. McAllister."

"And it further declares," the hired gun said, walking up to Redferne and pointing the pistol at his head, "that there is a hundred pounds reward for his capture."

A slight smile creased Preston's thin lips. "Dead or alive."

"Damned if you're not right, Captain," the gunman cocked the hammers of his pistol and pitched the broadsheet onto the ice. A breeze snagged it and impaled it on a frozen bulrush.

"Which do you prefer, outlaw, one in the back of the head or through the forehead?" He leveled the pistol.

A hand emerged from the rushes and seized the broadsheet, then Roger rose up and sighted along the barrel of a Brown Bess. A loud bang and the man in the buckskin breeches pitched backward onto the snow with a musket ball between his eyes. A volley of shots sheared off the tops off the frozen rushes, slamming into Preston and his men, pitching several from their horses.

The horsemen fled in all directions, some on foot, others clinging to their mounts. Reggie Preston, his left arm hanging limply by his side, spurred his horse into the pine trees and disappeared over the bluff.

Redferne pointed toward the trees. "Go after the bastard."

"Let him go," Blake said as he and his men emerged from the bulrushes.

"I suppose it goes without sayin' I'm glad to see yez all," Redferne said, cradling his wounded leg. Blake turned his head back and forth sniffing loudly like a dog pursuing a rabbit scent.

Redferne looked up at Blake. "Got a problem with your sniffer?"

"If I didn't know otherwise, I'd say Preston gave the condemned man a final drink before execution."

"Oh, that," Redferne said as Brendan and Roger helped him to his feet. "How do you think I survived all this time?"

"I'm aware of the medicinal properties of rum, but where the hell'd you get it?"

"Remember the smugglers' loot I stashed near the lake? Well, not to put too fine a point on it, but it saved my bacon."

"Surely you didn't exist on rum for the past few days." He sniffed again. "But from the way you smell, I'd say you did."

"That and a slab of fine Irish cheese pulled me through; otherwise you'd have found me stiff as a board in that little hut yonder."

"I'd say you had it better than many," Blake said.

"Say, how'd you find me?"

"You took off without leaving a forwarding address. Not an auspicious start for a new member with only one mission to his credit. In the army they call that desertion."

"I planned on coming back."

"Sure you did." Blake said. Roger and Brendan laughed.

"To answer your question: Word spread that someone matching your description killed the clachan chief of Kilmore, so we thought it might be a good area to start searching."

Redferne dropped his eyes. "I did it in self-defense."

"I'm sure there's a story behind it." Blake said. "In any event, we found your pistol in the Corvalus River. By a process of elimination and some lucky hunches, we tracked you across the lake. The musket shot helped us zero in on your position, and Roger took care of the rest."

"Chalk up one for the hawk, better than a guard dog."

"Say again," Blake said.

"*Naw bach lesh.* Don't worry about it."

They hoisted Redferne on one of the dead men's horses and retraced their steps across the lake. The storm had abated. On the way back to the safe house, Redferne recounted his struggle at the Corvalus River Bridge and his experience in the Kilmore clachan.

This most recent brush with death made him ponder his priorities. He needed to search for his son, to patch things up with Grace, but to do all that, he needed to stay alive. The fact that he would now be blamed for additional killings and the wounding of Reggie Preston contributed to his brooding. He was so distracted and disoriented by the worsening pain in his leg that he did not notice that they arrived at a different safe house.

Redferne awoke hours later soaked in sweat, muttering. "Gotta' get to Sligo and find Padraig."

"You're not going anywhere until this is seen to," Benjamin said, examining the wound in Redferne's thigh.

"How bad is it, Ben?" Stabs of pain shot up and down his leg.

"It would be a lot worse if you hadn't packed snow and ice around it, but from the looks of the swelling and the redness, I'm wagering it's infected."

Redferne tried to read the expression on Benjamin's face.

"I need to wash and clean the wound of any dirt or debris," he said, soaking a linen rag in a solution of warm water and carbolic acid. He dribbled it over the infected area. Redferne winced when Benjamin explored the wound with a metal probe. He panicked when he saw the blood. Everyone had heard stories of soldiers bleeding to death from superficial wounds or dying of untreated wounds that turned to gangrene.

"Don't worry," Benjamin said. "In this case bleeding is good. It will wash out the dirt I can't see, which should ease the pain and swelling. Your snow poultice kept the swelling down, but it deposited dirt and sand as it melted."

"Do you think I could lose it?" Redferne stammered.

"There are no guarantees in life, my friend." Benjamin applied a compress of lint saturated with linseed oil and warm water to the cut and wrapped it snugly with a bandage to keep it in place. "That's all we can do for now. We'll know more by tomorrow."

Redferne grimaced. "When will I see you again?"

"I'll be back tomorrow as soon as I can get away. Lord Preston has grown lax about my comings and goings, so it shouldn't be a problem." He touched Redferne's shoulder and followed Brendan to the waiting horses.

Redferne didn't like the state of uncertainty that Benjamin left in his wake, but decided to leave his worrying till morning and join his comrades in a mug of rum. Sligo would have to wait for another day. By the time the small clock on the mantle struck the half hour, Redferne's half-filled mug had slipped from his grasp onto the mud-packed floor. Soon he was dreaming about tunneling furiously with his spade beneath the door of a farmer's shed in Scotland.

When Benjamin returned the next day, he found Redferne delirious. Blake had plied him with rum to lessen his discomfort, which increased his raving. Several times he sat up in bed, shouting: "I let him drown. It was my fault." Sweat poured from his face and soaked his body.

Benjamin removed the bandages. Red streaks ran up and down Redferne's leg, indicating severe infection and possibly blood poisoning. He took a leather pouch containing several knives of different lengths and a metal probe from his small leather bag and spread them on a clean square of linen. In a dresser cabinet he found a large jar used for preserving fruit and filled it with a chlorine disinfectant of sodium carbonate and alkali. Next he selected a knife with a long blade and a metal probe and dropped them into a basin of boiling water. While the instruments soaked, he cleaned the skin around the wound with a mixture of rum and water.

"I'll need two of you to hold him down," he said to Blake. Reaching into his bag, he pulled out a round piece of wood that looked like the thin end of a chair leg and inserted it between Redferne's teeth. "Bite down on this. It will help with the pain." After disinfecting the knife and probe in the chlorine solution, he placed them on the linen square. "Well, gentlemen, I think we're ready."

At Benjamin's request, Blake and Roger transferred the patient from the bed to the kitchen table. "Hold him down." He traced along the outline of the wound with the probe to make an opening for the knife. Redferne screamed when Ben maneuvered the knife toward the bottom of the wound. Biting down on the wood Redferne struggled to break free. Benjamin withdrew the knife, pleased to see white pus well up through the incision.

"Good, good. It's beginning to empty." Taking a piece of wax he inserted it inside the cut to prop it open so it would continue to drain. Redferne was calmer now, and by the time Benjamin had washed the wound and applied a linseed poultice his breathing became more regular.

"Now all we can do is wait," Benjamin said as he washed and packed his instruments away.

CHAPTER 24

Captain Reggie Preston ate his breakfast of bacon, eggs, and kidney at the dining room table. He was in a foul mood. He rang the bell to summon a servant.

A young woman hurried to the table. "Yes, sir?"

"More coffee."

"I-t-it's on the table, sir." The servant pointed to the silver pot sitting on a stand beyond the captain's reach.

"Then pour it, fool." The servant's hand shook so badly that she overshot the rim of the cup, splashing coffee on the saucer and onto the captain's lap.

He jumped up and pounded his fist on the table sending the cutlery flying to the floor. "You incompetent imbecile," he roared, throwing cuts of toast and napkins at the servant who fled weeping from the room. "You are fired, fir..." His voice trailed off and he fell back into his chair out of breath.

He rested his forehead against his left palm and closed his eyes. His right arm hung helpless in a sling. His eye hurt. His nose throbbed. Redferne's face swam before him. The muskets and swords arrayed on the dining room walls among the coats of armor mocked his impotence, highlighting the activities he could no longer enjoy.

Although the hunchback assured him he was lucky that the musket ball had not severed an artery, he didn't feel lucky. He could hardly mount his horse and when he did, his arm throbbed so much from the bouncing that he had become a recluse confined to the Big

House. His father hardly spoke to him, seeming to push him aside in favor of Bannister, whom he noticed had grown quite friendly with Lady Preston.

Apart from a cursory investigation as to his whereabouts on the night of the break-in, the matter was laid to rest. With the re-establishment of the militia, his father had calmed the fears of the gentry, removing his greatest worry. He, however, was the butt of jokes among his friends. They ridiculed him for his poor showing against Redferne, whose reputation had grown fearsome in the popular imagination. Though Redferne had not fired the shot that wounded him, Reggie Preston blamed him for all his misfortune. Next time he would put an end to it, once and for all.

Bannister's brusque arrival in the dining room interrupted his brooding. He didn't knock on the door, another thing that rankled the captain. His underlings were beginning to disrespect him, especially Bannister.

"Good morning, Captain. How are you this fine morning?" Bannister sat at the table and rang the bell for a servant. Before Reggie could protest, a young footman entered, his eyes sweeping the room. Furious at Bannister for his presumption in front of the servant, Reggie did not challenge him lest underscoring further his declining stature.

Bannister raised his eyebrows. "Enda! They have you on double duty, I see."

Enda cleared his throat. "Some coffee, sir?"

"That would be fine." Bannister spoke to the servant with the assured air of someone used to running things.

When the footman left, the captain flared. "That was a damn impudent thing to do." He yanked the napkin from his neck and threw it on the table. "I fear, Mr. Bannister, that you have an exaggerated notion of your importance here, especially in the company of your betters."

Bannister's lips spread into a thin smile. "My most sincere apologies, sir. It was not my intention to step beyond my station. I had a dream last night that you should know about, Your Lordship."

"Please spare me your superstitious nonsense. I have no wish to be drawn into the murky realms of your imagination."

"With all due respect, sir, I think you'll be interested in the star performer of my sleepy vision."

"What have the concoctions of your fevered imagination to do with me?" The captain took another sip of coffee, staring intently over the rim of the cup at Bannister.

"The young woman in my dream complained of the cold. She appeared trapped in ice, but I could not tell where. When she raised her head, the ice shards slipped away revealing long red tresses. Next I woke up in a lather of sweat."

Beads of perspiration broke out on the captain's brow. "So this is your game; trying to scare me as if I was a child. God, I'll make you pay for your insolence." He jumped from his chair and drew his sword. Bannister kept the table length between them and moved back.

"Arm yourself, coward. I can take you even with one hand." The footman entered the room with Bannister's coffee, then dropped the tray and fled, splashing the hot liquid across the polished oak floor.

"So you and that bitch would like to pin this on me," the captain said through clenched teeth. He swept the breakfast things off the table to the floor with the flat of his sword.

"You've got this wrong," Bannister said drawing his sword, "I told you about the dream because of its mutual concern to us."

Ready to lunge, the captain stopped. Bannister faced him in a crouch, juggling the sword hilt from one hand to the other, as he cautiously circled the captain. The captain did not advance further, so Bannister backed away.

The captain grimaced and slumped onto one of the dining room chairs, holding the sword between his legs, tip to the floor. "How do I know you're not setting me up to take the fall for something you and that slut were equally responsible for?"

Bannister returned his weapon to its scabbard but kept his distance. "Because I can take you to where the body is hidden."

"That's going to make me feel safer?"

"This time we can do it right."

"Do what right?" The captain put his sword back in its sheath, the strain of the effort visible on his face.

"Bury it so no one will ever find it again." The anger and fight seemed to evaporate from the captain like air from a balloon.

Bannister came forward and assisted him to his feet. "Follow me, Captain."

Bannister stopped at the entrance to the service tunnel, lit a lantern, and moved into the gloom of the passageway. Rivulets of water dripped down the whitewashed walls. He moved at a fast pace through the serpentine corridor. The captain struggled to keep up. Every hundred yards or so, shafts of daylight shone through barred vents in the ceiling, casting shadows on the floor like prison cell bars. Preston's breathing sounded like a bellows.

They turned a corner to where a large wooden door blocked their way. Bannister fished an iron key from his pocket and inserted it in the old lock. He could not budge it with one hand, so he handed the lantern to the captain. After several tries with two hands, a heavy click. The door swung open and a blast of cold air froze the perspiration on their faces.

Once inside, Bannister lit the braziers around the circular brick wall, revealing a curved stack of ice. Bannister propped a ladder against it and with the lantern in his right hand, he began his climb. A mound of rubbly ice lay like a cairn on top. Setting the lantern down, he pulled aside a canvas cover exposing a trench about two feet deep. He moved the lantern closer, until the frozen face of Maureen Kelly looked back at him as if from the other side of a mirror. Bannister climbed back down to the captain, who stood as stiff as a statue at the bottom.

"Go on up, Captain."

"I'm not sure I want a better view," Preston whispered.

"Sometimes it's best to face your fears in order to conquer them."

He hesitated, then he climbed while Bannister ascended behind him. The captain lowered the lantern into the trench and gasped.

Bannister uncoiled a garrote and in one fluid motion flipped the waxed loop over the captain's head and yanked it tight around his neck. The captain dropped the lantern into the trench and clawed at the noose with his one good arm. His face turned purple. A dry rasping scream escaped his lips while Bannister strangled the life out of him and pushed him into Maureen Kelly's grave.

Exhausted, Bannister fell forward onto the ice stack. Despite the cold, he lay there for a few minutes breathing heavily until he smelled something burning. Preston's hair had caught fire from landing on the broken lantern. Using the edge of his palms, he scooped ice debris and snow from the cairn into the trench, quenching the flames. The stench of burnt hair stuck in his nostrils. He pushed the rest of the rubbly ice with his hands and feet into the grave until it was filled, then tromped the loose ice into place and poured a bucket of water into the cracks and hollows of the trench to seal the surface and make it less noticeable.

After the unpleasantness at the icehouse, Bannister took a long bath and then slept for several hours. Feeling refreshed, he arrived at Lady Preston's bedroom door a little before midnight in a clean linen shirt with billowing sleeves tucked inside a pair of buckskin breeches. A pair of riding boots with turned-down tan leather cuffs completed his attire.

He was through wandering the world offering his services to fickle despots and greedy noblemen for a mere pittance. Earlier that evening, spotting the first streaks of grey in his hair reminded him of time's grim advance. He had hitched his star to the Prestons. They were his best hope of escaping the cloying muck of destitution that threatened men of his profession when their looks and physical strength faded.

He tapped softly on her door.

She opened it, uttering one word. "Well?"

" 'Tis done."

A broad smile lit her face. She took his hand and led him inside her boudoir where a decanter of claret and two glasses sat on a table beside a roaring fire. She wore a light blue chemise that revealed her ample bosom. Her luxurious black hair tumbled freely down her back. "You're sure." She poured each of them a glass of claret. "He's not going to arise from the dead a year from now like that Kelly creature."

"Not unless Gabriel sounds the final trumpet within the year, and then it won't matter."

Her smile faded to a dark frown. "I'd prefer not to think about Judgment Day right now. If there is one, it won't be pleasant for either of us, will it?"

Bannister threw his head back and laughed. "Don't tell me you're getting religion. I thought Sunday services with the good Parson Stack had scrubbed your conscience clean of guilt or compassion for the wretched of the earth."

She stared into the dancing flames of the fire. "How ironic that listening to a gasbag like Stack prompts one to question God's existence and not affirm it."

"And even if God does exist," Bannister declared, "how smart can he be to pick such a dolt to be His earthly mouthpiece?"

Lady Preston laughed and took a long drink of wine. "In which case, why worry about God, even if He is floating somewhere in the clouds?" The blue chemise and the linen shirt spilled from the arm of the Medusa chair onto the floor when they fell into each other's arms on the canopied bed.

She woke him a few hours later in a panic. "What if someone finds the bodies before we move them?"

He yawned. "I thought of that."

Lady Preston waited for him to continue. Silence, then snoring. "Oh, for God's sake, wake up." She shook him by the shoulder, then jumped out of bed and lit a candelabrum with an ember from the fire before placing it on the bedside table.

He sat up, shading his eyes from the light. "You were saying."

He shook his head like a dog ridding its coat of water. "We can blame both deaths on Redferne. He had keys to the icehouse and the whole countryside knows that bad blood existed between him and the captain. People will see it as a revenge killing. He's an outlaw with a price on his head."

"What about Kelly? It will be harder to pin her death on him. This could get messy and slip out of our control, which could be dangerous for us. Unexpected details have a way of surfacing during a criminal investigation."

"And for that reason we have to make sure Redferne is caught and put out of commission." Bannister climbed out of bed and took a half-empty bottle of brandy from Lady Preston's night stand. When he offered her a glass, she waved him away.

"I've been thinking. Why kill someone if we can profit from his staying alive?" She twisted her long hair into ringlets with her index finger, then she cooed and stroked his hair. "A strapping man like Redferne would fetch quite a penny in Barbados."

"We need to catch him first. Your deceased step-son fell short in that endeavor more than once."

"I'm relying on you to solve that problem." She kissed him on the lips. "Allow me to suggest an idea."

"Go right ahead. I don't always think with my head when I'm in the embrace of a beautiful woman, especially at three in the morning."

"What if we get him to come to us?" She laid her head back on the pillow beside him.

Bannister raised himself on his elbow and studied her. "An interesting idea. You have a plan to get him to come knocking on our door?"

"He has a wife, doesn't he?"

"Yes, but they're separated."

"But she's the mother of his son, my dear," she whispered tracing his cheekbone with the tip of her finger.

Seamus Beirne

CHAPTER 25

Bannister sat on his horse peering through a hole in the blackthorn hedge at the little house in the hollow. He checked his pocket watch: ten o'clock on a moonless night, ideal for his purposes. He wasn't so much concerned about the time as the light that still burned in the kitchen window. For all their complaints about poverty, the poor still burned candles late into the night.

Eventually, the light in the kitchen faded and reappeared in the bedroom window. He took a black hood from his saddlebag and pulled it over his head. "What the hell's keeping her from getting into bed? It's not as if she can read."

The horse, sensing his impatience, pranced around. "Whoa, boy, whoa," he said, patting the gelding on the neck.

At last the light went out. He dismounted, tying his horse to the hedge, then feeling his way down the hill, he tiptoed to the front door and pushed it gently. It moved a bit. There wouldn't be the slightest problem kicking it in, but since he sought the element of surprise, he opted for a silent entry. Reaching under his coat, he pulled a long-bladed dagger from its sheath. Twisting the sharp point into the frail door, he opened up a hole big enough for his index finger and lifted the wire hook from the catch.

Quietly he shut the door behind him and waited until his eyes adjusted to the dark. By the light of the dying fire, he saw that the door to the little bedroom stood ajar. Snoring came from within. Removing his coat, he placed it on the floor close to the fireplace and gently pushed the door in. A few quick steps brought him to the edge of the bed overlooking the heaving bosom of Grace Redferne.

Her eyes shot open. Before she could scream, he clamped his hand over her mouth and the cry died in the hollow of his hand. She stiffened as he wrapped his left arm around her thin shoulders and pulled her to a sitting position. With his right hand still in place, he said, "When I remove my hand from your mouth, do not cry out or I will kill you, do you understand?" She nodded. He pulled his dagger and ran its blade across her throat.

"I've butchered deer with this and I will do the same to you if you lie to me. Do you believe me?"

In between gasps, she managed to say, "Yes."

"Where is your outlaw husband?" Before she answered, a spasm shot through her.

She sobbed. "He was here a week gone, but we got to fightin' and he took off. That's the God's honest truth."

He again put the edge of the blade against her throat, and although he didn't intend to, he drew blood. Fearing that she might not be getting the full impact of his presence, he ordered, "Get up and light a candle."

She scraped the floor beside her bed until she found the candlestick. He followed her into the kitchen where she lit a twisted piece of paper from the fire and touched it to the rush wick. "Now hold the candle up."

On seeing him, she sank to her knees, barely holding on to the candlestick.

He towered over her. "Where did your husband go?"

"He's with Blake and the others, but I don't know where," she continued to sob. "I've seen little of him in the last year."

"How come your son's not here?"

"When my husband left, we were close to starving. Parson Stack found employment for him in Sligo."

"Where in Sligo?"

"Parson Stack knows. Every month I go to the parsonage to collect the few shillings my son has earned. If it wasn't for that, I'd be a beggar woman walking the roads, Your Honor." She looked up at him through the dim candle light, a pleading look in her eyes.

"Put the candlestick on the floor." His fingers gripped the garrote in his pocket. He grabbed her around the waist and pushed her toward the kitchen table. She did not cry out when he bent her head over it, but wept softly.

He thought of killing Grace Redferne, but he needed her alive. She would get the word to Redferne that their son was in danger—that would flush him from his hiding place. If he was a typical father, he would go looking for his son, and Bannister would be there to meet him.

Seamus Beirne

CHAPTER 26

The next night, Bannister crouched among the headstones with a clear view of the parsonage and the skeleton of the new church rising in the background. Judging by the number of carriages outside his door, the parson was entertaining guests tonight. The coachmen passed a bottle around as they gossiped with each other or made crude jokes about their masters. In the fading light, it was difficult to read the inscriptions on the headstones. None of his kinfolk were here. They belonged to the lower classes and most likely were buried in unmarked graves. He did not want to end up like that. His eyes rested on the Preston mausoleum. He wanted to be laid to rest within that sturdy chamber.

A clamor brought his attention back to the parsonage where several couples had emerged onto the front steps and were saying good night to the parson and his wife. He hadn't thought about the wife. She could complicate things.

When the last of the carriages clattered out the main gate, he crept toward the house and peeked in a window. The parson poured himself a nightcap and settled into an armchair before a blazing log fire. The wife had disappeared. He figured she had gone to bed. He needed to strike before the parson followed her upstairs.

The parsonage, constructed from limestone, had doors and windows of stout oak. Gaining entry here would be more of a challenge than at Redferne's. He spotted a curtain flapping in an open window on the second floor. A quick check of the half-constructed church site yielded a ladder which he positioned beneath the window. Halfway up, he paused and put on his hood.

Apart from a gentle breeze stirring the leaves of the elm trees, the night was silent until he got to the window. Loud snoring. He had hoped for an empty room, but by the looks of things, he was about to meet the parson's wife.

He drew aside the flapping curtain and stepped inside. Could he cross to the door without waking her? If he couldn't, might it be better to silence her rather than run the risk of her waking up and screaming? The snoring built to a crescendo and stopped abruptly as if something blocked the sleeper's airway. He stood behind the window drape. The bedsprings squeaked. "Is that you, dear?" the parson's wife asked.

Bannister drew his dagger. Eventually she lay back down, apparently believing that her imagination was playing tricks on her.

When the snoring started again, he sheathed his dagger and crawled on his hands and knees to the door. Once on the landing, he felt his way down the stairs to the first floor. A shaft of light escaped beneath a door in the hallway.

Gently turning the handle, he pushed the door, but it stuck. He applied more pressure and it flew open with a snap. In spite of his gout and girth, the parson jumped from his armchair with the agility of a cat. He dropped his glass of sherry and backed toward the fire. "God's bones, who are you?" he asked, his eyes growing to twice their size.

Bannister drew his dagger. "The devil from hell if you don't cooperate."

The parson arched his brows. His lips quivered. He extended his great belly like a shield. "I am but a poor clergyman. I don't have much, but you are welcome to what I have."

"Seems to me, Parson, you live better than many of your flock." Bannister noticed the portrait on the wall opposite the fireplace, a knockoff of Caravaggio's painting of Abraham about to cut his son's throat.

"I depend on their generosity and God's favor."

"Let's hope God's in your corner tonight, Parson. Tell me about young Redferne."

The parson took a few steps away from the fire. "I don't understand."

"What arrangement do you have with the Sligo merchant?"

"That's confidential."

"Right now, Parson, you should be worried about your own protection. Where is the Redferne boy?" His voice was reminiscent of a mother soothing her child.

"Serving his time with a linen merchant to get him away from his scoundrel father. His wife asked me to help. I am not at liberty to divulge his precise whereabouts."

Bannister sprang like a ravenous dog and pushed him back onto the blazing logs. The parson's face registered pain before the scream came. "Please, please pull me out and I'll tell you." He extended a shaking hand.

It was all Bannister could do to get him upright. When he did, the parson dropped to the floor and rolled to douse the smoldering arse of his britches. Then, his breath coming in hoarse shudders, he grabbed the back of the sofa and pulled himself upright. Smoke curled around him, his voice escaping in gusts between sobs. "He's in the employ of Richard Lloyd, a linen merchant, located at Number 5 Drury Lane. He's a decent lad. Do not harm him."

"It's not him we're hunting, Reverend. Now I'll trouble you for a glass of your famous cognac, and I'll be on my way."

The parson bowed his head and stepped toward the Queen Anne dresser where he kept his liquor and a loaded double-barrel pistol. He retrieved the bottle of Rémy Martin and filled a tumbler which he handed to the hooded figure while holding the bottle in his other hand.

"You're not going to join me?"

"I should think not." On returning the bottle to the cabinet, he grabbed the pistol and struggled to cock the hammers, but not before Bannister looped the garrote around his neck. Because of the parson's great size, he put up quite a struggle, pulling Bannister to the floor on top of him. Panting for breath, Bannister had difficulty extricating the garrote from the folds of his victim's neck.

He stood up and stared down at the purple face with the bulging eyes, limp on the polished wooden floor. "You should stick to preaching, old man." He emptied the tumbler and returned it to the Queen Anne. As he rode away, the sound of stuttered snoring alternated with the snapping noise of the curtain from the second-story window.

CHAPTER 27

By the time Redferne was back on his feet, the snow had long vanished from the hills. Daisies, mayflowers, and cowslips carpeted the lowland pastures. It raised his spirits to see pink buds on the whitethorn bushes and hear the sounds of finches scavenging for nest material in the eaves of the safe house. His strength had returned along with spring, and he was anxious to be on the move again.

Soon after the operation on his leg, Redferne was shocked to discover that he was in a different safe house, a mountain hideaway not unlike the last one. It had a spacious kitchen with a room on each side and a storage area in the back. A painting of an Irish wolfhound hung on one wall and over the entryway, a Saint Bridget's cross. A large fireplace with an iron kettle hanging from a crane dominated the back wall, and above it a clothesline, sagging with shirts and trousers. The place smelled of sweat. Unlike the other hideout, this house had three glass windows.

While Blake and his men were away on operations, Redferne's only diversion was a pair of goldfinches chattering in a cage suspended from the ceiling. A splash of seed husks littered the table and the floor beneath them. Like the goldfinches, he felt caged-in, and he vowed to set them free before leaving.

He could no longer delay searching for his son. While he was laid up, his wife had been terrorized, Parson Stack was murdered, and Captain Preston had disappeared.

He shed no tears about Preston, but the intruder who broke into his house was after him, and willing to use his son to bait the trap.

159

He held his head between his hands. He had brought misfortune and danger to his family. He had gotten over his anger toward Grace. She deserved a visit now that he was mobile again, but his enemies expected him to do that. The parson's killing was no coincidence, most likely the work of the hoodlum who assaulted his wife. The obvious suspect was Reggie Preston, but the killing of the parson looked like the work of one man. Reggie was not a lone wolf. Was his disappearance a ruse to allow him to operate behind the scenes, or had Reggie himself fallen victim to some other sinister force?

One evening when Blake returned from a Whiteboy meeting, Redferne said, "I'm planning to head for Sligo in a few days."

"But you don't know where your son is lodging," Blake said, putting his musket into the gun rack and hanging his hat on a peg behind the door.

"That information I was planning to get from the parson, but..."

"Somebody got the jump on you."

"I'll have to beat the bushes in Sligo to find him."

"A stranger asking questions tends to attract attention." Blake rolled up his sleeves and dropped potatoes into a pot of water.

"It's a risk I'll take, Rory." Redferne rose stiffly from the chair and limped back and forth across the floor. He patted his leg. "Got to keep this in working order."

"There's another risk. The parson's killer may have enough resources to pay informants to tip him off on your arrival."

"I hurt my leg, not my head, so I get that. Wonder who's going to all this bother to find me, if Reggie Preston is out of the picture? Who else beside him have I insulted?"

Blake sat down heavily on a chair at the table and removed his boots. "Off the top of my head, I'd say the kinfolk of the chap who put that knife in your leg," he replied, taking off his socks and throwing them into an empty wicker basket.

Redferne threw up his hands. "I killed O'Driscoll in self-defense."

"Bet that makes all the difference to his family."

"You've a point."

Blake poured water into a basin and splashed it on his face. "Heat's a killer out there today. Remember, you killed the clachan chief, but not the real boss behind the smuggling operation."

"Forgot about him."

Blake took a large chunk of salted bacon from a press, then sliced it into strips which he dropped into the potato pot, along with a head of cabbage and several wild onions. "As I recall," Blake said, "you were the one who doubted that O'Driscoll was the kingpin of the outfit."

Redferne eyed the bubbling pot. "Enough there for two?"

"Enough for half a dozen. Why I keep feeding your lazy arse baffles me."

Redferne laughed. "Without me, you wouldn't have any bacon, sugar, or rum."

Blake went over and lifted the lid on the pot. "Things are coming along nicely. How about a shot of scotch whiskey before dinner?"

Redferne raised his eyebrows. "Scotch whiskey? Where'd you come by that?"

Rory ran his fingers through his hair and stared hard at Redferne. "I must tell you something that will make you as peeved as a trapped weasel..."

The clatter of shod hooves on the cobblestones outside sent Blake scampering to the gun rack. Redferne hobbled behind him.

"What in the name of?" Blake said, standing in the open doorway. Redferne followed him outside and encountered Roger, Brendan, and several others leading a train of horses and donkeys laden with bulging sacks up to the house.

Redferne's mouth dropped open and he stared at Blake.

Blake's face turned the color of a cock's comb.

He threw his hands in the air, still holding his musket. "Roger, what in hell are you doing here?"

Roger dismounted. "Sorry, Boss. We ran into a spot of trouble and this was the closest refuge."

"What, who?"

"The militia threw up a roadblock. Lucky we sent scouts ahead of us."

Blake's shoulders sagged. "Right. Get this stuff into the storage room." He turned to face Redferne.

"While you were up here sleeping away the hours for the last month, me and the boys hit the smuggling trains on several occasions."

Redferne spread his arms wide. "And you never told me?"

"You were sick and we didn't want to jeopardize your recovery. Besides, after the raid on the Tallford farm, I got the impression you didn't have the stomach for this."

Redferne's face flushed. "I've heard bullshit stories in my time, but this tops the list, Rory. You've kept me in the dark."

"You weren't fit to go on raids. That's the truth and you know it."

"I was fit enough to be in on what was going on, wasn't I? You've endangered my family."

"I did what?"

"You're hijacking their contraband. They've made the connection between Captain Freyney and me. They're out to settle the score for O'Driscoll. That's why they went after Grace."

Blake's hands curled into fists. "O'Driscoll has nothing to do with it. They're losing money and they're trying to shut down our operation."

"You mean your operation. I'm the one with the apple on my head." Redferne got within inches of Blake's face.

Roger and Brendan rushed between them. "Fella's, calm down. The last thing we need is this," Roger said, struggling to control Blake.

"Didn't mean to put you in danger," Blake said.

Brendan pushed Redferne against the wall of the house, startling the swallows from the eaves. By now all the other Whiteboys had gathered in a circle to watch the shouting match.

"It's odd they haven't moved against *you*," Redferne yelled over Roger's shoulder.

"They're afraid. We've ten more horses, dozens of Brown Bess muskets and pistols."

Redferne's mouth dropped open. "Ten horses! I've never

162

seen that many horses around here. Call me slow, but that I'd have noticed."

"Amazing what contraband money can do," Blake said.

The smell of bacon cooking wafted through the open door.

Roger sniffed. "I don't know about the rest of you, but I can taste that cabbage and bacon and I'm not waiting for an invitation. You two can stay here and beat the shite out of each other, but I'm heading inside to have myself a snoot full of whiskey before eats." Everyone else followed their noses, leaving Redferne and Blake standing sheepishly in the front yard.

Blake spoke. "I wasn't trying to shut you out. It's just that..."

Redferne raised his hand. "I think Roger is on to something, Rory. Let's finish this after dinner."

They congregated around the table, wolfing down the bacon, spuds, and cabbage. "Rory, this is better than me mother's," Brendan said, shoveling a forkful into his mouth. A chorus of ayes brought a smile to Blake's tense face.

"It's the wild onions, boys," Blake said.

"Here's to Rory." Brendan raised his glass of whiskey.

"To Rory," they all sang.

"I'm in for seconds," Roger said, filling his plate as the goldfinches went on a tear, spraying a plume of black head seeds all over his plate.

"Jesus Christ... I'm going to blow those fucking birds away before the night is out," Roger roared and threw his wooden plate into the leavings bucket. An explosion of laugher rocked the kitchen.

"Why doesn't somebody move that damn cage?" Roger shouted.

"Why don't you move to the other side of the table?" Brendan said.

More laughter.

Tears ran down Redferne's face and he leaned back in his chair and guffawed. Tension and anger lifted off him like mist evaporating from a lake on a summer's morning.

After the meal, Blake broke out the tobacco and everyone sat for a while smoking and discussing the close call with the smuggling heist. Roger paced the flagstones puffing vigorously on his pipe.

Gradually the group dispersed, some to tend to the horses, others to take up guard duty, leaving Redferne and Blake alone in the kitchen.

Blake nodded at the storeroom door off the kitchen. "Let's take a look at the latest haul." Redferne followed him, crunching through the bird seed splattered on the flagstones.

A small window allowed enough light to see canvas bags of contraband stacked against the walls, sharing space with farm implements and a stack of turf and logs.

"As you can see, there's not a lot of space here," Blake continued. "That's why we had to find larger stables to house the horses and store the contraband."

Redferne counted the bags with his finger. Ten in all. Not a bad day's work.

"Speaking of horses, does one of them have my name on it?" He cut the drawstring on one of the bags.

"They're common property. No one's name is on any of them."

Redferne felt embarrassed about the scene before dinner. He was a newcomer to the group—and a reluctant one at that. They owed him nothing. He owed them his life.

He pulled a bottle of scotch whiskey from one of the canvas bags and held it up to the light. "*Uisge beatha*, the water of life. Sounds like a hell of a business you're running, Rory, a little more profitable than school teaching, I'll wager."

"No comparison. There's a brisk trade in Dublin for Jamaican rum, tobacco, silk, sugar, and indigo at black-market prices."

"You've more money now and you're better armed, but you're not invincible."

"Neither are we as vulnerable as we used to be. We have over twenty armed riders. So they'll think twice about hitting us."

"But sooner or later they'll change their routes and then the jig is up," Redferne said.

"They already have, but we've been able to stay ahead of them."

Redferne narrowed his eyes. "This is not some cock and bull story you're feeding me, is it?"

"No, for the first time in my life, I've discovered the meaning of the phrase *money talks*. I'm paying several agents in Sligo who are close to the smuggling game to tip us off about new routes and delivery schedules." Blake rummaged in another of the bags. He held up a coil of rope. "Hey, look at this."

"They're smuggling rope?" Redferne walked over to Blake.

"The sweetest smelling rope I've ever come across," Blake said.

Redferne put it to his nose. "By God, it's tobacco."

Blake bit off a hunk and started to chew. "That should fetch quite a penny on the black market."

Redferne folded his arms and looked around the room. "So this is what muscle looks like."

"Yes, as long as we play the game smartly. We don't want to kill the goose that lays the golden egg, so we don't hit them as often as we could. After all, if they go out of business, so do we."

"With all of this money are we able to help our people?" Redferne asked.

"We've set up a tenant fund, run by Benjamin, to help the most destitute. We've succeeded in slowing down the evictions."

"By paying delinquent rents?"

"And by sending twenty armed horsemen to confront Bannister and his crowbar brigades."

"They'll up the ante, I bet."

Blake spat tobacco juice onto the turf stack. "They already have. A company of dragoons now accompanies every eviction operation, an expensive proposition for Lord Preston. Evictions have dropped by fifty per cent. Besides, the Tallford raid left a powerful impression."

Redferne felt as if Blake had punched him in the gut. "So Tallford didn't survive?"

"Unfortunately he did, but I'm told he's a changed man."

Redferne breathed again, and went back to examining a thin brown slab with a sweet odor, while trying to conceal from Blake how relieved he was.

"What you got there?" Blake said coming over.

"Don't know. I found it in this box with several others."

Blake bit into it.

"Chocolate. They're going crazy for this in Dublin."

"Never heard the like."

Redferne went from sack to sack like a dog searching for a buried bone, his face shining with excitement when he found something new. Was it all about the money now? He marveled at the vagaries of fate. One man's fortune was another's misfortune. He had found the smuggling route. He was the architect of Blake's good luck, but was he better off for all that?

When the light faded, the swallows stopped their nest-building in the eaves. Blake grabbed a small tub of scotch whiskey called a half-anker. "Let's celebrate. This is a fantastic haul." They left the storeroom and Blake padlocked the door.

Seated at the table, well away from the bird cage, Redferne said, "I've been mulling over the risk I'll be taking in Sligo. I thought it would be a question of going in and getting Padraig out."

Blake tipped the half-anker and filled Redferne's glass. "Sligo is a small place. Your tail would get the word the moment you entered the first tavern."

Redferne felt his jaw tighten. "That limits my choices."

"Maybe not. As I said, we have agents in Sligo. They could nose around and find out where your kid is."

"And you trust these men?"

"Money buys trust. Thinking of an old salt by the name of Jack Oldham. A worn out sailor. Scrounges a living doing odd jobs along the quays. He's our best bet, as his information to this point has been rock solid."

CHAPTER 28

Two days later Redferne set off for Sligo on a spirited black mare with a purse full of George II guineas. He had never had his hands on so much money in his life, or a more worthy cause on which to spend it. He reached the outskirts of the town on the evening of his second day of travel. Throngs of pedestrians crowded the streets, jostling for space with those on horseback. Carts, some hauling pigs, others with wicker baskets filled to the brim with shellfish, trundled over cobblestone pavements. Several urchins followed them, gleaning the shellfish that fell over the sides, to the great annoyance of the drivers who sporadically stopped and chased them away. Redferne was hard put to fathom why, since *they* were not about to gather up the fallen shellfish. Unless it was the need to demonstrate that a bunch of raggedy children could not take advantage of them.

He reined his horse off the main thoroughfare to avoid a contingent of dragoons. No use in tempting fate. Wanted posters carrying his likeness still floated around. He kept to the backstreets until he reached the quays at the mouth of the Garavogue River. The tide aided by a strong wind from the open sea surged into the estuary. A flock of seagulls kept up a cacophony overhead. Several ships rode at anchor, taking on merchandise before setting sail. One in particular, the *Kate O'Dwyer*, was loaded with what looked like bales of linen and wooden barrels, probably filled with butter or salted beef. He took a piece of paper from his waistcoat pocket with the words *Cochran's Tavern* written on it in Blake's neat schoolmaster's hand.

The quay, a warren of warehouses, taverns, and boarding houses, was a world unto itself. If not for the cleansing ocean breeze, the stench of discarded offal would have been overpowering. Crowds of sailors, peddlers, and revelers drifted in and out of taverns and boarding houses. It frightened him to think that Padraig might work in an environment like this. It hit him that being on horseback in a crowd of pedestrians wasn't the way to blend in. He found a stable down a side street next to a harness maker. The attendant, forking straw out a back door, wore a faded leather apron and communicated in grunts and one-syllable words.

After Redferne paid him a few shillings to feed and shelter his horse, he went next door to a saddler's shop. The place smelled of leather and horse hair. Bridles, saddles, and collars hung from its walls. Leather cuttings and strands of hemp littered the wooden floor. The owner, a stooped grey-haired man with an affable demeanor, looked up from a saddle he was stitching and took the pipe from his mouth.

"Aye, sure I can tell you where Cochran's tavern is, but I'm not certain a gentleman like yourself would find it to his liking."

Redferne chuckled at being referred to as a gentleman but didn't attempt to correct the impression. "I'm to meet a friend there, that's all."

"I'd question the judgment of your friend. It's nothing but a gathering place of rogues and thieves. First thing I would do, mate," he continued, putting the pipe back in his mouth, "is swap that fine top coat for something more in keeping with the clientele you're likely to meet there."

The kind of clientele, Redferne thought, more apt to have the information he sought. It made sense that Oldham would be more at home in a place like Cochran's than at Sunday Mass. Redferne exchanged his "gentleman's coat" with the stooped saddler for a tattered likeness that reeked of sweat. "I'll keep this until you return," the harness maker said, folding the coat and placing it on a shelf next to several rolls of hemp. Redferne gave him a sixpenny bit. "Godspeed."

He found Cochran's tucked between a dilapidated warehouse and a fish shop. He missed it on the way in because the *Kate O'Dwyer*, moored directly in front of it, distracted him. Judging from the number of sailors scurrying up the rigging, it appeared ready to weigh anchor. When he drew abreast of the fish shop, the smell of smoked herring set his stomach growling. He hadn't eaten since that morning. For tuppence he bought a herring wrapped in paper and went outside to eat it. He gawked up and down the waterfront at the passing parade, while picking the fine bones from the fish with his fingers. Some prattled in English, others Irish, and still more jabbered in languages he had never heard before. Out of the corner of his eye, he spotted a small boat pulling away from the *Kate O'Dwyer*. In the stern wrapped in a greatcoat sat Lord Preston's agent, Howard Bannister.

His first impulse was to run, then he remembered his reason for being here. This was a time to stand his ground, so he opened the door to Cochran's tavern and darted inside. It took a while for his eyes to adjust to the dim light. The place was loud with laughter and boisterous talk, and smelled of sweat and tobacco smoke. He found a spot at a table close to a window and got the attention of a barman with a week's growth of beard. He wore a white apron so splotched with beer and gravy stains that it looked more like a doormat. He ordered a pint and when it came, he finished the herring, marveling at how much the taste improved when washed down with slugs of ale.

His thoughts returned to Bannister. What was he doing here? Was his presence a coincidence, or of more ominous significance? He ordered another mug of ale. Bannister's appearance spooked him. Once he found his son, they would leave Sligo immediately.

Looking around, he realized that the description he had of Oldham could fit anyone of half a dozen chaps already on the premises. Large sections of the tavern were in semi-darkness from the shadows thrown by the candles. He walked around casually looking for an old salt of medium height, with a red beard, a leathery face, and a carbuncle on his left cheek. Not much to go on, since many of the revelers matched Oldham's description. The first person he asked gave him a blank look and muttered something in a language Redferne didn't understand. He moved to another table and had to shout above the clamor.

"I'm looking for Jack Oldham. Anyone seen him?" The din died down. One chap wearing an ill-fitting blue frock coat with several front buttons missing got to his feet. Putting a hand to his ear, he swayed a little and said, "Co-co-come again, mate?"

"I'm looking for Jack Oldham." Redferne leaned in and was nearly knocked off his feet by the smell of ale and sweat.

"So is the High Sheriff and ha-half the country for that matter." His mates guffawed. "Owe you coin, perchance?

Redferne curled his lip in disgust. Then the man in the blue frock coat stammered, "Jaysus mate, the-there he is at yon window."

Redferne followed the pointed finger. A red-bearded man with a leathery face sat at the table he had vacated. He sauntered over, trying to put on his most casual face. He extended his hand. "Hello, I'm Michael Redferne."

Oldham looked him over before responding and finally said, "So you're Blake's friend. I've been searching for you."

Redferne pulled out a chair opposite the man with the carbuncle on his cheek.

"Do you have what I came for?" Redferne signaled the barman to bring two mugs of ale for additional incentive.

"That depends on the size of your purse, friend," Oldham said unsmiling.

"The heft of my purse will remain a secret until I see my son." Outside the window, night had fallen like a black shawl. The bobbing lanterns of the ships moored on the Garavogue were the only lights visible through its dark weave.

Oldham took a long draft of beer and placed his mug back on the table before answering. "Then your long trip here will be for naught until I see the color of your coin." Redferne took out his purse and spread five gold guineas on his side of the table. Oldham reached out to grab them. Redferne seized his wrist.

"I repeat, you'll get the money when I get my son. Tell you what, though." He pushed two coins over to the other side of the table. "That much now, the rest when I lay eyes on my young fella'."

Oldham's face stayed expressionless as he picked up the coins and put them in an inside pocket. "Fair enough mate, follow me."

Redferne hung behind as Oldham made his way along the quays to the slop of the tide on the stone stairways. Had Padraig climbed up and down those steps loading and unloading ships? His heart beat faster at the prospect of wrapping his arms around him. Then the awful thought crept in. Would Padraig want to see him? Would he even want to return to Cloonfin? Lost in thought, he didn't notice Oldham turn down a side street. Hearing a shout behind him, he corrected his mistake and turned back to find Oldham waiting on a corner under a flickering street lamp.

They plunged into a warren of lanes bordered on both sides by warehouses, alternating with one-and two-story houses, some no better than shacks. After numerous twists and turns, Redferne lost all his orientation to the river. A ten-minute slog brought them to a large stone warehouse. Oldham banged on the big double door set in an arched opening.

A shaft of light emerged from a wicker door inset in the larger one. A man stuck his head out. "What's your business here?"

"Nothing that concerns you," Oldham said. "Tell Mr. Lloyd that Jack Oldham would like a word with him."

Redferne palmed the butt of the pistol in his belt through a hole in the pocket of his tattered coat. The doorkeeper cast a threatening look at Oldham. He shut the door and, in less than a minute, he was back beckoning them to follow him.

The interior, a large space lit by whale-oil lanterns that hung at intervals along the walls, was filled floor to ceiling with stacked bales of linen, chests of tea, and barrels of salted beef, butter, and other assorted goods. Men loaded merchandise onto drays, large wooden flat-bed carts, some of it destined for delivery to waiting ships, the remainder for distribution throughout the city. Redferne looked anxiously at the faces of the workers, hoping to spot Padraig.

The doorkeeper took them to the foot of a stairs leading to a large closed-in loft, with instructions to knock on the door at the top of the steps. Oldham did as directed and a footman ushered them into a spacious office. A bewigged gentleman somewhere in his sixties sat writing behind a big desk, cluttered with ledgers, bills of lading, and sheets of writing paper known as foolscap. A large nose with a prominent web of purple veins protruded from his unnaturally red face. He rose to meet them.

"Please be seated, gentlemen." He gestured to several chairs arranged along the back wall. "My name is Richard Lloyd. We have been expecting you."

Redferne's heart plummeted. He expected to see Padraig, but apart from themselves and Lloyd, the room was empty.

"Now to the matter at hand. Mr. Oldham, you may leave." He pointed to the door.

"God's blood if I will. Not 'til I gets me coin."

A clicking sound. Lloyd's right hand came from behind a stack of ledgers holding a cocked pistol.

"Get out, you scoundrel." He pulled a rope that hung from the ceiling. Two large men who looked like the patrons in Cochran's Tavern burst into the room armed with cudgels. The older of the two had a high forehead overlooking a scarred face and appeared intoxicated. He wore a dirty white neck sock that looked like a hangman's noose, and a green frock coat constrained from bursting at the seams by a solitary brass button. His partner had squinty eyes set in a baby face. His coat was red and could have been a hand-me-down from the English army except for the many multicolored patches that marred its appearance. Oldham protested and, at a signal from Lloyd, baby face knocked him down.

"Was it necessary to do that?" Redferne rushed to the old sailor sprawled on the floor. Blood seeped from a nasty wound on the back of his head. "It was my money he was after, not yours."

"Was it now?" Lloyd pointed the gun directly at Redferne. High forehead and baby face grabbed him from behind and pinned his arms.

"Mr. Oldham needs to learn he cannot serve two masters, but not to worry, he served his purpose."

"By getting his head beaten in for a few guineas?" Redferne said struggling.

"No, by bringing you to us." Howard Bannister came through the open door. Redferne's breath caught.

"The crooked agent and the thieving merchant. The partnership from hell."

"Not exactly partners, Mr. Redferne. Mr. Lloyd and I are only recently acquainted. Having discovered a common interest, we joined forces to solve our mutual problem."

Lloyd put the pistol back in the desk drawer and sat down heavily in his chair, indicating that the matter was now out of his hands. Bannister moved behind Redferne. "Don't do anything rash." he said, searching his pockets, "or these gentlemen will break your arms." He removed Redferne's pistol and stuck it in his belt. When he found the purse, he opened it and gave a satisfied grunt. "What a perfect solution. Mr. Redferne would like to compensate you Mr. Lloyd for all the bother he's caused you this evening." Bannister tossed the purse on Lloyd's desk.

Lloyd opened it with chubby fingers and smiled. "I thank you, sir." He bowed toward Bannister. "This about squares our account."

"Excellent, but I think Mr. Redferne needs to know what he's getting for his money. When my employer Lord Preston encouraged me to have a little chat with your wife, we were surprised to discover that Parson Stack knew where your boy was."

"What's Padraig to do with this?"

"As Lord Preston so wisely put it, 'Find the young whelp and you find the old man.' He was right."

"You're lying. His honor would have nothing to do with this."

"Ordinarily no, except that you repaid his generosity to you over the years by organizing an attack on his household."

"That's a fabrication. I was a prisoner in the Big House, hardly in a position to coordinate an assault."

"Be that as it may, I was directed by Lord Preston to contact Mr. Lloyd, and discovered that we were *birds of a feather*. Was greatly surprised when the good merchant revealed that your boy was no longer under his care."

The words hit Redferne like a boot to the stomach. His fear and grief exploded in a gut-wrenching roar. Breaking free of high forehead and baby face, he lunged at Bannister, knocking him to the floor. The ruffians, with a few well-placed kicks to the torso, succeeded in pulling him off their boss. They tied him to the chair as Bannister brushed off his clothes and tried to recover his dignity.

"As I was about to say when the parson told me…"

"You cowardly swine. He didn't tell you. You forced it out of him, then you murdered him."

"I'll let Mr. Lloyd tell you Stack's role in this story and perhaps your opinion of him may change."

Raising his heavy eyelids, Lloyd stared at Redferne., "Parson Stack sold your son to me as an indentured servant. He's a strapping lad so he got a fat purse for him. Apparently his financial needs conflicted with his pastoral principles. His church building program was in danger of faltering and he yielded to temptation."

"That's a lie! He gave my wife a portion of Padraig's wages each month."

"He could afford to, since he made out like a brigand on the transaction, so he paid her a few shillings monthly and no one was the wiser."

"I'm appealing to whatever shred of decency is left in your heart. What's become of my son?"

"I doubt Mr. Lloyd knows," Bannister broke in. "He in turn sold him to another, but I shouldn't worry too much about that, since there's a good chance you and he may be reunited."

"You cruel bastard, is your heart that black?"

"Unfortunately, I act on behalf of another, so it's completely out of my hands. I merely do my employer's bidding, for which I get paid handsomely. I suggest you take it up with Lord Preston when you return from your trip overseas."

A howl of laughter erupted in the room. Even the droopy Lloyd joined in.

Redferne slumped to his chair. He had brought nothing but

tragedy on his family—first his young brother, now his son. Everything he put his hand to turned to dirt. Finally, it had come to this; sitting lashed to a chair like a common criminal, about to be deported into the unknown.

In the long run, maybe it was best for everyone.

VOYAGE OF THE KATE O'DWYER

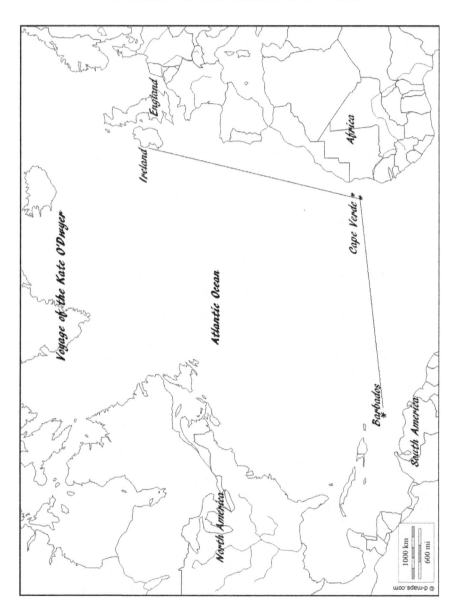

Source: http://d-maps.com/pays.php?num_pay=273&lang=en

CHAPTER 29

The brig *Kate O'Dwyer* cleared Sligo Bay a few minutes past midnight, heading into the North Atlantic on a southwesterly course, making good time under full sail. Captain Tolliver hoped to make the run to Barbados in less than forty days with a cargo of linen, butter, and salted beef for the American colonies and some discrete freight for Barbados. On the return journey, he planned to fill his holds with cases of Jamaican rum, chests of tea, sugar, flaxseed, and indigo.

The bright moon smeared a golden track atop the pewter-colored ocean all the way to the horizon. Driven by a strong wind, the *Kate O'Dwyer* seemed to be following that lunar pathway, but Tolliver knew that the moon was of little help in setting an accurate course. Without the ability to determine the exact longitude at sea, he had to rely on experience and intuition to get him to his destination. He ran the risk of ending up in the wrong port or worse still running aground because of inaccurate information.

A few weeks prior in the docks at Portsmouth, he purchased a wonder device that looked like a large pocket watch. The seller had been trying to unload it for weeks, but was roundly ridiculed when he explained that the device computed longitude at sea. Tolliver had been following a story in the newspapers about a Yorkshire clockmaker named John Harrison who made such a claim. When the seller knocked the price down to five pounds, Tolliver purchased it, suspecting he had a counterfeit, so its worth was questionable. If it was a hoax, he had only lost five quid. If it worked, it would revolutionize sea travel. He stood to make a lot of money in time saved on Atlantic crossings.

Tolliver consulted the longitude clock before departing the bridge at two in the morning and ordered Jules, the first mate, to adjust the fore-and-aft sail on the main mast.

Dressed in a black silver-trimmed frock coat that barely stretched across his broad shoulders, and a felt tricorne hat with a faille cockade, Jules looked more like a carnival barker than a ship's officer. His breath smelled of rum. Using a speaking trumpet, he gave the order to trim the sail. The wind humming in the rigging drowned out his voice and it took some time to complete the maneuver.

Down in his cabin, Tolliver picked up the course correction in the soles of his feet. When Jules was sober, there wasn't a better sailor on the high seas, he thought, lighting the three-pronged candelabrum on the upturned whiskey barrel. Selecting a book from a shelf over his writing table, he poured a glass of claret and settled into his armchair before preparing for bed. It had been a long, tense day, but he was optimistic about the longitude clock and the promise of a handsome payoff when he delivered his special freight to Barbados.

His association with Howard Bannister was proving more lucrative with every voyage. When he began to nod, he removed his coat and shoes, blew out the candles, and settled into his hammock. Moonlight flooded the cabin through the stern windows as he dropped off to sleep. Near the end of the fourth watch he awoke, waiting for the bell, but when it rang out, it sounded a general alarm, followed by shouting and the sound of running feet.

He threw on his clothes and ran to the bridge.

"What's all the fuss about, Jules?"

"British man o' war signaling us to heave to."

"Damn," he swore as he adjusted his telescope. "It's the *Guidance* out of Portsmouth."

"What's it doing off the west coast of Ireland?" Jules asked.

Tolliver pointed at a distant mountain "Why are we hugging the coast? I ordered a heading farther out to sea to avoid this." The first mate's unfocused eyes stared back.

"Take ten men and rearrange the cargo in the stern hold. I'll deal with you later."

"Right, sir." Jules raised a shaking hand to salute and rushed from the bridge. The *Guidance* sailed ten minutes off their larboard bow. Tolliver figured she was looking for smugglers, but why intercept an outbound ship? His optimistic feeling was gone. He had heard about *HMS Guidance*, but she was not known to come this far west. He had shifted his base of operations from the east to the west coast of Ireland to steer clear of her. If he were discovered, he would not be heading to Barbados, but to Spithead and a prison term. While the men fixed the helm and sail positions to heave to, he paced the bridge anxiously watching the *Guidance*.

Redferne woke in the darkness with a splitting headache, in chains. The last thing he remembered was Bannister and his thugs shackling him to a post along with several others in a secluded part of Lloyd's warehouse, and feeding them bread, cheese, and tea. Then his mind went blank. Now his head pounded, his stomach roiled, and he felt dizzy. His head cleared after a bout of vomiting as his bed swayed and pitched. He felt the warmth of another body chained beside him. All around were voices, punctuated by vomiting.

He tried to rise up in his bunk, but chains restricted his movement. Bannister must have drugged him. He had no memory of boarding a ship. He remembered the agent's remark about being reunited with Padraig. His son must have been shipped away to God-knows-where as well. His world had turned upside down and his newfound hope for a better life crushed beneath treachery and greed.

Standing in the shadows behind Bannister, apparently, was Lord Preston himself, projecting an image of civility and forbearance. Bannister did the dirty work while Preston reaped the benefits. One day he would have a reckoning with His Lordship.

He thought of his wife, Blake, and Oldham. All had unwittingly led him to this moment. Whether Oldham was playing both sides of the street, as Lloyd inferred by his remark, *serving two masters*, was unclear. At the least he misled, if not betrayed, himself and Blake.

His brief distraction over, reality returned with a vengeance. The manacles on his hands and feet chafed and the smell of vomit was overpowering.

He dozed and awoke again to see the hold flooded with light. Blinded, he turned away and rubbed his eyes. Men bounded down the hatchway, shouting obscenities as they slipped on vomit, swarming over the prisoners like ants. The crew soon had them gagged, bound, and barricaded behind a wall of linen bales and chests of tea. They placed additional freight on top of the bunks to conceal the chains and manacles. The gag bit into his mouth and he tasted blood as he struggled to breathe. The image of his young brother gasping for breath in the waves flashed before his eyes. He prayed that he would not throw up. The heat felt stifling. Though the ship slowed, it continued to pitch and roll causing more vomiting.

Through a crevice in the stacked linen bales Redferne observed men feverishly washing up the vomit with mops and buckets of water. A man wearing brown leather gloves scattered handfuls of a yellowish green powder across the floor. From its odor, Redferne figured it to be sulfur, but he was hard put to decide which was the more odious smell--it or the vomit. Either the captain was a fastidious gentleman, or he was expecting an inspection from someone who was. In the middle of the ocean no less. A tall man in a round grey hat and a full-length blue frock coat ducked down the hatchway. After a quick look around, he went back up on deck. The hatch slammed shut, plunging the hold into darkness again.

CHAPTER 30

"Longboat's in the water, sir," the first mate barked. The *Guidance* had pulled to within two hundred yards of the *Kate O'Dwyer*. The boat, manned by sailors and marines, quickly shortened the gap between them. Tolliver ordered the rope ladder lowered when the boarding party came up alongside. The captain of the marines followed by his men climbed up the ladder hand-over-hand. Their bright red jackets with yellow cuff bands and hip-high white leather gaiters contrasted starkly with the mishmash of apparel worn by the gawking sailors.

Once aboard they un-shouldered their muskets and formed a security circle. A young naval officer with prominent cheek bones and a sallow complexion stepped onto the deck, wearing a blue frock coat over a white waistcoat. On his head sat a low-crowned, flat tarred hat, with a black ribbon trailing down the back of his neck. The name *Guidance* was printed on the front of the hat. "I'm Lieutenant Sears," he said doffing his hat. "I wish to speak to the captain."

Tolliver doffed his hat and bowed. "Captain Tolliver, at your service."

"Captain Taylor of his majesty's ship *Guidance* presents his compliments and instructs me further to inspect your ship."

"By all means, sir," Tolliver answered. "Show the boarding party through the ship," he said to the first and second mates. Sears split his party in two, leaving half to stand guard while the other half conducted the search. Two of the marines on guard accompanied

181

the captain back to the bridge. The remainder stood on the lower deck facing inboard, muskets at the ready. Tolliver paced the bridge, stealing glances at the *Guidance* as the search party disappeared into the bowels of his ship.

His mind churned. Why was an outbound ship being searched for smuggled goods? Could it be an attempt to interdict slave running? Slave-running to Barbados had diminished, but it was in full swing in the American colonies. It wasn't as if the English government looked down on the practice of sending white men into bondage, either. In the previous century, under Cromwell, it had condemned thousands of Irish men, women, and children to labor in the sugarcane fields of Barbados. While large-scale white slavery had abated, it continued on a reduced scale.

Small-time white slavers like Bannister not only operated out of Ireland, but out of English ports like Liverpool, Bristol, and London as well. In general, the English government turned a blind eye to it.

Tolliver sighed, relieved when Sears climbed to the bridge and declared the *Kate O'Dwyer* clean. "One more thing," Sears said.

Captain Tolliver tensed.

"Can I see the ship's manifest?"

"By all means." Tolliver nodded to Jules who fetched it. Sears whistled through his teeth as he ran his fingers down the pages, then he stopped, his finger suspended over an item.

"Why stop in Barbados? Isn't that a rather roundabout way to get to Virginia, especially with hurricane season coming on?"

"The landed gentry of that island like fine Irish linen and silk from Lyon as much as the next and have the money to pay for both."

Sears laughed. "What a surprise. Poor buggers like you and me risk our arses to supply and protect them for a pittance."

"I'm afraid it's the way of the world," Tolliver said, wishing Sears and his party would leave.

Tolliver finally accompanied Sears down to the main deck where the rest of the boarding party waited in the longboat, oars upright.

As Sears climbed down the rope ladder to the heaving boat,

Tolliver called after him. "I'd be obliged if you could tell me what you were looking for?"

"Guns, Captain."

"Guns?" Tolliver shouted over the wind.

"Aye. Haven't you heard? The American colonies have taken up arms against us." He waved farewell and the longboat pulled away, the blades of its oars flashing like swords in the rising sun.

When the redcoats came to inspect the cargo, Redferne was bound and gagged so securely, he was unable cry out or make a noise. Through a crevice in the barricade he saw them move some of the bails and barrels, but this appeared to be a cursory inspection. The last man disappeared up the ladder and the hatch slammed down, shutting out the daylight and their one slim chance of rescue. His heart sank.

The stench in the hideaway grew unbearable. If they were not released soon, some of them would choke on their own vomit behind the gags. After what seemed like an eternity, the hatch flew open again and heavy footsteps pounded down the ladder. A lone voice urged. "Make haste before it's too late." Air and light penetrated the hideaway as the barricade was dismantled. The sailors loosened the gags and cut the ropes binding the captives. Released from their bonds, they surged from the hideaway coughing and wheezing and some fell on their knees from the effort. An angry roar went up. They rushed the rescue party who stampeded back up the hatchway. When the captives reached the deck, they found themselves staring into the muzzles of several dozen muskets with bayonets attached.

Captain Tolliver addressed them from the bridge. "I will not hesitate to shoot all of you if that's what it takes to restore order to my ship."

In addition to the musket men, two swivel-mounted, light carronades on the stern-castle were trained on the area around the hatchway. The gunners stood by with lit matches. Prisoners still coming up from the hold pushed Redferne from behind. Although the captain stood to lose a small fortune if they were killed, he would lose a lot more if a mutiny succeeded. Redferne knew that captains feared mutiny as much as yellow fever or scurvy.

Redferne shouted to his fellow captives in Irish, "Lads, hold up! We don't stand a chance. We'll wait for a better opportunity."

The pushing and the shoving stopped.

"What about them that died?" a voice from the huddled mass cried out. Apparently, what Redferne feared had happened.

"It's bloody murder," another said.

The rest took up the cry, chanting, "Murder, murder, bloody murder," and stamped their feet. The crew leveled their muskets and the carronade gunners panned the main deck.

As the chant continued, Redferne's bunkmate, Tom Gleason, a muscular young man with thinning hair and a reddish beard, shouted above the din. "Sean, where are you? Oh, mother of God, answer me."

Silence. Tolliver ordered his musket men to move the captives away from the hatch to the starboard side of the ship. To Jules he said, "Take two seamen and go back and search the hold."

Jules saluted. "Aye, sir."

They found the bodies of Sean Gleason and another young captive named Williams face down on the floor of the hideaway, suffocated by their own vomit. They carried the bodies up the hatchway and placed them side by side near the port bulwark. When Tom Gleason saw his younger brother, he set up a loud *ullaloo* which was taken up by the others. Redferne tried to join in, but a harsh croak came out. His heart pounded in fury. Some day he would make these bastards pay.

Captain Tolliver descended the stern castle, a look of bored indifference on his ruddy face. Tom Gleason asked permission to hold his young brother as a last farewell. Tolliver refused. Gleason tried to break through the cordon of musket men, but one of them clubbed him on the side of the head with the barrel of his gun. He crumpled to the deck a few feet from his deceased sibling.

Redferne could barely restrain himself, but it would be suicide to go for Tolliver facing all that firepower. "Isn't someone going to say a prayer over the poor buggers?" he shouted. "Even condemned murderers get that."

Tolliver smirked and said, "They won't need prayers where they're going. You, on the other hand will need all the prayers you can muster when you get to your journey's end." He withdrew a few paces and nodded. Two sailors grabbed each body in succession by the shoulders and feet, and with a "One, two, three, heave," tossed them like sacks of potatoes over the bulwark rail into the deep.

Someone started the "Our Father" in Irish and the entire group joined in. *Ár nAthair atá ar neamh, Go naofar d'ainim, Go tiocfadh do ríocht...* Many of the sailors in the shrouds removed their caps and bowed their heads as the bodies hit the waves. When the grim ritual was over, Tolliver ordered a contingent of sailors to douse the captives with buckets of seawater. Though cold, Redferne relished its coolness. For the first time in days, he felt normal as the vomit and the grime were washed away. Gleason stirred, pulling his legs toward him in a fetal position. Redferne and another captive named Diarmuid MacTigh, a tall blond man with angry red skin, moved to help him as the rest of the captives surrounded him in a protective wall. The strong sea breeze and the warmth of the sun soon dried their clothes and for a few moments, Redferne forgot their nightmarish situation.

When the captain left the deck, the first mate approached with the ship's blacksmith and helper in tow. "Sit down and stretch out your feet." The blacksmith and his assistant went from prisoner to prisoner, fitting them with leg irons. At an order from the first mate, the armed guard withdrew. "The carronades are still aimed at you, in case you get any ideas."

Each man then received a tin cup of water and a wooden bowl full of a porridge-like substance from a large tub hauled onto the deck by the ship's cook and his assistant. Redferne drank the water in one long gulp and attacked the porridge as if it was his last meal. He was amazed when the cook filled each man's bowl a second time and replenished his cup with water.

When he finished, he lay back on the deck and closed his eyes. Maureen Kelly's face flashed before him and he wept, not only for her, but for the child in her belly. What became of it? Was it born or did it die with its mother?

Now that their feet were shackled, they were no longer chained to the bunks, which allowed them to shuffle around in the dank hold during the day, but at night a guard re-chained them to the bunk posts. Redferne took stock of his surroundings. A double-high row of bunks ran along one side and, except for a clearing in the middle, most of the remaining space was given over to stacked linen bales and barrels of salted meat and butter. The air was foul except where it filtered through cracks in the deck and hatch, but in rough weather, sea water leaked in as well. A barrel of drinking water sat in a corner on one side of the hatch ladder, and in the opposite corner a slop bucket.

Diarmuid MacTigh shuffled to the bucket. "Excuse me, lads." His voice sounded as if it came from the bottom of a well.

"No cause for apologies, Diarmuid," Redferne said. "I expect we'll see a helluva lot worse before this adventure is over."

The others laughed.

With the death of Gleason's brother and Williams, eight captives remained.

The rest of the trip to the Cape Verde Islands, where they stopped to take on fresh fruit and water, passed uneventfully. For some, seasickness was their constant companion. Lying chained to each other, two to a bunk, guaranteed that if one got sick, everyone suffered. A level of brutality that would be condemned in civilized society was normal in the twisted world of the *Kate O'Dwyer*.

Rations consisted of two quarts of water, stirabout, and stale bread twice a day. Fruit was served until the supply ran out. They were allowed on deck for a half-hour morning and evening under the watchful eyes of the carronade gunners, a precaution Redferne thought ludicrous since they all wore leg irons.

The wound on Gleason's head healed with the help of the meager ministrations of his fellow prisoners. Redferne, being the oldest, reluctantly became their leader. Having lost the passion of his younger companions he counseled them not to dissipate their strength on useless anger, but to forge those emotions into a determination to survive.

He heard that their destination was Barbados from the blacksmith's helper, a young Irishman called Lawrence Craig, who befriended them by spiriting extra food and the odd bottle of claret into their prison. Craig was short in stature, with black curls dropping over his forehead, and a perpetually worried look on his pinched face. How he secured these supplies, Redferne didn't know. He sensed that their plight garnered sympathy among the crew, after seeing some of the men in the shrouds take off their caps on the day of young Gleason's burial.

Redferne doubted that the less robust among them would survive the long voyage to Barbados. Constant vomiting depleted their strength and the absence of a nourishing diet hastened starvation. One month out of Cape Verde, they encountered a storm that left half the prisoners so sick that they could hardly stand up. By the time the storm abated, three more expired and were cast over the bulwark rail into the deep. Five now remained.

During the storm, the cargo shifted, causing the ship to list. When the crew repositioned the errant freight, many of the sealed barrels ended up close to the prisoners' bunks. Redferne got an idea that called for a hammer and chisel. He lay awake waiting for Craig to come through the hatch with the tools he had promised. The penalty for being caught would be severe, especially for Craig. At worst he might be thrown overboard. At best he would get a flogging, but Craig seemed willing to take the risk. The hatch squeaked. A shadowy figure descended the ladder.

A hand reached up and shook his shoulder. "Redferne?

"Aye. Hope you didn't come empty handed?"

"I brought what you needed, also a lantern."

"Not much good that's going to do if I can't get outa the bunk."

"Hold your horses. One thing at a time." The click of a lock and the chains from his hands fell away. He rubbed his chaffed wrists.

"Hide this." Craig passed him a barrel key.

"What about the rest of us?" a voice above him said.

"Don't panic, we'll get to you."

Craig whispered to Redferne. "I brought a pair of pliers to get you outta' those leg irons at night."

"That would be a Godsend, but first things first."

"Right." Craig lit the small lantern and pulled out a hammer and chisel.

Redferne chose one of the sealed barrels and was ready to breach a seam when Roan Kilbane, a Galway native abducted during an eviction, said, "You'll need something to camouflage the sound."

"How about we all cough," Colin Noone, a carpenter's apprentice from Sligo, said.

Redferne laughed. "I thought half you fuckers were asleep and the other half sick or dying." A thin ripple of laughter came from the semi-darkness, accompanied by the rattle of chains. Redferne wrapped a piece of rag around the head of the chisel.

"Okay, on the count of three." He hit the chisel a sharp blow. Although many were sick, it seemed that robust coughing was something they could still do. A few more swings, and he penetrated the side of the barrel. Working the chisel head along a seam, he pried free a stave, revealing tightly-packed beef within. He unlocked the chains of his bunkmates and they squatted on the floor gorging on beef. When they were finished, Redferne replaced the stave on the barrel and hid it behind two rows of linen bales.

The next night they broke into a barrel of cheese and as the weeks went by, their physical condition so improved that seasickness was less frequent.

Three weeks from Bridgeport, Barbados, the cook surprised Craig one night as he raided the galley and had him hauled before the captain. He refused to talk until they tied him to the main mast and administered thirty lashes with a cowhide whip. He confessed to stealing food for the captives, but nothing else.

Redferne and the others listened to the sound of the lash, not realizing that their Good Samaritan had been found out. After the whipping, they cut him down and spread-eagled him on the deck face down. Then they doused him with seawater and left him to bake in the sun while the salt worked on his wounds. When he was near dead, they shackled him and threw him into the hold with the prisoners.

Seamus Beirne

CHAPTER 31

Redferne nursed Craig back to health as best he could, using their meager supply of water to wash and clean his lacerated back. The reason the rest of them escaped the lash was Tolliver's greed. They were getting close to Barbados, and he didn't want to deliver damaged goods and reduce his profit. Redferne concocted a plan that would not only cut into Tolliver's profits, but damage his reputation as well.

He asked Craig, "You think you can still remove the leg irons?"

"If you still have the tools I gave you." He smiled weakly.

"For what I've in mind you'll need to get the irons off three of us."

Craig stiffened. "Don't worry; your role is limited to using your skills as a blacksmith."

"Out with it, Redferne." Gleason said. "What's hatching in that brain of yours?"

"I'm thinking of dumping a little of Tolliver's cargo overboard every night until we reach Barbados."

"It'll be missed if they do an inspection?" Gleason said.

"How many inspections have they done so far? None, right?"

"I'll give you that, but nothing says they won't start," Gleason said, breathing heavily as he did pull-ups from the top rail of his bunk.

"Even if they do, we can move the cargo around, bringing the barrels in the rear up front to replace the ones we dump overboard," Redferne said, lifting one of the barrels to test its weight.

Craig's face tightened with fear. "What do we replace the rear barrels with?"

Redferne slapped one of the linen bales. "These. They're not about to go burrowing back into the stack and discover the void."

Craig wrung his hands. "Don't worry, Craig," Redferne said, "you only have to get these damn leg irons off."

Gleason eased himself to the floor. "When do we start?"

"Tonight. I overheard some of the crew saying there's no moon." He crawled under a lower bunk to retrieve Craig's wrench and pliers.

Craig lit the lantern. Redferne grabbed the chain to his leg irons and climbed the ladder to listen at the hatch. Apart from the roar of the wind in the rigging and the slap of the waves against the hull, the night was quiet. He returned to rejoin Craig and Gleason huddled behind a screen of linen bales examining Gleason's leg irons. They opened and closed on a hinge like an oyster shell secured by a nut and bolt.

"That nut is rusted on," Craig said, after several attempts to loosen it with the pliers. "It will be tough to get it off without some lubricant, which we don't have."

Redferne pointed "Yes we do. See that barrel. It's full of butter. I opened it earlier." The butter did the trick and in a matter of minutes Redferne and Gleason and Craig walked around the hold unfettered.

"The way I figure it," Redferne said, "it'll take two of us to carry the barrels and one to open the hatch and keep watch."

At the end of the third watch Craig climbed the ladder and edged the hatch open. Nothing but the slop of the waves against the hull and the chatter of dozens of seagulls and egrets resting in the rigging. He signaled Redferne and Gleason. They lugged the barrel up the ladder and crept out on deck, Craig crouched at the base of the main mast, partially concealed by the coiled lines hanging from the belaying pins. "Go," he said. They scampered across the deck in the shadow of the stern castle to avoid observation by the helmsman and hoisted the barrel over the rail. The whole operation took less than a minute. They made three more runs that night, and most nights during the weeks that followed, until they could remove no more barrels.

"This is about as far as we can go and still conceal the missing merchandise," Redferne said, sitting on an empty barrel.

Gleason ran his fingers inside the collar of his shirt. "The lads and I were thinking that as soon as we sight the coast we're going over the side."

Redferne slapped his forehead with the heel of his hand. "What? You'll never make it. That could be a two or three mile swim."

"There're enough empty barrels for us to use as life rafts."

Redferne's head spun. He hadn't thought of that as a logical follow-up to their caper. Even if they made it to shore alive, what were the odds of avoiding the manhunt that would follow?

"I've made this trip several times and I witnessed firsthand what happens to escaped slaves," Craig whispered. "If you're lucky, Tolliver determines the punishment. He would be deemed the legal owner, seeing as how you didn't get sold in the slave auction. In that case you might get off with a whipping."

"I'm willing to risk a whipping for the chance to get free," Gleason said, grabbing a bunk rail as the ship wallowed. The others agreed.

Then Redferne spoke. "If someone other than Tolliver decides their fate, what are we looking at?"

"I've seen escaped slaves nailed to the ground with wooden stakes and then burned," Craig said. "They begin by applying lit torches to the soles of the feet and slowly work their way to the head."

A collective gasp went up. The stricken looks on their faces told Redferne that several were having second thoughts, but after hearing Craig go on about the horrors of daily life in the sugar cane fields, they determined that jumping ship was the better option.

The ship wallowed and bucked some more and the timbers creaked as it boomed into the heaving waves. Wind whistled through the hatch. They could hear the sound of crashing waves on the deck. Water droplets ran along the seams between the planks above their heads. Everyone stopped talking and held on.

Everyone except Kilbane, who seemed to be enjoying it. His blue eyes danced beneath a mop of curly brown hair. "Don't worry. She's a hardy old girl. She'll pull through." The rest of them weren't as confident.

The *Kate O'Dwyer* rolled again, knocking over empty barrels as it fought the waves.

"Quick!" Redferne shouted, "They'll be down to check the cargo." Working feverishly, they stowed the empty barrels behind a wall of linen bales which they packed tightly against the ship's sides to prevent movement.

"Douse the light and hit the sack."

The deck vibrated with the sound of running feet. A lantern appeared in the hatch as first mate Jules and several others piled into the hold.

"Hold the light up," Jules said, examining the stacked linen bales. "Looks sound to me."

"Where are the barrels?"

"Behind the linen bales, I assume, unless this scum ate them," Jules said, to sneers and snickers. The ship wallowed again throwing Jules against Redferne's bunk. The smell of rum nearly caused Redferne to gag.

"Shouldn't we check?"

"Pull out one bale and be careful," Jules said. "Don't want to cause a slide."

Redferne's temples pounded. They pried a bale free and uncovered a barrel.

"Wonder how securely they're stowed," a sailor asked.

"There's one way to find out." Jules kicked the barrel and it shifted. "Damn, this could be a problem if the storm keeps up."

"Should we tell the captain?"

Jules inspected the wall of linen with the lantern. "No. What he doesn't know won't bother him. Rearranging things in this weather might be going from the frying pan into the fire." He shouldered the linen wall and it held.

"Gallant. Looks solid, no use in borrowing trouble." They replaced the linen bale in the stack and, after obscene comments about the weather and the prisoners, they trundled up the ladder and disappeared into the storm.

After a few minutes of silence, Redferne asked, "You lads still awake?"

"Awake? Damn near died of fright," Kilbane said.

"Almost pissed in my pants," Craig said. Everyone laughed. One by one they jumped down from their bunks and huddled in a circle on the floor. Standing was impossible with the roll of the ship.

"Any chance they'll come back?" Gleason asked.

"No." Redferne said. "Jules will be too drunk to make it down the hatch."

Gleason massaged his chin. "Which still leaves us with the question: Do we jump ship or take our chances?"

Redferne shook his head. "It's risky."

"We could sign on to a buccaneer ship," MacTigh said.

"It's true," Craig said, "pirate ships ply these waters, but there's no guarantee that there's one riding at anchor in some secluded cove waiting to pick up a half dozen runaway Irish slaves."

"But there must be other ships in the harbor looking for crew. We could sign on with them," Colin Noone offered.

"Assuming you make it safely to shore and aren't picked up by the manhunters," Craig said.

Redferne looked at Craig. "What are the odds of survival if we end up in the fields?"

"Once they brand you, it's only a matter of time before you are worked to death. Planting and cutting sugar cane takes its toll in the tropical sun. We Irish are ill-suited to such brutal temperatures."

At that moment, the ship took a deep roll and water spilled through the hatch. The eerie hum of the wind in the rigging, rising and falling with the strength of the gusts, penetrated the hold and heightened the climate of fear among the prisoners.

"Might be better odds than us surviving this storm," MacTigh said, his face frozen with fright. For a while no one spoke, as if their silence would help the ship right itself.

Redferne looked at each of the men's faces. Some were impassive, others showed fear. Hard to tell he thought, if that was from the storm or the grim prospects laid out by Craig. Kilbane was smiling. Still others looked resigned, as if the storm and the cane fields amounted to the same thing in the long run. "You've heard what the blacksmith said. It's up to each of you to make your own decision. I'm going to sleep on it and I'll give you my verdict in the morning, if there is a morning."

Redferne awoke at sunup to the cry of "Land ho," followed by the clang of the ship's bell saluting the announcement. The ship was steady again. Without warning, the deck reverberated with the thump of running feet and the cries of officers shouting commands to the sailors in the shrouds. For the men above deck, the prospect of shore leave and spending a week in the brothels and grog houses of Bridgeport put a spring in their step. For those in the hold, "Land ho" was a harbinger of a dreadful new chapter in their already-miserable lives.

"I've made my decision. I'm with ye," Redferne shouted to the dark hold. A jangling of chains accompanied a round of applause. When putting one's life on the line, he thought, best be with the committed, rather than with the fainthearted. The sound of the hatch opening signaled the arrival of the morning meal.

"Make sure the locks on your chains are in place. We don't want to blow it at this stage of the game," he hissed. The men scrambled to check their shackles. In the last two weeks, the quality of the food improved, a concession, he suspected to the demands of the slave auction. Instead of the regular mash diet, pieces of meat floated in a thin soup. Had Tolliver known that they had been burrowing into his profits for the past four weeks, he would not have been so generous.

After eating, they were marched topside for their morning exercise. Shredded lines, broken spars, and torn sails littered the deck. Sailors scurried to and fro collecting the debris and pitching it overboard. Redferne gazed at the land mass emerging from the mist in the southwest.

"Won't be long now, boys," a burly guard with missing teeth said. "What do you think of your new home? Wait till ye see those darkie women. Nothing too good for you Irish scum."

This was followed by a litany of obscene comments and jeers. They ignored the jibes, gazing at the barren vista taking shape before their eyes. Redferne sidled up to Craig.

"Not too hospitable by the looks of it. Not a tree in sight."

"The northeast coast is desolate. We're headed to the southwestern side, where Bridgeport is. That's on the Caribbean."

"It better be a hell of a lot better than this. A rabbit couldn't hide in that terrain."

"It's woodland and tropical forest on the southern side."

The rest of the men looked glumly at the bleak coastline slipping by on the port bow. Redferne waited until they were herded below decks to reveal what Craig had told him. Before he could speak, Gleason threw his hands up and swore. "Looks like bloody Connemara in the west of Ireland. We're screwed. We'd be spotted a mile off in that Godforsaken place."

Redferne dipped the ladle into the water barrel, took a mouthful and then spat it out. "Aaah! This stuff is rank. Tastes like someone emptied the slop bucket into it." A groan of disgust went up among the others. Redferne wiped his lips with the back of his hand and spat again before continuing. "According to Craig here, the southwest coast is much more agreeable."

"That leaves a lot of room for interpretation. Could you be more precise?" Gleason said, shuffling between the hatch and the linen wall to the doleful clink of his manacles. MacTigh, Kilbane, and Noone squatted, waiting for Craig to speak.

Craig sat with his back propped up against a lower bunk. "Palm trees, bush, swamps, good cover. Hard to find a man in there if he makes his mind up not to be found."

Redferne held his hands wide. "Look, we're caught between two horrible alternatives. There's no certainty that we'll make it through if we go over the side. But if we stay on the *Kate O'Dwyer*, we are bound for the slaughterhouse. I for one don't like those odds."

They stayed quiet as they evaluated Redferne's sober assessment. Then one by one they called out, "I'm in."

"Now that we've got that sorted, we need to formulate a plan. Craig, how much sailing time do you reckon to Bridgeport?"

"It'll be nightfall by the time we reach the southern part of the island. Maybe an hour or two after that to Bridgeport. They'll have to heave to until full tide to clear the coral reef. That could take another hour or two."

"That means we'll be going over the side in the dark," MacTigh said, alarm sounding in his voice.

"As opposed to going over in broad daylight. Easier for them to shoot our arses out of the water," Redferne said. A round of nervous laughter followed.

"How will we find our way in the dark?" MacTigh continued.

"The tide should carry us onto the shore," Craig said.

"Once we hit the beach, it'll be dumb luck after that," Redferne said.

"Hold on a minute." Craig dug under his straw mattress and pulled out a lump of charcoal.

"I need something to write on." They looked at each other.

Kilbane handed Craig a scrap of linen from the floor. "How about this?"

"Gallant." They gathered round as he made a rough sketch of Barbados. He identified Carlisle Bay on the sketch by its initials CB and a little south of that he marked Bridgeport with an X. "I'm for jumping ship in Carlisle Bay. That way we've a better chance of coming ashore, on the beaches north of Bridgeport, rather than being washed into the mouth of the Bridgeport harbor." He circled the X. "Where we'd easily be spotted."

"What are the conditions on shore?" Redferne asked.

"Miles of golden sand. Tropical forest a little inland and somewhere in the same region, a mangrove swamp." Craig blacked in the forest and the mangrove swamp on the map.

Several appeared preoccupied. Kilbane stared at the hatch; MacTigh and Noone sat on the floor with their heads in their hands. Before dark, each selected an empty barrel and made sure the lid was tamped down tightly. They also inspected them for leaks along the seams to make sure it was not one of those with the staves pried open.

No one knew how long they would be in the water, or if the barrels would hold up. As far as Redferne was concerned, going over the side was the point of greatest risk. "It's customary for captains to issue a measure of rum to the crew while riding at anchor waiting for the tide to rise," Craig said. "Most of the crew will be inside celebrating their forthcoming shore leave."

"Let's hope they knock themselves out," Gleason said rapping the hull with his clenched fist.

The plan called for each of them to line up along the rail before going over the top. They all claimed they could swim, a claim that would be tested when they had to cling to the barrels in the surging waves. Doing all of this at night complicated matters, but the disadvantages attending the darkness paled by comparison to the cloak of invisibility it would provide.

They were brought on deck again toward evening. Security had grown lax. Six men in leg irons weren't going anywhere.

As Craig said, lush green forests dotted the southern coast. Redferne whispered, "Memorize the terrain as best you can. Could prove useful later on."

Flocks of seagulls and petrels soared lazily overhead on the updrafts, diving toward the waves from time to time to scavenge flotsam from passing ships. Their shrill squawks, combined with the thrumming of the wind in the shrouds, reminded him of the tales told by Aunt Kate about the sinister screams of the Banshee.

It brought goose bumps to his arms.

As if on cue, flocks of birds exploded from the green canopy on the shoreline and melted back into the treetops, repeating the process over and over again. In the distance an unfamiliar rumble like the booming of far-off cannon guns. It took him a while to figure out it was surf pounding the beach.

Back in the hold they made their final preparations for escape. Gleason asked, "Is there a way to tie the barrels to our bodies? I can swim, but I'm not sure I can reach the shore. Listen to that surge."

Redferne jumped off his bunk and said to MacTigh, "Keep watch at the hatch. In all this freight, there must be rope or cord of some kind." He lit the lantern and raised it up to inspect the stack. The linen bales were in square canvas containers with drawstrings on top. Not enough string there to choke a chicken, but what about the linen itself? Cut in strips it could be braided into rope. Once it got wet it would cling to the barrel and make it easier to control. He reached up to the top bunk and retrieved a knife from Craig's tool kit. With Gleason holding the lantern aloft, they edged behind the façade of cargo. The void in back was spacious enough for an Irish *céili*. Had Jules kicked harder during the storm, the jig would've been up.

They untied one of the drawstrings and using the knife to start a tear, ripped the linen hanks into crude strips that they braided into ropes. "By God, lads, these are strong enough to hang a man from the yard arm," Redferne said as he and Gleason pulled on the linen braids to test them.

By the time darkness fell, all that remained was to wait for the *Kate O'Dwyer* to heave to when the tide rose. Redferne worried about Craig, who was still recuperating from the flogging. *Best keep close to him once we're in the water.* As if reading his thoughts, Craig said, "Redferne, I'm having second thoughts. I won't survive that swim. Maybe I should take my chances and stay on the ship."

"It wouldn't take them long to figure out you freed us from the shackles, you being a blacksmith and all."

"I'm aware of that, but I lied to you before when I said I could swim."

"Me and Gleason will help you. Without you none of this would be possible. We owe you."

"Aren't we a little premature with the appreciation? We're not off the ship yet and if we do manage to get away, I'll slow you down."

"If you don't come with us, Tolliver will hang or keelhaul you this night, mark my words." Redferne clapped him on the shoulder to reassure him. The look on Craig's face was more resignation than agreement, but this was something Redferne felt he had to do, since in the past his carelessness had resulted in the loss of life. Now he needed to make amends and try to save one.

The deck above came alive with the sounds of men scrambling into the shrouds, the squealing of lines through winches, and the creaking of sails. The ship slowed. Redferne turned to Craig. "Tell me again how long it takes for the tide to rise."

"Hour, hour and a half."

The activity on deck ended with laughter and cheers.

"This is it fella's," Redferne said, shaking each man's hand. "Before we go overboard we should decide on a meeting point on shore. Once in the water we'll be in the maw of the wind and the tide with no control over where we land. I'm going up top to reconnoiter. While I'm gone, start lashing yourselves to the barrels." As Redferne crept on deck, he realized that the ship was pitching and rolling more than usual, a sure sign that the ocean swells had grown bigger. He crawled on his belly to the port rail and surveyed the shore. Off to his right the darkness was peppered with dozens of lights. Ships in the harbor and houses along the docks, he reckoned. Best avoid that area if possible. Moving left, or north of that position, the coastal lights gradually thinned out until only one remained. He had found his compass point.

The noise from the galley was so loud that he failed to hear footsteps coming down the stern castle stairs until they were almost on top of him. He lay there and pretended to be drunk. "Here give us a hand up, mate," he slurred.

"What the hell," the sentry said and jumped back. "Didn't take you long to get walloped, you drunken sot, while I'm stuck out here parched to the world." He extended his hand. Before he knew what happened, Redferne had him in a headlock. He frog-walked him toward the bulwark rail, where he found a loose belaying pin. While he struggled to get the heavy wooden pin from its socket, the sentry yelled for help but no one heard him in the hubbub coming from the galley.

The sentry shouted again. Redferne struck him across the head with the pin and the cry died in his throat. He pushed him under the coils of line hanging from the pin rail, hiding him from view. Looking around, he detected no other sign of movement; everyone seemed to be in the galley. He dashed back to the hatch, taking the ladder steps two at a time. Lashed to the barrels, his mates looked like a bunch of pregnant women.

"Quick, help me get this on," he said to Gleason, lifting the barrel to his chest. "We need to get out of here before that sentry wakes up."

Gleason threw him a curious look as they followed him up the ladder through the hatch. They lined up along the bulwark rail a few feet apart so they wouldn't land on each other when they hit the water. Craig stood between Redferne and Gleason. The swell came heavy making it difficult to maintain their balance. "See that light to the extreme left," Redferne said in a hushed voice. "Try to aim for it. That will be our reference point. We'll wait for each other there."

"How will we identify ourselves in the dark?" Gleason asked. His breath came in short bursts.

"Shout the Irish word for home: *awalye*."

Grabbing the lines anchored to the belaying pins, they hoisted themselves up on the bulwark rail and jumped. Redferne and Gleason held Craig by the wrists.

Redferne thought he heard a shout before hitting the water but the impact winded him and he struggled to hold onto the barrel. Some landed in the troughs of the waves, others on the crests. The towering swells quickly dispersed them. They tried calling one another, but the wind tore their voices away.

Though the air was cold, the water felt warm and refreshing, a welcome change from months in the stinking hold. Given the force of the impact, Redferne was amazed that they managed to hold on to Craig.

Several sharp cracks made him turn his head. Flashes erupted from the *Kate O'Dwyer*, but in the darkness, he doubted that the musket shots found their mark. Swept to the crest of a large swell, he lost his grip on Craig when they slid down the other side.

Breakout from Sugar Island

MAP OF BARBADOS

Source: http://d-maps.com/pays.php?num_pay=125&lang=en

CHAPTER 32

Redferne couldn't tell how long he was in the water when the band of greenish-yellow fire appeared stretching along the shoreline. For a minute, he thought the beach was ablaze, then he recalled something he had read about the phenomenon of phosphorescence. He was headed in the right direction because the phosphorescence marked where the surf crashed against the shore.

He was having difficulty controlling the barrel and quickly became exhausted by the effort. He tried straddling it, feet trailing in the water on either side while holding tightly to the rim at the front. Like the horse on the frozen lake, the barrel seemed to have a mind of its own. At times, it drifted horizontally into the wave, then it spun around and broached the wave nose first. The linen rope loosened from water saturation, but it bound him tightly enough to the barrel to prevent him from falling off.

Every now and then, he shouted to his mates, but heard no response from the heaving blackness. Had Gleason and Craig been wrenched apart? How was Craig coping with the barrel? The belt of fire appeared and disappeared as he rose and fell in the troughs. As the pounding of the surf grew louder, a new fear gnawed at his gut. The coral reef. Would he clear it or be torn to shreds?

The cluster of lights loomed closer as he fought the strong current pulling him toward the harbor. The solitary light that was to be their guiding star had disappeared. He kicked with his feet to change the direction of the barrel, but it was a losing battle against the surge. He hoped that if he survived the reef, he'd have enough strength left to trek north to their meeting point.

But what if Tolliver had a welcoming party on the beach? The fiery surf came closer, and thunderclaps exploded on the shore. His arms grew numb from grasping the barrel. The dark outline of the forest emerged against the darker background of the night. Would it be a haven or a predator waiting to devour them?

The next wave launched him into the phosphorescence. The barrel hit the reef with a bone-shattering crunch and exploded in a snarl of hoops and staves. The impact catapulted him into the surf, which pulled him under and churned him head over heels several times before tossing him onto the sand.

He lay there breathless as the spent surf floated him higher up the beach. His body felt like it had been slammed against a wall. He wasn't sure if he could stand. The sound of voices from the harbor reminded him that danger lurked everywhere. He spat sand from his mouth and set off at a trot toward the north.

He spotted lights farther inland through the trees, but suppressed the impulse to head toward them for help. Intermittently he shouted *awalye* to no avail. He couldn't be the only survivor. Most of his mates were younger and hardier than he was, he reminded himself to keep his spirits up. At last, where the trees thinned out, his call was answered, and Gleason and MacTigh stepped from behind a sand dune. Seeing that Craig was not with them, his heart sank.

As if reading his thoughts, Gleason said, "Soon after you disappeared, he broke free of my grip. I tried to find him, but it was useless in the dark."

"How was he managing the barrel?"

"Struggling, but as I'm sure you discovered yourself, it was a bitch."

"It was indeed, but without it, we would never have made it in those seas."

They walked on in silence through the dunes until they spotted the solitary leaping light. It turned out to be a bonfire around which several forms danced and chanted in a language he had never heard. They had crept to within two hundred yards of it when they heard awalye. Noone and Kilbane emerged from the tall grass along the sand farther inland from the beach. Everyone was accounted for except Craig.

"Anyone hurt?" Redferne asked.

"A little black and blue from being tumbled on the sand," Kilbane said, "but nothing major."

Not knowing the nature of the activity around the bonfire, they settled down in the lee of a sand dune to wait for Craig, but as the hours wore on, it became apparent that he had not made it. If they didn't find him by dawn they would have to abandon the search. Tolliver's manhunt would be underway by then.

Barking dogs woke Redferne. The sun's rays infiltrated the clouds, back-lighting their cumulous mass with a yellow glow. The waves had lost their green fire. He roused his mates and they scampered for the cover of the forest. The bonfire people had melted away, leaving only a black patch of smoldering embers in the sand. They broached the trees, entering a world none of them had seen before.

Towering palms intermingled with trees draped in streamers of moss. Long sinewy vines drooped from others touching the ground, a springy carpet of decayed leaves and branches. As they moved into the interior, the canopy above filtered the morning sun. Strange red and green birds with curved beaks flitted through the branches, trailing discordant shrieks. When the barking grew louder, they plunged into the thicket. After running awhile, Redferne raised his hand and called a halt. Out of breath, they huddled beneath a tree.

"We need a strategy or we'll drop from exhaustion." He slapped the insects from his neck and shoulders. They looked a sorry lot-- hungry, tired, and lost in an alien world.

Gleason spoke and pointed upward. "We could pull ourselves up into the trees. Those vines seem sturdy enough to support a man's weight."

"Have you ever heard of the word 'treed?' " Redferne asked.

"Can't say that I have."

"It means to get trapped up a tree. The hunters wouldn't find us but the dogs would."

Gleason said, "We could be running out of the forest rather than into it."

"And for that reason we need to use the only constant available to us."

His mates looked at each other, continuing to swat at the insects buzzing around them.

"The one point of reference we now have is the barking of the dogs," Redferne said. "We'll have to stop running at intervals to check where the barking is coming from and run in the opposite direction."

They took off again. Sounds bounced among the trees, so plotting the position of the dogs was easier said than done. Redferne noticed the terrain changing. The soil grew wetter. Trees with root systems above the ground that looked like coiling snakes dominated the area.

As if from a dream, a band of bizarre individuals armed with muskets, spears, and bamboo sticks emerged from the tangled roots. They wore loincloths and red, blue, and green designs decorated their bodies. Their dark brown skin closely resembled Redferne's tan acquired from working summers cutting turf in the bogs.

A tall bare-chested black man, wearing blue britches and carrying a musket, stood among them. He didn't move when the Indians unshouldered their muskets and surrounded the white men.

Two of the painted warriors raised their voices. One pointed his spear at the intruders. The other gesticulated wildly. A heated argument ensued. An elder wearing a multicolored feathered headband raised his hand, while the others fell silent. He turned his head in the direction of the barking dogs before speaking. Redferne thought he recognized the language but couldn't place it. The tall black man looming beside the elder translated.

"Some of my people want to leave you to the man hunters. They say all white men come from the Evil One. Others say we should kill you and deprive the English planters of free labor. I say you should fight the white tormenters with us, shoulder to shoulder."

Redferne recognized the strange language as the one spoken around the bonfire back in the sand dunes. The barking sounded closer.

Redferne stuck out his chest. "Fighting the English is something we welcome. We come from an island that the English have pillaged for centuries. You have found yourself some willing soldiers." Gleason and his mates raised their fists and cheered.

The elder whispered something to the black man. "The chief said you must be 'red legs.' " The fugitives looked at each other.

"This is what we call the Irish who work in the sugar cane fields. They burn easily. The chief knows your reputation as fighters and he welcomes you." At a signal from the chief, they followed the natives into the swamp past the trees with the gnarled roots that looked like creatures from a nightmare. The sound of barking dogs grew fainter. Seeing the bewildered looks of the Irishmen, the black man explained that the gnarled trees were called mango, commonly found in swamps.

"The mango produces a sweet orange-yellow fruit about the size of an apple and is a favorite of the natives."

They walked in single file for a time through murky water up to their knees with spear-carriers in front and back of them, until they arrived at a small island lined with several beached dugout canoes.

Boarding the canoes, they wound their way around trees hung with curtains of mossy foliage that trailed on the water. An hour's paddling brought them to an island with a dozen or more huts made from bamboo and roofed with broad plantain leaves. Women and children crowded around when they went ashore.

The black man approached Redferne and holding out his hand said, "Isaac." Over six feet tall, he stood a head above Redferne. His face looked like it was chiseled from ancient Barbadian coral. When he smiled, the hardness softened and, apart from a missing lower front tooth, he was a handsome man. Like the other natives, he went barefoot.

"I escaped about a year ago from the sugarcane fields." He jerked his thumb over his shoulder. "The white men call these people Indians. They took me in and sheltered me. Without help, escapees seldom make it, and when they are caught, the consequences are horrific."

When Redferne told him about throwing half the ship's cargo overboard, Isaac howled with laughter and went to tell the chief their story. The elder's wrinkled face spread into a broad smile. Isaac returned and said, "The chief is pleased with your decision. He can use people with spirit. He used the word 'spirit,' but I believe he meant what we call imagination."

"I'm glad he appreciates our imagination, but what we would appreciate even more right now is a bit to eat."

They soon sat down to a feast of mangos, coconuts, maize stew, and what he later discovered was roasted green monkey. For the first time since leaving Ireland they began to feel human again; no longer chained animals. With the return of their dignity came the impulse to flee the island.

One morning two weeks later after the fugitives regained their strength and made friends with their protectors, Isaac showed up in their hut and shook Redferne by the shoulder. "Come with me." He led him to the water's edge, where they embarked with a dozen warriors in two canoes. The individual who had argued with the chief in the swamp the previous day sat in the lead canoe. Isaac carried a musket and the others carried an assortment of spears, long bamboo poles, and muskets.

Redferne pointed to the poles. "What are those for?"

"Blow guns. The bamboo has been hollowed out all the way through. It makes a formidable weapon, in some cases more effective than a musket."

"But how does... ?"

"Here, I'll show you." After a brief exchange, a warrior handed Isaac a bamboo tube and a fletched dart. The tube, about five feet long, shot a six inch-long dart with feathered tips notched around its end. Isaac handed the dart to Redferne. "Careful! Don't touch the tip. Sometimes they dip the point in curare-saturated resin to stun their prey."

Redferne gasped. He had never seen the like and handed it back to Isaac, who returned it and the blowgun to the native.

"Better let an expert show you how it's done." The man took the blowgun in his left hand, inserted the dart, and raised it to his mouth. With his right hand, he steadied the shank, taking aim at the foliage above, then he puffed his cheeks out, releasing a quick burst of air. A blur of red and green feathers...a squeal from above. The shooter had found his target. A small green monkey crashed through the foliage and landed with a splash in the water near the lead canoe.

"It's unusual for a monkey to succumb that quickly," Isaac said. "He must be a young'un. With adults, you can track them for an hour through the canopy before the curare immobilizes them." They fished the stunned animal from the water. A sharp blow to the back of its head with a stout stick put it out of its misery.

"I hope you like monkey. We'll be having it again for dinner tonight."

"That's fine with me as long as it's not poisoned. Even if we have it every night, it's better than ship's gruel. I've had my fill of that bilge."

"Not to worry, Irishman. The curare resin simply immobilizes the victim's breathing system. It doesn't taint the meat."

By the time the swamp gave way to solid ground, the sun's heat trapped under the canopy felt intense. A large black stain of perspiration saturated Redferne's shirt by the time the canoes scraped ashore. The hostile native, named Arpeche, lumbered toward Isaac and Redferne. His animal fur cap with the tail hanging down the back of his neck made his eyes look like an otter's. He divided his warriors into two groups, taking charge of one. Isaac took the other. Redferne stuck with Isaac. As they moved forward, brushing aside the curtains of Spanish moss from the bearded fig trees, Redferne tugged Isaac by the sleeve. "Where're we going?"

Isaac dropped down on one knee and put his forefinger to his lips. "Shh! We're almost there."

"How long are you going to keep me in the dark, Isaac?" Redferne whispered. "What's this all about?"

"We got word that several men are going over the fence today, so we're here to assist them."

"What fence?"

"You'll find out soon enough." Waving his hand, he motioned his party forward. The sound of voices ahead filtered through the trees. Isaac dropped to his knee again, which seemed to be the signal for the natives to fan out on either side of the path, disappearing into the foliage. Then an all-too-familiar sound: the rhythmic snap of a whip followed by an anguished cry. Isaac parted the foliage with the barrel of his musket to reveal a six-foot-high stockade of pointed wooden stakes, curving off to the left and right along the edge of the rain forest.

"Welcome to the Waldron Plantation, a hellhole of brutality. My home for over two years." The look on Isaac's face revealed that he was reliving the experience.

"What in the hell are we doing here?" Redferne pulled farther back into the foliage. The crack of the whip merged with cries of anguish. The blood pounded in his ears. "Let's get out of here, Isaac." He could all but see the twisted pleasure on Captain Preston's face, coming at him with the cowhide whip.

"Not before we do what we came here to do, Irishman, which is to help whoever makes a burst for freedom across that stockade."

Redferne glanced around. "Where did the natives go?"

"We don't know for sure where the breakout will occur, so Arpeche has stationed his warriors along the section of fence abutting the forest to lend assistance." The words barely escaped Isaac's mouth when he dropped his musket and slumped to the ground, choking and squirming. A dart protruded from his back.

Redferne whipped around to see the muzzle of the blowgun sticking from the undergrowth. He tried to swerve, but Arpeche's missile struck him square in the chest. He fell back writhing and gasping for breath. He made an ungainly effort to remove the dart, but blacked out. Overhead, green monkeys screeched and scurried through the canopy.

CHAPTER 33

Redferne's return to consciousness came with a huge gasp for breath, like a swimmer at the end of his endurance, broaching the surface to suck in a mouthful of air. Stinging pains lanced his chest and his buttocks throbbed from his recent branding. He made out the silhouette of a man in the dark sitting with his head in his hands a few feet away. Hearing Redferne stirring, the silhouette began to speak in short quick outbursts. "Stupid, stupid. Should have seen this coming."

Redferne sat up, which caused more pain in his buttocks. His leg irons rattled and instantly he realized where he was and what had befallen him.

"The signs were all around, but I ignored them," the bent-over figure said.

"Is that you, Isaac?" Redferne whispered, his voice reduced to a rasp from the effects of the curare.

"I should never have trusted Arpeche. I discounted the whispered rumors about him. I grew lax with my newfound freedom."

"No point in blaming yourself. What's done is done. Let's concentrate on getting outta' here."

"Don't be naïve, Irishman. You have arrived in the place you jumped ship to avoid because of my stupidity—the same hellhole I escaped from not six months ago."

Redferne's stomach muscles tightened. The horror stories about the sugar cane fields of Barbados enveloped him like an acrid black fog scouring his soul of the modest hope that his few days of freedom had conjured. He heard voices outside and then the door flew open. Two mulatto guards wearing only britches that stretched to mid-calf stomped in carrying cowhide whips. Their faces were blank, their eyes hollow as if they did not see or feel what they did to stay alive in the brutal world of sugar. They inflicted pain and they did it efficiently.

"On your feet," one barked. The other grabbed them roughly and pushed them out the door. Redferne pitched forward, tripping on his leg irons, landing on his hands and knees. The mulattos set upon him with their whips. He sprang to his feet with the speed of a wild animal fleeing a predator.

The sun had dipped below the tree tops as he scrambled after Isaac. A large wooden cross stood in the middle of the compound. Up close, the cross became a whipping post. The mulattos tied Isaac's wrists to its crossbar, suspending him so that only his toes touched the ground. A large throng surrounded him. The slaves were forced to watch daily punishments when they returned from the fields, to terrorize them into submission.

A murmur went up from the crowd when a figure dressed in blue emerged from the edge of the compound and approached the whipping post. "Waldron," someone whispered.

Mr. Waldron, a beefy plantation owner in his fifties, looked a picture of unrestrained appetite, never quite satisfied. Dressed in a blue silk coat with vest and breeches to match, his protruding belly hung over the top of his belt like a ring of dough over the lip of a bowl. He removed his tricorne hat and mopped his brow with a lace-edged silk handkerchief.

"It's been oppressively hot today, Isaac. But of course, you wouldn't know that since you and the Irish rogue slept through it."

Isaac kept his eyes averted. Looking directly at The Lord of the Manor could trigger additional punishment.

"You're an educated man, so I'm sure you know what the Bible says, Isaac. 'Give to Caesar the things that are Caesar's' etcetera, etcetera." He put the shaft of his riding crop under Isaac's chin and tipped his head back. "You violated that rule by depriving Caesar of what is legitimately his, didn't you, slave?" Then he retreated and signaled his overseer, Carew, to commence. Carew, whose muscled chest was crisscrossed with scars, wore a black sweat-rag knotted behind his head, the tails dropping to the nape of his neck. Like the slaves, he was barefooted. He ripped the ragged shirt from Isaac's back and then pacing off the distance laid on the first stroke.

The second lash crossed the first with a resounding snap. He continued the flogging until beads of blood spiraled off the whip on the backstroke, spraying the transfixed faces of the audience. Carew stopped when Isaac hung limp from the crossbar. His second-in-command doused Isaac with a bucket of cold saltwater, and the flogging continued until Isaac passed out again. They cut him down and pulled his body to one side to make room for the next unfortunate.

Redferne gritted his teeth as they tied his wrists to the crossbar. He'd show these sadistic English bastards how an Irishman behaves.

Waldron stepped forward once more. "A little something to put you in the right frame of mind, Mr. Redferne." He inserted snuff in both his nostrils with a flourish. "A pinch of attitude-alteration, so to speak, to help you adapt to our community." Redferne felt Isaac's sweat on the crossbar.

Waldron withdrew, and the first stinging stroke landed. Pain seared through him. In a vain attempt to distract himself, he counted the lashes: 23, 24, 25…He convulsed when the saltwater drenched his mangled back, but he did not cry out as they tightened the bonds around his wrists to pull him up on his toes once more.

The raggedy crowd stood hushed when the lash descended again, its hiss mingling with the night sounds now emanating from the forest. Through the miasma of pain, Redferne recognized the peculiar cries of the green monkeys scampering through the canopy. Fantastic green and red birds with curved beaks flew across his fading field of vision.

"Come." The soft Irish voice whispered in his ear as if in a dream. The heat of the bonfire seared his back. Maureen's soft breath brushed his cheek. "Come!" The voice, clearer now, said, "The rising horn has sounded; you must eat before we are away to the fields." He opened his eyes. In Maureen's place stood a young woman with a haggard face, partially concealed by a fall of long black grimy hair. She spoke again in Irish and held a wooden spoon full of a porridge-like substance to his mouth.

"*Ith do bhiadh!* We are not fed again till noon in the fields."

He tried to raise himself on one elbow. His back screamed with pain. "I'm in no condition to work. I can't put one foot in front of the other."

"You must," she said, "or they'll beat you again."

The threat of another lashing helped get him going. Mercifully, they removed his leg irons. But after hours digging holes for the new cane cuttings without a break, he was near collapse. He mopped his brow with an old handkerchief, stealing glances at this strange new world. The terrain alternated between flat and hilly, with long brown cane ridges snaking up the slopes from the valley floor like fat worms. Working the slopes was its own particular kind of hell, Isaac told him, but toiling in the valley was no picnic either. For part of the day luck placed him alongside a row of eucalyptus trees that operated as wind breaks between the fields, and gave him shade from the brutal sun. The work force, a mix of men and women, mostly Irish and Africans, labored in rows as they were goaded by the whips of mulatto drivers. Women and girls were expected to keep the same pace as men, and when they fell behind, they were flogged.

Pregnancy was no excuse. To ensure that the unborn child was not harmed during a flogging, which would be an economic loss, they nestled the woman's extended belly in a depression scooped out of the ground for that purpose. The mulatto drivers were particularly cruel to the Irish. He suspected that lording it over whites, no matter how lowly, provided them an indirect form of revenge against their white overlords.

At the meal break, he wolfed down his portion of *loblolly*, a maize-based seaman's gruel that most of the slaves disliked so much that upon seeing it, they cried out: "Oh, no *loblolly*, no *loblolly*!"

He couldn't afford the luxury of being picky. He slurped down his allotment of water in like fashion, surprised when the overseers filled his tin mug a second time. He had to maintain his strength if he was to survive, so when the dinner crew came 'round again with boiled sweet potatoes called bonaviste, he polished them off in minutes and licked his wooden bowl for good measure.

Although many Irish accents mixed with African dialects, he made no effort to communicate with his countrymen, nor they with him. At first, he thought it was because of a collective shame that proud people experienced at being reduced to a level lower than animals. But as the day wore on, he reasoned that the struggle to survive was uppermost. Any other expenditure of energy was a luxury none could afford.

Toward evening, the more experienced workers moved ahead of him. From the row on his right, a voice whispered, "Hey, Redferne, you better get a move on. They'll whip you, mon."

Isaac.

"Where did you come from? I was beginning to think they killed you."

"I'm an alumnus of this place. I've a friend among the drivers. He tipped me off that you were slacking. They don't give a shit whether you're new or not. They'll whip you, if you don't pick up the pace."

A commotion arose half a dozen rows over, and a woman was pulled from the line. An overseer appeared with a yardstick.

"What are they doing?" Redferne asked.

"Measuring the depth of the holes."

"What?"

"Each hole is supposed to be ten inches deep and two feet apart."

Redferne's eyes bulged. "Jaysus? First I've heard of that."

"Keep moving. Their inspections are done here. They'll move to another location." Isaac straightened and wiped his forehead with the back of his hand.

The woman wailed as the lash tore swatches of a thin cotton

shirt off her back. Rows of bent figures moved forward mechanically down the furrows. The rise and fall of a hundred burnished hoes flashed like broken glass in the rays of the sun, pounding out a doleful rhythm on the stubborn earth. The salt from Redferne's sweat seeped into the wounds on his back, causing fresh agony.

Buoyed by Isaac's presence, he made it to quitting time, having survived his first day—a grinding routine that would be replicated in all its brutality for a thousand tomorrows unless he did something. The black cloud descended again and he had to fight a numbing despair. He was a pawn in an exchange of one form of slavery for another: the chains of poverty and hunger in Ireland for the whip and manacles of Barbados. He had as much choice as a donkey or a dog. Like them, he wasn't free and like him thousands of others remained in thrall to power and greed.

That night as he lay on his belly on a bed of rushes to protect his still-tender back and buttocks, Isaac crept into his hut with a lantern and a salve for his wounds.

"This is going to sting, but it's an old African remedy and it works." Isaac set the lantern on a small stool, then uncorked a bottle containing a concoction of honey and tea brewed from sorrel leaves, dribbling the syrupy liquid across his wounds. Redferne's back blazed like fire and he had to clamp his teeth shut to avoid crying out. Sweat poured from his forehead. "Give it a few minutes and the stinging will pass and then you'll feel sweet relief."

"What about you?"

Isaac touched the bandages wrapping his chest and back. "Already taken care of. My back's like leather. Not as cut up as yours."

"You're a miracle worker," Redferne said as a soothing wave caressed his mangled back.

"That's an ability Father Josefa never attributed to me. Said I was blessed with the power of healing, but miracles? No. That would put me in the company of Jesus."

Redferne closed his eyes from fatigue and relief. "Father Josefa?"

"He was a Jesuit priest expelled from Portugal who ended up in Sierra Leone, where I was born."

"*Was* a Jesuit?"

"Yes," His voice grew thick. "They ran him through when he tried to shield us."

Redferne raised himself on an elbow, grimacing. "It wasn't a fair fight then."

"Josefa didn't have a chance against four armed slavers who burst in. Me and four others they clapped in irons and shipped to Virginia next day on board the *Green Hornet*."

"So Waldron knew you had some learning."

"I was his translator when he needed to negotiate with captains of foreign ships."

"A translator, imagine that." Redferne struggled to stay awake.

Isaac checked Redferne's back again. "Hmm." He went out and returned minutes later with a box of salves, ointments, and bandage rolls. He brought the stool with the lantern closer. "People don't believe me when I tell them I worked for Waldron until he discovered I planned to stowaway on an outbound ship."

"And then?"

"The flogging post, followed by an immediate transfer to the sugar mill."

Isaac cut several lengths from the bandage roll.

"Lucky you didn't end up like Josefa."

"My memory of Josefa was beginning to fade of late. Taught us Portuguese, Spanish, and English as well as how to read, write, and cipher. Our parents paid him in chickens and vegetables." He took a jar from his medicine box and with his knife coated the bandages with pink ointment.

"So how come you to be in Barbados?"

"Hurricane. The Green Hornet got blown off course and ran aground on the coral reef that girds the island. A few of us swam ashore."

"From one hell to another."

Isaac draped the bandage strips across his palm. "Rise up on your elbows. This is going to hurt at first."

"Ahhhhh!"

"Sorry." He wrapped the bandages around Redferne's back and

chest, fastening them with pins. "You'll be as right as rain by Monday."

"That feels wonderful."

"You're welcome."

"The *Green Hornet*, the *Kate O'Dwyer*," Redferne said. "I'm sorry Isaac, for you and all of us."

Isaac clapped his hands. "Enough of this depressing talk. Tomorrow is Sunday."

"Does Waldron expect us to be at church in our Sunday best?"

"No, but in one of his more remarkable turns of hypocrisy, he observes the Lord's Day and the biblical injunction to make it a day of rest."

Redferne laughed so hard that his back hurt again. The image of a pious, God-fearing Waldron sitting in the first pew nodding assent to a preacher's exhortation to "do unto others" almost made him vomit. "What a world we live in. Not only does it tolerate the exploitation of human beings in the name of profit, but it assumes that God's in on the fix."

"That's a new experience for the white man, but a way of life if you're black," Isaac replied, putting his salves and bandages back into his medicine box.

Redferne raised himself up again and looked around his new home. Isaac's shadow danced along the bamboo walls interwoven with branches as he moved around. Plantain leaves and palm thatch covered the roof. An earthen water jar and an iron cooking pot sat in a corner near a stool with the lantern. A few calabashes of different sizes, stacked on a rickety table, served as plates. His bed was a mat on the rush floor. When his elbow hurt, he lay back down and mumbled into the mat.

"Irishmen have been under England's jackboot for centuries. We don't take a back seat to anyone, black or brown, when it comes to feeling victimized."

"Great! The wretched of the earth, playing one-upmanship for the title of most abused," Isaac said, swatting a spider off his arm.

"Be that as it may, we need to put the Lord's Day to good use."

Isaac spoke. "If you're thinking of attending a church meeting, you can banish that notion."

"The rabble is forbidden to mingle with the gentry, even in The Lord's house, I take it," Redferne said.

"Don't forget The Lord is white in their eyes and he don't have no truck with blacks, be they African or Irish." He ran the tip of his tongue into the gap of his missing tooth.

"But I'm white," Redferne protested, grimacing.

"Like I said, the white man's God don't cotton to blacks."

"In that case, I'll present my case to the black man's God."

Isaac chuckled. "Won't do you no good. Black man's God don't have no truck with whites." His eyes danced.

Redferne raised his right hand above his head and let it fall to the floor with a smack. "The Irish are screwed. Is that what you're telling me?"

"Pretty much. Here they don't even have the status of a black man. That's pretty low."

"And they have fuck-all credibility with the deity of any stripe?" Redferne asked, trying to stifle a yawn.

"That's it. Now you've squared the circle." A slow smile flickered on Isaac's lips that Redferne barely detected in the semi-darkness of the hut. After a short silence, Isaac asked, "What's this about putting The Lord's Day to good use?"

"What I was about to say is that you're full of shite," Redferne said. Both men exploded in laughter and the chatter in the adjacent huts picked up, as if this burst of joviality lifted a weight from their withered spirits. The wind swooshed through the plantain leaves, flattening the candle flame in the lantern.

"What I wouldn't do for a tankard of Cloonfin beer."

"Can't help you with whatever-town beer that is, but I might be able to rustle up some slave-town hooch, "Isaac said going back to his hut. He returned with what looked like a bottle of water.

Redferne pulled himself up against the wall. "Courtesy of the dark continent?"

"Courtesy of Father Josefa." Isaac pulled the cork with his teeth.

Redferne thought his eyes might pop from their sockets. "The good priest taught you to make moonshine?"

"He taught us how to recognize certain plants and berries used in making jam."

"But he didn't make jam, right?"

"Not a spoonful." He brought the bottle to his lips and passed it to Redferne. "So you want to honor the Lord's Day with a meeting?"

"I was thinking of a meeting without a priest or a minister." Redferne whispered. "A meeting to talk a little treason," He took a swallow of Isaac's brew and closed his eyes. "Ah," then he raised his glass. "Here's to Josefa's recipe for jam." He smacked his lips and passed the bottle back to Isaac.

"Talk a little treason?" Isaac put the cork back in the bottle. "That salve was to soothe your back, not addle your brain."

"Addled is what I'll be if I don't get out of here, Isaac. Ireland was bad, but this place is beyond my wildest imaginings."

"Dead is what you'll be if you don't put that fool notion out of your skull. End up with your head on a sharp stake over the stockade gate, food for the vultures."

"Didn't stop you," Redferne said.

"Had outside help."

"The kind of help I'd hope to avoid."

"It was the kind of help that sprung me from this place. I'd still be sprung except for my own stupidity. If I ever worked up the nerve to try again, I'd only do it with smart people, not morons like me." He took another swig. "God bless Josefa."

"Do you think the chief was in on our abduction?"

"No! Chief Oxaxa didn't trust Arpeche. I don't think he had any idea what Arpeche was up to behind his back."

"Hoarding guns and gunpowder didn't arouse his suspicions?"

"It's a big swamp and apparently Arpeche and his cronies are effectively hiding their operation."

"It seems that Oxaxa might still be our best bet to get out of here then." Redferne grimaced as he moved.

"Only if I can get word to him what Arpeche is up to, otherwise Arpeche will turn any rescue operation into a manhunt," Isaac said.

Before Isaac left for his own cabin, Redferne said, "What kinda' brand is on my arse?"

"Same as mine." Isaac pulled down his britches. "Be my guest."

"*WS?*" Redferne's breath caught. "Oh, my God! What does it mean?"

"It's the plantation brand. We all have it. Stands for Waldron Sugar."

Redferne put his head in his hands. His sobs came in great heaves.

"What is it, Red? You're shocked that your pretty white arse has been defaced. Is that it?"

"She was here, she was here," he said. The identical mark was on Maureen Kelly's forearm when he and Padraig pulled her from the frozen lake.

Seamus Beirne

CHAPTER 34

Black smoke belched from sugar mill chimneys day and night during cane-cutting season, which ran from February to May. Hungry fires under vats of boiling cane juice hissed and crackled with the addition of more fuel.

Redferne was assigned to the number one, or "great" gang, which was composed of the strongest and most mature men and women on the plantation. This group bore the brunt of the hard labor, especially in cane-cutting season. During this period, it was not unusual for them to work far into the night, as there was a short window of time after which the cane would over-ripen. Whether from chance or cunning, Redferne had escaped further punishment.

Cane stalks stood six feet tall, a wave of undulating green, surging all the way from the valley floor until it blanketed the slopes. The tropical sun assaulted him as he moved along the cane rows, slashing stalks twice the thickness of his wrist with a machete. It reminded him of autumn days picking potatoes as a boy back in Ireland. How he longed to reach the end of that potato ridge so he could leave the field and play with his friends. That's where the comparison ended.

The end of a cane row held no such release, unless he dropped dead. He tried not to calculate the distance to where the cane terminated against the irrigation ditch. Putting his head down like a donkey pulling a load up hill, he forged ahead, making sure to keep pace with the people on either side of him.

He trudged on mechanically, bending to slash and rising to

cast the cut stalk into the furrow where it was gathered and loaded onto horse carts to be taken to the mill. Bending, slashing, rising, bending, slashing, rising. On it went, hour after hour. House slaves, mainly adolescent boys and girls, scurried up and down the rows with canteens of water.

Throwing his head back, he slurped from the canteen proffered by a young man. Water dribbled down his chin. When he lowered his head and returned the canteen, their eyes met. He dropped his machete.

Padraig!

The muscular, black-haired youth gazed back at him, astonishment written all over his tanned face. Padraig picked up the machete, handed it to his father and moved up the row to the next person without saying a word.

Redferne remained rooted to the spot, unable to speak. Did Padraig even recognize him?

"Better get a move on, Irishman," a man to his right said. "There's a driver bearing down." His knees shook so badly that it took him awhile to get back up to speed, but by that time, Padraig had disappeared. A huge burden lifted from his shoulders, and then the fault-finding began. If he had journeyed to Sligo sooner, things might have turned out differently.

If he had been a better father, a more attentive husband, a better provider, Grace would not have sent Padraig into service and eventually, without her knowing it, into slavery. He caught himself. That was water under the bridge.

He had to deal with things as they were, which looked a helluva lot better than five minutes before. He had found his son. Alive! Getting him out of this nightmare would become his consuming obsession.

As the sun cooled, the Africans started chanting, keeping time to the rhythm of the work. Soon the whole field sang, blacks and whites alike. He never thought himself a great singer. Not the kind who entertained people at *céilis* on summer evenings after work, but now he raised his voice with gusto. He had something huge to celebrate; he had found his son on the other side of the world. Joyful tears flowed down his cheeks and he outpaced his fellow workers, bending, slashing, rising, as he danced down the row to the irrigation ditch.

Cane cutting demanded considerable skill. Care had to be taken not to damage the buds from which ratoons, or new shoots, would grow the following year. A misplaced machete stroke resulted in a flogging. Although the work was hard, it had an upside. It provided the slaves with a tool that doubled as a weapon.

Redferne and Isaac noticed that the overseer didn't count the machetes at the end of the day. Every week for a month, they stole several and hid them in an irrigation ditch beyond the slave compound. Out of bounds to all slaves after dark, they were less likely to search it if weapons were missed. One night when Redferne made a run to the hiding place with two machetes under his coat, he heard voices as he entered no-man's land between the slave compound and the cane fields. He flattened himself in the long grass and listened. Hearing nothing more he moved into the field. At the end of the cane rows, he stowed the weapons in a cavity hollowed from the side of the irrigation ditch and hurried back. Halfway through the field, several men rushed from the cane stalks and jumped him. He landed face down in a furrow with someone's knee pressed hard against the small of his back. Others pinned his arms and legs.

"Are you spying on us, mate?"

"I'm minding my own business, that's what I'm doing." The knee dug deeper.

"If he reports us, our heads will be on spikes tomorrow."

"What now?"

"Kill the bastard. It's either us or him."

Blood pounded in Redferne's ears. "I'm Irish as you are. Why would I spy on my own countrymen?"

"Because you're a rotten tout. What's your name?"

"Redferne, Michael Redferne."

The knee snapped off his back. "Jesus, Mary, and Joseph."

Redferne staggered to his feet, brushing the dirt from his coat.

"Michael, it's me, Gleason."

Redferne swung and hit him in the mouth. "You fucking eejit, but I'm delighted to see you."

Gleason landed on his back and everyone laughed.

Gleason wiped the blood from his lip with the sleeve of his jacket. "Jaysus, I'm sorry Michael, but we thought you were one of Waldron's toadies. We're overjoyed it's you."

Redferne sat down in the furrow, trembling, his breath coming in great gasps. He looked up to see Kilbane, Noone, and MacTigh grinning down at him. "Sorry we had to meet again under such circumstances. When did you chaps arrive?"

"About two weeks ago," Gleason said, crawling over and sitting beside Redferne in the furrow.

"Arpeche still on the loose?"

"He nabbed all of us."

"Any word on Lawrence Craig?" Gleason shook his head.

Redferne turned toward Gleason. "What in hell are you doing out here in the middle of the night? Don't you know the consequences of being caught?"

"We can't take much more of this. We were scouting an escape route," Colin Noone said.

"So was I." Redferne stood up. "Follow me." He took a circuitous route back to the compound and entered Isaac's hut without knocking. "Look what the cat dragged in, Isaac."

Isaac's lips parted in a wide smile showing his missing tooth. "Gleason, Kilbane, Noone, and you with the funny name ah…?"

"MacTigh."

"Right, right. I shouldn't say it, but it's good to see you boys again." They pumped each other's hands. Redferne told Isaac about the incident in the cane field and although he tried, Isaac couldn't stop laughing. Everyone joined in except Gleason, whose lip had grown to the size of a small fish.

Isaac took a bottle of salve from his medicine box.

"It's a wondrous potion." Redferne said.

Isaac pointed to a burrow in the plantain roof and nodded at

Redferne. "While I'm working on Gleason, you get the other wonder drug. You'll find tin cups in the little cupboard."

Isaac's brew went down easily, and soon they were swapping stories and sharing their fears into the wee hours. Like Redferne and Isaac, the newcomers belonged to the great gang. They mulled over the ins and outs of escape but neither Isaac nor Redferne mentioned the arsenal. Redferne raised his cup for Lawrence Craig. "To a brave soul; may he rest in peace."

"Amen," they chanted.

Near morning, they returned to their huts to snatch a little sleep before the start of another brutal day.

Seamus Beirne

CHAPTER 35

Redferne got word from Padraig through a slave in the estate kitchens to meet him in the tack barn, a stone's throw from the Big House. Excitement stifled his fear when he set off after nightfall to rendezvous with his son whom he hadn't seen since that day in the cane field over a month ago. The wind rustled the fronds of the thatch palms, spraying the ground with seeds and desiccated fibers. The barn, a two-story red clapboard building with white trim, sat adjacent to a paddock with several white Arabian stallions. The Arabians whinnied and snorted, hanging their heads over the wall where Redferne cowered. His heart raced as he crept along the base of the wall and ran the remaining distance to the barn.

He inched the door open and crept inside. Moonlight streaming through a loft window glinted off the bridles and stirrups lining the walls. A wooden frame, crammed with saddles, collars, and horse blankets, ran down the center. On the right wall, a stairway ascended to a hayloft that extended halfway across the barn. He sat on the bottom step and waited, his pulse throbbing.

"Father! Up here."

His breath caught as he bounded up the creaking stairs. They wrapped their arms around each other. They did not speak for a while. Redferne ran his fingers through Padraig's hair and cried. "It's my fault, Son. I've brought misfortune to us all."

Padraig grabbed him by the shoulders and shook him. "It's not your fault. Blaming yourself won't help us now."

Padraig is right. This is no time to go soft. The loft held a haystack that nearly touched the roof. Pitchforks, rakes, and a broad-bladed hay knife leaned against the wall. They sat with their backs to the stack, facing a loft door used for pitching hay down to the stallions in the paddock. Redferne rose and opened the door to let in more light while Padraig retrieved a sack and a rope from beneath the hay.

Redferne looked at the rope and back at Padraig. "What's that for?"

"A quick escape route, if we need it." He nodded at the loft door.

Redferne's stomach tightened. "I pray it doesn't come to that. How long have you been on the Waldron spread, Son?"

Padraig laughed. "Fifteen months."

"And you're still alive. Amazing." He traced his fingers across Padraig's face.

"Wouldn't be if I remained with the 'little gang.' After arriving, I worked in the fields collecting cane trash to feed the boiler fires."

"Few survive being in that group. How did you manage it?"

"I scooped Waldron's young daughter from beneath the hooves of a runaway carthorse." Padraig opened the sack and took out a wicker basket with a cooked chicken, roasted potatoes, a loaf of bread, and a bottle of red wine. "Figured you could use a meal," he continued, taking two tin cups from his pocket.

Redferne's nose twitched and his eyes watered. He tore off a chicken leg and devoured it in two bites. Padraig poured him a mug of wine. "Ah. Pardon my manners, Son, but I haven't seen chicken since the one I poached from Preston's estate over two years ago." He slurped a mouthful of wine. "Your mother did a bang-up job on it too."

Padraig turned away. "How is Mother?"

Red paused with his mouth open, chicken grease and wine dribbling down his chin. He put the tin cup on the floor. "She was fine when I last saw her. I was hopping mad when she told me about you. We had another quarrel." An awkward silence followed.

Redferne looked at the remainder of the chicken. "Aren't you hungry?"

"No, Father. It's all for you. I already ate."

"You do look well fed, I'll grant you that. Waldron rewarded you then?"

"Assigned me to the kitchen staff. Worked my way up to assistant cook. Good food and inside work, except during cane-cutting season."

Redferne polished off the remainder of the meal and lay flat on the floor, his hand round the neck of the bottle, his feet sticking out the loft door, and his eyes staring at the stars. Orion sparkled like diamonds in the blackness. "Ever think about the stars, Son?"

"Do I ever look at them? Of course."

"No, I mean do you ever think of them? Beautiful, magnificent, so far away, free."

"Can't say I have."

"I do, especially since I landed in this cesspool."

He wrestled with the idea of telling Padraig about the escape plan, but held back. What Padraig didn't know couldn't be beaten out of him. He would tell him closer to the time.

Overhead, the wind riffled the thatch pines and, beneath his feet, the horses neighed and snorted.

"Give me your hand, Son. Who knows if...."

"Father, don't talk like that." Padraig lay down beside him and extended his hand. They talked some more. The stallions stamped their feet.

"Do you smell that?" a voice in the paddock said.

"Smell what?"

"Chicken."

"Too far from the Big House for that, but damned if you're not right, it's chicken sure enough."

"The loft door is open. Shouldn't be—Amos closes it every night."

"Let's go check."

"Perimeter guards," Padraig whispered.

Redferne grabbed the rope and handed a pitchfork to Padraig. "What are they doing in the paddock?"

"Horses have gone missing."

"Jesus! Why didn't you mention that?" Redferne knotted one

end of the rope around a wooden wall support. "They've got to walk in single file between the haystack and railing to get to us. I'll take the first one. You handle the second."

"Should we light a torch?" a guard said.

"And burn the fucking place down?"

Rapiers hissed from scabbards. Footsteps pounded up the stairs. Padraig's hot breath brushed Redferne's neck.

The footsteps stopped when they reached the top of the stairs. "Don't walk too close behind me."

"Probably one of ours, screwing a slave wench. Long gone, I bet."

"He's got the hay for it." They laughed. The footsteps resumed.

Redferne sprang as the guard passed the end of the stack, looping the rope around his neck and pulling him to the floor.

The second dropped his rapier and fled. Padraig took aim with the pitchfork. Redferne tightened the rope but he was unable to stop the man from rising and grappling with him. Feeling he was losing the battle, he grabbed the man around the waist and jumped out the loft door. When the rope caught, they were jerked upward. The guard screamed. Still clinging to the writhing body, Redferne turned his gaze from the purple face and swollen tongue. He released his grip and dropped to the ground, startling the Arabians that galloped around the paddock, their tails aloft.

Redferne cleared the paddock wall and ran to the front of the barn. He found Padraig standing over the second guard thrashing on the ground beyond the tack house door with the pitchfork sticking from his back. Padraig seemed mesmerized about what to do next.

"Father, he recognized me."

"What?"

"He called me Master Padraig."

"Get back inside the barn... go on, hurry."

Redferne pulled the pitchfork from the guard's back and raised it. The wind moaned in the thatch palms, sending a fresh spray of seeds and fibers to the ground.

When the guard stopped writhing, Redferne cast the pitchfork aside and ran to the barn door. "Padraig, we must be away. It'll be light in an hour." They circled back to the paddock. The body of the first guard bumped against the barn with every gust of wind.

"Don't look," Redferne said.

"For Christ's sake, I just killed a man." Redferne stared at him. "There'll be hell to pay come sunup. We need a plan."

"Release the Arabians. They'll think it's rustlers."

Seamus Beirne

CHAPTER 36

Redferne wanted to hold a meeting, but since the tack barn killings, patrols made sporadic incursions into the compound, making it risky to congregate in their cabins at night. The incursions seemed more from caution than suspicion that slaves were involved. As Padraig predicted, Waldron believed horse thieves killed the men. Blame fell on the stockade guards, some of whom, rumor had it, took bribes.

"Of all the rotten luck," Isaac said. "We've lost the only bit of privacy we had."

"Won't keep the patrols up forever, will they?" Redferne sat in Isaac's cabin, sampling his new rum concoction.

Isaac stopped his pacing and looked at Redferne. "Might do. At least long enough to frustrate our plans."

"What about meeting outside, walking around?"

"When is the last time you saw a black man and five white guys going for a stroll?"

Redferne took another sip. "This is good stuff."

Isaac dropped to his hunkers, picked up a rush from the floor and chewed on the end. "Maybe 'outside' is not such a hare-brained idea after all." He removed the rush from his mouth and spat the sap out the door.

Redferne raised his tin mug. "Drink to that."

"Next week is the start of spring planting."

Redferne scratched his chin. "What?"

"Never was much interested myself, 'cause I didn't want to stay around long enough to reap the fruits of my labor," Isaac said.

Redferne squinted. "I'm lost."

"Next Sunday you're going to help me plant my garden. Bring your friends."

The following Sunday Redferne woke to a hubbub of excited chatter. He stuck his head out the door. All around the compound people were digging and planting behind their cabins. He rounded up the *Kate O'Dwyer* men and headed for Isaac's cabin. Little bags of seeds covered Isaac's table and a large earthen jar sat in one corner.

"Forgot to tell you lads. One of the bright spots in a slave's life is his vegetable garden."

"They allow us to sow vegetables?" MacTigh's sunken eyes came to life. Isaac took up one of the bags. "Waldron figures it's a source of free food so he encourages it. He even provides the seeds."

"So now we're working on our only day off," Roan Kilbane said, brushing back his unruly brown curls. Always quick with a smile and a joke, Kilbane wasn't smiling anymore. He had a rasping cough that turned heads.

"Here," Isaac said, stirring a pinch of cloves and cinnamon into a mug of hot water which he handed to Kilbane. "By tomorrow you'll feel better." Then he led them outside. "Grab a spade and start digging."

The little gardens were alive with people laughing and singing as they turned the soil. Anyone who owned a colored shirt or a fancy dress had it on, so that blues, reds, and greens bobbed and weaved to the rhythm of moving bodies.

"Why are we doing this?" Gleason drove his spade into the sandy soil.

Redferne broke a turned-up sod with a hoe. "If they see the same people congregating on a regular basis inside their cabins, they may get suspicious."

"Not much to be suspicious of at this point, is there?" Gleason added.

Redferne studied Gleason as he spoke. His face looked drawn

and haggard and he wielded the spade awkwardly. The once-robust young man showed signs of fatigue and despondency after two months on the plantation. He looked across at Noone who followed MacTigh, breaking up the turned earth with a spade. All of them had the same sad sense of surrender in their hollow eyes. "You're right, Gleason, from the outside there's not much to be suspicious about, but Isaac and I have been busy behind the scenes. We're planning a breakout." All except Isaac leaned on their tools and looked at Redferne.

"Guard on the right," Isaac said. They concentrated on their work again until the guard moved on.

"Now you see why we're holding this meeting outdoors," Isaac said.

Kilbane bent over to cough. "This is a meeting?"

"Pay attention," Isaac said, tracking the guard.

"Over the past month, Isaac and I have managed to steal some weapons."

"What kind?" Gleason whispered, straightening himself.

"Mostly machetes." Gleason leaned in and his eyes widened.

"The night you lads jumped me," Redferne said, "I was hiding weapons, not looking for an escape route."

"You sly old fox," Kilbane said, a glimmer of a smile on his cracked lips. As if on cue, everyone straightened up and looked around. The forest beyond the stockade seemed closer.

After an hour of digging and tilling, they had a twenty by twenty foot plot ready for planting. The morning echoed with the squeals of children and the shouts and laughter of other gardeners happily engaged in an activity that might forestall death a little longer.

"Time for a break," Isaac said. "Before we start planting, let's have a little refreshment."

"Now you're talking," Noone said, leaning his spade against the wall of Isaac's hut.

"Mac—whatever your name is—I need your help." Isaac beckoned MacTigh.

Seconds later, they came out of the hut. MacTigh carried an

assortment of tin cups in his arms, and Isaac lugged the earthenware jar, placing it on the grass verge at the head of the plot. They sat down around it and held out their cups to Isaac.

Gleason took a sip. His eyes lit up. "What's this?"

"It's a brew made from the sorrel plant. Popular with the natives. Add a little ginger, some cloves, and a generous dollop of Isaac's special rum concoction and you have the perfect drink for a hot day."

"We got company," Redferne said. Two barrel-chested mulatto guards, each wearing red bandannas and carrying muskets and whips, wove their way through the throng of gardeners. One stopped in front of Redferne.

"Say, seen you somewhere before, haven't I?"

"Can't say I remember you, Boss."

"Could swear," he said, peering at Redferne before moving on. The others looked away and concentrated on their sorrel. Moments later the guard was back.

He shook his finger at Redferne. "Came to me. A young lad up at the Big House is the spitting image of you."

Redferne got a sinking feeling in the pit of his stomach. Amazing, no one had ever seen a likeness between himself and Padraig before. "Wouldn't know, Boss. Never been up there and no desire to either."

"Hmmm." The guard stared at Redferne as he moved away.

"Looks like you've seen a ghost," Isaac said.

"Must be the heat and the sorrel." Redferne clasped his hands to disguise their trembling.

Gleason got up and sat beside him. "When's the breakout?"

"Don't get ahead of yourself, man. We're still in the preliminary stages."

Gleason looked crestfallen. "Surely you've some idea."

"Rough guess, I'd say two months."

"Christ, we could all be dead by then," MacTigh said, wiping his watery eyes.

"That's a distinct possibility, if we don't plan this carefully. We won't get a second shot."

Isaac threw the heel of his drink into the plot. "Okay. Let's get some planting done. We can talk as we work."

"What are we planting?" Kilbane asked.

"Cabbage, beets, sweet peppers, calabaza."

"All mixed together?"

"Don't worry," Isaac said. "We're not planning to harvest them," First, they shaped the loose soil into rows about two feet wide, and then Isaac gave each of them a bamboo stick and a bag of seeds.

"It's a simple process. Bore a hole with the bamboo, insert a few seeds, cover the hole, and you're done." As they worked, he circulated among them, whispering. "Mind what Redferne said. And another thing, don't talk about it to anyone outside this circle, unless you want your heads to ornament the main gate."

Redferne's hands grew clammy. He regretted having revealed their plan. How many Irish insurrections had failed because of loose lips?

"How'll we get over the stockade?" Gleason pressed. "It's patrolled by armed guards with dogs."

"Haven't worked out the details yet," Redferne said, as he and Gleason worked down parallel rows, making holes in the soil and dropping seeds in. Noone came on behind them and closed the holes.

When they finished planting, everyone returned to Isaac's hut. Gleason asked, "What can we do to help?"

"Leave it to Isaac and me. We'll let you know when we need your help."

"Right now, you need to leave. Don't want to arouse suspicion," Isaac said, his fingers twitching as he stole glances out the door. After a final drink of sorrel, Gleason and the others left, leaving Redferne and Isaac on their own.

Isaac went to the door and looked after them "We don't have two months," he said, turning to Redferne. "That is, if you want me along."

"What are you talking about? Without you, we'll die here."

"We have two weeks to pull this off, not two months."

"We'll never be…"

"There's a slave auction in Bridgetown two weeks from tomorrow. Unless Waldron changes his attitude about runaways, I'll be on the auction block."

"Jaysus Christ, Isaac, how long have you known this?"

"Waldron thinks recaptured slaves are a security risk. He sells them at the first opportunity."

Redferne staggered to his feet like a stunned boxer recovering from a knockdown. The plantain leaves on the roof rose and fell with the wind, creating a flapping noise. Isaac faced Redferne. "I'm sorry, my friend. One of the drawbacks to being a slave. We're on borrowed time."

"But time's running out."

Isaac held Redferne in a steady gaze. "Luck is as important as time, Irishman. You can't plan for that, so we'll use the time we have and hope for the best."

Isaac didn't need to prove his resolve. But what about the rest of them, including Redferne himself? He recalled the wizened heads over the main gates of those who had tried and failed. Each passing day eroded their strength and their will to survive.

Even if they got across the stockade, they needed Isaac to navigate the swamp. Without his help, they would be picked up by Arpeche. He ran his fingers through his long brown hair that had grown to his shoulders. Then he thought about Padraig and that settled his doubt.

Isaac broke into his ruminations. "Let's prioritize our preparations tonight and work on the most important item tomorrow."

"Which is?"

"Won't get far without blowguns. If we can't silence the dogs, we haven't a hope in hell of getting across the fence in one piece," Isaac said.

Redferne gripped one of the bamboo supports of the hut. "We could remove some of these from the walls and cut them to the desired lengths, but where do we find the curare?"

"In the swamp."

Redferne burst out laughing and threw up his hands. "For Christ's sake, Isaac. 'In the swamp' might as well be in Bridgetown."

"Logging crews leave the stockade once or twice a week to cut wood for the boilers. Might be able to persuade my friendly overseer to assign one of us to that detail."

Redferne returned to his own place after dark. His body grew cold when he thought about the guard seeing the resemblance between him and the lad in the Big House. Would he make the connection and question Padraig?

Seamus Beirne

CHAPTER 37

Next day, Redferne found himself at the sugar mill offloading cane stalks from horse carts to be fed into huge rollers and crushed, thus allowing the juice to run into the vats below. A sharp axe lay against each of the crushing machines. Debris from the stalks choked the air, making it dusty, stifling work. Following the example of other slaves, he tied a moist cotton rag around his mouth and nose. The grinding noise of the rollers, the lowing of the oxen that powered them, and the shouts of overseers and horse-cart drivers made it almost impossible to communicate.

Whether from the noise, the swirling dust haze, or the frenetic work pace, the guards let the slaves be for the most part. Redferne took advantage of the lax supervision and swapped places with another slave assigned to a wood-cutting detail set to depart for the forest.

Relieved to escape the dust and the noise of the mill, his pulse quickened when a guard opened a gate in the stockade, allowing the horse carts to pass through. If the security at the mill was lax, the forest was a different story. Guards with muskets and dogs lined the cart track into the trees, taking no chances with twenty slaves armed with axes on the edge of a trackless swamp.

He paid close attention to the position of the guards as the tree felling began. Some grew bored and inattentive as the morning wore on, especially as the heat and humidity increased. Some gathered in groups of two and three and chatted, leaving areas on the perimeter unguarded. He worked his way down to one of these exposed places.

While wielding his axe against a stout mahogany tree, he surveyed the adjacent trees for the large heart-shaped leaves of the curare vine.

By lunchtime he spotted what he was looking for dangling up near the canopy. Skilled climbers harvested the curare by scurrying up other vines that drooped almost to the ground, but he was not such a climber. If he could not reach the vine, maybe he could bring the vine to himself. After devouring his lunch of *loblolly*, which he had grown to detest, he took his axe and hacked at the hardwood tree from which the curare vine dangled.

Its trunk was round and smooth with most of its leaves close to the canopy and the light.

Someone shouted from behind. "Halt." The hiss of a cowhide whip seconds before it curled around his upper torso. Dropping the axe, he put his hands up to protect his face as a stocky mulatto guard with silver colored earrings and bloodshot eyes rushed him.

"You don't decide when to resume work, the overseer does." He raised his whip again. Before he could deliver another stroke, a blow from a musket barrel across the back of the head felled him.

"Damned fool! When a man wants to work, let him; better that than sitting on his lazy arse eating the plantation's rations." The overseer, wearing a black hat without a brim, had a jowly face and a protruding belly held back by a wide leather belt. He looked down at the driver crumbled in a ball at the base of tree. "Get him on his feet again," he called to the other guards. "And you, what are you waiting for?" he said, turning to Redferne. "Start knocking that tree, before I take the whip to you myself."

Redferne retrieved his axe, thinking that his savior had to be Isaac's contact. After half an hour of strenuous slogging, he called out "Timber."

The big hardwood swayed like a drunk before tumbling, setting off a series of snapping sounds like musket shots as it sheared the branches of adjacent trees on its plunge to earth. Plumes of dust and debris surged up, visible in the shaft of light that shone through the wound in the torn canopy. The giant shivered and trembled as it settled onto the forest floor in a final convulsion. A ruckus of birds and monkeys screeched and squawked in apparent protest at the destruction of their habitat.

Since it was the biggest tree felled that day, the overseer ordered the rest of the crew to set about sawing it into logs and told Redferne to clean it of parasitic plants and creepers.

He set about the task with gusto, furtively stuffing the heart-shaped leaves into his pockets. His excitement at finding the curare made him forget about the lacerations from the whipping, but it reminded him of the precarious existence he and his fellow slaves led. Death hovered over them like a wild animal ready to spring. One had to be nimble and quick-witted to stay ahead of this stalking beast, and all the more cunning because it was human.

He walked with a lighter step that evening following the procession of timber-laden carts down the forest path and through the stockade gate. Drivers urged on the draught horses that strained under heavy loads. The rattling of cartwheels and jingling of harness took him back to his ice-gathering trips in Ireland, ambling beside his own horse and cart, with Padraig sitting on the shaft guiding the horse down the lane toward the lake.

Startled by a thread snake, one of the draught horses reared and slammed the back of the cart with the logs protruding from its rear into the stockade, leaving a three-foot section of the fence listing at a forty-five degree angle toward the rain forest. Being the last cart in the convoy, only Redferne, the driver, and the mulatto overseer were aware of what had just happened. The other carts had already crested a rise on their way to the mill boilers.

The mulatto, a stout man with a broad face, lifted his cap and scratched his head. Redferne could see the guard's dilemma. If he stayed to raise the fence, he would be late getting to the mill which could result in severe punishment. If he abandoned the stockade with a three-foot hole, he might be shot. Seizing the opportunity, Redferne suggested, "We can right the fence using the horse and cart. No one will be any the wiser. It can be repaired permanently later." The mulatto looked at Redferne, and then back up the hill where black smoke poured from the chimneystacks, then back at the fence. Without saying a word, he stepped through the breach, put his shoulder to the inclined section of the fence and pushed. It moved a little.

"Okay," he shouted, "let's do it."

Redferne and the driver slung a rope over the pointed stakes and fastened the other end to the back of the cart. "Easy does it," Redferne said as the driver, anxious to make up for lost time, flicked a switch over the horse's rear quarters. The horse, still skittish from the snake, resisted and backed up again.

Redferne grabbed the reins. "Let me handle it." The driver seemed happy to be relieved.

"Steady there, boy, steady." He whispered and pursed his lips, making kissing sounds. He stroked the animal's forehead. The horse settled and moved forward again, slowly pulling the damaged stockade section back into place. That temporary fix, Redferne hoped, would allow for easy penetration later.

"Hold, hold," the mulatto yelled. "That should do for the time being. Uncouple the rope and let's get a move on."

They entered the mill yard without incident and dumped their load outside the boiler house, where a crew cut the logs into pieces small enough to fit into the ovens underneath the copper vats.

The boiler fires had to be tended 'round the clock to keep the vats at an even temperature so that the impurities could be strained off from the cane juice. When sugar crystals formed, they poured wet clay over the mixture. As it seeped through, it separated the crystals from the molasses. Prolonged exposure to heat and smoke weakened the slaves' immune systems. Many fell victim to pulmonary ailments and other diseases.

The fact that all this pain and suffering took place to put sugar on the tables of the rich and powerful astounded Redferne. Sugar, or "white gold" was creating a whole new class of wealthy merchants and landowners while enslaving and consuming the lives of thousands of the less fortunate. He had seen sugar back in Ireland in the Big House, but never tasted it until finding it in the smugglers' sack. He recalled Grace wetting her finger and dipping it into the sugar bowl, fantasizing about Barbados. If she only knew. Someone called his name.

"Redferne." He turned to see Isaac and another slave lifting a copper vat from the oven top and placing it on the ground. Isaac was bare to his midriff, his body glistening with sweat. "That's okay, my friend will take it from here," Isaac said to his helper, a frail Irishman who struggled to catch his breath.

"Thank the Lord, I'm roasting one minute and freezing my arse off the next running back and forth between here and the cool house," the helper said, and sidled off.

"I was worried at not seeing you this morning," Redferne said.

"My friend Kijana thought it might arouse suspicion if he moved both of us at the same time."

"How come supervision is so relaxed in here? Haven't seen a whip or a driver since arriving, or is that what the axes are for?"

Isaac made a sweeping gesture. "This is where sugar is made. Every step of the process requires people with special skills, from tending fires to separating sugar crystals from the molasses. Management doesn't harass the skilled workers as long as they keep producing. Sugar is money. This is why we are all here."

Redferne narrowed his eyes. "And the axes?"

"Workers sometimes get their limbs caught in the machinery."

Redferne felt dizzy and he bent over to stifle the urge to vomit. "Oh, God!"

"Yeah, sugar's sweet, but the production process is brutal."

Redferne straightened up and took several deep breaths. "How did you end up here in the first place?"

Isaac inclined his head toward the ovens. "After being bounced as a translator, I worked the fires. When Kijana pulled me from the cane fields this morning, he assigned me to my old position. It's hot dirty work, so I inveigled a swap with someone who tended the vats and was anxious to make a switch."

"I'd sure as hell like to bollocks this whole operation before we get out of here," Redferne said as anger welled up inside him.

"Let's concentrate on the second part of your statement. Here—

help me carry this vat before someone discovers that we're neither skilled nor eager to work, and sends us packing back to the fields."

"Where are we headed?"

"To the bagging house where the sugar crystals are cooled and bagged for transportation to the docks."

The bagging area, a big barn-like structure, sat about fifty feet from the boiler house. When they pushed through the double doors, a rush of voices hit them like an ocean wave. Scores of slaves, male and female, bustled about in clockwork precision. Some bagged sugar, others loaded bags onto drays lined up along a platform. The only whips in evidence were carried by carters. Draft horses stamped their feet as if impatient to get out of the stifling heat of the building and get on the road to the docks.

Housed within the bagging area was the cold room, a small building with walls three feet thick and a slate roof insulated with layers of thatch and cane trash. Isaac led the way toward that building, where they deposited the vat.

Redferne beat his arms against his sides. "Damn, I never thought I'd complain about the cold, but this feels like the ice house back home."

"According to Father Josefa, the blood adjusts to extremes of heat and cold after a certain amount of time. You're getting acclimatized to Barbados."

Redferne pulled several heart-shaped leaves from his pocket and thrust them at Isaac.

"I was about to ask." Isaac rubbed the leaves between his fingers, his eyes blazing with excitement. "Tonight I'll be brewing a kettle full of curare tea."

They worked the remainder of the afternoon shuttling back and forth from the boiler house to the cool house, until a blast from the quitting horn rang through the compound. As he and Isaac left the cool room, Redferne turned around and gazed at the operation that had enough sugar to ransom a king.

CHAPTER 38

It sat in the sky like a big, black coiled boa, all day long. Flashes of red, blue, and yellow emanated from its dark heart as it swelled in size. The old-timers recognized it for what it was, an incubating monster of wind and rain that would unleash a maelstrom of destruction. The first drops landed with a heavy plop on the cane stalk leaves. Redferne crept between the huts of the compound toward the Big House with a sack of bamboo staves slung over his shoulder.

The Africans thought he was on a suicide mission. The words "Big House" caused them to cower in terror. Not so for the Irish, who spent a good part of their lives jousting with that establishment, albeit often unsuccessfully. Since their status was not quite as abject in their own country as it was in Barbados, the Big House held less of a psychological grip on their imaginations. For this reason when Redferne suggested going to the Big House to pick up a tool to smooth the bore of the bamboo staves, Isaac adamantly refused.

He waved his hands before his face as if warding off a swarm of bees. "Not me, mon. This is something you'll have to do on your own."

"If the bamboo staves aren't bored properly, our most important weapon could fail us—you know what that could mean."

"I also know what it means to be caught even within eyesight of that place. Not just a whipping. Crucifixion. I've seen a man spread-eagled in the cane field with stakes driven through his hands and feet, left to die under the burning sun for attempting what you are suggesting."

It was useless arguing, so Redferne set off on his own, picking this particular night because of the sky and the old-timers' prediction of a massive storm.

"Only a crazy person or a ghost would be caught out tonight. That a devil storm a' comin'," a wizened old man with a solitary tooth in the front of his mouth cautioned.

That's the point, Redferne thought. Given the history of these hurricanes, it was a safe bet that few would venture out. If he did encounter someone, he was ready for a confrontation, while his adversary would be caught unawares. The wind picked up and the fronds of the thatch palms streamed at crazy angles like shirts tugging on a line.

Then the rain came. Sheets of it. The howl of the wind intensified to nothing Redferne had ever heard before. The din grew deafening. Branches of trees, uprooted cane stalks, sea weed, and lumps of dirt filled the air, reducing visibility to almost zero. He struggled to keep his balance as the old man's words echoed in his ears. "There's a devil storm a comin'."

Pushing forward, he moved from one tree to another, seeking shelter. The whole plantation appeared airborne, as shed doors, farm implements, and wooden barrels joined the maelstrom.

He hadn't been candid with Isaac. He wasn't going all the way to Waldron's mansion, but to the boiler house to meet Padraig. The ferocity of the storm surprised him. The shape of the large structure loomed before him. He ran toward it. A red glow from the boiler fires shone intermittently as the wind whiplashed the heavy door open and shut, repeatedly, as if flipping the pages of a book. Timing his leap during the brief interval of light, he dove through the opening. The door slammed against the soles of his feet, sending him sprawling across the dirt floor.

He landed in an arc of light cast by one of the fires. Scrambling to escape the searing heat, he spied two figures standing in the shadows. Padraig was supposed to come on his own. Who was the stranger? The sugar mill and all its supporting buildings were off-limits to slaves after work hours.

"I'm seeking refuge from the storm," he shouted, hoping it would provide cover for his presence in the boiler house after hours.

"Father, it's me." Padraig stepped out of the shadows. Redferne gripped his son in a bear hug while gazing over his shoulder at the other figure beyond the light.

He whispered into Padraig's ear. "Who's with you?"

"I'll let my friend speak for himself," Padraig said. The figure in the shadows moved into the light.

Redferne clasped the sides of his head when he saw the pinched face. "Oh, my God! Lawrence Craig! We thought you were a goner, man." Redferne grabbed Craig's hand in both of his and pumped it with ferocious delight. Craig's face had filled out a little, his hair was shorter, but he still had a worried look.

"Thanks to you, I made it to shore but my barrel drifted into the harbor. I was hoisted out of the water by sailors from an English man o' war."

"Of all the rotten luck," Redferne said.

"I tried to lie my way out of it, but when the *Kate O'Dwyer* docked, I was returned to Captain Tolliver's custody," Craig said.

"Walked the beach for hours looking for you."

"Unfortunately, by that time, I was under lock and key in the hold of the *O'Dwyer*. Early next morning they had me on the auction block, and by noon the Waldron brand decorated my buttocks. One piece of good luck. I was out of Tolliver's custody before he discovered his gutted cargo." The two of them bent over laughing as they related the story to Padraig. Padraig looked stunned.

"Lucky for you Waldron needed a blacksmith, right?" Redferne said.

"They assigned me to the fourth gang with all the skilled workers, but I find no joy in making shackles for my own countrymen."

Redferne clapped him on the shoulder. "No, but now you can help liberate them, for the second time, I hope."

Craig pulled a long iron rod from under his coat. "This should solve our problem once it's heated to the right temperature." He inserted it into the glowing heart of the fire. Redferne pulled Padraig aside. "Did anyone comment that you looked like a field slave?"

"A guard, but I brushed it off with a bawdy joke."

"Quick thinking."

A clap of thunder sounding like the arch of heaven foundering shook the structure. Shingles peeled off the roof as wind and rain congealed into a mighty fist pummeling the boiler house.

"Quick," Redferne shouted above the maelstrom. He unshouldered the canvas sack and scattered the bamboo staves on the floor. "We better get this done before the building disintegrates." Craig and Padraig gazed upward at the flashes of blue and white forked lightning visible through large holes that had opened in the roof. Redferne grabbed the red-hot poker from the fire and ran it through the bamboo staves from both ends, burning away the obstructions at the joints. Craig and Padraig closed the door, but the rain cascaded through the roof. Loose wooden shingles rained down like leaves.

"Hurry, Padraig, gather the bamboo into the sack. Time to go!" Redferne wrapped the tail of his coat around the cool end of the hot poker, and ran toward a hole in the side of the building. They barely made it out before a deafening crash rocked the building. Rafters cascaded down on the boilers, overturning vats and emptying the contents across the dirt floor. Tropical rain peppered the spilled molasses like birdshot, sending plumes of steam hissing from the hot liquid. Across the compound sat the bagging house, a skeleton of its former self, except for the cold house that sat intact in one corner of the ruined building.

Redferne pointed at the stocky structure. "That's our best bet."

They ran to the cooling room door, dodging flying debris. Redferne felt around for the bolt and pulled it back, but it wouldn't budge.

"Damn," he swore as his fingers closed around a heavy padlock. "I should've known. This is the money house." They tried their shoulders against the door but it wouldn't move.

"It's like a bloody bank vault," Craig shouted.

"That's exactly what it is. After all, it contains gold. White gold."

They selected a fallen roof beam from the debris and rammed the door, knocking it off its hinges on the third try. Once inside they stood it back up and stacked sacks of sugar against it to prevent the wind from blowing it in. "We'll be safe here as long as the roof holds out," Redferne said. "That's the Achilles heel."

Craig pointed to the ceiling. "It's a slate roof well fastened to the rafters with three-inch nails. I helped the roofer repair it about a month ago. It's solid enough to support the weight of a draft horse."

"If the wind gets underneath it," Redferne said, "it'll rip it off like a dog tearing the last piece of meat from a bone." Though the hurricane winds blew warm, the cooling room felt chilly, so they huddled together. Redferne's heart sank. "This storm will tear the slave dwellings to shreds. No one will survive this."

Craig shook his head. "Not true."

"How is that possible?"

"During hurricane season, the slaves are allowed to shelter in the more stalwart buildings on the plantation. Waldron doesn't want to lose his work force. It would be more crippling than the loss of one season's sugar crop."

"Fine and good if people can make it to those buildings." Redferne had a worried look on his face.

"There's a backup system. Each of the huts is supposed to have a survival trench about six feet deep in or near it where several people can wait out the storm. It's covered over with a hatch made from tree branches lashed together. On top of that is a thick layer of clay under heavy rocks. A shallow tunnel provides access."

The wind and rain boomed through the outer building, but toward three o'clock, the storm began to abate. By then, Redferne and the others sloshed around in a foot of water that had seeped in under the door.

Redferne looked at Craig. "You've made several voyages to this island and are familiar with hurricanes, right?"

An uncomfortable look molded Craig's face. "Somewhat."

"What's the typical fallout from a hurricane?"

Craig massaged his chin and neck, looking off to one side. "Crops, people, and buildings are destroyed. Can be a grave economic loss for the plantation owner."

"How serious is the human loss?" Redferne's eyes bored into Craig.

"Not as bad as you might think, because of the shelters I mentioned."

"And the security situation?"

"That's a horse of a different color. Security in the aftermath tends to be erratic."

"Which means the best time for a breakout would be tomorrow while they're trying to dig out," Redferne said. Water in the cool room now reached their knees, swamping the sugar bags on the floor, but none of them paid any attention.

"Yes and no. After hurricanes, there's a policy of shoot first and ask questions later."

"Damn, so they'll be out in force tomorrow."

"Dogs, guns, the lot, but they'll be distracted depending on how severely the plantation has been hit."

By morning the storm had cleared and the water gorged with sugar smelled sweet. They pushed the soggy bags away from the door and stepped into a scene of total devastation. Nothing but the frame of the bagging house remained. They waded through a lake of liquid sugar. Large dray carts lay flipped over on their sides. Empty sacks floated on the sugar slush like bandages on a large molten sore. This year's sugar crop was gone. Redferne shuddered to think what might happen to the slaves if Waldron took out his frustration on them.

They made their way back to the slave compound amongst knots of people who staggered out of the stonewalled storage sheds. Some rose from holes in the earth like it was Resurrection Day. Others were not as lucky. Hands and feet protruded from piles of rubble, a grim end to a nightmarish existence. He scanned the faces of survivors, looking for Isaac and his other mates. As he did so, he realized what a miracle it was that anyone at all had survived.

He found Isaac near the spot where their huts once stood, observing the chaos. They embraced in silence.

"Meet my son Padraig," Redferne said. "And this here is Lawrence Craig." Isaac nodded, opening his eyes wide. He scrutinized Redferne.

"I suppose you'll eventually tell me how the boy came to be here."

"It's a long story. Right now we best focus our energies on the task at hand. We have a dozen clean-bore bamboo staves, thanks to their efforts," He gestured toward Craig and Padraig.

"When you left the compound last night, I thought you were walking to your funeral, but I was wrong, Irishman. Now I best brew me a mess of curare paste. Maybe your son would like to help me?"

"Have you seen Gleason and the others?" Isaac slowly shook his head.

"Right, then Craig and I will start looking."

A shadow flitted across Isaac's face.

Seamus Beirne

CHAPTER 39

Redferne and Craig came across a burial detail digging a mass grave in a depression at the edge of the slave compound for the bodies of twenty people--young, old, black, and white. These unfortunates had failed to reach the safety of the sheds in time, or neglected to excavate a survival trench beside their huts. In the life and death game of musical chairs that followed, they were caught out in the open.

Redferne jumped into the grave and clawed the cane trash from the faces of the dead.

"Hey, Redferne up here."

Gleason stood on the lip of the trench with a spade in his hand, his mates beside him.

Redferne looked up. "Praise be to God."

They pulled him from the trench and covered the corpses with clay. Relatives and friends looked on and when the grave was filled, they shuffled away. Some sobbed but, for the most part, few shed tears. Many envied the dead. At least their suffering was over.

After the burial, the Irish gravediggers had a joyous reunion with Redferne and Craig.

"It looks like the storm taketh and the storm giveth back," Gleason said, as he and his friends crowded around Craig, slapping him on the back as if his resurrection reassured them that in the midst of destruction, miracles could happen. When Redferne broached the news about a breakout that night, hesitation and uncertainty replaced their buoyant spirits.

259

Gleason scratched his stubbly chin. "Tonight! Do we even have a plan yet?"

"It may be the best chance we're ever likely to get," Redferne said as they rejoined Isaac and Padraig near the ruins of Isaac's hut. "Things are chaotic right now, but chaos could be our friend. They are more likely to get full security back up and running with every passing day. That would not be good for us."

"So we hit them while they are weak."

"Where they are weakest," Redferne said.

"After we break out, then what?" Kilbane asked.

"We'll have to figure that out on the run."

Isaac huddled over a small fire. A black pot hung from a tripod. The contents bubbled, and a skin of white froth formed on the surface.

"I'm a little nervous out here in the open, so the rest of you start building a shelter around me." Isaac stirred the curare juice with a broken wooden spoon. Redferne crouched beside him, picking up a stick and doodling in the dirt.

"The boys are anxious about the breakout and frankly, so am I." He didn't look directly at Isaac, not wanting to put him on the spot.

"So you should be. The odds of us making it are fifty-fifty, at best." He lifted the curare pot off the fire and put it aside to cool. "It'll take about two hours for this to solidify." A hut took shape around them. Gleason and his mates put the finishing touches to it by braiding plantain leaves onto a wooden frame of bamboo staves to form a crude roof.

"We'll need better odds than that if we hope to persuade Gleason and the others to jump so soon."

"So, what do you propose doing? Lie to them?"

"I don't want to deceive them, but I don't want to paint such a grim picture that they end up thinking this is a suicide mission."

"I wouldn't characterize it as that, but they need to be aware that once we cross that stockade there is no turning back."

"These are the same men who jumped into the ocean in the middle of the night with only a wooden barrel to assist them. They're not faint-hearted," Redferne said.

Isaac rose from his cross-legged position on the floor. "Now that that's settled, let's call 'em in and determine our next move."

A nervous spasm shot through Redferne's stomach. Beyond a skeleton plan, nothing had been thought through and they were supposed to leave tonight.

He called the others. When they positioned themselves around the walls of the hut, he was upbeat. Pulling the canvas sack toward him, he emptied the bamboo staves onto the floor.

"These are blowguns which we'll use to take out the dogs." He held up one of the bamboo shoots to be used as arrows that he and Padraig had gathered. "Once treated with curare, this packs enough wallop to bring down a cow."

"What about the man leading the dog? Gleason asked.

"One of us takes out the dog. Another the handler. All done in silence, hopefully."

"After that?" Noone asked, folding his arms.

"Then we head toward the damaged section of fence I mentioned before. They never repaired it properly, so a few of us should be able to push it over without too much trouble." Redferne looked expectantly at Isaac, who was fitting fletches made from feathers into notches on the ends of the bamboo shoots.

"If we breach the stockade by ten o'clock, that puts us ahead of the rising moon by about thirty minutes," Isaac said without lifting his head. He tightened a length of hemp around the notched end of the arrow and bit off the excess, spitting it out onto the floor. "Once outside the fence, we will head for the logging trail that takes us to the edge of the swamp."

A surge of excitement outside caused him to pause. "Dogs! Quick," he shouted, throwing armfuls of cane trash over the curare pot and the blowguns. "Disappear." The group fled, mingling with other inhabitants who wandered around foraging for food or searching for their meager possessions among the ruins. Thinking that theirs was the only reconstructed hut in the slave quarters, Redferne feared they might be discovered, but to his relief at least a dozen others had been rebuilt. A group of armed men with bloodhounds approached.

"Everyone on your feet and line up." The mulatto drivers urged the stragglers with cowhide whips. The injured, the sick, and the old were whipped into compliance until a ragged line of broken human beings stood amidst the debris. Two overseers carrying notebooks started at opposite ends of the line.

When they met in the center they tallied their figures.

"Fifty unaccounted for," one of the tallymen said to a portly gentleman wearing a green silk jacket and matching breeches tucked into a pair of riding boots.

Waldron!

He carried a riding crop in his right hand. His left was suspended in a sling.

Redferne's breathing came quick and shallow. Was Padraig in the lineup? Would Waldron recognize him? He looked up and down the jagged line. Padraig was about thirty feet away, looking better fed and clothed than his fellows. He thought the vein in his temple would burst. If Padraig did not come up with a plausible answer for being here, they would whip the truth out of him.

Waldron moved down the line, stopping to study the faces of the human wreckage standing listlessly before him. When he got to Isaac, he stopped and smiled. "Humph, Isaac, it seems nothing can kill you, not even the avenging hand of an angry God."

Isaac stood stock-still and did not raise his eyes.

"Get over there and stand with them," Waldron ordered, gesturing to a group huddled off to one side.

"Can't have men like Isaac on the loose, can we? Your kind stirs things up." A spiteful grin creased his face. Redferne's knees quaked when he realized that his friend was being removed from circulation, but his concern for Isaac evaporated when Waldron stopped in front of Padraig.

"Well, well, young sir, what are you doing among this rabble?" Waldron's face turned purple. "Is this is how you reward my kindness for removing you from these wretches, by seeking common cause with them?" He struck Padraig across the face with his riding crop. "Put him with the others!" He gestured toward the group where Isaac stood. "Let's see how you fare living the life you were destined for, you ungrateful whelp."

Redferne looked down when Waldron approached. The portly plantation owner passed by without even looking in his direction while Padraig and Isaac were marched off under armed guard. Barring a miracle, there would be no breakout tonight.

Seamus Beirne

CHAPTER 40

Lawrence Craig poked his head through a pile of sugar cane trash. Seeing the coast clear, he crawled out on all fours into the sunlight. No sense elevating his profile until he felt certain that the danger had passed. After fleeing Redferne's hut, he hid in the storm debris, knowing that if he were caught in the common slave quarters, his excuses for being there would be deemed seditious. His skill as a blacksmith put him in a privileged class whose treatment and living conditions were better than the regular farm slave. Had he been discovered among the lower-class slaves, his privileges would have been revoked or worse. That he had judged correctly was proven by the treatment meted out to Redferne's son.

He had to get back to his quarters undetected, which posed considerable risk since they were located close to the Big House. He moved from one blasted tree stump to another, ankle deep in rubble, until he reached the remains of the boiler house. One thing was beyond dispute—Waldron's operation was a goner, which would put him in a foul mood. He would likely take it out on his subjects.

He reached the security of his hut unchallenged, but his sense of relief was replaced by burning agitation. During the meeting in Redferne's hut, he had briefly tasted freedom and then it was wrenched from him. He smelled the open sea and its promise of liberation. Now the stomach-turning smell was that of decaying animals. Somewhere in this compound, Isaac, the one man who could resuscitate the dream of freedom, was being held captive. Without him, Redferne's plan was as dead as the occupants of the mass graves.

His status as a blacksmith allowed him to wander around the environs of the Big House without attracting attention, so he set off, determined to find Isaac and Padraig. He had walked but a few yards when an overseer yelled at him. "Report to the blacksmith's shop. They've been looking all over for you. Better come up with a story for your absence."

Before he got to the forge door, the familiar whiff of singed horse hoof assailed him. He went in to find the other blacksmith, Jack Gordon, shoeing a black mare.

"The boss has been lookin' fer ye, laddie." Gordon, a craggy-looking elder Scotsman with a thick neck and bulging arms, glanced around before continuing. "Ye best have a good excuse or you might be in for a whipping."

"I went down to check the boilers in the sugar mill. It's a mess down there."

"Whatever ye say, mate." He clipped a protruding nail point from the hoof.

"Why is he so all fired up about shoeing horses with the whole bloody place tumbling down around our ears?"

"Not horses he's worried about lad, but a breakout. He wants the likely culprits clapped in irons."

Craig's heart skipped a beat. Extra security would be laid on in the coming days, making an escape more problematic, but it might give him access to Isaac and Padraig. Right now he needed to find Isaac. He didn't have to wait long.

A commotion outside the forge signaled the arrival of a knot of slaves escorted by armed security. As the group trudged through the double doors, Craig tightened his face muscles to conceal a smile on seeing Isaac and Padraig. The overseer, a burly, bleary-eyed man in his forties, looked at Gordon. "Turn that horse loose. Mr. Waldron wants this scum ironed up!" He pointed to the huddled captives with the point of his whip. He approached Craig, slapping the whip's braided handle against his riding boot. When he raised it, Craig backed away, lifting his arm to cover his face.

"You've been missing for two hours?"

"Been checking the boilers, down at the mill. Knew Mr. Waldron would want a report as soon as possible."

At the mention of Waldron the overseer backed off.

"What are you waiting for then? Get over there and help Gordon." He booted Craig in the rear.

It took Craig and Gordon awhile to complete the job, despite the fact that in several cases, they used irons already on hand. The emaciated condition of many captives, however, required that their leg irons be heated and reworked. In all cases, they made the irons loose enough that with the aid of a lubricant like lard or butter, the prisoners could slip their bonds.

Seamus Beirne

CHAPTER 41

The moaning and weeping in the makeshift slave huts tapered off sometime after twelve. Earlier, Gleason and his mates retired to their quarters, defeat etched on their tired faces. More from frustration than resolve, Redferne spent the hours after sundown finishing the job Isaac started on the arrows. By midnight, he had nearly two dozen fletched and tipped with poison.

He almost jabbed himself several times with the poisoned tips after consuming a bottle of moonshine. He needed something to numb his fear and disappointment. His rage simmered to a boil as he lay in the dark listening. Even Nature was against the dispossessed. The hurricane had killed thirty slaves while sparing the privileged.

As his eyes adjusted to the darkness, he spotted the promised blue moon through a hole in the hastily constructed roof, hiding behind storm clouds that hung around longer than expected. On the edge of sleep, he sat bolt upright and foraged in the cane trash for his machete. Something agitated the green monkeys. He peered through a chink in the hut walls. Several shadowy figures carrying muskets with dogs in tow approached the compound.

He sneaked outside to reconnoiter. Dodging from one hut to the next, he reached the perimeter where he discovered Waldron's men not only patrolling the palisade, but surrounding the slave quarters as well. Whatever dim hope of escape he might have harbored died. The window had now slammed shut. Waldron acted more quickly and with more thoroughness than expected.

He crept back to his hut and lay down, unable to sleep. Then it hit him. Padraig must have broken under torture and the guards were here to round up the conspirators.

After freeing themselves from their shackles with lard Craig had provided, Isaac, Padraig, and the others broke out of the prison shed and dashed across open ground to the shelter of a cane field that had been spared by the hurricane. The stalks stood over six feet high and seemed to extend across the terrain forever. Craig awaited them there, but the look on his face told Isaac that something was wrong.

"Too late to be afraid now," Isaac said, thinking the blacksmith had gotten cold feet.

"We've a new problem."

"What, mon? Speak up."

"A second patrol with dogs has surrounded the slave quarters."

"Shit," Isaac said. "Are you sure of that?"

"Heard it from Gordon. He's well-connected."

Isaac shivered as a ghost wind rustled the cane stalks, making a sound like a thousand dried bones jostling each other.

"Getting through the palisade would be a challenge. Penetrating the cordon around the compound? Impossible," Isaac said. He couldn't see his companions' faces, but he felt their disappointment in the heavy silence.

"Why not bypass the slave compound altogether?" Padraig said. "Can't we get to the breached palisade by another route?"

"Only if we are willing to leave your father and the blowguns behind," Isaac answered in a tone insinuating the inanity of that suggestion.

"How about a diversion that would send the compound guards running back to the Big House?" Padraig said.

Isaac looked toward the voice in the darkness. "Go on."

"With guards on the palisade and around the slave quarters, the

Big House is lightly guarded, if at all, I'll bet."

"Which would leave it vulnerable to penetration," Craig said.

At first Isaac felt uneasy, given his fear of approaching the Big House. Seeing how desperate the situation was, however, he heard Padraig out.

"Craig and I know the layout of the Big House compound and I know a place to start some mischief."

Seamus Beirne

CHAPTER 42

A massive explosion wakened Redferne, followed by the high-pitched yelping of dogs and shouting guards. He poked his head out of the hut. A bright orange column of fire seared the darkness in the vicinity of the Big House.

As the guards rushed from the compound, he dug out the blowpipes from their hiding place. His gut told him that this was not some random accident on the heels of the hurricane. He sensed the hand of Isaac, although he was hard put to figure out how. The compound grew deathly still, but the commotion from dogs over by the swamp told him that all the guards hadn't left.

The compound came alive with voices as people rushed outside. When they saw the fire, a cheer went up.

"Hope the fucker burns to the ground," someone yelled.

"And everyone in it."

"Might be a good time to make a break," another excited voice shouted, and the crowd took up the chant. Tension gnawed at Redferne's innards. A stampede toward the stockade might pull the guards back into the compound, jeopardizing his plan. He joined the throng to gauge the temper of the escape talk. To his great relief it was more bravado than anything else. Few had the stomach to attack the palisade and wade into the swamp in the middle of the night.

"Ain't nowheres to run," A grizzled African said. "Water's up in the swamp after a hurricane. Wouldn't survive the night out there."

"Don't fancy having my throat cut by no damn savage, neither," another added.

"You'd rather have the savages in here do it for you, huh?" someone joked, bringing a round of laughter.

A roar went up from the crowd. People pointed. Redferne looked in the direction of the pointed fingers. The column of fire had turned into a raging inferno accompanied by a deep rumble and a massive explosion of sparks into the night sky.

"Maybe our luck has turned," Gleason whispered into Isaac's ear, his face lit up like a child expecting a new puppy.

"Can't leave without Padraig and Isaac," Redferne snapped. A disturbance at the edge of the crowd. The knot of jostling people separated, as Isaac, Padraig, Craig, and others came running up. He released a deep breath and gave Padraig a quick embrace.

"My head told me it was impossible, but when I saw the flames, my gut said you were behind it," he said to Isaac.

"I'm afraid this is one time your gut was off. Thank Craig for springing us and your son for starting the fire," Isaac said.

"Fine lad you are." Gleason clapped Padraig on the shoulder.

"A chip off the old block, I'd say," Isaac joined in, giving Redferne an approving look.

"You're responsible for that?" Redferne gestured toward the fire, pride and astonishment evident in his voice. Padraig looked away.

"I did more than wait on tables and trim candle wicks while working for Waldron. As footman to the Lord of the Manor, I had the run of the house."

"Sounds like you ran your nose into areas where it didn't belong, God love you," Redferne chuckled.

"I discovered the hiding place for the key to the gun powder magazine. So you can guess the rest."

Redferne wanted to know all the details but there was no time. They had to leave before this window of opportunity closed. It wouldn't be long until the captives were missed and Waldron connected their disappearance with the explosion. If they were caught now, executions would quickly follow.

They crowded around Redferne's hut after retrieving the weapons from the secret cache. Altogether there were twenty of them, twelve

Irish and eight Africans, all armed with machetes. The group had grown, which was a good thing in case they had to fight pursuers or deal with Arpeche. In addition to the machetes, Padraig and Craig had snagged a pair of horse pistols and several Brown Bess muskets before blowing the powder magazine.

Redferne spoke. "Isaac, a quick lesson on blowguns."

"It's going to be brief, because we must move." Isaac took a bamboo stave and inserted an arrow. "The main thing is not to scratch yourselves with the tip."

"How do we carry them?" MacTigh asked.

"We've made straw quivers which hold six arrows."

Isaac pointed the bamboo stave at the roof, blowing into it with an explosive puff of breath. The arrow embedded itself in the thatch.

Redferne continued with the briefing. "I'll get you to the weakened section of the palisade. Once there, we pick off the dogs and the guards closest to the exit point. They're stationed about fifty yards apart. If they're not dossing about, they move toward each other and then reverse, repeating the pattern throughout the night. We hit them when they're farthest apart. Outside the fence, Isaac takes over." Redferne paused and scanned the faces of the group. "That's it. Any questions?" Silence. "Good luck to us all."

They tucked the machetes inside their jackets and slipped out of the hut a few at a time. Nobody paid them any attention as those still outdoors stood transfixed, watching the inferno that engulfed the Big House. Ash floated down onto the roofs of the huts like black snow. Beyond the compound, they assembled at a prearranged spot in a cane field. Redferne took his son by the arm. "Stay close to me."

"Right, Father." Padraig handed him a horse pistol.

"Okay, let's go." They moved along the furrows between the cane rows in single file. Redferne raised his hand when they sighted the palisade.

Hunkering down at the edge of the field, they watched the guards, calculating how long it took for each of them to reach the midpoint of their patrol.

"We only need to take out two of them," Redferne whispered, "Right, Isaac?"

Isaac exhaled deeply. "All we'll have time for. Look up there." He pointed to a corona of light around the edges of a dark cloud. "Five minutes from now the moon will clear that cloud. It'll be like daylight around here."

One of the dogs growled and tugged its master toward the field.

"Quick," Isaac said, "Let's silence that brute or he'll bring the lot of them down on top of us."

Redferne followed Isaac on all fours through the tall grass.

"I'll take the guard. You take care of the dog," Isaac whispered, readying his blowpipe. Redferne did likewise and moved to a position beside him.

"You smell something out there, boy?" The guard pulled his pistol and moved to within ten feet of Redferne and Isaac. Isaac rose up out of the long grass and spat through his blowpipe, hitting the guard before he could raise his pistol. As the guard crumbled, a massive Rottweiler leaped. Redferne rose to a crouch, spat through his blowpipe, and hit the charging animal square in the chest, but it kept on coming, striking him in the midsection. The blow knocked him flat on his back and winded him.

The moon burst through the ragged clouds, painting the landscape in a yellow glow. Redferne grabbed the dog with both hands around the neck and strained to keep its snapping jaws from his face. They rolled and tumbled in the long grass, the dog growling and snarling and Redferne shouting and roaring as the instinct of preservation surged through him. The dog's hot breath smelled of fish, almost making Redferne gag. Then it whimpered and Redferne felt the pressure on his arms weaken. The Rottweiler's legs buckled and he teetered sideways and collapsed.

The other guard came at a run. Not finding his mate, he called out, "Ned!"

"I'm taking a piss," Redferne shouted.

"Must have consumed one helluva lot of beer last night to cause that racket. You might need to see the doctor if it hurts that bad."

Then, laughing, he turned on his heel and doubled back toward his starting point.

Isaac beckoned the others forward. "Hurry! Let's get through the fence before he returns." When they arrived, he said to Redferne, "Lead on."

Sweat glistened on Redferne's forehead. He scrutinized the fence. "Jaysus! I can't remember where the broken section is. It all looks the same in the moonlight." He handed his pistol to Isaac. "You and Padraig cover me while I look for it."

Isaac handed the pistol off to Gleason. "I'm going with you." They shouldered the fence in different places feeling for give, but it seemed solid as a stone wall. Intent on finding the opening, they failed to notice a guard approaching in the shadow of the palisade until he was almost on top of them.

"Halt!" he shouted, releasing the dog and offloading his musket. Redferne pulled his machete and held it in front of him. The dog lunged and impaled itself on the blade with a bloodcurdling shriek. Redferne dove to one side to avoid the musket trained on him. A shot rang out. The guard stumbled and collapsed face down beside the dog. Gleason ran up with the smoking pistol in his hand.

Isaac sang out. "I've found it." With an assist from Gleason they broke through the palisade. Padraig and the others ran for the opening. Shouts of "Breakout, Breakout!" rang out. Musket balls kicked up dirt behind their feet.

"This way!" Isaac shouted, leading the escapees down the logging trail into the woods. More musket balls whined above their heads and sliced into the trees. One dislodged a chunk of bark, hitting Redferne on the cheek. They stumbled along moonlit paths towered on either side by thatch vines for perhaps an hour. At the edge of the swamp, Isaac called a halt and took inventory. Everyone had made it through. Most stretched out on the forest floor, gasping for breath.

Green monkeys shrieked and swung through the branches up in the canopy.

Long streamers of Spanish moss that normally trailed on the ground now floated on the surface of the moonshine flood like green hair, undulating with the swell from the wind. Redferne washed his wounded cheek with swamp water and recalled the words of the grizzled black slave.

"Water's up in the swamp after a hurricane. Wouldn't last the night out there."

Redferne said to Isaac. "Don't think they'll follow us tonight."

"Don't bet on it. Waldron will be out for blood." Then turning to Craig. "Mr. Blacksmith, still have that sack of yours?"

"You didn't expect me to carry all of that weight on me own now, did ye?" He beckoned to Colin Noone, who produced three axe heads from a straw bag.

Redferne ran his fingers along the blades. They were razor sharp. "Good work, Craig. Where are the handles?"

"An axe handle is also a good weapon." Several men stepped forward and surrendered wooden staves.

"Let's get to work." They attached the handles to the axe heads. MacTigh looked puzzled. "Are we building a fire?"

"No, Irishman," Isaac said. "Unless you want to swim through the swamp, we're building rafts, so let's get moving." They placed sentries down the logging trail to prevent a surprise attack while they chopped down the straightest and thinnest young trees, cobbling together two crude rafts with vines and creepers.

"How sturdy are these contraptions?" MacTigh asked.

Isaac glared at him. "They don't have to be British man o' wars, mate, just robust enough to get us through the swamp."

"You had a more detailed plan than you let on," Redferne said.

"I didn't, but when the hurricane hit I knew the storm surge would turn the swamp into a lake."

"I thought when they took you and Padraig away, the jig was up."

"It turned out to be a stroke of good fortune. If Craig hadn't the foresight to hide, we would've been done in."

As they put finishing touches on their work, Padraig and Kilbane ran up, breathless. "Waldron's forming a pursuit party."

Isaac looked surprised. "You're sure of that?"

"Quite sure," Padraig said. "We scouted down the trail all the way to the palisade and saw men readying canoes."

"Shit," Gleason said.

"Any dogs?" Redferne asked.

"None that I could see."

"They don't want the barking to give their position away," Gleason said.

"Possibly, but a second party with dogs may be circling around from a different direction to cut us off," Isaac said with a worried look. "Let's hustle."

They set off on their flimsy rafts with Isaac in the lead, two helmsmen with long poles in each raft, one in the back, and another in front. Redferne and Padraig rode in the second raft. Water seeped up through the logs. Trees and vegetation in the swamp grew denser than in the wood, and the moonlight much dimmer.

Redferne worried more about what lurked ahead than what was coming from behind.

Seamus Beirne

CHAPTER 43

When the first rays of sunlight fought their way through the canopy, Isaac sang out. "Look sharp, we're entering Arpeche territory." A pandemonium of strange sounds erupted ahead of them. Redferne reached out and took Padraig's arm. Large screens of Spanish moss hung from the trees, making it difficult to see the way forward. The helmsmen pushed beyond the concealing foliage, emerging into a large lagoon with a small atoll crowned by a flock of large pink squawking birds with long curved necks, standing on long stork-like legs. Many of them appeared to have only one leg.

"Jaysus, one-legged pink turkeys!" MacTigh shouted. A clamor went up from the Irish.

"Keep away! Keep away!"

The Africans laughed.

"There's nothing to be afraid of, you chicken-shit Irishmen," Isaac said through a gap-toothed smile. "They're flamingos."

Redferne released his grip on Padraig's arm. "Well I'll be damned. One-legged birds. I never heard the like. How do they walk?"

Another burst of laughter from the Africans.

"The other leg is tucked into their plumage," Isaac said.

The rafts moved beneath the overhanging tree branches edging the atoll, but the strange birds didn't move, apparently content to share their piece of land with the strangers.

Arpeche and his men emerged like phantoms from among the flamingos on the rear slope of the atoll. Some carried nets with large iron rings for casting. Others had spears, guns, and machetes. The flamingos took to the air in a raucous exodus, hindering Arpeche's charge with a wall of flapping wings and dangling legs, giving the rafters time to get on their feet.

Isaac fired the first shot at Arpeche, but missed, dropping a large warrior running alongside him. The rafters appeared outnumbered two to one, but drawing first blood gave them a psychological advantage. They fought like she-wolves protecting their young, knowing there was no going back. Grunts, screams, and curses mingled with gunfire, and the steely ring of machetes and spears. Wild fowl took to the air and circled overhead squawking and screeching. Arpeche's attack faltered, and soon his followers buckled and fled leaving behind six dead and Arpeche surrounded. The rafters closed in.

Isaac raised his arm. "He's mine. Got a score to settle with this gent."

They circled each other like two hungry dogs contesting a piece of meat. Arpeche, squinting through bloodshot eyes, his face contorted in anger, yelled and hurled his spear at Isaac, who sliced the shaft in two with his machete. Arpeche unsheathed his knife and lunged. Isaac sidestepped the thrust, kicking Arpeche's feet from under him, pinning him to the ground.

"Finish him off," MacTigh yelled. The others took up the chant.

Isaac looked at Redferne.

"Padraig, give me your pistol," Gleason said.

"No," Redferne replied, "he's outnumbered. No longer a fair fight."

Gleason said, "We're letting him go?"

"We'll turn him over to the chief and let him deal with him."

"There's no time for that," Isaac snapped, tightening his arm around Arpeche's neck. "We're a bunch of escaped convicts, remember?"

"Not going to deliver him. Secure him here so the tribe can find him." Redferne said.

"How do we secure him?" Isaac struggled to control his irritation. Redferne pointed to one of the abandoned nets.

Isaac grinned. "Maybe I misjudged you. Make him sweat it out here in the hot sun until he is rescued."

"Or until the one-legged turkeys pick the bastard's eyes out," Gleason said. A cheer went up.

Isaac smiled. "Either way the Irishman has come up with an exquisite form of torture." Redferne felt uncomfortable when Gleason hogtied Arpeche. It reminded him too much of his own treatment on the plantation until he reflected on the number of victims Arpeche had delivered to Waldron, not to mention the deaths of two mates here on the atoll. Noone and Kilbane threw the net over him, anchoring it to the ground with wooden stakes driven through the iron rings.

After burying the dead, they left Arpeche to his fate and departed with Isaac again leading the way. This time Redferne was on the raft with him. As they pulled away the flamingos high-stepped it back to the atoll.

By mid-day, they emerged from the swamp on its eastern boundaries and hid the rafts in the foliage at the edge of a wood. Not a sign of Waldron, which surprised Redferne, since canoes were more agile than rafts in the swamp. He mentioned his concern to Isaac.

"Don't bank on that. They may have used another strategy."

Redferne rotated his finger. "Like an encircling maneuver?"

"Precisely. We'll have to move cautiously once we leave the cover of the wood."

"What's beyond the wood?"

Isaac shook his head slowly and looked at Craig.

"Whole lot a nothing. Long grass and sparsely treed all the way to the northern coast."

"What's your plan?" Redferne asked. "Hide out in the woods or get off the island?"

"No tellin' how many more broke for freedom. My guess is

quite a few beside ourselves, which means Waldron and the other plantation owners are going to comb the island until we're captured or eliminated."

Gleason, Padraig, and the others milled around looking uncertain, as Redferne and Isaac talked.

At last, Isaac gave the word and they followed an animal track through the wood, alive with squawks and chirps of multi-colored birds flitting through the trees. Monkeys swung through the canopy, shaking loose a shower of leaves and twigs.

"So our best bet is to leave the island altogether?" Redferne said.

"That depends on providence or sheer dumb luck."

Redferne's heart sank. "In my experience, God seldom answers the petitions of the destitute, and luck is a fickle thing. An escape plan with that as an essential component is hardly a plan at all."

"Not sure I agree with your logic, Redferne. Providence intervened in a major way. I wouldn't look a gift horse in the mouth."

Redferne scratched his head. "You've lost me."

"Providence sent the hurricane, didn't it?"

"Not sure I buy that, but I see your point. The hurricane helped."

"No, the hurricane is the reason we're still free. It caused so much disruption that the tyrant's attention is divided."

"Granted, but how is it going to help us flee the island?"

"It's not just prisoners who break loose during hurricanes; a lot of other stuff breaks loose as well."

"What else has broken loose that could help us?"

"Boats, man, boats. Hurricanes always litter the coastline with boats. Most of them are wrecks, but every now and then several survive intact."

"There are eighteen of us, man. It better be a big one."

"Or two small ones," Isaac said.

The track narrowed, forcing them to walk in single file.

Isaac called over his shoulder. "Stick to the path. If you get lost you're on your own."

"As long as it leads somewhere," Kilbane grumbled. "Could be going in circles."

"In that case you'll feel right at home," Gleason said, "coming from the trackless wastes of Connemara."

The Irish laughed; the Africans appeared bewildered.

Redferne looked behind to see where Padraig was.

"Two boats could be a problem," Redferne said. "That would split us up."

"Beggars can't be choosers, Redferne. I intend to get out of here any way I can."

"Not crazy about being cast adrift in a small boat, besides which, I can't sail," Redferne said, brushing a hanging vine away from his face.

"You can pull an oar, can't you?"

"It's a big ocean. We wouldn't stand a chance without a decent-sized boat." The rest of the group walked in silence except for the rhythmic slapping of hands on necks to squish attacking insects.

The awful memory of that day on the lake almost thirty years ago came surging back to Redferne. His younger brother would be thirty-seven had he lived. Loving husband and father to a few kids.

"Redferne, you listening?" Isaac shook him. "Let's pray we find a boat big enough for all of us, but either way I'm getting off this accursed island."

For the first time since they met, Redferne doubted the wisdom of putting himself and Padraig in Isaac's hands. Was he willing to throw caution to the wind in pursuit of a foolish risk? He could see no alternative. Isaac had gotten them this far.

Two red brocket deer darted across the track ahead of them and disappeared into the brush.

"Wouldn't mind a hunk of that right now," Noone said, "I'm tired and sick of eating mangos." A wave of mumbling went up and down the line.

"Let's take a break, Isaac," Redferne said.

"I'd like to get out of the wood first."

Another chorus of mumbling.

"No telling how long that might take," Redferne said.

Isaac pointed ahead. "See there, the trees are thinning out. Don't want to get stuck here after nightfall." More grumbling, but Isaac's argument won the day. They pushed ahead and a half hour more saw them on the edge of a large desolate area with tall grass and few trees, as Craig had predicted. Glad to be out of the confining closeness and stifling humidity of the wood, they sprawled in the grass and many fell asleep.

Redferne sat and studied the men he had jumped ship with: Gleason, Kilbane, MacTigh, Noone, and Craig. Even asleep, their faces mirrored the trauma of the past year—jagged lines, protruding cheekbones, and bloodshot eyes, along with cuts and bruises from the fight on the atoll. Padraig looked robust, having escaped the real horrors of plantation life. Isaac sauntered up and sat down beside him.

"Buck up, Redferne. We're better off now than this time yesterday."

"You coulda' fooled me."

The question of the boat came up again.

Isaac stood and looked out over the tall grass undulating in the wind. "I want off this island, whether in one boat or two makes no difference to me."

"Splitting up could be a disaster. Our survival may depend on sticking together." During this exchange, the sleepers began to stir. Some stretched; others sought the shelter of the wood to relieve themselves.

"If Waldron gets his hands on me, I'll be hung, drawn, and quartered. Anyone here ever see that?" Isaac asked.

No one answered.

"Well, I have!" He jammed his index finger into his chest several times, "Believe me, I'd rather take my chances with the ocean than face that, be it in two boats or one."

There was a murmur of consent. Even Padraig agreed with the others.

"You're right," Redferne said, covering his face with his hands. He wanted to say that he was looking out for his son, but that was a lie. He was thinking about himself. The prospect of taking to sea in a small boat frightened him. "What happens if we can't find a boat?"

"Then we go back to the Indian village and use it as a staging area for attacks on the plantation to break out more of our mates. When we build sufficient numbers, we'll commandeer a ship in Bridgetown and get the hell outta' here."

Redferne thought that was quite a grandiose plan and a hell of a long shot, but he kept silent.

"Waldron isn't going to sit on his hands. How do we handle him?" Padraig asked.

"We'll borrow a page from Arpeche's book and become invisible until the last moment. A hit and run strategy."

"Great good it did him," Gleason said.

"He'd have been okay 'cept he got fucked up by the one-legged turkeys," an African said. Everyone laughed, breaking the tension.

They rested a spell before crossing the desolate area between the woods and the northern tip of the island, eating mangoes which grew in abundance in the woods. They soon ran out of those as there were no mango trees in the region through which they were traveling. They needed to find food if they hoped to fight off pursuers or embark on a sea voyage. Since the terrain was flat, they ran, settling into a jog when they got tired. The long grass waved before the wind. The runners wheezed and panted.

There was intermittent cannon fire in the direction of Bridgetown. Had a slave revolt broken out? It seemed unlikely that big guns would be necessary against a ragged band of escapees with farm implements and machetes.

"Are my ears deceiving me or is that cannon fire getting closer?" Redferne panted, shading his eyes and looking out to sea.

"It's getting closer and that can only mean one thing," Isaac said.

"Naval guns?"

"Makes sense. Bridgetown hasn't moved."

They stopped running and listened, some bending over to catch their breath, their faces etched with concern. If the authorities sent ships to patrol the coasts, escape by boat would be problematic, but what were they firing at, groups of escaped slaves on land, or those fleeing by boat?

"The northern tip of the island is higher in elevation so we should have a clear view down the eastern and western coasts," Craig said. Having caught their breath, they set off again at a measured jog.

They reached the northern shore in the afternoon, an area of ragged cliffs overlooking the ocean. The last of the mangoes had been consumed hours before and they were weak with hunger. A corona of mist and foam blanketed the cliffs. Huge Atlantic breakers pounded the rugged coast. Small coves and inlets, each more picturesque than the next, notched the shoreline.

Gleason pointed in the direction they had come. "Look! A boat, run aground in yon' cove."

"And cast your gaze out to sea," Isaac said. "A British frigate, heading in that direction."

"Do you think they spotted it?" Padraig asked.

"Of course they have," Gleason said.

The frigate drew closer.

Isaac dropped his hand. "Down! Down! If they're using a glass, they can spot us too." Some scrambled for cover behind large boulders; others hunkered in the long grass.

"Are they looking for survivors, Father?" Padraig asked, stretched out beside him on the edge of the cliff.

"I doubt it," he answered, "but we'll soon find out."

"They've heaved-to broadside to the shore. Might be preparing to lower a longboat. Wouldn't be good news for us," Isaac said.

"Why?" Padraig parted the grass on the edge of the cliff for a better look.

"They may have spotted us and are readying a search party."

"I don't think they could've seen us in the mist."

"Let's hope you're right," Isaac said.

The boat in the cove, a two-masted brigantine, appeared abandoned but intact. The master of the British frigate wasn't concerned, apparently, whether it had survivors or not.

The port side of his vessel erupted in tongues of flame. When the smoke cleared, pieces of splintered planks, broken masts, spars, shredded rigging, and torn sail littered the water, all being carried by the undulating waves to be dumped unceremoniously on the rocky coast.

CHAPTER 44

"That answers the cannon fire question," Isaac said, eyeing the frigate. "They're moving up the coast sinking all the boats that broke anchor to prevent escapees fleeing the island."

"It also explains why there wasn't any aggressive pursuit by Waldron. He's waiting for the conclusion of the naval operation before committing to a full-scale chase," Redferne said.

"Maybe so, but his restraint doesn't make our task easier," Isaac said. "Let's get a move on before that frigate destroys any hope of getting away from here."

They headed down the southeastern shore keeping an eye on the frigate, which hadn't moved since it blew up the marooned ship. The terrain fell away before them in a gentle slope that leveled out into a strip of rain forest almost at sea level. Their spirits rose at the prospect of finding fruit.

Isaac pushed ahead, saying there'd be plenty of time to eat once they secured a ship.

"That's not going to happen with the men in their present condition," Redferne said, seeing the exhaustion on their faces.

When they reached the shelter of the forest, Isaac gave the go-ahead to fan out and look for anything edible. "Let's pitch camp here, and remember, no guns. Don't want to advertise our presence." Redferne, Padraig, and Gleason set off together, armed with machetes and blowguns. Kilbane, MacTigh, and Noone formed another group. Green monkeys scampered overhead, but they had neither the skill nor the energy to knock them down from far up in the canopy.

"Father, come here," Padraig shouted. "Look at this. Deer droppings. I recognize them from home."

Blowguns loaded, they followed the path and came upon two small red brocket deer munching on forest vegetation. The deer stomped their hooves and snorted before taking off at a run. Redferne and Gleason fired simultaneously. Both darts hit their mark but the animals continued into the brush. They found one a few hundred yards along the path, but the other was nowhere to be seen.

"I'll go after it," Redferne said. "You two take this one back to camp."

"Isn't one enough?" Padraig said.

"Not for sixteen people. No telling when we'll eat again, especially if we find a boat." He raced down the path in the direction he thought the deer might have taken, but after an extended search, he had to admit defeat. About to turn back, he heard a familiar sound.

Couldn't be, he thought. *The ocean is to my left, east of my position.* Then the faint crash of breakers directly in front of him, which was south. He breached the trees, and found himself in a small cove.

He closed his eyes thinking he was seeing a mirage, but when he opened them again, the sloop was still there leaning against a rock on a broad expanse of sand, its hull coated with a layer of marine growth. The tide appeared to be going out. The bay had a dogleg configuration, edged on both sides by forest all the way to the bend. Tide pools dotted the sand.

He retraced his steps and rejoined his mates who already had a fire going and were rigging a spit for the deer. "No luck then," Isaac said, skinning the red brocket. "Not to worry. Noone's crew nabbed one."

"Didn't find the deer," Redferne said, "but I found something more important." They all stopped and stared.

"Found a boat."

Their faces lit up at the news.

"Is it seaworthy?" Isaac asked.

"Didn't check to see what condition it was in. It has a single mast and it looks big enough to carry all of us."

A buzz of enthusiastic chatter erupted. Some wanted to check it out right then.

"No, better eat first. It will still be there after the meal," Isaac said.

"Unless the frigate discovers it first," Gleason said.

"Then it won't make any difference anyway," Isaac said.

Redferne glowered. "Don't stomp on their excitement, Isaac."

"I'm sorry, but most of these marooned boats are pretty banged up after a hurricane."

"Better a banged-up boat than no boat at all," Redferne said, joining Padraig, Craig, and Gleason, who were shucking stems from a potato-sized green fruit. "What you fella's got there?"

"Breadfruit," Craig replied, handing him one. "But they're better roasted," he continued, watching Redferne take a bite and spit the bitter fruit out.

"By God, I hope so." He grimaced. Once the young deer was skinned and prepared, they placed it on the spit and put dozens of breadfruit on the embers to roast with it. While their food cooked, Isaac stationed several men at the edge of the forest to stand guard.

Redferne stared into the fire. Its flames shooting into the darkness hypnotized him. "Come away with me?" a voice said in no more than a whisper. He closed his eyes to shut out the fire, but the voice faded away. When the meal was ready, they gorged themselves and it was everyman for himself, but there was plenty to go around and enough left over to take care of several tomorrows. The repast over, Redferne led them to the little cove, with Isaac's question echoing in his head. "Is it seaworthy, is it seaworthy?"

They left the trees and poured onto the beach like excited schoolchildren released from classes for a month, swarming all over the derelict. Because of the tilt they couldn't walk the deck easily but that didn't stop them from going below; all except Redferne and Isaac.

"What do you think, Isaac?"

"So far, so good." He walked around its exterior checking the condition of the planking, then rubbed his hand across the name *Susan and Mary* written in blue, barely visible on her bow. "What we have is a sloop and by the looks of it, she came through the hurricane in pretty good condition."

She had a gaff-rigged mainsail and a single jib attached to the bowsprit. Redferne reckoned her to be about seventy feet long.

He pointed to a longboat, its red paint flaking off, still lashed to her cradle on the sloping deck. "A little bit of extra insurance."

Isaac pulled himself into it. "It's double-banked. Looks like it could accommodate eight to ten oarsmen. Good to know." He climbed out and struggled up the sloping deck followed by Redferne. "Let's check the cabin."

It measured roughly six feet by six feet, with windows in the front and on both sides. A copper-colored lantern hung from the ceiling. A galley stove bolted to the deck occupied one corner.

"Wonder what type business she engaged in?" Redferne asked, opening a drawer in a wall cabinet.

Isaac unfurled a map he found on the floor. "From the looks of this, I'd say she was a privateer operating out of several islands in the Caribbean." He spread the map out on a table fastened to the wall beneath the front window.

Redferne looked over Isaac's shoulder. "How do you figure?"

"See all the red dots marking spots on St. Kitts, Barbados, St. Lucia, and the Grenadines?"

"How do you get privateer from that?"

"Just a hunch that these dots represent the locations of small bays or inlets where a shallow draft boat like the *Susan and Mary* could hide either before or after a raid."

Redferne went back to the drawer and rummaged some more. "What's a letter of marque?" He waved his find in front of Isaac.

"What did I tell you?" Isaac took the paper from Redferne. "This is a letter signed by the French Governor of Martinique granting a Claude Simon authorization to operate as a privateer against British and Spanish merchant ships."

"But she has an English name?"

"A captured prize. Simon never got around to changing the name."

"Safe to say she didn't drift here from Bridgeport."

"Almost a certainty."

A commotion came from below before the hatch flew open. Several men carrying bottles of wine crawled out of the hold into the cabin.

"Hold it, hold it," Isaac shouted." "Put the wine back. There'll be no drinking for now."

The Irish protested, casting dark looks at Isaac. "Why should we take orders from you?"

"You heard what the man said," Redferne shouted to his countrymen. "Put the damn wine back. It'll take a lot of work to get this boat righted and ready for sailing. The last thing we need is a bunch of drunks bollixing up the operation." After the men returned the wine to the hold, they bunched together on the sand casting threatening looks at the cabin.

Isaac looked down the open hatch. "Did you notice that their pant legs were wet when they came out of the hold?"

"Not a good sign." Redferne followed Isaac down the hatch.

"Close it behind you."

"Wouldn't it be nice to see where we're going?" Redferne said.

"I need the light closed off for a purpose."

At the bottom of the ladder, Redferne stepped into water up to his ankles, groping for the hull to feel his way forward.

"Do you see any light?" Isaac asked as he sloshed ahead in the darkness.

"No, not a stime, but my hands tell me there's enough wine crates down here to satisfy a small army for a month."

"My hunch is it's Spanish wine, not French."

"Aye, but where's the water coming from?"

"Most likely from a hole in the side resting on the sand."

They returned to deck and Isaac explained the situation to the men. Matt Kilbane spoke up. "Not the end of the world. We can careen her."

"What?"

"We pull her over onto her other side and work on the exposed section as long as the tide is out."

Redferne raised his eyebrows. "How do you know so much about this?"

"My father owned a Galway hooker, a boat similar to this one."

"If we locate the hole, can you repair it?" Isaac asked.

"Not without pitch or something like that."

"You'll find no pitch here," Craig said, "but there's a substitute that the natives use for the same purpose."

"What is it?" Gleason asked.

"Sap from the breadfruit tree, and it's all around us."

Redferne glanced across the bay. The crash of breakers. Out of sight around the dogleg. "I'm a little concerned that we haven't heard from that brig in the last few hours. She could come sailing in here any minute," He shaded his eyes with his hands and moved a few paces to get a better look out to sea.

"Not with the tide out. The water's too shallow for the brig's draft. Probably moved down the coast in search of bigger game," Isaac said.

"Might have a problem getting out of here at high tide." MacTigh said.

"Not likely since the sloop got in here to begin with," Kilbane said.

"Aye, but the storm surge could have carried her in," Isaac said.

"I hadn't thought of that. Might as well play the odds and forge ahead," Kilbane said. The boom of cannon echoed across the bay. Flocks of seabirds startled from the rocks, circled overhead, squawking loudly. Everyone stopped talking and looked out to sea.

Isaac shaded his eyes. "That shot came from the southeast. They've missed us."

"Sounds are hard to track over water," Redferne said, inclining his head as if waiting for another shot.

"Can't be a hundred percent certain," Isaac said and turned to Craig. "Take Noone with you and start collecting sap. The rest of us will work on getting this old girl back on her feet."

"Before we tip her," Kilbane said, "better remove the seaweed and barnacles from the hull. It'll increase her speed and maneuverability."

They set about that with machetes and knives and within an hour they had the hull free of crustaceans. That done, they tied one end of a rope they found on board to the mast, and threw the other end over a tree branch. Using the tree branch as leverage they all lined up along the free rope end like a tug o' war team and heaved, raising it off the sand.

Water poured out from a six foot gash between the seams. After pausing to let it drain, they resumed heaving and swearing until the boat rolled over on its other side. A short while later, Craig and Noone rushed out of the forest with two bucketsful of sap that was fast congealing into a white paste. They looked panicked.

Noone gasped for breath. "Someone was watching us in the bush. We drew our pistols to flush him out and he took off."

"Did you get a look at him?"

"Only saw his back, but we found this in his hiding place." Craig handed a blowgun dart to Isaac.

"Damn, one of Arpeche's men."

"He might be a scout for a search party." Redferne said.

Gleason bared his teeth. "Knew we shoulda' killed that bastard."

"Makes no difference now. We need to hustle." Isaac placed several guards armed with muskets facing the rain forest.

The rest positioned their weapons near them as they scraped the remaining marine layer off the hull. Kilbane and Craig filled the voids with breadfruit paste, checking periodically over their shoulders. They finished the job and settled down to wait for the tide to come in. Several tense hours passed before the surging waves lifted the sloop off the sand. "Hope the paste has hardened sufficiently," Kilbane said.

Isaac glanced at the rain forest. "We'll have to take our chances."

By ten o'clock, the tide was fully in and the *Susan and Mary* bobbed gently on the swell. A short while later, with their supplies of food and water onboard, they pulled the guards off the beach, hoisted the sails, and got underway. Kilbane's caulking job was holding.

Since Kilbane was the only one among them with knowledge of sailing, he became the helmsman and navigator. As he guided the *Susan and Mary* toward the dogleg, everyone crowded on deck to see what lay beyond the bend. Had the Indian scout enough time to alert Island authorities? Would the frigate be waiting for them? Was the *Susan and Mary*'s draft shallow enough to clear the reef?

Once around the bend, the broad Atlantic lay before them. The frigate was nowhere to be seen. No sooner had they begun to relax than Isaac, up at the bow, shouted. "Reef coming up." Kilbane's demeanor changed. Beads of perspiration appeared on his forehead and the knuckles of his hands turned white from gripping the wheel spokes.

"Over the reef now," Isaac yelled. The *Susan and Mary* shuddered all along its length. Then it broke free into clear water, the bow rearing and bucking as it fought the incoming breakers.

Isaac ran back from his place at the bow. "Let's check for damage."

Lighting two oil lanterns, he and Redferne climbed into the hold. Redferne held his breath, fearful of what they might find, but it looked as if the *Susan and Mary* came through unscathed. They ran the lantern light along the newly-caulked seams and found no seepage.

"Jaysus, I thought for sure we had torn the arse out of her, captain," Redferne said, clapping Isaac on the shoulder.

Isaac chuckled. "Captain? Ain't that a lick."

"You're the best man for the job."

"We shall see. We shall see." He lit the way out of the hold into the cabin.

"Good job, Kilbane," Isaac said to the helmsman when they went up on deck. "Everything's shipshape below."

Kilbane, more relaxed now, asked, "Isn't it about time, Isaac, you told me where we're going?"

"The nearest island, St. Lucia, is about ninety miles northwest of here. It's mostly a barren volcanic place, but it's the first place they'd look."

"So Lucia is out, what next," Redferne said.

"Our best bet is St. Kitts for three reasons. It's French-ruled, it's several hundred miles from here, and best of all, it's a haven for buccaneers, many of them escaped African and Irish slaves."

"Let's hope Claude Simon isn't on the dock to greet us," Colin Noone said.

"That's a risk we'll have to take."

Kilbane grinned. "Now you're talking. St. Kitts, here we come— as soon as someone tells me how to get there."

Redferne turned toward Isaac, who shuffled his feet and walked to the ship's rail, grabbing it with both hands.

"That's the problem," he said over his shoulder. "I'm not exactly sure."

Seamus Beirne

CHAPTER 45

Redferne felt like chastising Isaac for this lapse in planning but thought better of it.

"Hold a minute," he said to Kilbane and went looking for Craig. He found him inspecting the longboat and brought him to Isaac.

"Craig's been to St. Kitt's."

"The *Kate O'Dwyer* stopped there on one occasion to take on water," Craig said.

"Do you know how to get there?"

Craig looked startled. "I'm a bloody blacksmith, not a navigator."

Isaac threw his hands up.

"Here, take the wheel," Kilbane said to Redferne and disappeared inside the cabin. The sound of rifling through drawers and cabinets. "Aha," He came back with charts and a compass. The wind caught the chart and nearly ripped it from his grasp, so he spread it out on the deck and had Isaac and Craig kneel on it to keep it down.

Looking bemused, Redferne said, "Wouldn't it make more sense to do this in the cabin out of the wind?"

"It would if I'd ever been known to have much sense," Kilbane replied, running his eyes back and forth across the faded paper. "St. Kitts, here we are, seventeen degrees north, sixty three degrees west. Looks like it's about three or four hundred miles to the northeast."

After setting his compass, he reclaimed the wheel from Redferne and adjusted his bearings. The swells came larger and farther apart, but the *Susan and Mary* took them in stride. Seagulls and petrels circled overhead, some coming to rest on masts and lines. A few of the men stretched out on the deck. Others lolled along the bulwark rails watching the rolling sea. Redferne stood near the prow, holding on to the rigging, filling his lungs with salt air. Isaac and Padraig stood beside him each lost in their own thoughts. Large fields of seaweed slopped against the sides of the sloop.

"This might be a good time to break out a few crates of the grape," Redferne said to Isaac.

"Good idea."

A cheer went up from the men when they heard the news. Not having a corkscrew, they drove the corks into the bottles and started celebrating.

Redferne took a long draft and handed a bottle to Isaac. The label read, *Rioja*, product of Spain. He smiled and took a mouthful. "Sweetest brew I ever tasted." He wiped his lips with the back of his hand. An ear-splitting noise roared over the *Susan and Mary*. A cannon ball plunged into the waves, about thirty yards off their prow, unleashing a twenty foot geyser into the air.

The frigate came at them from their starboard side. Men dropped their bottles and scattered, looking for cover. Several slipped on the spilt wine and skidded toward the bulwarks. The deck looked blood-red from half-empty bottles rolling back and forth.

"Can't stay on this course or he'll cut me off," Kilbane shouted.

Isaac cupped his hands. "Do whatever you must to get us out of here." Kilbane headed due east but the next cannon landed astern of them. The *Susan and Mary* held her own against the bigger ship, but the odds of out-racing her were slim.

"Redferne, take the wheel again," Kilbane shouted. He ran toward the bow, then came back yelling. "She's rigged for a second jib. Spread out and look for another piece of canvas." A mad scuffle ensued as the men combed the ship. Redferne glanced behind. Tongues of flame spiked from the frigate's fighting tops. Musket balls gouged the deck, shattering wine bottles and hurling a fusillade of splinters and shards of glass across the ship. Screams of pain filled the air as the lethal hail shredded human flesh.

Padraig ran toward Redferne from the bow, his face chalk white.

"Son, get down, get down!" A musket ball tore into Padraig's arm and hurled him across the deck. "Oh, God, no!" Redferne abandoned the helm and ran to his son, pulling him off the exposed deck into the cabin. With no one at the helm, the sloop lost the wind and slowed. Another geyser erupted on their port side.

If he didn't return to the helm, all could be lost. He called for help but the few men remaining on deck cowered for safety in the shelter of the bulwarks. The rest were down below looking for the sail. He looked at his son. His face had turned grey. He was losing blood.

Ripping off his own shirt, he gathered it into a ball and pressed it against the bubbling wound, then he undid his belt and fed it under Padraig's arm, wrapping it tightly around the balled-up shirt, before racing back to his post at the helm.

"I got it," Isaac yelled, racing from the cabin to the bow with the sail under his arm. Musket balls chewed the deck around their feet as he and Kilbane rigged it to the forestay alongside the other jib.

The ship leaped forward as the second jib sail ballooned with wind. Redferne crouched in the shelter of the taffrail. Grabbing one of the wheel spokes, he kept the sloop heading into the wind. Another round of shot tore into the taffrail, keeping him pinned down. The enemy musket men were targeting him. He kept one eye on the helm and the other on the cabin door. Behind it unattended lay his son, quite possibly bleeding to death. "Mother Mary, help us…someone get out here…Isaac, where the hell are you?" He was about to abandon the wheel when Kilbane dashed from the cabin to assist him.

"Get back inside. I'll take over," Kilbane yelled.

"About bloody time," Redferne ran for the cabin. As the *Susan and Mary* gained speed, the musket balls fell short, hissing like angry snakes on hitting cold water behind them. She gradually outpaced the frigate and eventually moved beyond the range of her guns. As Redferne entered the cabin, Isaac stuck his head out the door and shouted, "Kilbane, stick to your present easterly course. Can't risk turning toward St. Kitts until we are out of range of that frigate. Everyone out of the cabin except Redferne and Craig."

Isaac turned his attention to Padraig, who lapsed in and out of consciousness. "Nice work on the tourniquet," he said to Redferne. "You managed to staunch the bleeding." He probed the wound with the tip of his knife but failed to retrieve the ball which was too deeply embedded in the arm. After cleaning it as best he could with cold water, he disinfected it with rum and bound it with a strip of shredded linen curtain from the cabin window. "This will have to do 'til we reach St. Kitts. I don't have a forceps." Then he gave Padraig several shots of rum to deaden the pain. Padraig's eyes grew heavy and he drifted off to sleep as darkness descended.

Worry lines creased Redferne's face. "What if he goes into shock before we reach land?"

Isaac threw up his hands. "I'm not a physician. We'll have to deal with that if and when it arises."

"I'm sorry, Isaac. I don't mean to be critical, but I'm scared for…"

A shout. "Lights on the horizon."

They rushed outside. Lights bobbed on the horizon.

"Could they be lights from land?" Redferne asked.

"No," Craig replied. "I've been on enough ships to know that these are stern lights."

"Coming toward us or moving away?" Gleason asked.

"They're stern lights."

Gleason blushed.

"Is it possible we're gaining on it?" Redferne said.

"Those lights weren't there ten minutes ago." Craig replied.

"Makes no difference no how," Isaac said. "It's about time for us to swing northwest toward St. Kitts."

"No!" Redferne shouted. "That ship might be able to help my kid. If we're gaining on it, it's a hell of a lot closer than St. Kitts."

"What if it's a British man 'o war or a slaver? What then?" Isaac countered. A murmur went up from the men.

"Not worth the risk," Noone shouted.

"Believe me Redferne," Isaac said, linking his fingers and lowering his eyes. "We're all rooting for Padraig. You gotta' know that, but it's one life, and as precious as it is to you, to the rest of us he's one of sixteen."

"Since we are gaining steadily on yon' vessel and running without lights, couldn't we steal up on her unobserved?"

"And what then?" Isaac asked.

"All the ships I've known display their names on the taffrail. With the aid of a spyglass and the two stern lights we should be able to identify her without getting so close as to put us in jeopardy."

Isaac scanned the faces around him. "Hey, Mac what's-your-name, go aloft and see if you can identify that ship."

"Right, Boss." MacTigh scurried up the rigging. They followed him until he morphed into a swaying silhouette against the starlit sky.

As if on cue, the wind picked up, every plank, line, and spar creaking loudly. Isaac cupped his hands.

"See anything?"

A ragged voice descended as if from the heavens. "Jaysus, I forgot the bloody glass."

They all laughed, except Redferne.

"Here it is." Kilbane came forward from the stern. "Noone, take the helm."

Kilbane started to climb.

They waited. "She's got two square-rigged masts—a brig by the looks of her," Kilbane shouted.

Isaac cupped his hands again. "Can you see the name?"

"No."

Isaac struggled to maintain his footing on the heaving deck. "It's getting rough. Come on down and don't forget MacTigh."

Back on deck, Kilbane handed the glass to Isaac. "I'd say she's a merchant man."

"How could you tell?" Isaac asked.

"British navy seldom runs brigs across the Atlantic."

"Suppose we discover that she's the *Bellerophon* out of Plymouth, what then?"

"It confirms she's not navy, otherwise she'd be the *HMS Bellerophon*," Kilbane interjected.

"And if she is *HMS Bellerophon*, we pull away. She won't be any the wiser," Redferne added, his chest heaving in anticipation.

Craig spoke. "With the extra jib, we're faster than she is. Making good our escape shouldn't be too much of a worry."

Redferne took heart at Craig and Kilbane's support. Being the only ones on board with sailing experience, it was likely their words carried some weight. Redferne sensed the group leaning to his side once they were confident that the *Susan and Mary* had the ability to outrun the other ship.

Isaac surveyed the gathered faces. "So what are we saying?"

"I say we go for it," Kilbane said. "Give or take an hour and we should be in a position to read the name on the taffrail."

That seemed to settle the argument. The sloop ploughed on, closing the gap between herself and the mystery ship. Redferne thanked the group and returned to the cabin to check on Padraig.

A short while later, Isaac adjusted the spyglass and gave a low whistle. "I'll be damned. Isn't that the—I'll let you take a look for yourself." He handed the glass to Redferne who trained it on the phantom ship, its dark bulk now barely a quarter mile away.

He adjusted the glass and sucked in his breath. "Craig, you're not going to believe this; it's not the *HMS Bellerophon* out of Plymouth. It's the *Kate O'Dwyer* out of Sligo town."

Gleason snatched the glass from Redferne. "Here, gimme' a look at that. Christ on a cross, it's him. That bastard Tolliver. This changes the situation entirely. Can't wait to board that accursed brig."

"Aye, aye," the Irish lads sang out in unison. All of them had arrived in Barbados compliments of Captain Tolliver.

"You must be out of your mind. You told me yourself that this ship carries carronades. Could tear us apart with canister shot in a heartbeat," Isaac said.

"Aye, but we know where they're located," Gleason said. "The first order of business once we're on board will be to commandeer them. Control those and you control the ship."

A wave of excitement coursed through the sloop, catching the Africans in its wake. They didn't know Tolliver but they were familiar with ships like the *Kate O'Dwyer*, having themselves arrived in chains on similar vessels.

"I think you're the luckiest man in the world, because if there's one thing that could have gotten these men riled up—Africans and Irish alike—you've found it," Isaac said. "For many of my brothers, me included, the *Kate O'Dwyer* might as well be the *Green Hornet*."

"Is Kilbane a good enough helmsman to bring us alongside the *O'Dwyer* without ramming her?" Redferne asked.

"He's not and neither is anyone else," Kilbane answered. "What you suggest can't be done in these swells. We'll have to come up with another plan."

"A smaller boat could pull it off." Redferne pointed to the longboat lying on the deck in its cradle.

"Might work if it got up enough speed, which I doubt it could do with one sail," Kilbane said.

Redferne lifted an oar from the bottom of the longboat. "With help from four sets of these, it might. There's a doctor on that ship. He may be a drunkard, but he has medical instruments Isaac could use to help Padraig."

It took another half hour to iron out the details. Once aboard the *Kate O'Dwyer*, their weapon of choice would be the blowgun. It was silent and effective.

Craig went over the layout of the *Kate O'Dwyer*.

"The carronades are located on the stern castle. That's where the wheel house is as well."

"It's also where the helmsman and the man standing watch at the stern will be," Redferne added.

"There are night watchmen in other areas of the ship as well, especially on the forecastle deck at the bow," Craig continued.

"We won't bother with them," Redferne said. "First we capture the carronades, take over the helm, and then seize the captain. We do that, we control the ship."

"The only problem is that *they* may be inclined to bother with us, if we bump into them," Craig replied, a little huffed.

"We need to prepare for contingencies," Isaac said.

"That's why we have blowguns and machetes," Redferne snapped.

"Slow down, Redferne, or you'll jeopardize all of us," Isaac said. A chorus of ayes forced Redferne to pull back.

He turned to Isaac and said, "Maybe I am inclined to jump the gun a little, so what's your plan?"

Isaac gave him a cold stare. "To begin with, you Irishmen will have to darken your faces so you don't stand out like a bunch of harlots in church."

"With what?"

"Coke from the galley stove. Let's get a move on. Better they think we're demons rising from the depths. Scare the hell outta' them," he added, helping Craig darken his face. After the rest of the Irish completed their blackening job, Kilbane maneuvered the sloop alongside the *Kate O'Dwyer*, keeping it at a safe distance.

They launched the longboat, with Redferne and Isaac pulling oars in the prow and three more sets of oarsmen back of them. Craig manned the sail. One African named Keon stayed with Kilbane on the *Susan and Mary*. Almost immediately, the longboat dropped astern of the sloop.

CHAPTER 46

The first streaks of light scuffed the sky. It would be dawn soon, which was not good. Darkness was their friend, but they were about to lose it. It took the rowers a while to get their rhythm, but when they did, they began gaining on the brig.

Even in the chilly dawn, with wind gusts flailing, sweat trickled down their faces. The hundred yards to the big ship, rising and sinking in the swells, looked like a quarter mile. The wind blew fickle too, occasionally leaving the sail flapping like a shirt on a line, then puffing it out it out like a gander's chest. It felt like the wind mocked them, keeping the *Kate O'Dwyer* beyond their reach, until a robust squall propelled the longboat within grappling distance of their quarry.

A blizzard of salt spray sluicing from the prow of the brig drenched them as it carved into the waves. They maneuvered along her starboard side until they drew amidships, all the while struggling to avoid a collision. The wind trilling in the rigging of the brig and the slop of the waves against her side made it difficult for them to hear each other. It also camouflaged the sound of the first grappling hook they launched over the rail.

They had assembled grapplers from extra rope and hooks found in the hold of the sloop and wrapped them in strips of their cotton garments to deaden the sound of impact. They tied the rope from the first hook to the bow of the longboat to keep it from drifting away. Then Redferne took a second grappler and lobbed it. He and Isaac were the first over the side of the *O'Dwyer*, followed by Gleason and MacTigh. Isaac and MacTigh would secure the carronades while Redferne and Gleason made their way to the captain's cabin under the stern castle.

On a signal from Redferne, Craig, Noone, and the rest of the men would board later. No sense in exposing them before it was necessary. They encountered no opposition as they crept toward the captain's cabin and entered through the unlocked door. Loud snoring greeted them which stopped abruptly at the sound of a heavy thud from the deck above. "What the hell?" the captain shouted, grabbing his pistol off the nightstand. He leveled it at Redferne, who wrested it away, but not before it went off, burying a lead ball in the ceiling. A fist in the face snapped Tolliver's head back against the headboard.

"Suck on that, you bastard," Gleason said.

When they hustled him up to the stern deck, the ship reverberated with cries and the sound of running feet. Redferne relaxed when he saw Isaac and MacTigh in control of the carronades. The crumpled body of the watchman lay head first over the top step of the port stairway, a blowgun dart stuck in his neck. Not waiting for Redferne's signal, Noone, Craig, and the others stormed over the rail and engaged the alarmed sailors who came staggering from their bunks onto the main deck.

They put up a half-hearted resistance before fleeing back to the forecastle. "Up here!" Redferne yelled. The Africans and black-faced Irishmen cheered and charged up the stern castle ladder two steps at a time. A half-dozen musket men in long johns assembled on the forecastle and aimed their muskets at the stern. Seeing the captain in Redferne's grip with a knife to his throat they hesitated, but one of them discharged his musket, grazing an Irishman in the head. Isaac touched a lit match to the carronade fuse and raked the forecastle with a deadly hail of canister shot. Some of the musket men were catapulted into the ocean like rag dolls. Several sprawled bleeding and moaning on the deck.

Redferne dragged the captain to the rail overlooking the main deck.

"Throw down your weapons or many more of you will be killed." He tightened his grip on the captain and pressed the knife blade against his Adam's apple. "Tell them," he hissed.

"Do as he says," Tolliver ordered, his pitiless face now chalk-white.

"This ship, under this captain, has carried hundreds of human beings to slavery and death in the cane fields of Barbados," Redferne shouted. "As of today, this stops. Those of you who don't want to join us are free to take to the longboats and take your chances on the open sea." Cutlasses, pistols, and muskets clattered to the deck.

"Not him, not that son of a bitch," Gleason yelled, training his carronade on the captain.

"What's going on, Redferne? Don't remember this as being part of the deal," Isaac said, his deep-lined face pinched in disbelief. "Aren't we heading for St. Kitts?"

"Hear me out. We have a choice. Head back to St. Kitts and sign on with some buccaneer, or stick with this ship and run our own operation."

"We don't know nothing of running a ship this size," MacTigh said.

"No, but some of the present crew are bound to stay on, especially after we explore the hold and take stock of the cargo. I have a hunch it's worth a pretty penny." Tolliver twisted his head to glare at Redferne, a look of disbelief on his face.

Gleason nodded toward the captain. "After we take care of this monster."

"Back off, Gleason," Isaac said. "The last thing we want is to fight among ourselves. Right now we need to find that doctor and attend to Padraig."

"I don't trust that doctor. Look! It's early morning and he's already falling down drunk." Redferne pointed to a bleary-eyed, unshaven man standing unsteadily among the prisoners, dressed in a greasy black frock coat with a grimy pair of long johns protruding underneath.

"No, Isaac. Get his instruments and you attend to Padraig." While Isaac was thus engaged, they hogtied the captain and locked him in his cabin.

Redferne stood at the taffrail watching the sun peek over the horizon. The *Susan and Mary* tagged along about three hundred yards off their stern. He waved to Kilbane and ordered the sailing master of the *O'Dwyer* to "Heave to."

The sailing master, an old salt with a slight stoop and weather-beaten face by the name of Windham, came up the ladder puffing a white chalk pipe. "A piece of advice, laddie," he rasped, pulling the pipe from his mouth and addressing Redferne. "Launch them longboats on the double, so that them that has a mind to go can do so. Mark my words, the longer they stay on board, the greater the likelihood of trouble."

"And will you be one of those departing?"

"I'm a swabbie who likes to keep an eye out for a new opportunity. My gut tells me such an opportunity may be in the offing. So, if it's okay with you, Cap'n, I'll be staying put." He saluted.

"You understand you'll be charged with mutiny if you fall into the hands of the British."

"That's a risk I'm willing to take, especially since I know firsthand the kind of cargo stowed below decks."

Once the business of heaving to was complete and the vessel was almost at a standstill, Redferne gave the command, "Lower the longboats." Two-thirds of the crew decided to leave, along with the captain.

Gleason protested. "This man is a criminal. He murdered my brother. You're going to let him escape like that?" He kicked shut the wheelhouse door.

"Gleason, there are times when pragmatism gets in the way of justice," Redferne said. "This is one of them. The cold truth is, we need the cooperation of the remaining crew members to get us where we're going. Instinct tells me that executing the captain might not be the best way to secure that."

"I think in this case Redferne's got it right," Isaac added, "much as I hate to see a slaver walk free. My hunch is that Tolliver's career is over once the word gets back to his bosses that he not only lost the entire cargo, but the ship as well."

"Since we don't know how this caper is going to end," Redferne said, "I'd as soon not be charged with the execution of a ship's captain on the high seas."

He scanned the faces of his mates, looking for a reaction, but got only shuffling and coughing.

"All those in favor of a hanging, raise your hands." Four Irish lads including Gleason and Craig shot their hands into the air. Redferne paused then said, "All who feel Tolliver should be cast adrift, raise your hands."

The rest of the crew assented.

As the longboats pulled away from the *Kate O'Dwyer*, Tolliver, dressed in his blue frock coat, sat slumped in the lead boat. Redferne wondered if the captain could come back to haunt him. Isaac's insistence on blackening their faces had been inspired. Tolliver, beyond identifying them as Irish from their accents, did not appear to recognize any of them, not even Craig, his former crewmember. Windham joined him at the taffrail.

"What are the chances any of them will reach dry land alive?" Redferne asked.

"Every chance in the world." He puffed hard on the chalk pipe clenched between his teeth.

"That's a little optimistic, don't you think?"

"We left Bridgetown less than twelve hours ago, averaging four knots an hour. That puts them sixty or seventy miles from land."

"God's blood," Redferne said. "That's close enough to get rescued and send a fast frigate on our tail."

"Not to worry mate," Windham said. "We have a new-fangled navigational instrument on board called a chronometer that will get us to our destination faster than any pursuer."

They spun around at the sound of a musket shot. A man up in the rigging, his feet planted firmly in the shrouds, took aim at the longboats. Gleason. Having missed, he was attempting to reload, but the rocking of the ship made it difficult. He succeeded and raising the musket to his shoulder and aimed again at Tolliver.

Isaac started up the rigging with a blowpipe in his left hand. "Gleason," he yelled, "what the hell are you doing?" Gleason ignored him, struggling to counteract the rocking of the ship and adjust his aim. Isaac's dart struck him in the arm. The musket slipped from his grip, landing with a clatter on the deck. He grasped his wounded limb and looked at Isaac, his face frozen in disbelief.

"Don't worry. I didn't use curare. You'll live."

When the last of the longboats departed, Redferne and Isaac rowed out to the *Susan and Mary* that lay hove to some distance away. With the aid of the doctor's forceps, Isaac extracted the bullet from Padraig's shoulder. Then they transferred him to the *Kate O'Dwyer* and put him in the captain's bed. By the time they closed the door behind them, he was snoring.

"Apart from being a little drunk, he pulled through it okay," Isaac said.

Redferne clasped his hand. "I have total trust in you, but when you used the blowgun on Gleason, I thought you had gone over the edge."

"Tolliver was a sitting duck in that blue frock coat. Knew I couldn't reach Gleason before he got another shot off. His arm will sting for a few days, but other than that he'll be fine."

For the next hour, Redferne, Isaac, and Windham explored the hold and discovered a cargo of sugar, tea, tobacco, rum, and flax seed. According to Windham's estimate, it had a market value of over ten thousand pounds. "Amsterdam is your best bet to move this stuff, Irishman," Windham said, his eyes sweeping the hold. "It's a pretty open city and I think you could get a good price. Since the Dutch have been supplying the American colonists with loans and gunpowder, there's bad blood between themselves and the English. The Dutch burghers are unlikely to ask too many questions, if you get my drift."

"Mr. Windham? Can you excuse us, I'd like to talk with my mates," Redferne said.

Windham took his leave reluctantly, judging from the squint in his eye. Redferne gathered his men on the forecastle deck and disclosed Windham's estimate about the value of the cargo. They buzzed with excitement. "I don't need to tell you that this transaction could make us all wealthy men. And that figure doesn't include the sale of the ship. More important than that—we now have the means to return home."

Isaac spoke. "Europe is not Africa, which I doubt many of us want to return to." He looked around at his black mates, who nodded. "Europe, be it England, France, Spain, or Ireland is hardly a hospitable place for a black man; an escaped slave to boot. How long would we survive in the white man's land before being clapped in irons and returned to Barbados, Virginia, or some similar hellhole?"

"You're forgetting something," Redferne said. "You'd be wealthy."

Isaac and the other Africans laughed. "Black men with wealth. They'd accuse us of thievery and hang us on the spot. I'm afraid this is where we part company, friend." He looked at Redferne. "Besides, us black folk are best suited to the tropics. Don't want to spend the rest of our lives freezing our arses off in some frigid European climate." Chuckles followed, but they were forced.

Redferne felt crestfallen.

"Don't look so dejected, Redferne. It's not as if we're leaving empty-handed. We have a boat, with a hold full of wine and coffee." He gestured toward the sloop. "Once the *Kate O'Dwyer* donates a little sugar, and a swallow or two of rum, it should hold us until we go into business for ourselves."

Redferne embraced him. "You old scoundrel. I suppose you're going into the shipping business."

"As soon as we dispose of our cargo, get additional crew, and a new flag."

"I hear Tortuga is open for business," Redferne said.

"So I'm told."

It took about two hours to load the sloop, and by late afternoon, the *Susan and Mary* sailed away. Redferne stood at the taffrail as she turned for Tortuga. According to Kilbane's reckoning, it lay six hundred miles to the northwest. As the distance between the ships grew, Isaac turned and waved. Redferne returned the farewell. Would he ever see his friend again?

Seamus Beirne

CHAPTER 47

With the aid of the chronometer and Windham's expertise, the *Kate O'Dwyer* made a fast Atlantic crossing. Three weeks after separating from the *Susan and Mary*, she dropped anchor in the port of Amsterdam at a dilapidated wharf near the entrance to the North Sea.

A week later on an overcast day in a cavernous warehouse filled with barrels and bales of merchandise, two streets back from the Keizergracht Canal, Redferne, Gleason, and Windham sat at a table with a Dutch merchant named Johan Zoutman. This was their second meeting, having allowed Zoutman to inspect the ship and cargo two days previous.

A balding man in his fifties with an unkempt black goatee and a ring in his ear, he wore sailor's slops under a shabby purple frock coat with torn pockets. The squint of his ferret eyes belied his smile. He looked nothing like the businessman he purported to be, but more the front man Windham knew him to be for a smuggling cartel based in Rotterdam. An ink pot holding a quill and a stack of foolscap sat on the table in front of him.

"You can't be serious," Redferne said, after Zoutman offered five thousand pounds sterling for the *Kate O'Dwyer* and its cargo. Redferne looked for reassurance from Windham.

Zoutman stroked his straggly goatee and stared at Redferne with a blank face like a poker player assessing the competition. "Gentlemen, I assume you landed on my doorstep because I'll not ask questions. A no-questions-asked deal comes with certain conditions. We call it a take-it-or-leave it-transaction."

Windham slammed his fist on the table. "Look mate, you're not the only take-it-or-leave-it player in town. We can always take our business to Lodewijk van Bylandt."

A flicker of concern crossed Zoutman's face. "His offer will undercut mine, I assure you."

"Then he'll get the great deal you passed up, because let me tell you when you piss off these Irishmen, they'll not come crawling back to you, Herr Zoutman," Windham shot back.

"My financial backers are likely to ask for confirmation of lawful title to the *Kate O'Dwyer*, which I assume you can produce."

Redferne rose from his chair. "Title my arse. Stop playing games and make a realistic offer, not one that would barely purchase the longboats on the *O'Dwyer*."

"If producing a title was a requirement among you chaps," Windham said taking Redferne's lead and standing, "your backers would be eating shite with the hogs a long time ago."

Gleason looked from Redferne to Windham and back again. A door opened behind them and the grey afternoon slithered in like a damp cloud ahead of two individuals who looked as if they spent their time keeping order in a grog house. Redferne reached for the pistol in his waistband. Gleason and Windham followed suit.

"Gentlemen, gentlemen," Zoutman intervened, "there's no call for hasty action." He waved off his visitors. "Two of my runners is all, come to receive their assignments for the day. I'm afraid their manners aren't up to snuff, barging in like that." Redferne let out a mocking laugh.

Only after Zoutman handed over a leather bag containing 9,000 pounds sterling did Redferne agree to take the new owner to the *O'Dwyer's* hiding place in IJ Bay on the North Sea.

After dividing the proceeds among them, the former slaves went their separate ways. Craig, Gleason, and Noone choose to accompany Redferne and Padraig back to Ireland. MacTigh opted to stay in Amsterdam, and still others including Kilbane and Windham heeded the call of the open sea once more.

"Methinks I'll go in search of old Isaac." Kilbane winked

before turning on his heel and following Windham. "He may need a good helmsman."

A sad smile creased Redferne's weathered face. "If you find him, tell him I hope we'll meet again someday." Kilbane waved without turning, holding high the chronometer from the *Kate O'Dwyer*, then disappeared into the crowd milling on the wharf.

The next day Redferne and company boarded a packet ship from the Hook of Holland bound for Dublin.

Two days of rough sailing saw them through the North Sea into the English Channel, where they rounded the Isles of Scilly off southern England and entered the Irish Sea to fair weather. Two days later, they sighted Howth Head at the entrance to Dublin Bay. When they tied up at the Liffey docks, Redferne had a knot in the pit of his stomach at setting foot on his native land for the first time in two years.

The expressions on the faces of his companions showed similar emotions. At first he thought it was the fear of returning to the old oppression. After all, this was the birthplace of their misfortunes.

They moved cautiously along the docks, jostling with sailors, merchants, and laborers. Although 2,000 miles from the Sugar Island, the mentality of slavery, suspicion, fear, and insecurity lurked within them like poison seeds ready to sprout. They must learn to live again like free men, but not like the freemen they used to be; this time freemen of means. Redferne touched the money belt around his waist. It felt good.

The smell of bacon frying brought them to a halt. Without a word, they followed their noses along the quays and arrived outside the door of the Travelers' Friend tavern.

Redferne looked up at the jovial fat man on the sign holding a plate of steaming pancakes in one hand, a tankard of beer in the other. "Don't know about you boys, but I can't think of a better way to celebrate our return home than with a good Irish breakfast of bacon and black pudding."

"Jaysus, I didn't know I was so hungry until I smelled the blessed bacon frying. After that slop on board the packet, I could eat a baby's arse through a sugan chair," Gleason said to general laughter.

Once inside the tavern they ordered the biggest breakfast on the bill of fare: sausages, bacon, kidneys, black pudding, and mugs of tea. A large circular bar surrounded by stools filled the center of the room. Most of the stools had occupants, even at this early hour, chatting in foreign languages. Tables and chairs took up the remaining space, with few empty spots remaining. Waiters and waitresses hustled through the swinging kitchen doors, releasing a draft of breakfast aromas with every swing.

Redferne patted his chest as they settled into a corner table. "This is on me."

"Can you afford it?" Craig asked. They laughed like children surprised by Christmas gifts they never thought of receiving.

"A toast," Padraig said, raising his mug. "Farewell to *loblolly*. May we never eat such slop again."

They put their mugs down, clapped their hands and shouted. "No more *loblolly*, no more *loblolly*," pounding their fists on the table. The breakfast patrons took up the chant: "No more *loblolly*, no more *loblolly*." The foreigners at the bar joined in. When the commotion died down, they fell silent.

Then Redferne raised his mug. "A toast to all the friends and kin we lost," he nodded to Gleason, "and to those still slaving under the devil sun and the rawhide whip." They all drank. "And those that sent them there," he said under his breath, "are here on this island." For a time, the only sounds were the slurping of tea, the grinding of teeth, and the rattle of knives and forks as the new freemen made up for lost time.

"It's time we turned our faces toward our current situation," Redferne said breaking the silence.

The others paused in their eating and looked at him as if they could not deal with such a decision until they satisfied their hunger.

"Padraig and I are heading home to Cloonfin in County Roscommon to clear up a few loose ends." In case he was mistaken, he wanted to double-check the brand on Maureen Kelly's corpse.

Craig straightened in his chair. "I'm going south to my home county of Tipperary as soon as I buy myself a fine horse." As he uttered the words "fine horse," a smile lit up his face.

Colin took the mug of tea from his mouth. "Me too. After I get a horse, I'll be going back to Sligo to buy a few acres of land for my parents and siblings."

Gleason spoke. "I'm heading home to my parents in Monaghan to break the news of Sean's death."

Redferne recalled the grim scene of the younger Gleason's burial at sea. "Right then, I suppose we better be shoving off." He lowered his head, uncomfortable at the prospect of saying farewell.

They lingered awhile longer, promising to keep in touch, now that they had the means to do so, but a heavy feeling hung in the air like a dense fog, so they quickly shook each other's hands and went their separate ways.

Seamus Beirne

CHAPTER 48

The clerk at the Bank of Ireland on Capel Street in Dublin, a little man with darting eyes, adjusted his ruffled neck sock and brushed the lapels of his immaculate green frock coat when the two shabby individuals asked to open an account. The older of the two wore a scruffy brown jacket over a frayed waistcoat with several buttons missing. An unkempt beard covered his deeply-tanned face. The younger looked as ragged.

"One minute," the clerk said, backing away from the pair as if they had leprosy. He retreated into the recesses of the building, returning a moment later with a bewigged gentleman in a gunmetal grey coat with brass buttons arrayed down each side. A pince nez clung to the bridge of his nose. "This is the manager, Mr. Steele."

"May I help you?" Steele asked in a tone one might use with an uninvited guest at the first ball of the season.

"That remains to be seen. Yer man here acts as if we stumbled into the wrong establishment," Redferne said, tipping his head toward the clerk.

"This is a bank, sir. Again, how may we assist you?"

"An establishment where one can borrow or deposit money, right?"

The manager closed his eyes and sighed. "Let me guess. You've come to borrow, right?"

Redferne unbuckled his money belt and set it on the counter. "No, we're looking for a place to stow this. Over £5,000 in it."

The manager's eyes grew to twice their normal size. "Yes, yes, of course, sir, please follow me." He opened a section of the counter and, all but tripping over himself, led them into a back office through an oak-paneled door.

Half an hour later, the two liberated slaves emerged with bank notes totaling a thousand pounds in several denominations, with the balance locked away in the vault.

"Son, we need to find ourselves a barber and a draper if we are to play our new roles as gentlemen convincingly," Redferne said as they headed toward Sackville Street in search of self-improvement.

The mail coach from Dublin pulled into Longford at five in the afternoon on a glorious spring day. No one paid attention to the two strangers emerging from the carriage in their finery. Next day they bought two horses and set out for Cloonfin, twelve miles to the south. For fear of attracting the attention of highwaymen, they changed back into grubby attire, looking more like traveling linen merchants than gentry.

They rode along through an expanse of bog purpled in heather, all the way to the mountain known as Sliabh Bawn. They strained to see a skylark soaring invisible against a blue sky, its song clear and vibrant. Rabbits ran across their path; children chased each other laughing around clamps of turf. It was as if time stood still. Had Maureen Kelly traveled this road on her journey home, only to have her life snuffed out soon thereafter? Having survived the horrors of Barbados, her unexpected appearance must have posed a mortal threat to her abductors.

He thought of the "WS" brand on his buttocks to steel himself for what lay ahead. Turning to Padraig, he cleared his throat and said, "Son, we're coming to Preston territory. The first thing we have to do is find your mother and get you both to safekeeping."

Padraig kneed his horse's flanks. "I can take care of myself. Remember the tack barn."

Redferne chuckled. "Believe me, I haven't forgotten. You've had a brutal apprenticeship in survival. That's why I'm entrusting your mother's wellbeing to you, because if my plan succeeds, there may be reprisals."

Redferne lapsed into silence as they rode in single file along the rutted road. The familiar scent of the heather drifting on the wind smelled intoxicating, conjuring up deeply buried images and memories. Soon they were at the outskirts of Cloonfin. Redferne reined his horse off the road at the bridge and followed the meandering river toward the Big House.

Padraig pulled sharply on his reins. "Isn't this the last place we want to be if you're so concerned about my safety?"

"Can't risk going through the town. Someone might spot us. Too soon for that yet."

"But we're headed straight to..."

"We're not going up and knocking at Preston's front door, if that's what's spooking you—not yet, at any rate."

They reached the large mound that was the ice house. It rose up among the beech trees like a giant abscess, sinister in the half-light of the setting sun. Redferne broke out in a sweat and old fears came rushing back. They dismounted and hobbled their horses to a low-lying branch, now clothed in full spring foliage. The horses swished their tails and shook their manes to shoo away gnats and midges swarming about their heads. Redferne stepped toward the door in the arch.

"Aren't you forgetting something, Father? You no longer have a key to this place."

"Be patient." He ran his hand over the archway, stopping near its crest. "Funny how the fingers never forget the feel of something." He removed a rusty key from behind a loose stone and inserted it in the old lock. "I told Preston I lost it. When he replaced it, I hid the original above the archway. If things got desperate, we could find refuge here from the elements and Ben Strange could rustle up something for us to eat."

After pushing and pulling, they managed to push the door in. "Seems it hasn't been opened in a long time," Redferne said. A draft of cold air hit their faces. Before entering, they checked their surroundings and listened. The only sound was the jingling of harness as the horses foraged for grass beneath the trees.

"Padraig, go back to the saddle bags and get the candles and flint box," he whispered, not sure why he lowered his voice.

After several tries, he managed a spark and got the tinder to flame. They lit the candles and placed them in the lanterns on the wall inside the door. Then they made their way down the circular stairs, casting eerie shadows on the curved brick walls. At the bottom, Redferne foraged until he found an ice pick. Raising the lanterns over their heads, they viewed the ice stack sitting sphinx-like before them, much as they left it.

"This last part I must do on my own." Redferne leaned the ladder against the stack. Taking the lantern and ice pick, he climbed to the top and chipped away at the area where he laid Maureen to rest. Chunks of ice exploded against the brick walls. Beads of sweat oozed from his forehead.

After twenty minutes the ice pick struck a metallic object. He yanked it out. Its tip had pierced the reservoir of an old lantern. Oil bubbled to the surface like embalming fluid.

"Oh, God." Someone else had been here after him. He clawed around until his fingers closed on what felt like string or twine. "Padraig, come up here. I need a second light."

Padraig held both lanterns over the trench. "Jesus, Mary, and Joseph," Redferne said, looking down at the fistful of frozen hair in his hand. He stared transfixed at the once-handsome face of captain Preston, now shriveled to the texture of frozen butter. Whoever killed him surely discovered Maureen's body beforehand. Had the killer or killers suspected that he had hidden her body? It might explain why he was shipped off to Barbados, but why kill the captain? The captain's murder dethroned him as the central figure in Redferne's misfortune. Would old man Preston kill his own son? He made a quick sign of the cross at the thought.

He hadn't the stomach to dig deeper. Since Preston's body was higher up in the trench, he assumed that the killer had simply dumped the captain on top of the corpse beneath. "Let's get out of here," he said after filling the trench up with ice rubble. "There are no more answers here."

Climbing down from the ice stack Padraig turned to go up the stairs. "No," Redferne said. "We have to enter the belly of the beast." He opened the interior door and they crept down the subterranean passage toward the Big House. Moonlight filtered through the ventilation bars, giving the whitewashed walls a translucent glow.

Seamus Beirne

CHAPTER 49

"Let's get rid of him and be done with it." Lady Preston paced back and forth between her writing desk and the floor-to-ceiling windows overlooking the parkland. Catching a glimpse of herself in the mirror she froze. Her customarily coiffured hair looked disheveled, and the worry lines on her face competed with the first rivulets of age nesting under her eyes. She scowled and turned her attention again to the letter written in her uncle's neat hand. "*Kate O'Dwyer* overdue; feared lost." She slammed it down on the desk. What he didn't say, but implied was, "Kiss your monthly remittance goodbye."

Bannister stared out the window at a red fawn scampering among the beech trees under the watchful eyes of a doe. A dark cloud lingered above Sliabh Bán threatening rain. Yesterday, he spotted the first streaks of grey in his hair. The vagaries of time and fortune could snatch away youth and wealth in the blink of an eye. Lady Preston was becoming a scourge. For the first time, he entertained a sympathetic thought for Lord Preston. The Lord of the estate, now broken in mind and body, spent his days confined to a wheelchair under the stern gaze of his dour ancestor with the bullethole in his chest.

Lady Preston stamped her foot. "Are you listening to me?"

"Unfortunately, yes, and what you suggest is madness."

"Do you have a better plan?"

"Killing another Preston is not going to solve our problems and could bring everything—what's left of it—crashing down on our heads."

She grabbed the letter and waved it. "Everything already has crashed around us: the rents, the smuggling runs, the Whiteboy menace, and now this."

Bannister conceded that the loss of the *O'Dwyer* was a huge problem, cutting off two major sources of revenue, the smuggling and the slave trade, but killing Lord Preston was tantamount to suicide.

She tossed the letter aside. "So you are going to let misfortune roll over you like *him* instead of fighting back. Wonder how long before we'll be in Dublin outfitting *you* for a wheelchair."

Bannister slapped her across the face with such force that it sent her flying back against the window, where she landed in a heap in the alcove.

He jabbed his finger at her. "Listen to me. I'm not following you down this crazy path. What's called for here is calm, not panic. Killing the head of the Preston estate who is also the High Sheriff of the county is not like killing his wayward playboy son." She lay among the folds of the draperies, whimpering. Blood trickled from her nose leaving red blotches on her white ruffled collar. He thought about helping her up, but the impulse faded. He turned his mind back to the dark cloud that threatened to engulf them.

The Preston property rested precariously on the trap door of the Encumbered Estates Court, with a fast sale being the only option left to avoid penury, but the Lord's pride would not let him do that. Lady Preston would inherit everything, but there was one big fly in that ointment: the bank would seize a hefty percentage of the proceeds. As the estate agent, he realized that. Lady Preston, on the other hand, had only a vague notion of what that entailed. The only way out was to implement his original plan of mass evictions, but the Lord had resisted, and the newly-energized Whiteboy Organization fought against them.

Times had changed. Fear of a French invasion seized the country when British forces departed Ireland to deal with insurrection in the American colonies. An aggressive volunteer movement had sprung up to handle crises on the home front, emboldening landholders to react brutally to the slightest threat to their security.

Now might be the perfect time to rid the estate of its tenants, most of whom were apt to go over to the French in the event of an invasion. Letting the freeloaders starve on the roadside would address that problem in short order. He could consolidate a good percentage of the cleared potato plots into grazing for the more lucrative enterprise of dairy farming.

Would the Lord cooperate, or would misplaced feelings for his tenants overrule his common sense yet again? With arms behind his back, he walked over to Lady Preston's writing desk and poured a glass of claret, then returned to the window to study the grazing deer. If he acted precipitously and failed, all his schemes could explode like wizards' touch powder. He massaged his stubbled cheeks with thumb and forefinger. Maybe there was something to what Lady Preston was suggesting after all.

Removing the Lord would mean dealing with his widow. While they both wanted power and money, they differed on the best approach to achieve those ends, but she was persuadable. He went over, lifted her into his arms, and carried her into the boudoir.

Seamus Beirne

CHAPTER 50

Redferne emerged from the service passageway and made his way to the door of what he assumed was still Benjamin's room. Padraig remained concealed in the shadows as lookout. He put his ear to the door. Loud snoring from within. Could he be sure it was Benjamin? There was only one way to find out. He gently turned the pewter-colored knob and inched the door forward. Thankfully, it didn't squeak. The snoring stopped and a frail voice whispered, "No need to tread so lightly, friend, this blunderbuss will find you in the dark."

"Benjamin, it's me—Redferne."

"Either you are a knave, or I've crossed over to the other side where I'm suffering the torments of hell, but the heft of this weapon says otherwise. Who are you?" His voice sounded hoarse from sleep.

"I tell you Ben, it's me, Michael Redferne, returned from a place far worse than hell. I'm no ghost. I'm alive and so is Padraig."

"Back up and find the candle in the alcove near the door. Light it from the fire and raise it to your face."

Redferne did as instructed, all the while glancing nervously in the direction of the voice and the blunderbuss. Such a weapon could blow a hole the size of a mature sheep in a barn door. Definitely not to be trifled with. He raised the candle shakily to his face and prayed that Benjamin had his wits about him—if it was Benjamin?

"Higher," the voice said.

He complied and spotted the flared mouth of the gun moving erratically as if its owner was struggling to keep it steady. Sweat broke out on his face. "Careful with that thing, Ben."

They came soft at first, and then the sobs grew louder. At last, the muzzle dropped.

Redferne lowered the candle and moved closer to the frail form of his old friend propped up in bed with the muzzle loader by his side.

"Pray tell me I'm not dreaming," Benjamin wept as Redferne bent down and put his arm around the old man's hunched shoulders.

"It's me Ben, sure enough." His throat tightened as he tried to strangle his own sob. "I'll go and get Padraig now."

When Padraig entered, Benjamin clasped both his hands. "What a strapping young lad you've become."

Redferne raised the lantern and looked around the room where Captain Preston attacked him two years before. Nothing had changed except Benjamin, who looked frailer and more hunched over than before.

He placed the lantern on the mantelpiece and removed his hat and coat. Benjamin got out of bed, added turf to the fire, and filled the kettle for tea.

"You'll find three mugs and a jug of milk in that wee press. Sorry I haven't anything more substantial to offer you."

"Ben, don't worry about it. We ate in Longford less than three hours ago, and anyway you weren't expecting visitors in the middle of the night."

"As I get older, I find my appetite decreasing, so I normally don't eat after supper." When the tea was ready, Ben settled into his chair at the fire. Redferne and Padraig pulled up theirs and sat beside him, each cradling a mug of strong tea.

Redferne poured out his story and Benjamin followed intently, reaching out occasionally to grasp each of them by the arms as if to reassure himself that his midnight visitors were real. On hearing about Captain Preston's fate, a look of sadness crossed his wrinkled face.

"I care not for him, but I'm sorry for His Lordship's sake. He has been good to me. His son's disappearance eats at him like a cancer."

"Maybe this discovery will bring him some peace," Redferne

said, feeling like a hypocrite in light of the hell he was planning to bring down on the Prestons.

Benjamin looked into the fire and whispered. "May it be so, may it truly be so."

The pit of Redferne's stomach tightened as he studied Benjamin's face. He didn't reveal Bannister's allegations about Lord Preston's part in his enslavement. When he concluded his story, he asked Benjamin, "How are things here?"

Benjamin raised his eyes and looked directly at him. "Worse than when you left, at least for some."

"Where is my mother?" Padraig asked.

Benjamin looked from one to the other before replying. "No need to tell you that things can go awry."

Padraig gasped and Redferne's knees went wobbly. "For God's sake, out with it. Don't leave the boy guessing."

"When Parson Stack was murdered, people blamed Grace for directing the killer to him, although by all accounts she did it unknowingly." A fit of sneezing seized Benjamin. He pulled a faded handkerchief from his right cuff to blow his nose. "It happens every spring, when the flowers bloom." He stretched his face so that his eyes opened wide before stuffing the handkerchief back in his cuff.

Padraig got a blanket from Benjamin's bed and draped it across the old man's shoulders.

"Benjamin, please?" Redferne said.

"The snubs, the slights, and the ostracization got too much for her, and in the end they drove the good lady off. Last I heard, she was staying with an uncle somewhere in the County Galway."

"In Athenry, with Grand Uncle Seamus?" Padraig said.

"Athenry, I do believe that's correct," Benjamin said.

Redferne hugged Padraig and let himself breathe again. "You will have to find her, Son. When I finish my business here I'll join you."

An old clock on the mantle struck one, time to depart, but Benjamin wouldn't hear of it.

"I have much yet to tell you," he said.

"Before you go further I need to ask you where Rory Blake was when my Grace was going through rough times? Did he try to help her? Before I was transported, he and the Whiteboys were benefiting handsomely from the smuggling operations."

"That's part of the 'much left to tell you.' He tried to help her, but as the Whiteboys' power grew, he became more absorbed in running the group than helping the unfortunate."

Redferne felt his face grow hot, this time not from fear, but from anger. Padraig's head dropped. At Redferne's suggestion, he curled up in a quilt and stretched out in a corner of the room.

"He's grown big and strong," Benjamin said, looking at the sleeping lad. "His mother will be overjoyed to see him."

"That she will. Ben, we may have to bunk with you for a few days until we get ourselves situated." Redferne added, stifling a yawn with the palm of his hand. Fear flitted across Benjamin's face and he fidgeted with his hands.

Redferne shifted uneasily. "What's the matter, Ben?"

"You may recall my earlier answer that things had gotten worse for some. Well, include me in that category." His voice trailed off into a whisper.

"I thought His Lordship was good to you?"

"Indeed he is, a real gentleman. Unfortunately, he's no longer master of his own house. Lady Preston and Bannister are in control now. They run the place with an iron fist. Lord Preston spends most of his time confined to a wheelchair in the library."

"Have they threatened you?"

"People walk around whispering. There is no joy here anymore. Suspicion reigns. That's why I keep the blunderbuss."

"But you keep your door unlocked. Odd behavior for one who's afraid."

"In their paranoia, they have imposed a curfew and do room checks from time to time."

"What in the hell are they afraid of? They're the top dogs in the county."

"Everything. The Whiteboys, their declining fortunes, fear of rebellion among their tenants."

"So they see the staff as potential allies of the tenants in an uprising."

"I suppose. Who knows? They don't need a reason."

"Believe me, I understand that. It seems the world is one big prison for poor folk, from Barbados to Ireland. Skin color may be different, the weather may vary, but starvation and fear seem to be universal weapons of the powerful. I intend to change that."

"Don't do anything rash, I beg you," Benjamin said, joining his hands as if in prayer. "Bannister moves quickly at the slightest provocation as do the other landlords. He particularly resents me because he thinks I have influence with Lord Preston."

"Then why do you stay here? Surely Rory Blake can take care of you. He owes you that much and more." Benjamin became uneasy. Redferne sensed that he wasn't telling him everything. He pressed him further. "Why not tell Rory your time of service is at an end and you need his support?"

"I could do that, but that would leave me with another...ah, shall we say, a certain responsibility I feel I can't walk away from."

"And what would that be?"

He looked away. "Lord Preston needs me to look after him." There it was again. Once his sworn enemy, Preston was now Benjamin's friend. It complicated things. Didn't Benjamin suspect that Preston was a wolf in sheep's clothing?

"What in hell obligation do you have to a family who physically maimed you and kept you in bondage most of your existence?"

"Life's not as simple as that. The Lord's health has taken a turn for the worse in the last few days. I have to figure out what's causing the sudden change."

"If he's been in a wheelchair for the past year, isn't it just the natural progression of whatever ails him?"

"That's what worries me. What put him in the wheelchair was worry, disappointment, despair, and shame for what he considers his failure to ensure the prosperity of his family and his ancestral estates. It was more mental than physical."

"Why hasn't he been sent to an insane asylum. Isn't that where loonies are sent?"

"I don't expect you to understand this, but not everyone who has a problem of the mind is a lunatic. A lunatic doesn't suddenly start losing his hair and have his skin turn pallid. Something else's afoot."

Redferne didn't want to press the issue further, so he rose and shook Padraig. "Come on, Son, it's time we were on our way."

Padraig staggered to his feet rubbing his eyes. "But I thought we were..."

"Our presence here could put Benjamin in danger, so we best seek lodging elsewhere."

Benjamin sat staring into the dying fire. Before opening the door Redferne pressed a twenty pound note in Benjamin's palm. "Don't worry friend, I'll be back."

Benjamin glanced down at the paper in his hand and his mouth cracked open. "I feel like the lowest of cowards running you off like this." He clasped Redferne's hand in both of his.

"Don't concern yourself with that. It's a lovely night. We'll sleep outdoors if we have to. Besides, we can always head for Rory Blake's safe house, if it's still operating as such." Benjamin became animated and lurched to his feet.

"It might be best if you first call on Andrew Hicks at the Cock and Bull Tavern. He will do right by you."

CHAPTER 51

"Stay back a ways. I'll go on foot from here," Redferne whispered, dismounting and handing the reins of his horse to Padraig. A pallid moon roamed the sky trying to hide behind threadbare clouds. He checked his pocket watch. It was a few minutes to two in the morning. A thin breeze came in fits, rustling the leaves of the birch trees overhanging the Cock and Bull Inn. As one might expect, no lights shone in the windows at this hour, which did not necessarily mean that no one was watching.

Wanting to bypass the front door, he detoured around the side through a stand of trees that flanked the inn. The curmudgeonly, Andrew Hicks, proprietor would not be blamed for thinking that anyone sneaking up on his establishment at this hour might be up to no good. Redferne watched where he placed his feet to avoid snapping fallen branches. Hicks kept a loaded blunderbuss at the ready. One did not want to surprise him, especially half-asleep.

He exited the trees near the horse stable and went in. He found a lantern hanging near the door and lit it. Little had changed. It smelled of hay, tack, and horse dung. A carriage stood in a far corner with its door standing open as if someone was getting ready to disembark. He paused and listened with his hand closed around the butt of his pistol. Along the right wall ran a bank of stalls with horses in the first four, contentedly chomping hay. Rather than disturb Andrew, he and Padraig would be comfortable enough here until morning. After stabling their horses in two of the empty stalls, they found another for themselves behind the coach and settled in for the night on a bed of straw.

Redferne quenched the lantern and soon drifted into an uneasy sleep filled with sounds and images. The voice in his dream seemed to come from afar, yet it felt familiar. The noise of the hurricane roared in his head and the voice receded, then surged back like a wave crashing onto a beach, saying, "Wake up Red, wake up!" He recognized it as the voice of Isaac. Other voices sounded more distinct.

"What a bloody wild goose chase that was," one said.

Redferne woke covered in sweat. The predawn light streaming through the double doors painted the stable with a pale hue, as if the world drained of its colors had been reduced to a primitive tint that transformed everything into a drab grey. Padraig snored gently beside him.

"I say we go back and finish him off," another voice said with a tone of urgency. The sounds of horses being saddled filled the stable. This was no dream.

"It will look like a robbery, so why bother?" the first voice said.

"But he knows who we were looking for. The boss is going to be steamed if that news gets out." Redferne drew his pistol and peered around the corner of the stall, seeing three men, but he could not make out any distinguishing features in the grey atmosphere. "I thought we were the only guests in the inn last night," the first one said, "but here are two more horses now."

"What's so strange about that? It's an inn, isn't it?"

"It wouldn't be, except we locked the inn doors after we checked in last night, or has all that free grog addled your brain?"

Redferne nudged Padraig awake. "We have company."

"Yes, but Hicks could have let someone in after we finished our meal," a third said.

"Still, it makes me uneasy," the first voice said. "We better give this place the once over."

Redferne gestured to Padraig to crawl under the carriage with him.

"Whoever these gents are, they have money. These are two fine horses." Someone stepped into the carriage. Showers of dust rained down on Redferne and Padraig with every step the searcher took.

338

"Okay, let's mount up and get out of here."

"Shouldn't we search the inn? After all, that's the logical place to find this pair."

"We already searched the bloody place."

"This is awful strange, that's all I can say."

At the sound of shod hooves on the cobbled stone floor, Redferne released a long breath as the interlopers led their horses outside. Then. "I'm going to silence Reid."

"Jesus Christ, Howard, he'll croak before anyone discovers what happened."

"In that case, I'll hurry things up."

"Have it your way, but make it clean and silent, and while you're at it, check again for those phantom guests."

"Bring my horse 'round to the front. I'll catch up with you later."

"You're taking an unnecessary risk, mate."

"I'll be fine. I have my lucky rabbit's foot."

"Great good it did the fucking rabbit," someone swore.

They clattered out of the stable with their mate's horse in tow. A shadowy figure headed for the back door of the inn.

Redferne pulled off his boots. "I'm going after him. Don't stir from here and keep your pistol cocked."

"I'm going with you."

"No. This is something I have to do myself." He stalked the would-be assassin in his stocking feet through the back door, unsheathing his dagger. The house lay in semi-darkness as he shadowed the man to one of the upstairs bedrooms. He reached the open door as the would-be killer raised his knife over Hicks, bound hand and foot to a chair. In a quick movement, Redferne cut his throat from behind. The heat of the blood startled him when it gushed over his hand and sprayed the innkeeper's head and shoulders.

Redferne untied the innkeeper and helped him to a bed where he spooned him sips of water. Some of the bruises were seared black, indicating that they were caused by a red-hot poker.

"Who were these thugs, Andrew?"

"Can't say for sure," Reid whispered through bloodied lips, "but when they told me who they were looking for I laughed at them because I thought they were insane."

"Who were they looking for?"

"They were looking for someone who apparently has come back from the dead. You."

CHAPTER 52

Redferne's thoughts raced as he spurred his horse up the mountain road to the safe house, travelling by night to avoid detection. After securing help for Hicks, he sent Padraig in search of his mother. Given Padraig's experience in Barbados, he knew that he could take care of himself, and hopefully plead his father's case before her.

He turned in his saddle several times to check behind him. The starry night, dominated by the Plough constellation, barely lit the road ahead, winding its way through stands of mountain ash. How did the intruders know he and Padraig were headed to the Cock and Bull? No one knew they were even in the country except Benjamin. His mind rebelled at the thought of betrayal. Benjamin *had* acted odd when Redferne suggested seeking shelter with Rory Blake, directing them to the Cock and Bull instead. Had Benjamin been compromised?

Redferne didn't know whom to believe, but with the news of his return already out, there was a gaping hole somewhere in the loyalty of his old friends. Hitting a dark patch where the trees arched over the road, he dismounted, fearing an ambush. He walked his horse till the Plough shone through again. Benjamin said that much had changed, but Redferne had no idea that basic alliances had shifted. Had Benjamin arranged to have him killed?

Could he trust Rory Blake? He recalled the biblical reference to a *nest of vipers*. Ireland was supposed to be free of snakes—except the human kind. The last quarter mile up the mountain trail ran steep and dangerous, so he dismounted as much to sort his own thoughts as to spare his horse.

Benjamin assured him that the safe house was in the same location, but when he got to the little valley, he was surprised to see that Blake had added more stables and barns. Lights glowed in several of the windows, not the signature of a dwelling trying to pass unnoticed. He tied his horse to a tree and sat beneath it, taking a slug of water from his canteen to ponder his next move. This was supposed to be an outlaw hideout, but it didn't look like one. Did Blake's hedge school still have a bag for a door? Was Blake even in the school mastering business anymore?

A rustle of branches behind him.

"I didn't know ghosts needed horses," a voice said from the darkness.

Redferne jumped up. "And I didn't expect you'd be tipped off to my arrival, Rory,"

"Wasn't. You happened to get here during my watch. Simple as that. No skullduggery involved. I'm on from midnight to three."

"I'll bet. Seems like you have a lot to watch over. The place looks like the Big House, not an outlaw hideout."

"Not what you might call a friendly greeting for an old friend," Blake said, stepping out from the shadows of the trees with a musket in his hand.

"Not sure I can call you that anymore, Rory. The last time I relied on your advice, I ended up going overseas."

"Jack Oldham was a sailor, not a saint. I say *was*, because after his encounter with you, nobody has seen hide nor hair of him."

Redferne palmed the butt of his pistol. "And you left it at that, huh?"

"Myself and a few of the lads went to Sligo. Combed the docks and taverns. Talked to sailors and shore men for days, but no luck. You and Oldham had vanished without a trace."

"By the looks of things here, the smuggling business seems to be ticking along nicely," Redferne said.

Blake gestured toward the compound. "I want you to know that none of this would have happened without you."

"Damn right it wouldn't, and from the reports I've heard, and what I see with my own eyes, I'm wondering why I fought O'Driscoll to the death in the freezing river."

"You've been talking to Benjamin. He tends to sees things in black and white. Unfortunately life is a little more nuanced than that. Something he doesn't understand." He leaned his musket against a tree trunk.

"Not impressed by your big words, schoolmaster. Apparently, Benjamin, one of the smartest men in the county, is no longer capable of understanding the complexities of life. Spare me the bullshit and explain why you failed to help my Grace in her hour of need."

As the sun rose, Redferne got a better look at Blake. His once salt and pepper hair had gone almost completely grey. His face looked full and jowly and his midsection bulged a little over his belt. Living the good life, Redferne thought, while I labored under the whip in the devil sun.

Blake's voice constricted. "Not easy to help someone who spurns your help."

"And why would she spurn your help, pray?"

"You'll have to ask her that yourself. Maybe she lost faith in men, given the one she had to put up with those many years."

Redferne swung and caught Blake under the jaw, tumbling him down the hill toward the house. When the Whiteboy chief struggled to his feet, Redferne pounced on him, punching with his left and right. All the pent up rage of years exploded in a torrent and engulfed Rory Blake. Blake was no match for Redferne, who was lean and muscled from two years dodging death on the plantation. The commotion attracted the attention of those within and Roger and Brendan stormed out and pistol-whipped Redferne across the head.

Redferne woke with a splitting headache. A bird cage, hanging from the ceiling, creaked back and forth as the two squawking goldfinches skirmished, spraying the table with seed and husks. The musty smell of damp laundry twitched his nostrils. Rory Blake handed him a mug.

"Drink it. It's just spring water mixed with tobacco juice. It's good for a headache."

Redferne took the mug. "How do I know it's not poisoned?"

"Could already have done that had we a mind to. Though God knows, given the mess you've made of my face, I'm not sure why I hesitated."

Redferne rubbed the egg-sized bump on his head and sipped the bitter concoction.

"I apologize for that," Rory said nodding, "but Roger and Brendan didn't recognize you right off. They thought I was being attacked by a lunatic."

Redferne avoided Blake's glare. "I'm not sure what's worse, my headache, or this piss you're giving me to drink," By the looks of the black eye and the cuts on Blake's nose and lower lip, he had altered his face all right. He wasn't proud of it, but couldn't muster the courage to apologize.

"Piss or not it'll help your sore head. I'm right glad to see you. Gave you up for dead a long time ago." Blake held out his hand. Redferne shook it and felt relief, but not enough to lower his guard. He still had a lot of unanswered questions about Rory Blake and the Whiteboys.

Over the next few days as they both recovered, the tension between them subsided. Running the Whiteboy outfit took up a lot of his time, Blake confided. He admitted that to some extent he had lost control of it. "When it was Brendan and Roger, life was simpler, but we've grown in number since the smuggling money rolled in." They succeeded in curbing mass evictions, he said, by attacking Preston estate middlemen and subsidizing the rents of the destitute.

"You may have heard that Bannister is cock o' the walk since Lord Preston's son disappeared. Our resistance has pressured him into being more cooperative with us," Blake said.

"Resistance? Meaning attacks on middlemen like Tallford?"

"That and raids on the smuggling trains. We think Bannister is up to his eyes in moving contraband." Running his tongue over the cut on his lip, Blake took several sheets of paper from a dresser drawer and spread them out on the table top. He beckoned Redferne over. "These are rough maps of four smuggling routes. Two come from the port of Sligo and two from Galway." He traced his finger along the routes. "The two from Sligo pass through Cloonfin, the other two end up in Athlone, on the river Shannon."

"What's their ultimate destination?" Redferne asked, sitting at the table and pulling the maps toward him.

"Dublin."

"I can see why you might implicate Bannister in the smuggling trains from Sligo, but what's his connection to the Galway operation?"

"At first we thought there wasn't any till we shadowed a train leaving Galway to a pleasure craft on the Shannon River in the village of Tarmonbarry." Blake got up and walked to a window pulling the curtain back to peek outside.

"Something wrong?" Redferne asked.

"No, just the swallows in the eaves, but they make a hell of a racket. Checking to be sure." He let the curtain flap back and returned to the table. "After loading the boat, the smugglers hoisted sail and headed south on the Shannon."

"Dublin is southeast of Tarmonbarry, not due south," Redferne said.

"Right, but you know what is south? Shannonbridge, where the Grand Canal intersects the river. On a hunch we rode there overnight. The boat headed east on the Grand Canal."

Redferne gave a low whistle. "And the Grand Canal ends up in Dublin."

"You got it. Quite a slick operation. The authorities would never think of searching a pleasure craft for contraband."

"Great piece of detective work, but how does this point to Bannister?"

"We spread a little money around in Tarmonbarry, and guess who owns the boat? The Prestons."

Redferne slapped the table. "Nailed them."

"There's no doubt." Blake took two chalk pipes and a plug of tobacco from a box on the mantelpiece and handed a pipe to Redferne.

"Does Bannister know you're behind the raids on the smuggling trains?"

"No hedge schools in the Preston townlands have been disrupted since we started the raids. Plus evictions are way down," Blake said.

Those sounded like weak arguments to Redferne, but he pushed on. "And in return, what's Bannister getting out of it?"

"We've limited our attacks on his smuggling operation, focusing on opportunities further afield."

"So Bannister benefits from Whiteboy restraint."

"We're trying to avoid killing the goose that's laying the golden egg," Blake said.

"Where is Lord Preston in all of this?"

"Since he owns the boat, he's gotta' be in on it."

Redferne could easily accept this assessment, given Bannister's mocking comments to him before he was transported: *I merely do my employer's bidding...take it up with Lord Preston when you return from your trip overseas.*

After filling his pipe with tobacco, Blake passed the plug and a penknife across the table.

Redferne cut slivers from the plug and filled the bowl, but a central question still churned in the pit of his stomach. What was Blake's connection to Bannister? Blake passed him a flaming ember from the fire and Redferne puffed vigorously until the bowl glowed red. Soon the fragrant smell of tobacco replaced the musty smell of damp laundry. "Are you aware that young men and women have been disappearing off the streets and boreens around the Preston estate for the past two years?" Redferne watched Blake through the blue haze of tobacco smoke.

He whipped the pipe from his mouth and spat into the fire. "Heard these rumors. It's a myth. There's so much displacement from evictions and immigration that it's a short step to thinking that people who up and left were kidnapped."

"But you haven't investigated these missing people then?"

"There's not a shred of evidence to support such fantastic claims."

A chill went through Redferne. Was Blake turning a blind eye to the kidnappings? Either he was woefully out of touch as a result of his change of fortune, or he was stonewalling.

"What about Maureen Kelly then?" Redferne manipulated the shank of the pipe with his teeth and stared at Blake.

Blake looked startled. "Maureen Kelly? I presume she's in America"

A draft of air blew down the chimney, scattering an ash cloud into the kitchen, setting both of them coughing.

"Damn, I keep telling Roger to clean that flue. Some night we'll be suffocated in our beds," Blake said.

Redferne's eyes watered. "What if I told you…" He wiped his eyes with the heel of his hand, "that she was kidnapped, and that she spent some time in a slave colony on Barbados. Would you take these disappearances seriously then?"

"Not sure. It could be an isolated event that doesn't warrant jumping to conclusions. How would you know that, anyway?"

"I know it and so would you, if you had asked me a simple question when I came in here," Redferne answered.

Blake frowned. "What kinda' question?"

"This kind: 'Michael, what happened in Sligo town?' I would have said, 'Rory, I was kidnapped by Bannister, along with several others, and sent as a slave to work in the cane fields of Barbados, as was Padraig my son.' Remember him?"

Blake stuttered and fumbled and in general resembled a cornered rabbit. "Look, Michael, I felt guilt about your disappearance, because I felt responsible. Maybe I placed too much trust in Oldham? Fact is I didn't know him all that well, but I guarantee you I had nothing to do with your or your son's terrible ordeal."

"Did you know about Bannister's part in this?"

"Absolutely not."

Another blast came down the chimney, chasing them both outside.

Seamus Beirne

CHAPTER 53

Next day, Redferne fled the safe house without telling Blake, although he suspected it was only a matter of time before Blake tracked him down. Figuring it best to stay out of sight, he rented a little farmhouse from a financially-stressed middleman who asked no questions and stocked it with enough provisions for a month; bread, tea, eggs, potatoes, a half side of bacon, flour, and assorted vegetables. A bag of sugar sat on a shelf behind the shop counter, but the thought of purchasing it nauseated him.

It took him a week to track Gleason down and the better part of a day to win him over to his scheme. He expected him today. The whinnying of a horse in the front garden alerted him that Gleason had arrived. When he entered the little kitchen with a "God save all here," the two former slaves clasped each others' hands and embraced.

"Nice little place you got here." Gleason looked around and pointed to the ceiling. "It's a long way from plantain leaves and bamboo."

"Woven thatch. Walls two feet thick, a proper fireplace, and a well out back. Storms, but thank God no hurricanes in this part of the world."

"Half expected to see Isaac here."

Redferne paused hanging Gleason's coat behind the door. "Miss that man." He gazed out the glass window with two-feet-deep whitewashed sill. "I find myself talking to him every now and then."

"Since I've come home, I indulge myself in the luxury of washing up, so if..."

349

Redferne laughed and pointed to a little table with a soap dish and a basin. "Pardon my manners. You'll find a bucket of water and a ladle underneath it."

While Gleason splashed water on his face and washed his hands, Redferne busied himself setting the table. "Your timing is perfect," he said over his shoulder. "I figured after a long journey you could do with a little dinner. It's about ten minutes away."

"You figured right," Gleason said, throwing the contents of the basin out the back door. "Some of the slop that passes for food in these roadside taverns is worse than *loblolly*."

"By God, you've become a snob. Isn't it amazing how a bit of money raises one's standards?"

"Speaking of money, I hope you spent some of it on quality spirits. I want none of that moonshine piss." He came forward and sat beside the fire.

"I'll have you know that the *poteen* in these parts is the best in all of Ireland. Myself, though, I'm partial to Jameson." He took a five naggin bottle and two glasses off the dresser and joined Gleason beside the fire.

"Now you're talking."

They toasted each other's good fortune. When that round was over, Redferne raised his glass. "To our new business venture, may it put an end to tyranny in these parts."

Gleason's expression grew serious.

Redferne served up a meal of potatoes boiled with bacon and a generous helping of cabbage, and then he set a large pot of tea on the table.

Gleason shoveled forkfuls of potatoes and cabbage into his mouth. "So run this by me again. You're attempting to solve a murder, end the local slave trade, and reduce the most powerful landlord in the county—who is also the High Sheriff—to destitution."

"That's it in a nutshell."

"And this plan involves telling none of your old friends or acquaintances."

"Right again."

350

"I hope you're not biting off more than you can chew."

"I warned you it's not going to be easy, but I think I can hit the landlord where he is most vulnerable."

"I hope I'm not being naïve, but aren't you exaggerating your clout a little?" Gleason said.

"How so?"

"At the end of the day, you're still a peasant with money."

"Aye, but money is king, remember that."

"It may be among the lower classes, but it's not the sole measure of success among the gentry."

"I don't care how the high and mighty measure their success. I can live with their contempt as long as I get what I want," Redferne said.

"That's my point. They may block what you want."

"I'm afraid you're confusing me."

"Let me put it another way. What happens if a poor man finds himself out on the side of the road without money?"

"He'll starve to death."

"Precisely. Now when was the last time you heard one of the gentry starving to death for lack of money?" Gleason asked.

"Can't say that I have."

"Because in their minds, pedigree and social standing are far more important than money. They'll take care of their own."

Redferne poured himself and Gleason a cup of tea. "If the gentleman in question, Colonel Preston, doesn't accept a peasant's money, he will lose the entire investment of his ancestors going back two hundred years. He's up to his neck in debt with the banks. They won't bail him out, and his fellow landlords can't spare the money to save him." He put the teapot back on the coals and returned to the table.

"So you think you have him over a barrel."

"Yes and no. That's where you come in."

"Hold your horses a minute. I sure as hell am not throwing my money into a lost cause."

"Not asking you to do that."

"Then what are you on about?"

351

"Right now you'll need to trust me. I'll let you know in due course. Your main job will be to take my place. We're going to Cloonfin this afternoon to do a little bit of surveillance. It's market day."

"I need another shot of Jameson's, because if I'm going to impersonate you in the town you were born in, it'll take something a helluva lot stronger than tea," Gleason said.

"You'll be playing you, which in reality is me behind the scenes."

"So you're the puppet master, which makes me…?"

"Stop getting ahead of yourself. We'll take this a step at a time."

CHAPTER 54

They showed up in Cloonfin's market square that afternoon. Redferne drew quizzical glances from some in the crowd as if they recognized him but weren't quite sure, then noticing his powdered white wig and expensive clothes, they lost interest. He couldn't rely on the deception holding up, hence the need for Gleason, a complete unknown.

Along with the typical mix of pigs, turkeys, vegetables, and potatoes, the square buzzed with the shouts of weavers jostling and pushing each other to get the attention of the linen merchants. With a shrewdness honed by years of haggling, these men examined the hanks of linen the weavers placed before them, checking the weave, texture, and workmanship. Most importantly, they looked for the seal of the Linen Board. Without that, merchants would not make an offer.

Redferne nudged Gleason. "Look around, who do you think is the most important man in this market right now?"

Gleason appeared befuddled at first and then said, "I would have to say the linen merchants. They are the chaps with the money, not the weavers."

"Take another look. Where do you see the longest queue?"

"Over there near the market house."

A knot of people jostled for position in front of a one-story red brick building that flew the union flag of Great Britain.

"Right, let's sidle over there and check it out."

A tall, gaunt man in his sixties, wearing a black coat and matching black britches that stopped below the knee, stood behind a long table handling hanks of brown linen. Moving down the table, he held up each hank to the sun. After a thorough examination he either pushed it aside or inserted the edge of the linen between the jaws of a pincer-like implement to imprint his seal.

"You can see by his demeanor that this chap knows he has power," Redferne said. "Notice he is small on chitchat. He looks condescending and imperious."

"Who the hell is this guy?"

"Without his seal, these linen hanks might as well be turned into dish rags for all the good they'd be."

"I'm not arguing with you. Yon' unsmiling individual seems to be cock-of-the-walk in the linen business."

"You can say that again," Redferne moved through the crowd of weavers stealing glances at the man in the black attire. "This gentleman is called a Seal Master, appointed by the Linen Board. Without his stamp of approval, months of hard work are all for naught."

"So?"

"I want you to be him."

"I thought you wanted me to be you." Gleason stopped his mouth agape.

"I want you to be me playing him. I brought you here to see how he operates, how he moves, to get a sense of him, and to hear what he sounds like."

"He's a man of few words. We're not going to make much progress on that front today," Gleason said.

"Like most seal masters, he has a north of Ireland accent, which is what you have. That's why I picked you for the job."

"Should I drop on bended knee and thank you for your confidence in me?" Gleason said with a wild look on his face.

"Let's go over to Gavin's on the corner. I'll treat you to one of Cloonfin's local ales."

"I hope it goes down easier than what you're trying to con me into doing."

"There are three breweries here, so we can sample the product of all three if you have a mind to."

"If my mind was in the right place, I'd be saddling my horse and heading back to County Monaghan."

Redferne threw back his head and laughed, trying to make light of Gleason's comment. He ceased laughing when he remembered that last month, three chaps from a neighboring town were sentenced to be hanged for stealing linen webs drying on the commons. Gleason's crime would be another order of magnitude.

Redferne picked a table with captain's chairs in the back of Gavin's, commanding a view of the room. Already merchants and traders filled every stool at the oaken bar top. Behind the stools, a knot of men shouted drink orders across the shoulders of those seated. The noise from the market entered in short bursts as the door opened and closed, ushering in others who left muddy boot tracks on the sawdust. When their beers were served, Redferne reached into his pocket and pulled out a notebook.

He opened it and pushed it across the table. "What you're looking at is a drawing of a Linen Board seal."

The words *William Bradshaw of Dungannon*, arranged in a circle, surrounded an image of a harp. A British crown adorned the top of the circle. Underneath it, the words: *Official Seal for brown linen. Trustees of the Board of Linen and Hemp Manufacturers of Ireland.*

"This is only a piece of paper."

"The real deal is back at the farmhouse."

"And you stole this or had it stolen from this William Bradshaw?"

"William Bradshaw doesn't exist; not until you assume his name."

Gleason put down his drink and gazed out the window fronting the square. Seeing him wavering, Redferne said, "If we pull this off, we find out who killed an innocent woman and bring down the tyrant I believe responsible for sending you, me, and scores of others to the island of the damned."

"So I am to be William Bradshaw, seal master for the Linen Board?"

"Your reputation is so well-established that you have your own seal."

"How did you come by it if Mr. Bradshaw doesn't exist?"

"A counterfeiter from Falls Road in Belfast persuaded by a donation of a hundred pounds brought the gentleman to life."

"When do I assume my new identity?" Gleason drained his glass and Redferne signaled a barman for another round.

"Monday. Take some rooms at the Cloonfin Arms Hotel for a few days as befits a gentleman of your stature. Spread the word you're looking to lease land for flax growing." The round arrived and he slid the server a two-shilling piece. "Cloonfin has a reputation for quality linen rivaling that of the linen triangle in the North of Ireland."

"I'm not going to sound like a fool if I make that claim, am I?"

"Trust me, no. Flash your seal around, but keep away from any of the seal masters currently working the Cloonfin market until they leave town, which probably will happen over the weekend." Redferne raised the mug and took a long draft. "Best beer in the country." Forgetting his new station, he wiped his mouth with his sleeve. "Don't be too obvious, but hopefully the word gets back to the Prestons. If they accept the bait and contact you, get in touch with me right away."

Over the next few days, Gleason studied flax growing and linen production from books he found in the hotel. Redferne hadn't requested it, but it occurred to him that the person he was claiming to be would be well versed in such matters. Monday afternoon, a bellhop brought a note to his room announcing that a gentleman in the hotel lobby requested to see him.

"Something to do with linen, I do believe, sir," the bellhop said. Gleason glanced at the name Benjamin Strange written on the note. It wasn't one of the names Redferne had furnished him from the Preston estate.

Descending the stairs, he observed two men in the middle of the lobby talking loudly. From their attire, he took them for farmers and headed in their direction. An older gentleman seated on a leather armchair in an alcove off the lobby stood up with some difficulty and called, "Mr. Bradshaw?"

"Yes, indeed," Gleason said, trying not to look too eager. He offered his hand.

"My name is Benjamin Strange. I must say your reputation has preceded you." Strange slowly settled back in his chair. Amazing, Gleason thought, since he only started working on his reputation a few days previous.

Gleason settled in a comfortable chair opposite Benjamin, who laughed nervously and shifted in his seat. "So you're interested in linen production, I hear."

"Gracious, no, not me personally. I am here on behalf of my master, Lord Preston. He requests the honor of your presence for a light tea this evening. I have a carriage at your disposal outside the door right now, if such short notice doesn't inconvenience you. My master is unwell and has to conduct his business whenever his health permits."

About to beg off because he wanted to contact Redferne first, Gleason reconsidered on hearing of Preston's precarious health. Better seize the brass ring when it was offered. Benjamin led the way to the phaeton parked along the cobbled footpath. Within minutes, they passed under the large Gothic arch that framed the entrance to the demesne.

After following the gravel avenue through groves of beech and chestnut trees, they stopped before an array of steps that led to a portico overlooking the main entrance. Gleason followed Benjamin to the library, where Lord Preston greeted them from his wheelchair. After the introductions, Benjamin said, "I will take my leave now, M'Lord, and fetch the tea."

"No, Benjamin, stay right here. I want your opinion on what Mr. Bradshaw has to say. I have already arranged with cook to take care of the tea." He pulled his blanket more snugly around his thin shoulders.

Though it was almost the end of May, a fire burned in the grate. The picture of the patriarch over the mantel piece still had a hole in its chest. Observing Preston's pallid color, black fingernails, and the odd patches of baldness on his head, Gleason worried that he might not be well enough to enter into an agreement, especially the kind Redferne was looking for.

A knock ushered in a footman bearing a silver tray with evening tea. Benjamin took the stoneware teapot and poured a cup for each of them. The cup was so small that Gleason had difficulty getting his fingers through the handle, but over the course of an hour he managed to put away six of them, as well as a generous helping of scones slathered in clotted cream and strawberry jam. They talked about flax-growing, linen production, and skilled labor. He found Preston quite knowledgeable about the industry and said a silent prayer of thanks that he had read up on the topic.

"At what stage in the growth cycle do you prefer to harvest the flax, Mr. Bradshaw?" Preston asked, suspending his cup over his saucer.

"I find that when the leaves are yellow is the best time to harvest. The fibers are most flexible at that stage and produce higher quality linen."

"We are in agreement, Mr. Bradshaw; I think it's a harbinger of good things to come."

Gleason didn't have a clue what *harbinger* meant, but from the context, he suspected it meant something positive.

The servant brought a second pot of tea and The Lord pressed Gleason to have another cup.

"Don't mind if I do, sir." He reached his spoon toward the sugar bowl and then stopped.

Out of the blue Benjamin said, "Quite a young man, Mr. Bradshaw, to have achieved such a high vote of confidence from the Linen Board. A seal master no less. An honor, I'm told, accorded only to a few."

Preston looked at Benjamin and then at Gleason, who began to sweat. He felt the seal in his pocket. Pulling it out, he placed it on the table as a diversion to give him time to think.

"May I look at it, sir?" Preston asked.

"By all means." He pushed it over, noticing Benjamin's eyes still on him. The stooped old man had not been distracted by the maneuver. Had Benjamin noticed his hesitation over the sugar?

"In answer to your question, Mr. Strange. This responsibility has been in my family for three generations. It was first accorded to my grandfather, who passed it on to my father. Now it rests with me."

That seemed to satisfy Preston, who quickly turned to the matter of finances. "I can give a thousand acres over to flax if the price is right." He sipped his tea and put clotted cream on his scone.

"If the soil conditions meet my standards and you set aside a barn to dry the flax stalks after plucking, I can go as high as five pounds an acre," Gleason said.

"We would, of course, require a deposit," Preston said after a pause.

"I understand, and because of the uncertainties relating to weather, the availability of labor, drainage, etc., I'm only prepared to contribute fifty pounds to the purchase of seed."

"Mr. Bradshaw," Preston said leaning forward. "I will need time to digest your offer. You will be hearing from me before the week is out."

"Don't leave it too long. The growing season is fast approaching and I don't want to be caught wrong-footed."

"You shall have your answer presently."

Redferne looked out the little farmhouse window as he listened to Gleason recount his conversation with Prescott and Benjamin. It was the last week in May and the days grew longer. In a few weeks at the summer solstice, they would reverse themselves and contract a little every day as the summer rolled on. The flax-growing window extended from June to August, which was almost upon them. Not much time left to play around.

At first he thought Preston had taken the bait, but when Gleason repeated Benjamin's question, he realized it wasn't at all certain Preston was hooked. Did Benjamin smell a rat?

"As far as I could tell, Benjamin seemed satisfied with my answer," Gleason said.

"Benjamin is a smart fellow. Should he pursue his suspicions, he will discover you're an imposter."

"That raises the question, will he pass it along to Preston."

"Depends on where his loyalties lie."

On Friday of the same week, the hotel footman brought an envelope to Gleason's room. Closing the door, he slit open the flap with his penknife. Enclosed within was a letter written on parchment, bearing the three lions of the Preston coat of arms, dated *the 25th of May, 1776.*

We have an agreement contingent on an increase of £50 in the seed money allotment.

Yours faithfully,
Lord Charles Preston

In anticipation of such an eventuality, Redferne transferred a sum of money from his bank in Dublin to William Bradshaw's account at a bank in Belfast, then he wrote a draft from that bank to the Honorable Charles Preston for the specified amount, which Gleason delivered the next day, sealing the deal with a handshake.

CHAPTER 55

Bannister got the word from a rider sent by Lady Preston while on the road back from Carrick Fergus with a hundred head of cattle, most of them milk cows. He rubbed his eyes in disbelief. "Hurry home. Disaster in the making."

He waved the note in the rider's face. "Do you know what this is all about?"

"Oh, no, sir," the startled young man said.

Leaving the cattle drive to his drovers with instructions to push ahead with all speed, Bannister galloped off. He was a day's ride from the Preston estate. When he arrived, saddle weary and hungry, the scene that greeted him looked worse than his wildest imaginings.

Hundreds of acres of prime pasture had been put to the plough in his two-week absence. Even some of the parkland in the demesne had been turned. He spurred his tired mount toward a ploughman guiding a team of horses pulling a silver blade that cleaved into the green grass, laying bare a moist ribbon of brown loam that glistened in the sun.

He dismounted and yanked the reins from the ploughman's hands. "Stop, stop. Who authorized this?"

"Lord Preston, sir."

"And Mr. Bradshaw," a second ploughman volunteered.

"Who?"

"Mr. Bradshaw."

"Who the hell is he?"

"All we know is, we were told by Lord Preston and Mr. Bradshaw a week ago to prepare the ground for planting flax, Your Honor."

"Flax?" Bannister's face turned chalky white. He threw up his hands, leapt on his horse, and rode up and down among the teams of ploughmen, shouting at them to stop. If this flax project took hold, it spelled disaster for his dairy farming scheme. Trembling with rage, he galloped off toward the stables. After all his meticulous planning, the old coot had stolen a march on him.

Arriving at Lady Preston's room, he pushed the door open and stormed in to find her standing at a window observing the scene unfolding below.

He grabbed her by the shoulder and spun her around. "Why didn't you get word to me sooner?"Her face flushed with anger as she brusquely pulled his hand away.

"Because I just returned today from Dublin, or don't you remember?"

"Dublin! That's all you think about. Well, think of this! If our grazing project goes south, there won't be any more Dublin."

Lady Preston waved her hands in the air and shouted. "You said this was settled before you left to buy the cattle. How was I to know? You made the call!"

He grabbed a half-empty bottle of claret and poured himself a glass, splashing it all over the sideboard. His hand trembled as he guided the glass to his mouth.

"I thought he was fading fast by the time I left to purchase the cattle."

"Apparently, he got a second wind."

"And apparently your medication is not as effective as you thought it was, otherwise he'd be slobbering all over himself, blabbing nonsense to that damn portrait in the library," Bannister said.

"Someone must have helped him. He was in no condition to make such a decision."

"Flax will consume the best grazing land on the estate. We have to stop him."

"How?" Lady Preston asked. "He's still the owner of this estate and appears to be in control of all his faculties."

"Who is this Bradshaw? Where did *he* come from?"

"He's a linen merchant and a seal master from Dungannon, traveling the country looking to buy large quantities of linen."

"And your husband struck a bargain with him?"

"Apparently so. I find it interesting that suddenly you refer to him as *my husband*."

He slammed his glass down on the nightstand and stormed out. God knows what sort of deal the old fool made with this merchant. This would have to be stopped. The purchase of such a large herd of cattle, not approved by Preston, had cut into his own resources. It was the only way he could see to revive the fortunes of the estate. He had thought of flax and dismissed it as too much at the mercy of the weather, and an uncertain market. The dairy business was booming. The export of Irish butter increased dramatically with the opening up of British and European markets. That's where the money was to be made and he wanted in on it.

He could try to persuade Preston to see the merits of his plan, save for the fact that he had not informed him beforehand about this new venture, thinking he would be out of the picture by now. Coaxing him into agreements only to have him renege on them later, like he did with the mass eviction plan, was a fool's game. When he thought Preston was going loony, he initiated evictions on his own. So far Whiteboy resistance had been minimal. But it cost him a pretty penny in smuggling revenue. Preston had to be stopped at all costs.

The following morning, the herd of cattle, goaded on by the whistles and ash plants of the drovers, mooed its way down Church Street's broad thoroughfare and passed beneath the Gothic arch into the demesne. People crowded the footpaths and stood in open doorways gaping at the spectacle. No one had ever seen so many cattle.

"What the hell is going on behind those walls?" Bernie Clayton wanted to know as he and his partner Joe Mannion loaded large bags of flour onto drays from a store house. With sacks draped over the backs of their heads and shoulders, they looked like cowled monks. "They're planting hundreds of acres of flax and now they're bringing in this large herd."

"That's why evictions are up, so these bastards can profit from the misery of the poor," Mannion said.

"Hould on Joe! There might be a silver lining to this yet. Those cows gotta' be milked, right?"

"Aye, Bernie. I can't see Preston or his lot setting their arses down on milking stools, can you?"

"Which means it'll be up to our kind to squeeze those teats."

"Right you are," said Mannion. "And get paid for doin' it."

"There could be a lot of eating and drinking in this, sure enough, if those loony bastards know what the hell they're doin'," Clayton said.

They took one last look at the herd of cows, and then turned back to their work, shaking their heads in apparent disbelief at the ways of the crazy Protestants.

Despite Benjamin's best efforts to restore Lord Preston to health, he had deteriorated by the day. His eyes were sunk in his head, his fingernails discolored, and he was losing his hair. He did not buy the doctor's diagnosis that His Lordship's illness was seated in the mind and beyond the capabilities of traditional medicine. The doctor's conclusions were based on the assumption that the enormous stress from Lord Preston's collapsing fortunes and his son's disappearance were at the root of his problems. This nervous disorder, as the physician called it, had leaped from the colonel's diseased mind and preyed on his body.

However, Lord Preston had bounced back sufficiently to engage with Mr. Bradshaw and establish a course for the recovery of his estate. It was a temporary respite and his malady soon returned in a more virulent form. The white lines on His Lordship's nails were the first real indicator to Benjamin that the origin of his patient's distress was physical rather than psychic. He researched *The Anatomy of Humane Bodies* by William Cooper for an answer, to no avail. Then he turned to his own medical journals, notes, and observations he had jotted down over the years.

Finally, under a heading dated second of October, 1765, he came across a startling entry. He had accompanied Lord Preston to visit the mining country of north Yorkshire in England to investigate the efficiency of a new steam-powered water pump, with a view to solving a drainage problem on the estate. Written in his neat hand was an observation that some of the miners were suffering from arsenic poisoning, displaying symptoms of vomiting, confusion, hair loss, and white lines on the fingernails and toenails. Local doctors blamed it on coal dust inhalation.

Was someone trying to poison The lord? Since the hour was late, he did not disturb his patient but set about looking for an antidote in the medical books.

From ancient times, charcoal was used to arrest the effects of arsenic once the source of the poison was detected and removed. There were no mines in the Cloonfin region, so there had to be another source. Why hadn't others fallen ill?

Next morning before the kitchen staff arrived, he removed several charcoal briquettes from the firebox. He waited till the cook came in and watched her preparing breakfast. She made a big pot of porridge or stirabout, fried some bacon and eggs, and moved the lot over to a warming plate. He filled a bowl of stirabout for himself and another for His Lordship. Seeing the second bowl, the cook said, "In need of some extra fortification this morning, Benjamin?"

"Agnes, you know I think highly of your cooking, but in the case of stirabout, one bowl does me just fine."

She frowned. "But what's the second…?"

"Oh, this," Benjamin laughed, holding up the other bowl of stirabout. "This is for His Lordship."

Agnes's face darkened. She looked around her. "Lady Preston will have a conniption if she finds this out. Since His Lordship's illness, she insists on checking his food before it is served."

Seamus Beirne

CHAPTER 56

It was ten minutes after twelve when the sheepdog growled and rose from beside the fire, sniffing its way to the front door as if following an invisible thread. Redferne motioned Gleason to go into the bedroom. He wanted both ends of the house defended, in case it was an intruder. If it was a late night caller, he couldn't afford to be seen in the company of Mr. William Bradshaw.

At night, as a security precaution, he relied solely on the light of the fire to move inside the house. With pistol in hand, he slipped out the back door and crawled on his belly to the copse of trees that bounded the house in the front. Somebody lurked near the entrance.

He approached the figure from behind. "What is your business at this hour, stranger?" He cocked the hammer of the pistol.

"I apologize for the hour and the manner of my approach, but I had to be certain I was not followed," Ben Strange said, turning toward him.

"Can you be sure of that, Ben?"

"I've been hiding in the trees for about fifteen minutes. I'm relatively certain that I am alone." Redferne led the old servant to the back door. When he entered the kitchen, he made enough noise to alert Gleason to their presence. "Hang your coat on that peg behind the door while I resuscitate the fire and wet the tea. I'm sure you could use a cup."

Benjamin settled in beside the fire "I'd be most grateful, God's blessing on you."

"I could use some of God's favor, especially in the explanations department, Benjamin." Redferne poured boiling water into the teapot and set it on a circle of crushed coals to draw.

"I owe you an explanation about the incident at the Cock and Bull, which is part of the reason I came here tonight. A most unfortunate event for which I was unwittingly responsible."

"That might be a good place to start, Ben. It almost cost me and my son our lives, not to mention Andrew Hicks." He returned the tongs to the wall ring in the hob.

"Again my deep regrets. I've come to regard Lord Preston as a noble gentleman who resisted the advice of those who counseled mass evictions to solve his problems."

Redferne handed Ben a steaming mug of tea and sat down opposite him.

"Could I trouble you for a little milk and sugar?"

Redferne's jaw clenched. "Milk, yes. Sugar, no."

"Of course. Forgive my insensitivity."

"Get on with it," Redferne said placing a milk jug on a stool beside Benjamin.

"His Lordship has been ill for almost a year, and it has fallen on me to be his minder and physician, which I gladly do." He sipped the tea slowly, warming his hands on the mug.

"Did you tell him I returned, Ben?"

"I'm afraid I did, Michael, but with no malicious intent. My master and I talk about local and world events. Since I am his conduit for news, I shared an incident with him which would interest him greatly."

"You told the man responsible for my enslavement that I escaped and was back on his estate?"

"Michael, His Lordship was quite unaware of this. When I told him your story, he was outraged by Bannister's involvement."

Redferne threw back his head and laughed. "So outraged that he sent his goons to kill me, Padraig, and Hicks? To another man I would say, how stupid can you be, but you're not a stupid man, Ben."

"When I heard of the incident at the Cock and Bull, I confronted His Lordship. He assured me that the only one he confided in was

368

his dear wife." He slurped another sip of the hot tea, his eyes fixed on Redferne

"And that didn't tip him off that maybe his *dear wife* might not be everything he thought she was?"

"In my conversations with him I delicately inferred as much, but he dismissed it saying that while she was a nagger and a spendthrift, she would never be involved in something of that nature." He took another swallow of tea.

Redferne leaned in. "Spoken like a true cuckolded husband, a situation of which, no doubt, you are aware."

Benjamin averted his eyes. "Yes, but I was ignorant until now that it was common knowledge."

"Not common knowledge, perhaps, but whispered in the halls of the Big House and the country taverns."

"Be that as it may, events have moved far beyond that. It's another reason I've come to see you. I've already mentioned my master's deteriorating health. It became critical within the last week. To make a long story short, Lady Preston has been lacing His Lordship's food with arsenic for the last six months."

Redferne's breath caught. He got up to put more turf on the fire. "Do you think she's acting on her own?"

"My guess is her lover Bannister is waist-deep in this."

"Is Lord Preston aware of their conspiracy?

"I had to tell him why I was feeding him charcoal fragments several times a day. He is biding his time until his health improves, which I am happy to say shows a marked turnaround already."

"Biding his time or lacking the courage to move against them," Redferne said, settling the sods of turf behind the fire with his bare hands.

"You've heard the phrase, give a man enough rope and he will hang himself. That's my master's plan," Benjamin said.

"It occurs to me that a man who buys a hundred head of cattle without his boss's knowledge, and tries to sabotage his boss's flax enterprise, might not be easily intimidated by that same boss," Redferne said. The sheepdog moved from the back of the kitchen and, lying down on the hearth beside Redferne, he put his head between his paws and moaned.

Benjamin raised his eyebrows. "For a man who is supposedly lying low, you are surprisingly well-informed."

"I have visited some country pubs where I'm not known, and I can tell you it's a common topic of conversation."

"Then let me tell you something you do not know, nor does Bannister. Lord Preston is about to seize Bannister's cattle. And speaking of flax." Here Benjamin paused and fixed Redferne with a cold stare. "Do not harm my master. He does not deserve this."

Redferne's assessment of Benjamin in the brains department was correct. Trying not to let his facial expressions reveal his feelings, he said, "If what you've told me about Preston is true, why would I hurt him? I admit, I came home full of hate, thinking he was responsible for my misfortune. Now it appears I may need to turn my attention elsewhere."

Benjamin put the empty mug on the stool beside the milk jug and rose stiffly. "The tea was a godsend. Now, I'll take my leave."

"Cannot let you go on your own in the middle of the night. I'll see you to the Big House. Where's your horse?"

"About a hundred yards from here in a copse of trees."

Redferne rode with Benjamin all the way to the equine cathedral, mostly in silence. There wasn't much more to be said, but a lot more thinking to be done. Funny, he thought, how one's cherished assumptions can be knocked into a cocked hat in the blink of an eye. How things once thought solid turn out to be a mirage.

As Benjamin dismounted, he pulled the reins over his horse's head and looked across his saddle at Redferne. "You know, of course, that the Honorable William Bradshaw is an imposter. Like you, he has an aversion to sugar." Then turning on his heel, he led the horse into the shadows of the stable.

CHAPTER 57

When Lord Preston's newly-planted flax fields exploded in a riot of blue and white, the dark cloud of depression surrounding him lifted. It promised to be a bounteous harvest and it instilled in him a hope he hadn't felt in a long time. In another month, the stalks would be at their peak and for the first time in years his estate was at peace. Bradshaw's crop provided months of employment for his tenants: plowing, harrowing, digging drains, and planting the flax. More months of work lay ahead for the peasants as they dried, cleaned, and retted the stalks in preparation for spinning and weaving the flax fibers into brown linen.

He had spent his survival reserves of cash on wages, regarding it as an investment and a goodwill gesture undergirding his contract with Bradshaw. The fruit of his agreement with the seal master would more than cover his expenses, with enough left over to meet his monthly loan obligations. Even more important, some of his outlays were flowing back to him from tenant rents. It came as somewhat of a surprise to discover that people, even the destitute, met their obligations when they had the wherewithal to do so.

Under Benjamin's care, his health improved along with a renewed confidence and a resolve to tackle the intractable problems strangling his estate. He cut off Lady Preston's allowance, put an end to lavish banquets, sold off his stable of hunting horses, and the large pack of dogs that went with them. Squeezed out by the large flax-growing operation, Bannister was forced to rent land from middlemen on the fringes of the estate to accommodate his dairy herd.

One evening late in June, Lord Preston called Benjamin to the library.

Benjamin tapped on the door and let himself in. "Yes, M'Lord."

"Have Harold bring up the phaeton and drive you to the constable's house in Cloonfin. Instruct him to round up several deputies and return here forthwith." Seeing the look of hesitation on Benjamin's face, he said. "Don't worry; here is a letter containing the instructions I've spelled out to you."

"Yes, M'Lord." Benjamin bowed and withdrew.

Within an hour he returned with Constable Taylor and two deputies. Taylor, a man in his late fifties, wore a grey serge suit that had seen better days, knee-high stockings, and black hobnail boots. Appearing uncomfortable in the elegant library, he removed his tricorne hat, revealing a shock of unruly grey hair. His face looked weathered and unshaven. "Constable Taylor," Preston said. "As sheriff of this county, I've called you here to arrest and detain certain members of my household."

Taylor shook his head like a dog ridding his coat of water. His bloodshot eyes darted in all directions.

"And now, gentlemen," Preston said, "if you will please follow me. You too, Benjamin." He led the way through the great hall with the medieval suits of armor, past the large fireplace with the brass firedogs, up the circular stairway until he reached his wife's apartments. Knocking once, he opened the door and walked in, followed by the others.

Lady Preston emerged from her boudoir, hair wrapped in a towel. Her face froze in fright on seeing the visitors. Recovering, she turned toward her husband and blurted, "What is the meaning of this outrage? Am I not to have privacy in my own bedroom? What is this rabble doing here?"

"Mr. Taylor, please proceed."

Looking uncertain, Taylor drew himself up and stammered, "Me Lady, on the orders of the high sheriff of the county...y-yer' husband, Ma'am, I'm placing you under arrest." Lady Preston's bosom heaved as if it were about to explode. She stared at her husband, eyes wide.

"Charles," she said, "what's going on here?"

Preston handed Taylor a sheet of foolscap from his inside pocket and instructed him to read it.

Coughing to clear his throat, Taylor commenced. "Madam, you are being charged with the attempted murder of yer' husband—an... and adultery. You are to be tried a month hence by the magistrate's court. Until that time, you will be confined to the jail in the basement of the old market house."

The color drained from Lady Preston's face. "This is preposterous! What shred of evidence do you have for such outrageous accusations?"

Preston looked to Benjamin, who withdrew a small flat box from his waistcoat. He took a pinch of the white substance from the box between his thumb and forefinger and held it up. "This, Ma'am, is white arsenic, an extremely toxic potion I detected in your husband's food."

"These are all lies! You are trying to frame me."

A quick search of Lady Preston's boudoir uncovered a jar half-full of a substance similar to that produced by Benjamin. The previous week, during her absence, Benjamin had searched her room and found the damning proof. Lady Preston collapsed at her husband's feet and sobbed.

"Please, Charles, Bannister threatened to kill me if I didn't go along."

"So he forced you into his bed, is that it?'

She covered the absence of a reply by a renewed outburst of sobbing.

Preston looked at the woman at his feet, then turned to the constable. "Remove her."

As a deputy led her away, Preston took a small double-barreled pistol from his inside pocket and instructed the constable and his deputy to ready their weapons. Reversing his route, he headed into the connecting corridor between the main house and the servants' wing. At the entrance to the servants' quarters, a farm hand carrying a sledge hammer joined them, following them to a room on the third floor.

There Preston cocked the hammers of his pistol. Taylor and his deputy followed suit. Finding the door locked, Preston motioned to the man with the sledge hammer. "Break it down, Mr. Lytle."

The slamming of the sledge against the door echoed like cannon fire throughout the building, knocking chunks of plaster off the walls and ceilings, scaring frightened occupants from their rooms. Gaining entry, they discovered that Bannister had escaped through an open window.

"M'Lord, the bedclothes are still warm so he cannot have gotten far."

"Ring the fire bell and have the buildings and outhouses searched from top to bottom. I want everyone involved. Constable, head back to town and alert the residents that there is one-hundred-pounds reward for Bannister's capture."

A two-hour search came up empty, but Bannister's horse was still in the stable.

After a week's confinement in the damp cell, subsisting on a diet of potatoes and gruel, Lady Preston began to sing. The final messages of condemned men, etched in the soft limestone walls of the basement jail, moved her to portray herself as the manipulated ingénue of a devious lover, rather than the ruthless instigator of his crimes. In quick succession, she squealed to the shocked constable about the clandestine slave operation and the smuggling. She also fingered Bannister for the killing of Maureen Kelly and Captain Preston. Disposed to believe the word of a gentlewoman, the constable reported the prisoner's accusations to Lord Preston in the great hall of the Big House.

"Since there may be weight to what M'lady is saying about Mr. Bannister, M'Lord, I'm doubling our efforts to track him down, but he seems to have disappeared like a leprechaun."

Preston shook his head. "Constable, a woman who attempts to kill her husband is hardly a credible witness. She's trying to save her own skin."

"I'm sorry, M'Lord, but…"

"Mr. Taylor, there is no need to apologize. You have done well. After I've had time to mourn my son, I will deal with the brigand who led my boy astray. In the meantime, be vigilant with your prisoner." Preston returned to the library and shut the door, sitting down heavily in a chair. He put his head in his hands. A summer wind blew through the open windows, rattling the shutters and lifting the long muslin curtains like streamers, balancing them delicately in midair before releasing them to caress the old shutters as they fell.

Lord Preston tightened the collar of his greatcoat against the cold wafting off the ice stack. When they lifted the stiff body of his son into the light, he bent over and cried, tracing his fingers along the contours of Reggie's frozen face. Benjamin held him by the arm as they lifted Maureen Kelly's corpse from the ice and laid it alongside the body of her killer on the ice house floor. A "ullaloo" went up from the Kelly relatives when they each bent to touch her.

Maureen's father and two brothers carried her body up the winding staircase into a summer day among the beech trees. A hearse awaited them. Maureen Kelly was finally going home.

They took the body of Reggie Preston along the winding passageway into the Big House. That evening, according to his father's wishes, he was buried without ceremony in the family crypt in the Protestant graveyard adjacent to the unfinished church.

Seamus Beirne

CHAPTER 58

Redferne screwed the lid off a jar and held it up to the light. The curare paste had congealed into a thick jell, its moisture having evaporated with age. He suspected that it was potent enough to kill a horse, so he diluted it with water. The trick was how to arrive at the proper proportion of paste to liquid so it acted as a tranquilizer rather than a lethal potion. He wasn't sure how to do that, since Isaac mixed the original concoction.

Only one way to find out. He took his blow gun, went to the edge of the wood near the farmhouse, and lay in wait beside a rabbit warren. His first few tries were disastrous. All of the creatures he hit crawled away and died. Gradually, he fine-tuned the mixture until a half hour after he dropped a young cow with a dart to the neck, it struggled to its feet and staggered away. A cow was not a human being, so he refined the mixture. Based on their relative weights, he settled on a blend he hoped would stun rather than kill an average-size man. The only question now was where and how to trap his victim?

The militia scoured the country for two weeks looking for Bannister, but he seemed to have vanished without a trace. Redferne mulled over the circumstances of the fugitive's disappearance. His horse was still in the stables the evening of Lady Preston's arrest. Lord Preston had placed a guard on the stables that night and the next day, but Bannister never showed up, leaving him with two options: steal a horse or try to escape on foot. The estate's horses were all accounted for and no horse thefts were reported in the surrounding townlands.

If he was on foot, he couldn't have gotten far, unless he had help. What were the odds of that? The tenants hated him, and much of the town's people feared him. His allies would be few; possibly the middlemen or the neighboring landlords, but having been charged with the murder of Lord Preston's son, it was highly unlikely that any of them would risk the hangman's noose to help him. Someone had to be hiding him—but who and why? The answer to the first question was still a mystery, but the answer to the second was simple: money, or the promise of it.

Given his revenues from the slave trade and the smuggling, he figured Bannister to be wealthy. He could pay someone to hide him, especially if that someone didn't have a lot to lose. Money was a powerful motivator. Men were known to risk an awful lot more to get less than Bannister could pay.

He rose with the sun on the day of Maureen Kelly's funeral. After saddling his horse and stowing the blowgun in his saddle bag, he struggled with the idea of making an appearance at the graveside. He couldn't bring himself to do it. By now, the word was surely out that he was responsible for hiding her body in the ice house. The Kellys would want to know why he hadn't informed them. Since he didn't have a convincing answer, he decided to take the cowardly way out and not go. Someday when it was all sorted out, he would call and pay his respects. Right now, something else gnawed at his gut.

He mounted his horse and headed down the lane to the little crossroads where he took the fork leading to the mountains. The pungent smell of heather brought him back to a period, half a lifetime ago, when he spent long summer days under the sun cutting turf for hire with his shirt off. The suspicion needling his insides like a pebble in a shoe distracted him, and he failed to spot two men hiding in the heather until they rose up and pointed their guns at him.

"That's far enough!" a young fellow with red hair and several days' growth of beard shouted. His horse reared. By the time he regained control, the redhead grabbed the reins. The other, a broad-shouldered, stocky individual, with unkempt brown hair down to his shirt collar, stood off to the side leveling his Brown Bess. Thinking he was being set upon by highwaymen, Redferne said, "I've little but you're welcome to it." He dug around in his pockets.

"Not interested in your money, mate," the redhead growled. He had a clipped north of Ireland accent that Redferne found familiar.

"Then you have me at a disadvantage. Am I trespassing?"

"Who are you, and what's your business here?" the one pointing the gun said.

"I'm a friend of Rory Blake's and last time I traveled here, this was a public road." The lookouts, because now that's what he figured they were, exchanged quick glances with each other.

"Is he expecting you?"

"Didn't think I needed an appointment; never had one before."

"Things have changed," the redhead said. They took his pistol and escorted him up the mountain road, one in front, the other in back. When they reached the safe house, he noticed other guards stationed around the perimeter. Security had been beefed up since his last visit.

Blake appeared from one of the stables and waved when he saw Redferne.

"Didn't realize you owned the bloody road, Rory, or have the Whiteboys replaced the local militia?"

"Seems every time we meet, Red, we have a set to."

"Might help if I didn't get my head bashed in or threatened every time I get within pissing distance of your place. I feel like I'm back in the prison colony."

"Might help if you hung around long enough so my men recognized you."

"I had business to attend to."

"You boys can leave," Blake said to the lookouts.

"Hey, you, how about my pistol?" The redhead turned and threw it in Redferne's direction.

"Where'd you get him?" He fell into step behind Blake.

"That's Clyde. Came down here from the north looking for adventure. He's handy with a gun. Happened that we needed his services at the time."

"Can't say I like his manners, nor the cut of his jib."

"This is a rough business. Not much room for the faint-hearted."

Redferne followed Blake to the safe house kitchen. Once indoors, Blake went into the back room and came out with a bottle of Armagnac brandy. He held it aloft. "You don't see this in our neck of the woods often." He opened a cupboard and brought two glasses to the table.

"How'd you come by it?" Redferne took the strange bottle in his hand.

"It fell off a Dutch vessel that docked in Sligo." He laughed and filled the two glasses.

Redferne took a sip and smacked his lips. "Jesus, this tastes better than cognac." He settled into a chair and looked around. The goldfinches were still here, squabbling as usual. Six or seven men sat at a corner table playing cards. Blake hadn't offered them any brandy. Something else seemed odd. Redferne didn't recognize any of them. Since this was a local organization, it struck him as peculiar.

Redferne nodded. "I don't know any of these chaps. What happened to Roger and Brendan?"

"Roger and Brendan are my right-hand men, but like most of the other locals, they come from small farms or conacre plots, which as you know, have to be tended."

"So you call them on an as-needed basis?"

"That's the way it works."

Redferne gestured to the others. "Why keep this many around?"

Blake passed the Armagnac glass beneath his nose and sniffed. "Sometimes we have to respond to things that can't wait until we mobilize the local boys. Like a surprise eviction, for example."

Mercenaries, Redferne thought. Young men whose loyalty belonged to the highest bidder. Not a desirable situation. *Is Rory Blake losing his edge, or drifting to the other side?* On the way here, he had wrestled with the idea of telling Rory what was bothering him, but he decided to keep it to himself, because what was bothering him was Rory Blake, and this fresh encounter did little to alleviate his fears.

Redferne spent the evening sipping Armagnac and dodging questions from Blake about his plans. He told him nothing about his plans or his wealth. A residue of tension hung in the air that superficial conversation or Armagnac couldn't dispel. Before it got dark he went to check his horse. Blake accompanied him. Was he tagging along to keep an eye on him?

They walked to a squat building with a thatched roof. More than a dozen horses munched hay from a stall that ran the length of the stable. A little tipsy from brandy, he had difficulty locating his horse, but not so tipsy that he didn't recognize Clyde slipping out the other door of the stable. Redferne's saddle hung from a peg on the wall behind his horse and draped over it, his open saddlebag. Redferne hadn't opened it.

Blake stroked the horse's back. "Satisfied we're taking care of her?"

"I need a reliable mount. Don't forget I'm still a man with a price on my head."

"Not after Lady Preston's confession, you're not."

"I was charged with orchestrating the attack on the Big House. To my knowledge, she did not clear that up."

Blake looked tense. "Surely Benjamin will set His Lordship straight on that."

"He hasn't up to now. My hunch is that Prescott will wait until after the trial to address it. Until then, I'm fair game for any bounty hunter in the area." He stepped outside the stable and Blake followed. Clyde had disappeared.

"Can't argue with you there," Blake said. "Sometimes the law moves slowly in those matters, so I suggest you stay here until this thing is settled."

Redferne didn't say it, but he thought he might be in greater danger here by the looks of Blake's companions. "Do you think Bannister will hang if they catch him?"

Blake laughed as they walked back to the house. "They're never going to catch him, so it's a moot point."

Redferne studied Blake's face, but could discern nothing. "You seem sure about that."

"I believe in the power of money and he has plenty of it. It's more potent than the law. Even the Romans had a term for it. '*Pecuniam obediunt omnia*—All things obey money.' Nothing much has changed in the last eighteen hundred years. My hunch is that Bannister has paid his way out of the country by now."

Suddenly Redferne felt ravenous. "I know you're not running a hotel, but if I don't eat soon, I'll pass out."

"I got dinner on," Blake said, opening the door, and within half an hour they all sat down to a meal of boiled rabbit, cabbage, and potatoes. When they finished, Blake broke out the Armagnac again. By nightfall, he was slurring his words. Redferne slowed his own consumption, pretending that he was drinking more than he actually was. When he went out to piss, he took his glass along and emptied it into the grass. For the first time he was willing to think that Blake might be hiding Bannister.

Blake was too cocksure that the agent had fled the country. Given the devastation that Bannister had wreaked on the tenants, whom Blake was supposed to be championing, Redferne expected the Whiteboys to be involved in tracking him down, but he detected no such inclination and little concern that he had escaped.

When the conversation slowed, Clyde pulled out a pack of cards and invited his mates to a game of chance called *faro* involving several players and a banker. Redferne declined the invitation, saying that he was too drunk to make a good showing. He marveled at the number of silver shillings that crossed the table. As the game ebbed and flowed, it grew loud and boisterous, with winners and losers. Tempers flared from time to time. One of the losers complained that his bad luck was the result of having lost his lucky charm.

"You mean that smelly foot you sling around your neck?" one of the gamblers asked.

"It's kept me out of trouble on more than one occasion." A chorus of cheers and hoots went up, mocking the speaker.

"That's a bunch of superstitious shite," Clyde, who was acting as the banker, jeered. "It didn't help the rabbit much, did it? Ever think of that?"

Redferne had been lightly dozing, but came wide awake. The hair on his arms stood erect. From the beginning there was something familiar about Clyde's voice. Now he had no doubt.

Seamus Beirne

CHAPTER 59

Redferne shared a room with Clyde and another Whiteboy that night. He tried to avoid the arrangement, but Blake insisted, saying, "An empty bunk is a hell of a lot more comfortable than that old armchair you're slouched in."

"Okay, have it your way," Redferne said, "but with the amount of booze I've consumed, I may be dancing over bodies to get outside to piss."

"Then piss out the window," Blake said thickly. Redferne staggered to a room off the kitchen, bringing a round of laughter from the diehards who were finishing up their last round of *faro*.

He lay on the bed on top of the blanket, and put his pistol under the pillow, but did not undress. One of his roommates was already snoring loudly. Redferne could hear Clyde's distinctive northern accent at the card table.

He lay silent trying to decide whether he should stick around and try to untangle Rory Blake's involvement with Bannister, or flee through the bedroom window. Clyde came into the room singing a rebel ballad about a wild rapparee.

"Lift your glasses friends with mine, and give your hand to me, I'm England's foe..."

It was a halting rendition, but the clarity of his voice struck Redferne, not a boozy version as one might expect from someone who had been drinking half the night.

Redferne reached under the pillow, rested his hand on his pistol and pretended to snore, keeping pace with his bunk mate. Clyde went to the window and raised the bottom half, then turned around. Redferne felt his eyes upon him. *"...I'm Ireland's friend, I'm an outlawed rapparee."* Clyde hummed the next few bars. Redferne eased back the hammers of his pistol, hoping the clicking sounds were camouflaged by the loud snoring. His bunk mate stopped snoring with a snort. Without thinking, Redferne followed suit. Now the only sound came from the heavy breathing of the shadow standing over him.

Whether the silence unnerved him, Redferne was not sure, but Clyde turned and climbed out the window, disappearing into the darkness. Redferne went to the window and listened for the sound of pissing, but only the chirp, chirp of crickets disturbed the quiet. If Clyde wasn't taking a piss, then he was leaving the safe house, no doubt in the direction of the stable.

He climbed out the window after him and surveilled the stable from the shelter of the trees until Clyde came walking out with a horse. Once out of earshot of the house, he jumped in the saddle and headed down the mountain. For a man supposedly under the influence, Clyde had remarkably good coordination.

In the length of time it took to saddle his horse, Redferne was on his tail. If he didn't catch Clyde before he reached the crossroads at the foot of the mountain, he would lose him. He had enough starlight to travel at some speed without breaking his neck, but not enough to overtake someone with a five-minute lead, so Redferne dismounted and led his horse off the road into the heather.

He took a short cut through the bog, allowing him to bypass the winding mountain road. The descent was steep and pockmarked with quagmires, so he proceeded with extra caution, reaching the crossroads in time to see Clyde take the left fork toward the river. He followed at a distance. By the time he reached the river, Clyde was no longer in sight.

Did he follow the road south toward the bridge or north to the foot-plank crossing? The foot-plank was closer and less traveled, but would not accommodate a horse. The bridge allowed for a safer crossing. Redferne listened to his gut and struck out for the foot plank. A gentle whinny revealed Clyde's horse concealed behind a clump of sally bushes. He secured his own horse and crossed onto the cracked limestone plateau. Visibility had increased significantly, showing Clyde some distance ahead negotiating the treacherous fissures. He shadowed him to a hazel wood where he entered a thatched hut in a small clearing.

Loud voices came from inside. Removing the blow gun from his shoulder bag, he fitted a dart into the barrel and crawled to the rear where he found a crack in the mud walls enabling him to see inside. An oil lamp sat on a crude table lighting the interior. Clyde and someone with a long black braid squatted on the floor. It was Bannister! Not the powerful land agent, nor the dashing lover of Lady Preston, but an unshaven, disheveled individual who seemed broken by his weeks on the run. Clyde had brought the fugitive a meal.

Redferne's dart hit Bannister in the base of the neck as he raised the wine bottle to his lips. He fell face forward gasping, hitting his head against a post. Before he could get a second shot off, Clyde dashed for the door and disappeared into the hazel wood. Redferne drew his pistol and gave chase, but he was unable to pick up his trail in the dense wood, so he returned to the hut.

After removing the dart, he tied a swatch of linen round Bannister's neck to staunch the bleeding, then checked his pulse; still strong. Thinking he had little time to tarry before Clyde returned with Blake and his crew, Redferne took a quick survey of the hut. A sunken post with manacles and chains attached to it stood in one corner "What the hell went on here?" Then it hit him. A holding pen for human beings. His heart thumped at the memory of his own enslavement.

He toyed with the idea of chaining Bannister to the post, to give him a dose of his own medicine, but relented. No time for that. He would stow him in the farmhouse as he had he planned. He pulled his watch from an inside pocket. Seven o'clock. Time to move. After checking Bannister's pulse again, he hoisted him over his shoulder like a sack of potatoes and headed out.

The plateau was a treacherous place with its depressions and fissures, but it offered concealment. What if Clyde was out there waiting in ambush? But it was also the shortest route to the river, so he took the risk. Halfway across, his breathing grew labored and his legs wobbled. The extra strain of having to jump some of the wider crevasses took its toll and he began to sweat profusely.

He contemplated stopping to rest, but he might not have the strength to hoist Bannister back up on his shoulder, so he staggered on. Almost within sight of the river he caught his foot in a fissure and pitched forward, dumping Bannister onto the limestone slab. "Fuck, I hope I haven't killed the bastard. He can't get off that easy." He crept over on his hands and knees to inspect his captive. Apart from a nasty gash on his forehead, he seemed okay.

As he repositioned Bannister on his shoulder, Clyde rose up from a crevasse. He leveled his pistol. "What's your preference? One between the eyes or through the belly. Myself, I favor the belly because it will take you a long time to die."

A shot rang out. It surprised Redferne. He always thought you never heard the shot that killed you. Clyde staggered, dropped his pistol and pitched backward into the crevasse. Redferne struggled to remain upright. A dark shape emerged from the tree line at the edge of the plateau. He took a deep breath and tried to focus.

It was Rory Blake, smoke pouring from the barrel of his Brown Bess. "Given the grief and abuse I take from you, I wonder why I keep saving your arse."

"Take him off of me before I collapse." Redferne sat down heavily on the limestone, relieved to see the man he had come to fear.

"So I reckon that makes three of us who were stone sober last night," Blake said, taking a small bottle of Armagnac from his coat pocket and taking a slug. "Let's make up for lost time." He passed the bottle to Redferne.

Redferne put the bottle to his lips. "All I can say is you had me fooled. Thank God in hindsight, I apparently didn't fool you."

"I've made some stupid mistakes and grew negligent when the money started flowing in, but betraying our cause was never one of them."

Redferne handed the bottle back. "How did you find me?"

"I've been suspicious of Clyde for weeks, so I kept track of his movements. Unfortunately, last night I was a little tipsier than I thought and dozed off. Luckily I woke up as you were leaving the stable, but even luckier, I had saddled my horse an hour earlier and hid him behind the house for such a contingency. I put the wee bottle of Armagnac in my saddlebag in case of an emergency." Blake stretched out full length on the limestone and put his hat over his eyes. "I could sleep for a week." He took another nip of Armagnac.

Redferne laughed. "Keep slugging that and you will. Not up to hauling two of you back to Cloonfin. Hope you don't blame me for distrusting you."

"You'd have been a fool not to, but before I said anything I had to confirm my suspicions about Clyde."

"So he was Bannister's informant."

"For the past month, the smuggling trains managed to steer clear of our ambush sites. That's when I suspected we had a spy among us."

"I'm sorry. I was convinced you had crossed to the other side."

"Don't feel too sorry. The mistrust was mutual, especially after you arranged Tallford's release from the pit." Blake coughed, knocking the hat from his eyes and sitting up.

Heat flushed Redferne's face. "You knew about that?

"Was watching you from the hill. When you offered to torch the hay stacks, I suspected something, given you were at best a reluctant soldier."

"But you never did anything about it."

"No, for fear of what might befall you if the group got wind of it...or maybe I was relieved that Tallford survived, but I couldn't admit that to the others."

Blake, the fire and brimstone man, had a soft spot. He didn't want anyone else to know about it.

Blake drove the cork back into the bottle with the heel of his hand, then hesitated. "Sorry, you want another shot?"

"God, no. I'm not sure I'm steady on my feet as it is. I appreciate you telling me about Tallford. It confirms a suspicion

I've had for awhile. There's not much in this world that's black and white, is there?"

A sad smile wrinkled Blake's face. A recognition perhaps of an intuition that came too late. He sluiced the ramrod up and down the barrel of his Brown Bess in preparation for loading. "Not by a long shot."

A morning breeze swept the plateau, scouring the dry leaves and debris from the limestone fissures. For a while, neither of them spoke until Blake walked over and took a look at Bannister. "What did you do to him? He seems to be in a coma."

"It's a trick I picked up from the Indians on Barbados." He showed Blake the blowgun and the curare darts.

Blake's eyes opened wide as Redferne explained how it worked. "By God. Never heard of such a thing."

"Deadly efficient too."

"So what are you planning on doing with him?"

"I want him to know the terror of waking up on the high seas bound for the unknown."

"How are you going to achieve that, with the whole county looking for him?"

"By spiriting him to the port of Sligo at night where I've arranged with a certain ship's captain to take additional cargo. For a price of course."

"Getting him to Sligo unnoticed may be a problem if he doesn't cooperate," Blake said.

"He won't notice. He'll be in a sweet curare dream."

"By God that's diabolical. Almost like black magic."

Redferne thought of Isaac and smiled. "Right. So give me a hand getting him back to my place before the morning gets any older and someone discovers us."

" 'Fraid I can't do that, Redferne. This bastard needs to be tried in Ireland. He should hang, not get shipped out of the country under cover of darkness."

Redferne's hand closed on the butt of his pistol. "If this is a joke, it's a bad one."

"Hear me out. The people of this town need to see justice done publicly. You're not the only injured party here. What about the Kellys, the others like you who were kidnapped and—dare I mention it?—old man Preston himself?"

"I'm concerned about me."

He was shocked by his bold-faced admission. Was this who he was? An adolescent nursing grievances. A hypocrite. Was his chronic guilt a camouflage for the pain of disappointment and unfulfilled dreams? Were his wife and son, his dead brother, and Maureen Kelly only on the periphery of his concern? He felt ashamed.

"It's bigger than you, Red. He's harmed the people of this community. They need to decide," Blake said, ramming a steel ball down the barrel of his musket with a scouring stick.

"And you think the magistrate's court represents this community?"

"It's all we've got," Blake said. "Besides, old Ben Strange's got the High Sheriff's ear, I'm told." Bannister moaned. Redferne readied another arrow, but Blake persuaded him not to use it.

"Let him come around. He needs to know the fear of being caught, especially being caught by you."

In the end, whether from a genuine change of heart or the fear of public reproach, Redferne agreed to turn Bannister over to the authorities. They led him across the plank and put him astride Clyde's horse while he was still groggy. Blake rode ahead to alert the town. As Redferne led his captive down the broad main street, the Angelus bell tolled, an unusual occurrence at nine in the morning, bringing young and old into the street.

A cheer went up when they recognized Bannister. "Hang him now!" they shouted until the arrival of the phaeton carrying Lord Preston and Benjamin calmed them. They looked in wonder as The Lord of the Manor shook Redferne's hand. Constable Taylor manacled Bannister and dragged him away.

Seamus Beirne

392

CHAPTER 60

At five o'clock on a morning in mid-August, Michael Redferne sat astride his horse studying the flax field. Hundreds of asymmetrical stacks, looking like tiny church steeples in the half light, spread haphazardly across the field to dry. At that moment, he finally decided to go through with his plan. The consequences could be dire. These stacks represented months of labor and held out the prospect of prosperity, not only for Preston but for the peasants whose toil and sweat were heavily invested in this crop.

A dark wall of lumpy beech trees stood shoulder to shoulder like giant sentinels along the fields' boundaries, as if daring him to carry out his destructive scheme. He reined his horse away from the lush summer grass along the verges and set off for a rendezvous with Gleason. With the apprehension of Bannister, the price on his head had been lifted and he could come and go as he pleased, but he could not afford to be seen with the seal master. As the day of reckoning approached, Gleason grew more nervous and refused to meet Redferne in the farmhouse anymore for fear of being seen in his company. Concealed under the bridge of a dry riverbed, Redferne glanced at his watch. When Gleason finally rode up, an hour late, he appeared more agitated than usual.

"What took you so long?" Redferne asked.

"Trying to make certain I wasn't being followed."

"It's all in your head. Why do you think anyone would be following you?"

"Sooner or later someone is going to discover what's *in* my head.

393

That would not be good for either of us." He dismounted and let his horse join Redferne's, munching grass along the banks, and then he sat down on a rock, rubbing his face with his hands.

"I thought we went over all of this. It's a little late to be getting cold feet with the flax-gathering only days away."

"I thought it had already been gathered."

"Into stacks in the field it has. The next step is to move the stacks into the barns to dry faster. And that's where you come in."

"The more I think about this, Redferne, the more I'm convinced that what you're about to do is wrong."

Redferne picked up a stone and threw it down the riverbed, watching it ricochet off the rocks. "What's wrong is sending people like you and me into slavery. Throwing hundreds of people out on the side of the road to die of starvation. Being forced to educate our kids in hedge schools. That's what's wrong."

Gleason drew up his shoulders. "How will harming those same people further improve that situation?"

"How do I take Preston down without causing some harm in the short run to those who work for him?"

The sound of galloping made them pull their horses out of sight under the bridge. They covered their ears as the riders thundered over the arch. After the commotion faded, Redferne scrambled up the bank. A company of dragoons disappeared around a bend in a cloud of dust. He slid back down. "A patrol. No need to panic. We're freemen."

Gleason appeared more nervous than ever. "It was Bannister and Preston's wife, not Lord Preston, who were responsible for your misfortune."

"Not directly, but indirectly he was."

"He seems like a decent old skin to me."

"Preston is sitting atop a corrupt and evil system. It's as wicked as the cane fields of Barbados," Redferne said.

"If you go through with this, you'll ruin him."

"And if I don't go through with it, he'll ruin us by passing his estate to someone not as understanding or as decent as he is."

"What about Benjamin? I've been walking on eggshells these past two months fearing he might turn me in."

"He'd have done it by now, if he was going to do anything. I made a promise to him that I would not harm Lord Preston, and he trusts me," Redferne said.

Gleason mounted his horse. "Speaking of being turned in, I'm assuming you've heard that Bannister and Lady Preston have been remanded to the Assize Court in Roscommon town. The trial's scheduled for next week."

"I've heard, and I'd like to have our business with Lord Preston concluded before the verdict is in."

Gleason shook his head and pulled up on the reins. "I've a bad feeling about this," he said, then he spurred his horse and cantered down the riverbed, climbing up the bank at a low spot onto the road.

A slow burn of worry smoldered in the pit of Redferne's stomach.

According to the agreement with William Bradshaw, Preston moved the flax from his fields into the barns to hasten the drying process. Preston invited Bradshaw to dinner when the work was done to celebrate the successful completion of this phase of the operation. They sat down to a meal of lamb, roast potatoes, and carrots garnished with butter and parsley in a little dining room off the great hall. Lord Preston bragged that the entire meal was home-grown. He offered the first toast with a glass of local beer.

"To our continued partnership, long may it flourish."

"Long may it flourish," Gleason replied as they touched glasses.

The Lord's wheelchair was nowhere in sight. Thanks to Benjamin, the color had come back to his cheeks, and he spoke with renewed vigor.

"I must say, in the beginning, I was a little skeptical of our arrangement."

"You doubted the word of a seal master?"

"Heavens no," Preston said sounding flustered. "Some of the old timers thought that bringing flax inside to dry was a little unusual. It dries quite well outdoors."

Sweat dampened the palms of Gleason's hands. He suspected that one of the old timers Preston referred to was Benjamin. Luckily, it was a question Redferne and he had anticipated, so they had worked out an answer in advance.

"That is the traditional way of doing it, but when I visited Holland last year I saw them bring the flax indoors. They claimed it was a faster and safer method of drying."

Recognizing the reputation of the Dutch in the linen industry, Preston backed off. "I told them that I had complete confidence in a linen merchant with his own seal, which in any case was irrelevant, since as a gentleman I gave my word to another gentleman." Preston rang a bell and a servant entered carrying a bowl of mixed fruit compote on a tray. Preston took the bowl and placed it on the table. "We grow the fruit for this fabulous dessert in our own gardens, which I must show you sometime. It also contains the only ingredient of the meal that did not originate on our farm."

Gleason took a spoon of compote. "This is truly delicious, but there's one flavor I can't quite identify."

"Aha, the secret ingredient." Prescott lifted a silver cloche from a tray, revealing a bottle of Armagnac brandy. "One of the finest brandies in the world, courtesy of Bannister's illegal operations."

After several glasses of Armagnac, Gleason's pulse slowed, but he could not wait for the evening to be over.

On the surface, it sounded like Preston had taken the bait, but what if he knew that Gleason was a fraud and was waiting for the opportune moment to have him arrested. But to what purpose? The solvency of Preston's estate rested on the genuineness of the flax contract, and his behavior gave every indication that he believed it to be so. Nevertheless, Gleason remained tense for the rest of the evening. He was hoping his nervousness didn't show through. Preston was in a celebratory mood. By the time the meal was concluded, after many more rounds of Armagnac, His Lordship was too much under the weather to sense Gleason's unease.

Preston's ebullient mood continued into the next day. He asked Benjamin to organize a celebration among the workers, a premature harvest festival. He supplied all the food and drink as well as wood for a large bonfire. On the night of the festivities, Preston was in high spirits. He walked among the crowd of workers shaking hands and slapping people on the back.

"You'd think he was running for a seat in parliament," one wag was heard to say, but that comment was in the minority. In general, everyone seemed to be having a good time. Peasants who had never met him approached him, albeit timidly.

"Thanks, your Grace," they offered shyly. Some of the women curtsied. More forward among them, a willowy, red-haired girl with sparkling green eyes, said, "We should do this every year, your Grace."

A murmur of disapproval went up from some in the group.

"No, no, I think..." He paused. "What's your name, young lady?

"Molly, Yer' Honor," she said blushing.

"I think Molly's right. Let's make this a tradition."

A cheer went up and then the dancing began. With a tankard of ale in one hand and a chalk pipe in the other, Preston sat before the bonfire, smoking and sipping his ale. Dancers circled the blazing pyramid of logs.

Benjamin sat behind his master. Lord Preston appeared contented, a man from whose shoulders a heavy burden had been lifted. Benjamin wondered how long the dream would last before reality came crashing through.

Seamus Beirne

CHAPTER 61

Redferne watched from the shadows with a mixture of envy and regret. He steeled himself by recalling images of Barbados and the suffering that still existed there. The bonfire was an unbelievable piece of luck that would deflect any suspicion from a malicious perpetrator. He thought of Maureen Kelly dancing around the bonfire at the crossroads the evening prior to her departure for America. His eyes teared up but he shook it off.

He waited until the last of the revelers departed before sneaking toward the spent fire. Its burning embers cast a muted red glow in the darkness. He had blackened his face with charcoal and donned monk's clothing to mimic the ghostly friar of the Preston estate.

He carried a sack full of torches dipped in pitch. Not wanting to expose himself in the dim light of the dying fire, he snatched a half-burnt ember and retreated into the shadows. Opening the doors of a flax shed he touched the ember to the tip of a torch and threw the flaming brand inside.

After fermenting for a week, the damp flax had generated methane gas that exploded into flames. He ran to the other sheds repeating the procedure. It took less than five minutes to incinerate three months' work. As he retreated into the trees, the air came alive with the crackle and pop of exploding flax bolls. Ragged sheets of flame leapt from the buildings like caged animals released from a thousand years of bondage, scarring the night with an angry red glow.

By morning the contents of the sheds were reduced to a layer of grey ash a foot deep, spread across the cobbled floors. The red brick walls were blackened like the interior of a forge and the slate roofs had crumpled, their remains buried in ash. Preston bent down and scooped up a handful of the grey powder and slowly let it run through his fingers, hardly noticing that it was still hot. It was all that was left of his dream, and he wanted to touch it one last time. His final chance of holding on to his beloved estate had gone up in smoke.

Turning to Mr. Bradshaw, who had made a great show of hurrying to the scene of the disaster, he said in a barely audible voice, "I am deeply embarrassed, sir, for reneging on my pledge. It would appear that Providence has turned on us. Regretfully, I will be unable to fulfill our agreement."

"Not Providence, My Lord, but an unfortunate accident."

"We tempted the Gods and they turned the fire against us." Gleason found himself at a loss. He felt unclean and wanted to get far away. A large crowd of laborers and townspeople gathered at the smoldering pyre, including Redferne and Rory Blake. Accusations were hurled at those who attended the previous night's celebration as if they were to blame for the catastrophe.

"It'll be a tough winter. Without the work, we'll starve for sure," someone said.

A chorus of voices murmured, "Aye."

A wizened old lady wrapped in a black shawl wagged her finger in the face of a young woman with a plump face and rosy cheeks. "That's what happens when a bunch of drunks violate God's law. The man above will not be blasphemed."

"Shut up, you bloody ejit," someone replied. "The man above has more weighty matters on his plate than seeking revenge on a few poor folk out to have a good time."

Blake looked askance at Redferne. "I don't know for sure what happened here, but I recall when we were kids you liked to set stuff on fire."

"And since you don't, Rory, why indulge in wild speculation?"

Redferne caught up to Benjamin who was following Lord Preston back toward the Big House. "Ben, might I have a word with your master?"

Ben did not change his pace or look around. Undeterred, Redferne followed him to the back door of the servants' wing. As he reached up to press the latch, he turned and faced Redferne.

"You put me in the terrible position of having to choose between loyalty to my own kind, and betraying a good and decent man."

Redferne shifted uneasily on his feet. "I only promised that I would not hurt him."

"You broke your promise to do no harm."

"No, I kept my promise not to hurt him."

"You sound like a cornered politician playing word games. You harmed him but you didn't hurt him? You've ruined him. You insult me with such sophistry. Be gone," he said, turning toward the open door.

"You might change your mind about that if you hear me out."

Ben hesitated on the threshold and turned around. He looked tired and suspicious, as if he had heard one too many lies. "Say your piece."

"I have a proposition for your master that might interest him."

"And what could you have to say that might alter the present reality?"

"I returned from Barbados a rich man. I didn't tell you that when last we met."

"Two years, being worked to death as a slave and now you are rich? Is that what you expect me to believe?"

Checking left and right before speaking, he told Benjamin the circumstances of his escape and how he and his mates came by great wealth. Benjamin listened politely as one might to a beggar at one's door, while Redferne laid out his proposition for Lord Preston.

"If this is true, I will arrange for a meeting with His Lordship. If it turns out to be otherwise, I will kill you myself." He slammed the door in Redferne's face.

Seamus Beirne

CHAPTER 62

Redferne moved his feet nervously under the mahogany table as he sat across from Lord Preston and Benjamin, under the stern gaze of the patriarch's portrait with the hole in its chest. The first thing he would do he promised himself, if they reached an agreement, would be to repair that damned hole.

The late evening sun streamed through the windows casting a soft yellow sheen along the table. Redferne could see all the way to the old church at the edge of the demesne. In its shadow, Bannister's large herd of milk cows, seized by Lord Preston, grazed undisturbed on the rich parkland grasses. Benjamin's face appeared impassive. Preston looked like he had aged ten years since the fire. Hunched over with his elbows on the table, he bore a striking resemblance to the old humpbacked servant sitting next to him.

The Lord cleared his throat. Straightening, he placed his hands one on top of the other on the table, as if waiting for the daily report from his estate agent. "Benjamin tells me you desire to purchase my estate, sir," he said without offering any formal greeting.

"It is as he told you." Redferne thought he would have the upper hand here, but was taken aback to discover that he felt otherwise.

"You will not be surprised, I hope, that I require solid evidence to back up the genuineness of your intentions."

Redferne withdrew a large purse from inside his coat and emptied its contents on the table. Preston drew back as if dazzled by the heap of golden guineas spread before him.

"I went to my bank in Dublin last week to obtain a good faith deposit. There is £5,000 here. The rest will be forthcoming in the form of a bank draft for £3,000 more if we reach an agreement."

Preston's shoulders sagged even more. He seemed to collapse inward as if someone had let the air out of him.

"But surely you realize that while such an amount is sufficient to remove the encumbrances from the estate, it is insufficient to buy it outright." He turned an accusing look on Benjamin. "Such an offer is an insult and a short step from daylight robbery," he continued, pulling a handkerchief from his cuff and dabbing his moist brow.

Benjamin's jaw tightened. "You already have my master at a disadvantage, so it is discourteous of you to try to humiliate him further."

"It is not my intention to embarrass Lord Preston, as it was never my intention to buy the estate outright. My goal is to work out a compromise so that we both achieve part of what we want."

Preston straightened his shoulders. "Proceed."

"For clearing the property of its encumbrances, I want a controlling interest in the estate—60-40. Decision-making power will rest with me. You will be a silent partner and will be uninvolved in the daily running of the estate. Furthermore, with the exception of the servants' wing, you may retain ownership of the Big House, plus the demesne and parklands that surround it." Redferne paused and looked across the table before continuing. "That, sir, is my offer."

In the silence that followed he heard every creak and groan of the old house as if it were registering its disapproval. Benjamin's labored breathing added to the surreal atmosphere. After a whispered conversation with Benjamin, Preston excused himself and they left the room together.

Redferne rose and stood before an open window overlooking the demesne. The long summer evening was beginning to wane. Soon it would be lamplight time, an interval of shadow and indecision. He hoped his own dark odyssey was finally winding down and a new chapter beginning. He hadn't heard from Padraig. Had he found his mother in good health? He could provide for her now. Would she have him back?

Was Preston too proud or scared to go into partnership with a former peasant of his own estate? Would pride push him toward financial suicide rather than collude with the lower classes? After all, Preston belonged to a society that built hidden tunnels and staircases to avoid even accidental contact with servants.

If Preston turned him down, his whole scheme would come to grief, but Benjamin was level-headed, shrewd, and had his master's ear. Much of the decision, Redferne suspected, rested with him.

Turning from the window, Redferne's gaze fell on the portrait above the fireplace. The old patriarch was probably turning in his grave at the mere thought of what his great grandson was contemplating. The long-case clock struck ten; they had been gone almost an hour. What was keeping them?

Footsteps. The door opened. Preston entered followed by Benjamin carrying a writing tray. They resumed their places around the table.

"Benjamin, will you review the terms of Mr. Redferne's offer to avoid misunderstandings?"

Benjamin took a sheet of foolscap from the tray and commenced reading. Redferne fidgeted with the buttons of his waistcoat. Benjamin finished and passed the document to His Lordship, who adjusted his glasses to peruse it briefly. Then he spoke.

"Mr. Redferne, I accept the terms and conditions of your offer as set forth herein, with one caveat."

"Damn," he thought, "what now?"

"Benjamin stays with me. You can take all the other servants, but not him." Redferne started to breathe again, then burst out laughing. That was never one of the conditions, but the mention of it was evidence of the high esteem Preston had for his servant.

A broad smile crossed Benjamin's face. His master signed the document with a flourish. After dripping beads of hot red wax on the page beneath the names, The lord imprinted the Preston coat of arms onto it with the estate seal. Redferne signed his name under Lord Preston's with a shaky hand.

Michael Redferne Esqr.

Given at Cloonfin on this third day of August, in the year of Our Lord, 1776.

The signing completed, Preston rang a bell. A servant entered bearing a silver tray with a bottle of Spanish brandy and three glasses. Preston filled them and handed one each to Redferne and Benjamin. He raised his own and paused. "To the Redferne-Preston Enterprise, long may it prosper!"

"Long may it prosper!" the others intoned.

Redferne raised his glass. "To the opening of this estate and the liberation of its people. Here's to the dawning of a new day."

A look of panic flitted across Lord Preston's face, but he gamely raised his glass and joined the others in the toast.

"To a new day," they said in unison and downed their Spanish brandy.

EPILOGUE

On the tenth of August, 1776, one week after the agreement at the Big House, the Magistrates' Court handed down its decision in the matter of Lady Preston and Bannister. Both were condemned to death. They were to be taken to the public square in Roscommon town and hanged the following day. Through Lord Preston's intervention, however, this was later commuted to life in prison. Whereupon they were shackled and taken under guard to the port of Sligo, and from thence transported to the Sugar Island.

ABOUT THE AUTHOR

Irish-born writer, Seamus Beirne, lives in Irvine, California with his wife Ann and their dog Lucy. Their three grown children are gainfully employed and live away from home. The stress of retirement is alleviated by frequent visits from their two grandchildren!! Seamus spent twenty-five years as a high school English teacher and administrator. *Breakout From Sugar Island* is his first novel.

http://www.seamusbeirne.net/

For the Finest in Nautical and Historical Fiction and Non-Fiction
www.FireshipPress.com

Interesting • Informative • Authoritative

All Fireship Press books are now available through Amazon and via leading bookstores and wholesalers from coast-to-coast.